THE FIRST

THE FIRST

THE WAR OF SOULS

BOOK TWO

CHRIS A. JACKSON

Cover Design by S.H. Roddey

I would like to dedicate this novel to all of those who are fighting to save our planet from the slow-motion apocalypse of man-made climate change. Though it is unlikely to progress as far as I've projected in this work of fiction, it is real, and we are at the brink of a precipice. With the immanent collapse of the north Atlantic currents, which influence climate all over the world, especially in Europe, we are destined for a drastic change to our planet's global ecology, and in fact, are already seeing those changes. We are the frog in the pot, and the water is warming up. We can, however, tip the scales back, repair the damage. It will be a monumental task, but some of the most brilliant minds in the world are working on it. The question isn't if we can save our planet, the question is if we have the will to do so.

1
HUNTING DEVILS

I stand in a crowd of hundreds of protesters, facing the Cabell Federal Building in Dallas, Texas, invisible in the rowdy throng. Our shouts of protest come out in clouds of steam, a Texas norther the likes of which no cowboy or Native American of previous centuries has ever seen putting a minus-ten Fahrenheit nip in the air. The cold gives me cover, for everyone is bundled up in scarves, hats, and coats. I'm also disguised, thanks to Jeri's efforts and the wonder of anonymous online shopping. Cosplay is an interesting culture... God bless them. What little is exposed of my face is deep brown, my nose broad, with a plasti-flesh prosthetic, my brows thick and unplucked, my mouth full and cheeks fuller. Even the best AI facial recognition software in the world won't recognize me.

Why I'm risking my life and freezing my ass off, is complicated.

For the first time in my five-thousand years, I am the hunter instead of the hunted. It's a role I find difficult to adjust to. I am a healer, after all, a saver of souls, not a banisher of them. While I have taken lives, far too many, I always depended on God to sort out their souls. I must remind myself constantly that these are not human souls, but Nephilim, the spawn of the angels banished to Hell, determined to corrupt all of mankind. They're damned already; I'm simply sending them where they belong. I've finally been given a weapon to make this possible. A weapon that could win the war. That concept, winning, still bewilders me after so long.

But to use this weapon, I must first find my quarry. Not so simple in a world of ten billion humans, any one of whom could be a Nephilim. Hence the freezing my ass off.

I hold a sign demanding human rights, keeping my face averted from the ranks of NAFAS federal troops stationed along the street. We're confined to the park across the street, the gathering technically legal but tightly contained; free speech is still supposedly a right in NAFAS, but a carefully regulated one. The irony of policing free speech for misinformation, while the government spews propaganda like offal from a slaughterhouse, is something I've seen too many times to appreciate. I keep my cover, wait, and watch, huddled under a bulky threadbare coat and knit hat, my free hand thrust into one pocket clutching the cold cylinder of a smoke grenade, my last-ditch escape should I be identified.

In the six months since we banished our first two Nephilim, Gippy and I have remained hidden in the sea of humanity that is the mega-city of Atlanta. The Nephilim are still hunting us, still arrogant in their superiority, but we're invisible, two grains of sand on a world-sized beach. We have not spent those months idly, however. I've taught Gippy all I can in the short span. He is an apt pupil, determined and tireless. Jeri, also, I've schooled in the arts of war. She is less apt, less steady, as yet unbaptized by fire, but also determined. And as ironic as it might sound, I've learned much from them both as well. This world is more theirs than mine, after all, for I am a creature of millennia past.

Oh, for the good old days... I get a flash of deja vu, the 1960s, protesting war in bell-bottom jeans, a tee-shirt, and sandals, flowers in my hair, without a worry about being recognized by my enemies, facing the leveled rifles of National Guard. *What glorious fools, protesting a war waged half a world away...* Every generation believes the world is more violent than in the past. Not in my experience. *China, Russia, North America, Africa, the Amazon... indigenous people slaughtered like vermin.*

Steady spirit... I concentrate on those I love... also something so new to me that I'm baffled by my own emotions. I've allowed myself, once again, to love and be loved. Our relationship is complicated; Gippy and I are as mother and son—or so I would imagine, for in my five thousand years I have never borne a child—while Jeri and I are passion and intensity and fulfillment. Jeri and Gippy are each other's safe harbors, comfort and solace. There is no jealousy between us, for we are family now. They give me hope and strength to continue the fight.

And we have had our victories, two more Nephilim souls banished to Hell. Only one-hundred-ninety-five more to win the War of Souls, a conflict that has raged throughout the recorded history of humanity. I still don't harbor much hope of victory, for as far as I know, I'm still the last of my kind. But I've been gifted hope, and that's a powerful thing.

Today, we will try for one more.

"They're coming out." Gippy's voice is tinny and remote in my earpiece, broken but audible through the static. He's inside the courthouse, posing as a member of the NAFAS Free Press Service—talk about an oxymoron.

I check my position and work my way forward, keeping my eyes low, my face averted from the dozen or so cameras watching the crowd. Commerce Street is blocked off to regular traffic, four vehicles waiting at the curb for the federal judges along with a dozen black and gold NAFAS cruisers. The crowd is pressed tight now, good cover, but this is the most dangerous moment. They'll be watching the crowd closely, cameras taking a thousand frames a second, matching them to a million faces in the terrorist registry. If I'm identified, I have little doubt that they'll order the troops to open fire regardless of innocent bystanders. Hell, they hit St. Louis with everything short of a tactical nuke in an attempt to take me out. *Memories of months hiding in rubble, healing the poor fools I led into a fight they couldn't win, eating garbage, living... surviving... and finally fleeing.* I am the last of the Ageless offspring of the Seraphim, the only one staving off the final judgment. Unless... *Cora...*

The crowd's chants rise in pitch and volume, and I snap out of my reverie as the first of the judges is escorted out of the building. My ability to sense the hatred radiating from a Nephilim is limited by distance, but I'm close enough, I hope. The crowd surges forward against the row of transparent riot shields, off the curb and into the street. We've broken our containment; this protest is now illegal and we could all be arrested, but I go with it, only one person away from the troopers. I raise my voice with the others, wave my sign, and press forward. The closer I am, the more sure I can be of my target. The judges, three men and a woman are escorted to their vehicles one at a time. Gippy and I have researched them all as deeply as the ultranet will allow.

The first to emerge is Judge Thomas Hollins, Caucasian, fifty-six years old, married, four children, wealthy from his parents' fortune, highly schooled at the finest institutions money can buy. He's barely twenty feet away when he gets into his car, and I feel nothing. He is not my quarry, but then, I didn't think he was. While Nephilim often rise to powerful positions, they cannot choose the humans they inhabit. Since less than one percent of the human race holds anything approximating real wealth, for a Nephilim to be born into a wealthy family is rare. Hollins is just an entitled white man who thinks the world would be a better place if run by entitled white men.

The second is Kenzie Raymark, a tiny mixed-race woman, forty-seven years old, married with two children from her second wife. A rarity in Texas, she's a hard-nosed liberal in a conservative state, in a conservative empire. She is also, obviously, not a Nephilim.

The third to venture out is Anthony Wick, another white, powerful, conservative; sixty-one years old and single widower of a rich wife. He has twenty-five years on the bench with a voting record that would have made Hell proud. Hard core NAFAS supporter and imperialist hawk, he is the reason I'm here. He walks out to his car... and I feel nothing.

Damn!

I grind my teeth. I'd been so sure; Wick has all the earmarks of a Nephilim: born of unassuming parents who died young, well educated, married rich, wife died unexpectedly and left him everything. But I'm wrong; even from twenty feet away, I should have felt something. As his car pulls away, I start to turn, then a faint wave of hatred and malice washes over me like heat from a distant kiln.

I fix the fourth judge with my eyes as he emerges, concentrating on him, focusing. The burning malice is unmistakable. It's either coming from him or one of his entourage. I doubt the latter. Nephilim seek positions of power; one would never deign to serve as a human's lacky. His eyes are fixed forward, a smug smile on his face. The hatred cuts off as I watch him get into a small limousine with his assistant and two security goons. I assess automatically, seeing everything, running the numbers, clicking off the threats, the risks, the equations of bullets tearing through living flesh...

These surgical strikes Gippy and I plan are tricky, for we can't just kill the Nephilim or risk killing them while neutralizing their security assets. *Don't forget the driver... Four bystanders... One Nephilim...*

I turn away and start threading a path through the dispersing crowd, reviewing what I know of the fourth Judge. Ben Martinez, a moderate, Hispanic, young—only thirty-eight—new to the bench, a successful lawyer for a private firm before being appointed. Married, no children, moderately wealthy, but only from his own earnings, and rising in power and influence. At his age, he may be aiming for a Supreme Court appointment. Not who I expected, but he's definitely a Nephilim.

"Empa, did you make him?" Gippy asks over our comm.

I key the mic under my lapel. "Yes, but it's not Wick. It's Martinez."

"Martinez? But he's a moderate! What the fuckity fuck?" One thing Gippy hasn't lost is his penchant for street profanity; it's something he's taught me to appreciate, in fact.

"I know." A young woman in the crowd eyes me suspiciously. Too shabbily dressed to be talking to myself with no apparent phone. She probably suspects that I'm a NAFAS spy. "We'll talk in the car."

"Right."

Ditching my sign, I walk three blocks through the city to where we parked, making sure I'm not followed and keeping my face averted from the ubiquitous security cameras. Gippy's already in the car, a late model Dodge that we acquired two days ago in Fort Worth. He looks like a professional in his suit and tie. I still can't believe the changes in him that only six months have wrought. He's put on muscle, kicked his addictions, and learned to read, write, shoot, drive, and keep his head on straight in a firefight. The last bit you don't teach, but Gifford has survived and stayed sane through his baptism. Of course, I healed a lot of the guilt he feels for taking human lives, even if they were trying to kill us at the time, but I have to give him credit. He's transformed from a strung-out street kid to a warrior in an amazingly short span, a badass in every sense of the word.

I get in, and he pulls away from the curb, giving me a skeptical look. "So, Martinez? *Really*?"

"I can't be absolutely sure, but I think so. Either him, a bodyguard, or his assistant, and that's usually not Nephilim MO."

"I would have bet on Wick."

"So would I. He's why we came here, after all, but we've got some homework to do if we want to take Martinez."

"I *hate* homework," he says with a scowl.

"You'd hate getting electrocuted by a security drone more." I pull up the specs on Martinez's house.

"Can't argue with that," he says.

We drive to our creepy little motel room just outside the city, passing tent cities of refugees fleeing the Arctic winter. Instead of letting the homeless live in abandoned apartment buildings, Texas bulldozed entire city blocks and cordoned them off with chain link as "temporary refugee shelters" fifteen years ago. They supplied uninsulated prefab huts and tents, poor shelter from the bitter cold winds racing down from the north. About ten percent die every winter, but their number never diminishes. Spring is coming, but we're due for our eighteenth bomb cyclone in three weeks. Mythical climate change is kicking North America's ass, the new normal.

I wonder if the Nephilim engineered climate change or if it was just a happy coincidence for them. It seems too perfect for their agenda of despair, hopelessness, and hate. They don't want to simply murder humanity, they want to corrupt it. When the last of human hope dies, the last good soul turns to evil, and the last Ageless is exterminated, the four horsemen will come.

Over my dead body... probably literally.

For the rest of the day, we're glued to our phones, looking for a weakness in Martinez's security. Unfortunately, his house is a fortress. He has four security people active at all times, and a CCTV system and motion detectors all over the property. An intruder alert would launch a dozen Taser-armed drones. His assistant lives in an apartment on his property, over the garage, originally designed for a caretaker or in-law. Half a dozen domestic servants—butler, maid, cook, gardener, driver, and maintenance specialist—round out the staff. None of those live on-site, but security knows them all right down to their DNA, and they come and go through a gate with armed guards and retinal scanners. We have zero chance of impersonating one of them. Infiltration, either by force or stealth, seems impossible.

Martinez and his wife do get out of the house regularly, however. Part of climbing the network of power involves socializing with the right people, and the Martinezes are good at it. He's young and charismatic, his wife younger and gorgeous, and they attend two to four social engagements a week. Cocktail parties, fundraisers, dedications, the symphony, opera, theater, and sporting events. They always have at least two security people with them, and the driver in the car.

"The car," Gippy says, not for the first time. "That's the weakest link with the lowest chance for collateral damage."

"The driver seems our best opportunity," I agree. "We snatch him, get into the vehicle, rig it, and we've got them in a box."

"Think we can do it without killin' anyone?" Gippy's always trying to keep killing to a minimum, and I'm proud of him for it. I've seen far too much killing. *Africa, Europe, Cambodia, Central America... the smell of blood and decomposing human flesh... the hoarse cries of feasting crows...* This time, however, he gives me a skeptical look. "Even if we gas the whole car, it'd be dicey. You said one goon sits up front, the other in the back. That's not good."

"No, it's not, and there's a partition between the two. If they're at a social engagement, they'll get in the car in a public place." I think of his lovely wife, perhaps the most innocent one in our threat arena. "A valet might not notice a different driver, but the second they get in the car, things will get ugly."

"Gotta be a way..." He chews his lower lip. "Can you remember if the guard who sits in front got in the car last?"

I think back to the court house. "Yes, he ushered Martinez in, closed the door, and got in the front. What are you thinking?"

"Snatch the driver, I take his place, Tase the front seat guard when the door closes, then you gas the back compartment from the trunk as I drive away. Maybe rig the back doors to stay locked. Problem is, we've gotta take Martinez down before he or any of his goons can make a call."

"Yes, we do." We'd had a close call in that regard once, when a target pressed a panic button that called in NAFAS police.

"So, four other people in the car, and who knows how many bystanders outside if shit goes sideways." Gippy shakes his head and gets up, pacing the threadbare carpet. "They're high profile. Places they go gonna have private security. Shit goes down, they'll shoot first. That's gonna turn into a bloodbath, and we'd be in the middle of it. Even if we drive away, take out the bystanders, switch cars, and stuff Judge Hell-spawn into our car, they'll get a call out and down comes the shitstorm."

He's not wrong. "I know, but I don't see any easier way."

"Maybe drug him and pick him up in an ambulance?"

"Not a bad idea, but that would mean infiltrating a restaurant or social event to slip something into his food or drink, and we'd have to make sure it went to *him*, not someone else."

"Complicated." Gippy shakes his head again. "This gettin' *way* too complicated, E. We need simple."

"Everything *starts* simple..." I sigh; our other two victories were far less difficult: a high-ranking police captain in Kansas City and a pharmaceutical executive in Phoenix, neither of them high profile.

"What's that thing you taught me Musashi said? From one thing..."

Gippy's question brings back memories and lessons from centuries ago. "From one thing, know ten thousand things."

"Right. That. So, what do we *know*?"

"Martinez is a Nephilim."

"We know that for *sure*? You got no doubt?" Gippy stops his pacing and fixes me with a hard stare. "You said you was like twenty feet away."

He has a point. "It was either him or one of his group. When he got into his car, the... feeling I get from them disappeared, so I assumed it was him."

"But we weren't even *here* for Martinez. We thought it was Wick."

"But we were wrong; that I *do* know for certain."

"Exactly!" Gippy's eyes widen, and he wags a finger in the air. "And it don't make *sense*! Martinez's a moderate. Wick's a hardcore right-wing psycho dick. He's why we *came* here."

"But he's not a Nephilim, I *am* sure of that!" I'm not sure where he's going with this.

"Okay, but what are the chances that a hawk like Wick *isn't* one, but a moderate like Martinez *is*?" He shakes his head, lips a hard line. "Somethin' ain't *right* here, E."

He has another good point; something about this feels wrong. "Okay, back to basics. I do know that one of Martinez's group is a Nephilim. Either him, his assistant, or one of his security people."

"But you said it's not likely to be some flunky, right?"

"Not *usually*, but..." A niggling suspicion tickles the back of my neck. I delve the ultranet with my phone again, looking up personnel records, dates, employment histories. Personnel files aren't exactly public records, but they're not very secure, and we're into the district databases already from our research on Wick. Gippy's tapping his phone, too, but I pay him no attention. Suddenly, I see it, and the light dawns. I gape at my screen for a heartbeat, momentarily speechless. "You're not going to *believe* this, Gip!"

"The mutha-fuckin' *assistant*!" Gippy shows me the screen of his phone, a middle-aged woman smiling and shaking Wick's hand. The same woman I saw with Martinez. "Penny Saunders! She used to work for *Wick*!" A grin lightens his face like a lighthouse on a stormy shore.

"Bingo!" I grin back.

His smile clouds with confusion. "What's that?"

"Sorry. Nothing important." I often forget he's a child of modern times and our life experiences often don't translate well. "It's *got* to be her. It makes sense. She corrupted Wick for six years. Her work there is done, so she moves on. She's a hider, an influencer. It fits."

"And Martinez is young, and she can sway him. He's the tie vote on the court. With him bent toward the right, the court's tilted three to one." Gippy pauses and fixes me with another piercing look. "But we gotta be *sure*, E."

I nod. "You're right. We do, but she'll be a much easier target to get close to. She's not under constant surveillance. She'll go out alone eventually."

"We're back to simple. I like it!" Gippy reaches for his long jacket. "Stake out?"

"Stake out." I grab my heavy coat, and we're in the car in less than a minute.

Saunders lives at Martinez's house, so she's easy enough to find. It's a nice neighborhood, all high fences and video cameras, big houses, sprawling grounds, shiny cars. Gippy looks up her personal vehicle and the layout of the house as I drive, and we stake out the front gate from half a block away. There's a service entrance in the back, but a judge's personal assistant wouldn't use that. Our old Dodge is a little out of place here, but there are enough cars parked along the streets and in driveways to camouflage us. It's also after work hours for the people who live affluent lifestyles, so there's not much traffic. We take shifts watching, and Gippy jostles me awake to a dark sky and rain mixed with snow.

"Bingo!" He points through the rain-streaked windshield at the gate.

"I thought you didn't know what Bingo was." I blink myself awake. A shiny GM coal-emulsion coupe is pulling out from the Martinez residence.

"Looked it up. Gotta do somethin' to keep sharp. She's goin' out." He starts our car and pulls out, following Saunders' a block back in the non-existent traffic. "No security, so Martinez is still home. Unless she's goin' out with the missus or someone else, we got her alone."

"Unless she's meeting someone." I reach under the seat for a canned cappuccino. It's not real coffee, but there's enough caffeine in it to jump-start a rhinoceros. "Want one?"

"Nah, I'm wired like a cheap radio." I know he doesn't mean anything stronger than coffee, but Gippy is an addict. He's been clean for months but told me he still has occasional cravings, especially under stress conditions.

We follow from a distance until we progress into a higher traffic area, then he closes the gap. I keep track of our position on my phone and suspect where we're going even before we pull into the shopping district. Most of the big retail stores failed with the shift toward online shopping, but this is a wealthy suburb, and rich people have always liked to shop. A flash memory: *ancient Rome, I walk several steps behind a white-robed senator, one of his entourage as he peruses the markets, commoners bowing and groveling for a few thrown denarii.* Here, a few high-end stores and restaurants have kept this place thriving. Saunders pulls into a parking spot and walks down the block to a clothing store without even looking over her shoulder, confident, secure in her anonymity, ignorant that she's being stalked.

We park nearby, and I follow her in. Gippy stays in the car, ready to play his part should our suspicions pan out. Inside the store, I take interest in a rack of sport jackets near the exit. I don't spot Saunders, but chances are she'll leave by the same exit. Even Nephilim are creatures of habit.

After about a half hour, a flood of hatred sweeps over me. I don't have to look up to know a Nephilim is close. I have to be sure, however, and turn just enough to watch the big glass doors with a sideways glance. Saunders strides past with two bags in hand, smiling and thanking the door guard as he ushers her out. The instant the door closes behind her, the feeling vanishes.

I key my mic. "It's Saunders. No doubt. We're a go."

"I'm on it," Gippy replies.

I leave the store and spot Saunders heading toward her car. I start toward ours. The GM pulls out and starts down the street. I get to our car and find Gippy behind the wheel.

"Done?" I ask as my door slams closed.

"Easy as kissin' yer sister." He pulls out and we follow.

My sister... I had one once, five millennia ago. I remember her face, the feel of her soul. I remember feeling her die from an infected rat bite, the simple bacteria that I could have destroyed easily had I known what I was at the time. My gifts didn't come with an instruction manual. My human family died before I learned how to heal others with my father's legacy.

Focus, Empa. Steady spirit...

Saunders makes it a block from the shopping district before she realizes she's got a flat tire. The caltrops we use cause slow leaks, giving us time to close in. She pulls to the curb and gets out as we slow to make our approach. Staring down at the flat tire, she pulls her phone and starts to use it, probably calling her auto club. I do a quick scan of the street; there's almost no traffic, and half the street lights are out.

"We're good, Gip. As soon as she's off her phone, do it!" I pull up the collar of my coat and free the bulky weapon from the case at my feet.

"Hang on." Gippy pulls up behind the Nephilim's car, headlights bright in her face. As Saunders turns away from the lights and moves to get back in her car, he turns to pull up beside the shiny GM.

I toggle my window down—malice from the Nephilim hits me like heat from an Auschwitz furnace—and position the muzzle of the weapon over the lip of the door. "Car trouble?" I ask as we pull up to her.

"Nothing I can't—"

As she turns to face me, I flick the safety up, which activates the laser sight, put the red dot on her torso, and pull the trigger. The Taser cracks, and the heavy XP probes pierce her Kevlar jacket. Fifty-thousand volts hit her, and every nerve in her body fires, seizing her muscles in spasm. I'm out of my door before she even hits the pavement. The Nephilim is convulsing but struggling to rise; they're far tougher than humans, but her muscles aren't working. Her phone lies beside her twitching hand, and my heel comes down on it, smashing it to pieces. Her other hand is fumbling in her suit jacket. I'm on her before she can free the pistol, flipping her onto her face and planting a knee between her shoulder blades. I wrench the small-caliber weapon away and tuck it in my pocket, then pin her arms behind her back before she can regain control.

The moment we touch, I get her and she gets me. She knows she's trapped by the very last Ageless daughter of the Seraphim, and I know I've found the daughter of Suphlatus, the fallen angel of dust and concealment. Her strategy makes sense to me now, remaining in the background, hidden, weaving misinformation and lies into weapons that humans will wield for her. I free a pair of zip cuffs and cinch them tight on her wrists.

She mutters slurred dead languages, becoming more coordinated by the second. Gippy kneels beside me to stab a ten-gauge needle into her butt and injects ten CCs of ketamine in one push. The drug is one of the fastest acting anesthetics available, often used for large animals. Still, it takes about a minute to take effect, and we can't wait. Gippy caps the syringe and pulls a handful of cable ties from his pocket, securing her legs at the knee and ankle. I pull a roll of duct tape from another pocket and shut her up. We haul her up and fling her bodily into the back seat just as another car pulls up, bright headlights illuminating us.

"Shit!" Gippy slams the door and faces the lights, his pistol in one hand held in shadow. I didn't even see him draw it, and I'm proud.

I hope he doesn't have to shoot anyone but reach for my Glock. If this is a trap...

"Hey! What the hell are you doin'?!" someone yells.

"They're not police." I keep my face averted, hurrying around the front of our car to the driver's side. If someone puts a picture of my face on the net, the next thing I hear could be the shockwave of an incoming missile.

"I got this, E." Gippy steps toward the lights and holds out a black bill-fold, a shiny home-printed badge gleaming in the headlights. "Federal agents! Get back in your car!" He raises his pistol.

Someone swears, and I hear a door slam. Saunders is struggling and screaming through the tape, but she can't escape. I take the wheel, and Gippy backs up to the passenger door. He slides in, and I stomp the gas pedal to the floor. Before we hit the highway, the ketamine kicks in, and the Nephilim quiets down.

"Think they got any pics?" Gippy asks.

"Couldn't see past their lights." Anyone with enough resources to own a car would have a phone, but taking pictures of federal agents is now against the law, and penalties are harsh. "Even if they did, they probably won't share them. Too dangerous."

"Never thought I'd thank the naffies for oppressing freedom of speech."

"Irony's a bitch, ain't she?" Something about slipping into Gippy's vernacular makes me smile. He's taught me some valuable lessons. I check our captive; she's breathing fast, but completely out. "Remind me to send a thank you note to Taser International."

"And whoever makes ketamine, and zip ties, and three-D printers, and anonymous online shopping..."

"All the modern conveniences..." I stifle a smirk as I turn onto Highway 80. In half an hour, just past the little town of Forney, I turn off onto a dark blacktop road, then onto a dirt track that leads to a long-abandoned farm. The wind is kicking up icy snow from the dead field, hazing the air, the tires crunching as I slow. I drive up to the disused barn, and Gippy gets out to open the doors. I drive in, the headlights illuminating our preparations, a white sheet draped over a folding table, everything we need for the exorcism stacked on another table. I shut the car down, and he closes the doors.

"Let the festivities begin!" Gippy grins, and I clamber out of the car to help retrieve our prize from the back seat. “Express elevator to Hell, goin’ *down*!”

I chuckle at the movie reference; I’ve shared all of my favorites with him and Jeri. It’s amazing how some things age well, while others don’t. They didn’t understand *Blazing Saddles*, for instance, but loved *Casablanca*. Go figure.

“Grab her legs.” I heave with him, but the sheer magnitude of our looming task still daunts me. “Only one hundred ninety-four to go.”

2
ASHES TO ASHES

"Audio journal entry one; May eighth, twenty fifty-two." I clear my throat, swallowing tears, and grip the wheel in white-knuckled fists. *Coward! You could have stayed!* But I know in my heart that I've made the right decision. I can't deny God's hand in this any longer... *Pregnant! You're pregnant!* Running away is the only way I can keep my child safe—the first child born of an Ageless in five thousand years.

"I... don't know why I'm making this recording, or where to begin. Maybe just for someone to talk to, even if you're not here yet. I hope you find this useful, my love, but..." *Don't terrify the poor kid, Terpsichore! Tell them the truth!* "If you're listening to this, my beloved child, whoever you are, you need to know who your mother and father were, and what a miracle you truly are, the first of your kind. I hope it'll help you understand."

I check my mirror as my old Tesla climbs the arch of the newly built span to the mainland. The car's on its fourth battery, and better than it ever was. The new carbon fiber one can give me six hundred miles per charge, and I'm full up, my escape well planned. Behind me, Brown University and the man I love recede in the distance. I'm reminded of fleeing Paris before the Nazis arrived, fleeing Rome after barely escaping the fire that consumed the city, fleeing San Francisco in flames, leaving

New Orleans as the waterfront warehouses were put to the torch, burning bales of cotton floating down the Mississippi as the Union ships approached. I seem to leave everything I love behind me in flames, and I feel like a coward. My heart breaks once again. I wonder if I'll ever learn, but know it's not likely. This time, at least, I didn't leave an entire city in ashes, only the heart of the man I love.

Pregnant... pregnant... I'm fucking pregnant! I can think of little else now, who this child of Heaven and Hell will be, and how I can keep them safe.

I wipe away tears and record as I drive. "I don't know when I'll give this to you, but I think not until you're old enough to grasp a few things. The first thing I'll tell you is that you were conceived in love, and that your father is a wonderful man with a heart of gold. Unfortunately, or maybe *fortunately,* he holds something inside him that is dreadful and dangerous, which is why I had to leave him. I never thought it possible that my union with him would conceive a child. The hidden designs of God have taken root in me in ways I don't yet understand."

Pregnant... How, for the love of God...

I swallow the lump in my throat and continue. "Ahead of myself again! Ha! Well, my darling, if there's one thing you probably already know about me, it's that I'm about as organized as a train wreck. If you don't know already, my real name is Terpsichore. I'm what's known as an *Ageless,* which doesn't really explain much other than I don't age. The *reason* I'm Ageless is that my father is Israfal, Angel of Music, one of the Seraphim." *...when the Angels of God came unto the daughters of men, they bore the Angels children, who became the mighty of legend, the heroes of renown.* Heroes... all dead now. All but me. Even I sometimes find my own origin hard to believe. "If you're hearing that for the first time, you're probably thinking, 'So, Mom's a nut, I guess.'

"I assure you, love, that I'm not crazy." I hit *Pause* as I take the onramp onto Highway 6. Traffic is light, so I blink away tears and tap *Record* to continue.

"I'm not going to tell you your father's name, simply because I'm sure you'd try to find him, and that would be dangerous for both you *and* him. You see, the reason you were born is the darkness that resides within your father. This is going to be hard to explain without giving you the entire picture, and you're going to hate me for it, but here it is: Your father holds a Nephilim, the offspring of one of the Gregori, an angel cast out of Heaven, within himself. As far as I know, he's the only one ever to survive being occupied by a Nephilim. All others have perished, their souls destroyed, but your father was... *is* special, and his unique soul may be the salvation of mankind." I shake my head with the memory of that discovery, my own disbelief. *Such a beautiful soul holding such evil within...* I almost fled right then, for I have little doubt that the Nephilim within him, Azkeel, recognized me as an Ageless. But the Beast's minion was impotent, trapped, and Emil is such a selfless, caring person. I had to find out how that happened.

"I know, TMI, right?

"I'm sorry, love, but your life is destined by your very origin to be both complicated and dangerous. That's the other thing you need to know, in case you haven't figured it out yet. The entire world is at war, but most humans don't realize it. The War of Souls has been raging for more than five thousand years, my entire life, the offspring of the Seraphim and Gregori fighting over the fate of mankind. If Heaven wins, which is doubtful, since I may very well be the last Ageless still alive, mankind has a chance. If Hell wins, Armageddon will fall, and the Earth will be wiped clean. Judgment day."

I swallow hard. "I'm sorry. No pressure, right?

"I don't know for certain that I'm the last of my kind, but I haven't heard from any of my cousins in a long time. I've found something that... may help us, but communicating is dangerous these days, with NAFAS in control of the Internet and monitoring all cellular traffic, not to mention all the other draconian measures that will undoubtedly follow." I can see the storm of totalitarianism on the horizon as surely as if I had a political weather map. This isn't my first rodeo. I wonder if I should say anything about the potential weapon that my relationship with Emil has uncovered, but realize that it won't matter. Time will lessen the chance that this will ever matter, that Emil will survive, that I will, that my child will even be born, that Earth will survive at all.

Still, my discovery gives me hope, unfounded though it might be. *Tell them, Terpsichore. They deserve the whole truth.*

"I'm leaving some things with your father that, if found by one of my cousins, will ensure that what I've learned and cannot investigate, the one chance we may have against the Nephilim, will be put to use." I wince. "Sorry. That sounded stupid. Suffice to say your father harboring a Nephilim and surviving suggests some way to protect humans from possession, or even to banish the Nephilim to Hell. This may be the key to victory. If you survive to adulthood, I'll continue my investigations, but your life must come first, for I don't know yet what you are, or what God's plan is for you." *Shit, lighten up Cora! You're scaring the poor kid to death!* "Sorry again if this is too much to wrap your head around. I hope I'm there to explain things to you fully in person, but I'll try to make these recordings more coherent in the future. Right now, I'm a little frazzled."

I hit *Pause* and punch up navigation to the nearest place I know where I can disappear, at least until I can make some kind of a plan. *Plan? Come on, Terpsichore. You know how your plans usually turn out.* Still, I need a refuge, funds, and a shift in identity. I know that I can find all three in Nashville, city of music. There, I can regroup, draw on resources, and decide where to go. *Three recharges, maybe nineteen hours driving...* I plan out my stops, keeping off the main highways, out of large cities, where I can pick up money, weapons, documents, work out contingencies if things go badly... as they always seem to do. No plan survives contact with Terpsichore, but I have to start somewhere.

I hit *Resume* and continue. "I must find a place to live in secret, to raise you in peace. Someplace remote, I think, and warm. The climate of this world is beyond crisis, and I despise the cold that these exacerbated seasons bring every winter.

"I pray that you don't judge me too harshly for keeping your father from knowing you. I love him, and I love you, my dearest, but the fate of mankind hangs in the balance between you and he. One day, perhaps, you'll meet him. I urge you to be careful if you try to find him, for you *will* be hunted, as I've been... and am being."

Gippy pulled the Dodge up beside their big Buick and they got out without a word. After four hours of exorcism, their job was done, the Nephilim permanently banished to Hell, but they were both exhausted. Gippy unlocked the Buick, and they started shifting their weapons and duffels from the Dodge, and two large aluminum suitcases from the trunk of the Buick to the other car. They'd boosted the Dodge in Fort Worth, and when they were done here, nobody would be able to trace it back to them. One of the aluminum cases went into the front seat, the other into the trunk. He tried to ignore the lifeless corpse of the Nephilim stuffed into the trunk. That, too, would be unidentifiable when they were finished.

Chemistry, baby... It never ceased to amaze him what could be made from a few chemicals mixed together, and the ultranet had everything you needed to get that mixture right.

"Want me to drive?" Empa lifted out their rifle cases and followed him. They hadn't used the long guns on this trip, but she'd taught him that having a weapon and not needing it was better than needing one and not having it.

"I'm good for a while." He helped pile their gear in the massive trunk of the Buick and slammed the lid, thoughts of Jeri warming his heart. "Home in twelve hours..."

"I'll set the timers." Empa turned back to the Dodge, leaned in, and he heard the aluminum cases slamming closed. She shut the doors and trunk as well, and strode back toward the Buick. He could see the fatigue in her stride, but she still had that cat-like walk, awareness, poise, that had impressed him the first time they met. *Rain, the woman in the trench coat, beautiful and terrifying, Lennie lying at her feet, bleeding out...* He shook off the memory and focused. "We can pick up coffee in Sulphur Springs."

"Gotta feed your demon, eh?" He grinned at her again, and she smirked.

"You *really* want to see a demon, take away my coffee." They got in, and he fired up the Buick, moved his Glock to the side-seat holster, and turned on the heat full blast.

Empa clipped her seatbelt with a sigh. "Home, Gifford."

"After two weeks on the road, you ain't gotta tell *me* twice." The car display said three forty-two am. He drove away at a sedate pace. They were five miles down the little dirt road when the thermite and napalm charges detonated, reducing the Dodge, the corpse, and any trace of him and Empa to unrecoverable ashes. *BBR, burned beyond recognition... Nothing cleans up a crime scene quite like fire.*

"One hundred ninety-four more." Empa sighed again and leaned back in her seat, rubbing her eyes.

"Don't be a pessimist," he chided.

"Listen to you using such language." She punched him lightly in the shoulder.

"Good teacher." Gippy had spent the winter months studying and training constantly. Literacy, tactics, marksmanship, close fighting—something Empa called Krav Maga—and the Lessons of the Five Rings kept him more than busy, but fulfilled him in a way he'd never dreamed. She had given him purpose, an enemy to fight, crafting him into a warrior for Heaven in the War of Souls. Hell currently had them outnumbered by a lot.

"Let me know if you need a break. I'm going to—" Empa's phone vibrated on the console, a message flashing up on the small screen, "Text Msg From Daddy."

"Don't he *ever* sleep?" Gippy muttered.

"Not much anymore, I'm afraid." She pulled up the message and said, "He's carrying a lot of baggage, Gip, and it's been a long winter for him."

"I know, but what are we supposed to do, drop everything and go chasing after his old girlfriend?"

Father Farrell messaged them at least once a week about their progress searching for Empa's cousin, Cora, who he'd known as Teri about twenty years ago. Finding out she left because she was pregnant with his child had hit him hard. It had hit Empa just as hard, since the children of the Seraphim couldn't bear children... until now. Gippy couldn't imagine having a child, that much responsibility. His life was complicated enough already.

"Yes, we are, but not until the weather breaks." She tapped a message and put the phone down. "Maybe next week, if New England doesn't get hit by another blizzard."

"I fuckin' *hate* snow." He pulled onto the on-ramp to I-30 and accelerated to the speed limit, clicked on the cruise control, and stretched his neck.

"Summer's coming. Then you can complain about the heat."

"Never. *Love* the heat. Bring it on." He laughed at her glare. "Seriously, you think we got a chance in... at all of finding your cousin?" A chance in Hell of finding an angel's daughter seemed blasphemous. Hanging around Empa had changed Gippy's view of things like that. Heaven and Hell were real, and human souls were the currency of both; Hell damned them, and Heaven redeemed them. He still wondered, with all he'd done, where his soul would go when he died. *Keep fighting the good fight, Gip. You'll get there...*

Empa shrugged. "I doubt it, but we have to try, for Emil, and there's only one place to start looking."

"So, Rhode Island... Is it really an island?"

"Brown University is now, but it didn't used to be."

"More boats?" Gippy didn't like boats.

"There's a bridge, and one thing universities are good at is keeping records. If there's anything to find, they'll have it."

"And if that fucker we banished from Father Farrell told every demon in Hell about where he met Cora, they could be waiting for us, right?"

"Yes." She shook her head and rubbed her eyes again. "Yes, they could be."

3
ON THE ROAD AGAIN

I hear Jeri close the upstairs door, her boots trundling down the stairs to the basement. I pull two wooden bokken from the rack of training weapons and advance on the downstairs door that I left ajar, girding my tumultuous nerves. *Such sweet sorrow...* Parting isn't anything new for us, but that never diminishes the anguish, the fear that we'll never see each other again. My life seems sometimes to have been nothing but a long string of final goodbyes. I pray to my grandmother that this won't be one.

But first things first. Steady spirit. As Jeri pushes the door open and enters, I pitch one of the bokken to her.

A smile flashes as she catches it by the hilt, glances around the dojo, and closes the door behind her. "So, *that's* how it is?"

I don't reply, don't return her smile, and take up the Chūdan stance, the point of my practice sword aimed at her throat.

Her smile wavers and dies. "Empa, I don't feel like—"

I *Kiai* loud enough to rattle the heavy sound insulation lining the walls, and strike.

Jeri parries reflexively, and I'm proud of her instant transition from calm to battle. Six months of intensive training has changed her from the street-smart punk terrified of the world into a competent, if not highly proficient, young warrior. She's still not faced true battle, except for the one time she saved my life with the stroke of a sword, but she's progressing nicely, no longer frightened of weapons, though she still doesn't like guns. She understands that we're at war, and that pacifism is not the path to survival. She does, however, love swords, despite having been run through with one. I have indulged her love in more ways than bladed combat, but this might just save her life.

As our wooden blades clash, I recall my first encounter with the man who taught me to fight properly with a katana, and whom I taught to love deeply and fully without losing himself. *He stands in his garden holding two practice swords, scrutinizing me without looking directly at me. I am unarmed. Before I can bow, he throws a sword to me, as I just have Jeri, and our first sparring match begins. He beats me badly, but there is surprise in his eyes as I take blow after blow without faltering. I earn his respect... and I fall in love.* Miyamoto Musashi was so much more than a warrior. A true Kensai in every sense of the word; a philosopher, artist, strategist, and Ronin fairly worshiped by other Samurai for his prowess. Also, a deeply private and solitary man, he taught me how to lead a life of solitude, and I taught him to love without letting pleasure cloud his philosophy of emotional control. I remember our last goodbye, his refusal to allow me to heal the persistent neuralgia that was plaguing him with pain every waking moment. He knew death personally already, and was unafraid to face it. My heart was broken, but he never gave into despair, yet another useless emotion in his opinion. His grace and training have saved me more times than I can count.

I press Jeri for a quick exchange, and finally rap her smartly on the shoulder. "You're *dead*, Jeri!" I lower my bokken.

"Gip said you wanted to *talk*, not kick my ass!" She rubs her sore shoulder, glaring at me.

I step up, put a hand on her bare forearm, take the injury, and feel her anger with me. I step even closer, our faces a hand-span apart. "*Feel* is for art, or music, or making love, Jeri. Where is your spirit?"

She nods, her temper vanishing in an instant, her lessons reasserting themselves. "Steady spirit."

"Good." I don't let go of her forearm, just to feel her soul, her insatiable eroticism, her undying love. I know she feels mine, but I remain stoic, steady, holding her gaze. "Now, tell me what you see."

"Everything. Close when far. Far when close." Her eyes remain fixed on mine, begging me to delve her soul, but I resist. "The targets are arranged in a line on the far wall, the black one in the middle. The mats are stacked on the right hand wall beside the practice dummies. Only three practice weapons are missing from the rack on the left hand wall. There's nobody else in the dojo, and there's nowhere someone could hide. You're wearing a business suit, silk shirt, light makeup, green contacts, no shoes, and—" She inhales through her nose. "—Alizarin."

"Good." I finally let myself smile. "I'm proud of you, Jeri."

She smiles, blushes, and swallows hard. "And you're leaving again."

"Yes. In the morning."

"How long will you be gone?"

"I don't know. We're going to try to find my cousin." I haven't told her where we're beginning our search, and she knows why. What I don't tell her, the Nephilim can't torture out of her. As for the rest, there's only one more thing to say. "I love you."

"*God,* I miss you when you're gone." Jeri drops her bokken, wraps me in her arms, and squeezes so tight I can't breathe.

I squeeze her back, since it's my only defense. I relish the feel of her, the heart beating against my ribs, her insatiable thoughts plaguing me, screaming erotic visions into my mind. *How I ever fell in love with a sex addict...* But I know that loving Jeri has been good for me. She taught me that I could love once again, fully and without reserve, and have that love returned. Both she and Gippy have saved my life in more ways than one. They give me hope, both for our struggle and for myself.

We finally break the clinch to breathe, and she stares into my eyes with tears pooling in hers.

Her mouth quirks into a mischievous smile. "Can I tear off your clothes now?"

I laugh and kiss her, my fists knotting in her spiky hair. She moans into my mouth, the metal studs piercing her tongue clicking against my teeth. I feel her the desire to torture me with those damned things.

I break the clinch. "Jeri, I have to say some things to you."

"Okay." Her nimble fingers start working on the buttons of my blouse. "Talk fast."

"Jeri!" I step back. "Please, just one second."

She stops, realizing I'm serious again. "Okay."

"I don't know where this search will take us, but it's going to be dangerous. If the Nephilim found Cora, they'll be watching her back trail. The Nephilim that was in Emil *certainly* knows she was an Ageless, and will have spread the word to watch for us wherever they were together." This, of course, is a huge hint where we're going, but nothing the legions of Hell don't already know. "*That's* the trail we have to follow."

"I understand." I see in her eyes that she does. "But you can be invisible now." She has a natural talent for makeup, hair, and fashion, and has become quite a master of disguises. She's spent a fortune outfitting us with dozens of different identities.

"We can try, but we'll have to ask questions, hack networks, delve into records, and if they're watching, they'll probably discover our investigation." I pick up our dropped bokken and take them back to the rack. "I just want you to know, this isn't like one of our hunting expeditions. This is going to take time and could expose us." I turn to her. "It might even expose *you*. You need to be ready to vanish if we get caught."

"You won't get caught." She steps up to me again, her face set in iron. "I refuse to consider that."

"You *have* to."

She shakes her head, and her tears spill. "Why?"

"Because I need to know you're *safe*, Jeri." A deep breath, and I can feel the fear of losing me emanating from her. "This is why I tried for so long to remain alone, why I didn't risk... being with someone, anyone. It's not just the emotional attachment, it's the danger, the fear of bringing Hell down on others. That's why I've been pushing your training so hard. I need to be able to focus on our job, not worry about your safety constantly. And I need to know that *you're* focused, that you're paying attention to your surroundings, seeing everything..."

"Awareness is a constant state," she nods. "I *am* focused. I promise. I just..."

"I know." I step up and raise a hand to brush her cheek, and she leans into the caress. "I know leaving will hurt, the not knowing, the worrying, but we'll be able to message and... you *know* I love you."

"I know." She coughs a tearful laugh, and turns to kiss my hand, reaching for me. "So, *now* can I tear your clothes off?"

I kiss her hard, eyes open, delving her soul, pulling her into mine, and sharing what I am with her, *everything* I am. I feel her shudder in my grasp, and pull back just far enough to speak. "Yes."

"Fuuuuk, *yes*!" She grabs my blouse, and buttons rattle to the dojo floor.

~

Gippy held Jeri at the door to the garage, not wanting to let go, not wanting to leave, but knowing he had to. "Sorry, Jer. The job."

"I know." She broke the clinch and sighed. "You two better hurry back. This celibacy shit sucks."

"We'll try, but no promises." He knew her, knew she was as much of an addict as he was, but her addiction was sex. Even being with both him and Empa didn't quash her desires. Addictions were something he understood. "If you need to scratch that itch..."

"Shut up." She kissed him and pulled back with a grin. "I'll manage. Ain't nothin' a few handy home appliances can't handle."

Gippy laughed. He'd seen her collection of toys, and they'd even played around some with them. "Just don't hurt yourself."

"No worries." She let him go and turned to embrace Empa. They'd both assumed new identities and looks. Empa wore a wig and makeup that made her look convincingly Afro-Asian. He'd gone for a trans persona that he felt comfortable with: makeup, jewelry, plucked eyebrows, wig, and a few additions to his underclothes that gave him a convincing figure. Jeri had suggested it and helped him with his walk and mannerisms. "You two take care of each other."

"We will," Empa assured her. "And you two stay sharp, please."

"We're on it. You watch your *own* backs." Hank, the old veteran who had accompanied them from the St. Luther's shelter, gripped Gippy's hand hard. He might be seventy something, but he was the healthiest septuagenarian on Earth, thanks to Empa. "And don't shoot your dick off."

"Right." Gippy grinned at Hank and even managed to match the man's iron grip. Months of training and good food had paid off. "Thanks, *really*."

"Ain't no thing, brother." Hank clapped him hard on the shoulder. "Fightin' the *good* fight, you know." He'd told Gippy about his time as a soldier, the not knowing whether they were going to be allowed to go after the actual bad actors, or if some political bullshit would pull them back... again. Now, he knew he was on the right side, and that meant everything.

"Here." Empa reached under her long coat and pulled the black-scabbarded length of her katana from the sewn in pocket, the sword she'd been given by Miyamoto Musashi. She held it out to Jeri. "Keep this."

Gippy's mouth fell open. He knew how much Empa treasured the weapon, her last remembrance from the man she had loved above all others in five millennia.

"Really?" Jeri stared at the sword for a moment, unwilling. She knew what it meant to Empa. "You *sure?*"

"I'm sure." Empa pressed the cherished weapon into Jeri's hand. "It's only a tool, a piece of metal, not a person." She glanced to Gippy and winked. He'd told her that once, and she'd said later that Musashi himself had said as much. "Keep it handy. It's better than a pistol for close work, and you're better with a blade."

"I..." Jeri nodded and took the sword, pulling it a few inches from the scabbard to peer down at the silvery metal. "I'll keep it for you."

"*Practice* with it. The balance is slightly different than the bokken."

"We on the road, E." Gippy reached for the door to the garage, knowing prolonging the moment would only make it hurt more. "We'll be in touch."

"You better be!" Jeri said with a scowl. "I love you both, you know."

"Yeah." Gippy swallowed the lump in his throat and shared another glance with Empa. "We love you, too, Jer. Just be safe."

"We're safe," she assured them, stepping back to nudge Hank. "Safe and sound. You two get to work."

"We'll keep the light on for ya," Hank added with a casual salute.

"Thanks." Gippy followed Empa into the garage and they got into the old Buick, Empa behind the wheel.

The car doors slammed, and she stabbed the garage door opener. The engine rumbled to life, and they backed out without a word. Half an hour later, they were on Interstate 85 North.

Gippy's phone vibrated in his pocket, and he pulled it and logged in. Jeri had sent him a warmly pornographic "Miss You!" emoji that made him smile. He replied, then loaded their route and tweaked it a little. "About two days?"

"I think so. Best if we don't hurry. We'll detour off the freeways to fuel up and get some sleep."

He nodded—cameras were always a concern—then pulled up a weather app. "Cold as fuck up there still."

"But not snowing anymore, and the roads should be clear."

He looked to her critically, knowing they needed to focus on what lay ahead, not what they were leaving behind. *Steady spirit...* "Think we'll find anything?"

"Something, but I don't know if it'll lead us anywhere. More than we found in Emil's closet, anyway. There are records of Cora, or *Teri Timmons,* being enrolled at Brown. We just have to get access."

"But without faculty credentials we're fucked," he reminded her.

"A Brown faculty affiliation *would* make it easy, but we'll see. Universities tend to share, but personal information is strictly controlled, at least if you're not a naffie."

"Right." Nephilim were hip deep in the NAFAS military and secret police. They already knew they'd have to be careful, so he changed the subject. "You gonna be Doctor Ellen Winston again?"

"I'll try that first. We may have to do a little electronic or *actual* B-and-E if we get stonewalled."

"Sounds like fun." He stretched and slouched in the seat. "What about me?"

She shrugged. "Research assistant, cop, wife... you choose."

Gippy couldn't imagine pulling off the casual intimacy that would be required for assuming the identity of Empa's wife. "Research assistant."

"Perfect. Get some sleep, and we'll work on your identity when you wake up."

"Fine with me." He put his head back and closed his eyes, images of Jeri playing through his mind as he drifted off. He dreamt of her, of course, but in the midst of their intimacy, she transformed into a demon.

"Journal entry five. May eleven, twenty twenty-two." I yawn and blink at the exit signs. "I think I'm dictating more to stay awake than anything else at this point. Sorry if it's a little disjointed. I'm coming into Nashville, which is one of my favorite cities in the world."

I take an exit and turn left onto Demonbreun Street. Here, at least, I don't need a map or a computer to find my way. "Music is a way of life here, so I fit in. I spent years here a century ago, playing in little dumps, spreading my gift, giving people hope... I don't think I can afford the exposure of doing that again. Too many people recording everything on their phones these days, but I'm hoping my stashes are still untouched." I cringe at the condition of the buildings, the filth on the streets, the homeless camping out under the freeway. "The place sure ain't what it used to be."

I tap *Pause* and pull into a dilapidated motel. A shoulder bag and a beat-up guitar case are my only luggage. I have some other things in the trunk, but carrying only these two here helps me blend in. I pay the surly manager cash for two nights, take a shower, set an alarm, and get some sleep. I dream of being pregnant, waddling around with a distended belly, childbirth, pain... and the life Emil and I created being gifted a soul. We greet our baby as mother and father... then both Emil and our child fade away, leaving me alone, heartbroken.

At two am I wake to my alarm, sit up, then hurry to the bathroom to throw up. Washing my mouth out and brushing my teeth, I check my new look in the mirror. A stranger with red hair, blue contacts, and freckles looks back at me. I look young but feel old.

I pull my phone on impulse and hit *Record*. "Morning sickness. Thanks a lot. If you're a girl, I hope you go through this, too. Not for revenge, just for the experience. I never get sick, and now I'm puking up my guts every morning. It's early for this kind of thing, and I hope everything's all right. I can't go to a doctor for a check-up."

I pause the recording and put on some non-descript clothes; jeans, tee shirt, denim button down untucked, and a light jacket too thin for this weather. The weight of a short barrel .38 revolver in a Velcro holster at the small of my back is completely undetectable. A stocking cap pulled low over my ears, and I'm out the door, carrying only my guitar case this time. The case is light because I left the instrument on the bed.

A quarter hour walk and I find a brew-pub in place of a nightclub where I used to play. It's changed hands half a dozen times in a century, but still stands, as most of the old clubs do. It's now called "Tunez and Brewz," obviously still playing to the music crowd, and even this late I can hear music from within. I step inside, scan for cops, and stagger my way to the bar.

"Any chance for a coffee. It's freezin' out there." I put my best southern twang into it, and the bartender nods.

"Sure thing!" He smiles at me, his eyes roving predictably. "You need a better jacket, gal. Freeze those tits right off in a wind breaker!"

I grin at him. "Ain't froze off yet, and I been a lot colder." *Denmark in winter, German 88's hammering the frozen countryside, nothing but a thin wool blanket for warmth...* I thank him for the coffee, sip, and cringe. It's instant. The climate's playing hell with crops all over the world, and the tropics are being drowned, a deadly new fungus killing coffee plantations by the hundreds of square miles. *Searing hot coffee in a tiny cup sipped in summer heat of Constantinople, strong, syrupy, and black as night...* I struggle not to weep into my cup.

There are only a few customers at the tables, and those are mostly intoxicated, including the poor young man trying to work his way through a song that he undoubtedly wrote himself. The melody is nice, but he's fumbling the chords and his lyrics are clumsy. I transform it in my head out of habit.

"Another?"

"I better not." A notion comes to me unbidden; I need a reason to linger and as usual, my answer is music. "I'm tapped out. Just pawned my guitar in fact."

His eyes narrow, and he nods to my empty cup. "You gonna stiff me for that, then?"

I wave a hand at the stage and the struggling youth. "Mind if I sing for my supper?"

His eyebrows arch. "If it's okay with Joey, sure."

I scooch off my barstool and haul my empty guitar case up to the stage, shrugging out of my wind breaker. I catch the young man's eye as he finishes his tune. "Mind if I join in? Payin' fer a cup of joe." I hook a thumb to the bar.

The young man blinks at me, and his eyes settle on my chest, then rise to my face, and he blushes. "Sure."

"Hocked my guitar." I step up onto the low stage and point to his spare. "Mind if I borrow?"

"You serious?"

"I can play anything you can name, pardner." I grin and pick up the old twelve string, strumming a chord and adjusting the tuning by reflex. My next strum comes out perfect. I settle my ass on a stool, and peal off a riff of notes straight out of my head. We've drawn some interest from the inebriated patrons. "You start, and I'll join in."

He grins. "All right, then, darlin'. Cetch me if ya can!"

He begins, and I follow easily, smiling at him, feeling his love for his songs. This is original stuff, his own, and I embellish here and there as the tempo increases. The meager crowd perks up at our antics, interest spreading through the room like a wave of warmth. I soak it in, feeling it, breathing in the notes, exhaling melody and love. Joey glows with it, suddenly stone sober and tearing it up, shifting tempo again. My fingers dance, and I follow, picking around his notes with plenty of time to improvise. He laughs, and I shine with it, reflecting the love back. Someone in the now rapt crowd whoops as we rip into Bluegrass, tearing up and down, chasing each other.

We continue for a solid ten minutes, and Joey begins to miss notes out of fatigue. I slow the tempo for him, and we wind down and wrap it up with a flamenco riff.

The sparce crowd howls, applauding wildly. Joey staggers off his stool and lets his guitar drop on its strap, thrusting out a hand to me.

"Joey Marks."

"Corey Sallanger." I shake his hand. "You're good!"

"You're *better*!" He barks a laugh. "What the hell you doin' in a dive like this, darlin'?"

"Travelin'. Tryin' to get south. Dunno where yet. Just out of the damn *cold*." I lean the loaned guitar against my stool. "I gotta hit the can. I'll be a few, but I'll play another set with you if you like."

"*Hell* yeah!" He grins and joins the sparse crowd as they applaud me off the stage.

I take my jacket and guitar case with me as I head to the back and downstairs to the bathrooms. The place hasn't really changed much with the years, at least architecturally. I find the old store room right where it was a century ago, and pull a folding knife from my back pocket to jimmy the simple latch.

Inside is dark until I flick on my pen Maglight. The room's full of junk, but navigable. I make my way to the back and find the old iron panel set into the brick wall, an ancient ash door when the place was still heated by a coal-fired boiler. My knife works the rust off the latch, and I pry the door open. The hinges are really rusted, and I have to pull hard; it makes a horrible screech. Inside is a nest of cobwebs, cockroaches, and mouse droppings. I grit my teeth and reach in and up to the shelf where I stowed my stash so long ago and find the long metal box. It's heavier than I remember.

I pull the old stainless steel safety deposit box down and open my guitar case. I'll open it later, but from the look and weight, nobody has touched it. Inside are nestled three hundred one ounce Krugerrands, each worth about three thousand North American Dollars. Currency may rise and fall, and banks can fold, but gold seems always to climb in value, especially now, when reserves are scarce and economies are in the toilet. I have stashes like this one all over the world, but rarely have to delve into them. Music has always been my currency, and has kept me alive when those around me have starved for lack of work. *The Irish famine, whole families gaunt, eating grass soup, hollow eyed...* Now, I have a legitimate emergency. Money means safety, and if I'm going to bear a child, that is what I need above all else.

I lock my guitar case on my trove and head back upstairs. I'll play another set, then head back to my room. I need more sleep and a good meal before I continue south. But where to go? Where can I find a haven where my child can grow up safe?

My child... The thought terrifies me.

4
NEEDLES IN HAYSTACKS

Can't believe they saved so much," Gippy mutters as we top the Highway 6 span across the risen Providence River.

"Nothing like the New Hope Seawall, but they did manage to keep some." The view from the top of the span is both heartbreaking and inspiring.

Most of Providence is submerged. The skyline was never much to look at anyway, but the seawall that shields the new island in the fork of the Seekonk River reminds me of the Great Wall of China. This one, unlike New Hope, doesn't face the direct brunt of the North Atlantic, and has survived. That it was largely built to preserve a university gives me a warm glow of the remaining value humans place on knowledge and learning. I remember one of my cousins, the daughter of Camael, Angel of knowledge, and how she burned trying to save the legendary repository in Alexandria. Here, at least, we can chalk up one win in the War against Education.

Our tires crunch old snow as we descend over the seawall surrounding the university district and take the first exit onto Waterman Street. There's almost no traffic, of course, and a few bundled-up passersby stare at us. I brake gingerly and turn left onto Brown Street. Thirty years ago, I never would have found a parking spot, but there's no trouble at all pulling the Buick to the curb in front of the administration building. I could probably park in a red zone and not even get a parking ticket.

"This is it?" Gippy shifts his weapon to his belt holster and reaches into the back seat for a heavier overcoat. After struggling into the coat, he hitches his bra back into place and checks his makeup in the mirror. "Game time."

White teeth flash as he checks them for lipstick, and I suppress a smile. *Welcome to my world...*

I'm impressed how well he pulls off the trans persona, the walk, the mannerisms, nothing overt, simply feminine. Jeri's done a good job coaching him. He's asked me a dozen times if he looks like a drag queen, but I assure him that he doesn't. He even draws some interested looks from students as we get out and start for the administration building. Maybe the padded underwear helps, but there isn't a facial or gait recognition program on Earth that would recognize him. I, on the other hand, keep my hood up and affect a slight limp as we slip-slide up the icy steps and enter the building.

A directory tells us where to go, up one floor to the records department. There, we face a bored-looking young man behind a glass barrier.

He glances at us both, his eyes lingering where young men's eyes usually do, and his eyebrows arching. "May I help you?"

"I hope so." I produce my altered Johns Hopkins ID and slide it through the slot. "I'm Dr. Winston, Johns Hopkins. We're searching for information about a woman who was enrolled here some time ago. She was a patient in one of our clinical trials."

He examines my ID without much interest. "Is she currently a student?"

"No. She was a non-degree post graduate in fifty-two but left the program. She's fallen off the grid, and we need to contact her." I can't get much of a sense of him through the glass, but he's clearly doubtful. I don't give him the name Cora was using yet. If he stonewalls us, I don't want to send up any flags for our enemies to trace. "There have been some... unforeseen long-term side effects to the medication we were testing."

"We can't give out any personal information, I'm afraid." He slides my ID back through the slot.

"Same old story, Doc." Gippy pouts and shakes his head sadly. "Nobody cares anymore, even if people are dying of lymphoma."

Gippy's comment scores a hit, and the young man's face flushes. "Now, wait just a minute..."

I wave his protest off. "He's just following their rules, Genie. That doesn't mean he doesn't care."

"That's right." The young man nods to me, then looks back to Gippy. "I *care*, but I can't give you any personal identifiers. I could lose my job."

"We've got all the personal identifiers we need." Gippy rifles his pocketbook and comes up with a sheet we printed from the university database. This is where things become dangerous. If Nephilim have hacked Brown's computer system and uploaded trace software that keys on any searches specifying Cora's former identity, we could end up on the receiving end of a missile strike. "This is her, Terisa Timmons, age twenty-eight, non-degree grad student in the music program. Her address when she was here is right there." He slides the printout through the slot and taps a lacquered fake nail on the paper. "We just can't *find* her."

The young man takes the paper and reads it carefully. We have his attention, or Gippy does, at least.

"All we need is a forwarding address, or anyone who might know where she went. A phone number, next of kin, even an old boyfriend would help." I put as much of me as I can into the plea for help, but I don't think much gets through the barrier.

"Please, could you just look her up for us?" Gippy pleads. "Her *life* may depend on it."

"I'll look, but I can't give you any of her personal information." He turns to a terminal and taps in Cora's assumed name, her student ID number, and department. Then he shakes his head. "No forwarding address. No next of kin or contact information. Not even banking info. She paid her tuition in cash."

"Cash? That's odd, isn't it?" I know it is.

"Yes, but not unheard of. That was... a troubled time, and many students still prefer to keep their financial information private." He sighs and scrolls through screens. "The only thing I've got is her advisor's name. Maybe you could contact her."

A flicker of hope kindles. We'll run into less bureaucratic red tape with Cora's former advisor, if she's still alive. "Well, that's something, I guess."

"Anything would be helpful. *Thank* you!" Gippy flashes him a heartfelt smile, and the guy blushes.

"Glad I can help. Her advisor's name is Miriam Donley." He pulls a pen and scratches something on the sheet Gippy gave him. "I'm just writing her phone number on here so I won't get in trouble. She's retired, but still lives outside Old Baltimore. I'll put my personal number on here, too, in case you have any more questions." His blush intensifies as he pushes the paper back under the glass, his smile warm and welcoming, clearly interested in more than information about a woman who once attended Brown.

"Thank you!" Gippy gushes, taking the page. "You're a *darling*."

"No problem at all, Miss..."

"Johnston, Genie Johnston. Nice to meet you..." Gippy beams at him, earning another blush.

"Robert, but everyone calls me Bobby. Here's my card with my email, just in case you're ever in town and need anything." Bobby slides the card through the slot.

"*Well*, next time I'm in town, I'll look you up." Gippy takes the card and flashes him another glowing smile, and I have to suppress one of my own.

Score one for the Gipster...

"Thank you, Bobby. I hope this helps." I nudge Gippy and we head for the office door. If we tripped some kind of cyber alert, there could be NAFAS squad cars already on the way. Outside, I pull up my hood and give Gippy a nudge. "Nice job."

"Thanks. More bees with honey, you know." He's glowing with his success.

"Much more honey, and he'd have asked you out."

"If we weren't in a rush, I might have asked *him* out!" Gippy flashes that smile again. "He was *cute*."

I know he's only kidding, but can't keep from giving him crap about it. "And poor Jeri sits at home alone while you're out seducing cute guys."

His glow dims. "Just flirting a little. I'm not serious. Ain't every day I get a guy to look at me when *you're* in the room."

"I'm kidding. The flirting worked. Use any weapon you've got." I get in the driver's side and Gippy pulls up Miriam Donley's number on his phone. In minutes he has her address.

"Eight hours!" He sighs and struggles out of his overcoat, moving his weapon to the seat holster. "I'm sick of this car already, E. It's like we fuckin' *live* in this thing."

I can't disagree. "We'll break it up, stop for the night in Allentown."

"Good! This damn getup is killing me." He hitches his bra again with a grimace.

I can't help but laugh. "Welcome to *my* world, bitch."

"Journal Entry ten. May twenty-first, twenty fifty-two. I'm crossing the Mississippi at Memphis, another music city. I stopped long enough to regroup, play a couple of clubs, and pick up another of my stashes. I'm sick of road food already." I nibble on a salty cracker to settle my tumultuous stomach and cringe at the grey water flowing sluggishly under the Memphis-Arkansas Bridge. Even through the skim of ice, I can see the floating plastic waste. I realize I'm dictating to someone who may know nothing of geography, and back up. "Sorry. The Mississippi is the biggest river in North America, the watershed for about a third of the nation that used to be the United States. The Big Muddy's not what she used to be, choked by pollution. I hope I can find someplace in this decaying empire to raise you that isn't a *complete* disaster."

Environmental advocacy is a thing of the past, it seems, with the dissolution of the EPA, one of the first acts of the unified NAFAS government. Regulations were slashed, and corporations re-tooled in a matter of a few years. The greatest river in North America is now dead, murdered by runoff from industrial agriculture, manufacturing, fracking waste, and coal mine tailings. Thirteen times the Ohio River caught fire before humans finally realized that oil and water don't mix and legislated change. Now things are worse than ever before. I have no confirmation that Nephilim are behind the destruction of this world's ecosystems, but it fits their modus operandi. Pollution, illness, cancer, despair... They all go hand in hand.

I gird my tears and shift the subject. "Faced with Jackson Mississippi or Little Rock Arkansas, I chose the latter, the lesser of two evils. Neither state's human rights records are shining examples of brotherly love, but I have no choice. Texas won't be much better, but I have to make some stops there to buy supplies." Another NAFAS deregulation was the sale of firearms, and it seems like Texans are more in love with guns than their own children. Unfortunately, I have to protect myself, and there I can buy what I need with no questions, no ID, no cameras, and no waiting period. I will avoid Dallas out of fear of being recognized, and Houston is half-drowned, but Austin and San Antonio aren't so bad. At least they weren't the last time I attended the regional music festivals. Even with every dime of federal funding to the arts cut off, some culture remains. I wonder, briefly, if I might find a place in rural San Antonio to settle down, then discard the idea.

"Finding a place for us to live is turning into an exercise in futility, I'm afraid. Large cities have more music culture, which I can use for cover and income, but these days they also have a much larger police presence and constant surveillance. The use of facial recognition software is on the rise, and I must be careful." I glance at myself in the mirror, still a freckled redhead, and wonder how to change my look, or if I should. A white woman is less of a target for harassment in the south than a Latina or Asian, even these days, but I have little doubt that my picture's on every police network in NAFAS. "I need someplace rural, but not too rustic, warm enough to avoid the worst of winters to come, but out of the hurricane belt, on the grid, but not on the network. Christ, I may as well be looking for an honest politician."

I cringe at my own blasphemy, but I know my dear lost uncle would understand.

"Sorry if I'm coming off as a cynical old crone, but I've been around a long time, and some things just never seem to change. I know I can't shelter you entirely from the evils of the world, but I hope you can at least grow up in a safe, happy environment." *If there is such a thing in this forsaken world anymore.*

I pause my recording and turn on some music to lighten my mood. I'll be in Texas in a few hours, so I choose some good-old fashioned country twang. The mournful lyrics don't do my temperament much good. I'm battling loneliness as much as I am the Nephilim. I am, if anything, a creature of human culture, and without human contact, I'm bereft. The music does give me some ideas for my next persona, however.

"I need a damn cowboy hat and a pair of shit kickers!" I put some Texas twang into my voice, easy as putting on a pair of blue jeans, which also go onto my mental shopping list; boot cuts with a snug backside, I think. Something to keep those Texan eyes on my ass, not on my face. "No online shoppin' for this ol' girl, though. I need some duds that have some miles on 'em." I'll have plenty of off-freeway miles from Shreveport to Austin. Surely I'll find a Goodwill store somewhere along my route.

"Goodwill..." The word strums chords of irony in my heart. I wonder, sometimes, if there is still much goodwill left in the hearts of humans.

Then I remember my sweet, generous Emil, and my heart breaks anew.

5
A RAY OF HOPE

They'd called ahead, so Donley knew who they were and why they were there when they walked up the sidewalk to her drab, one-story brick house in the suburbs of Baltimore. When Gippy pushed the doorbell, however, loud barking resonated through the thick door, followed by a harsh metallic rattling sound. Something large scratched furiously at the other side of the wood.

Gippy staggered back a step and just about lost his footing on the icy walkway and the damn high-heeled boots. "Mutha..."

Empa steadied him. "Shh. Just dogs. Probably for protection if she's living alone."

"Sounds like a whole *pack* of 'em." Big dogs made him nervous; too many run-ins with canine security during his years on the street. He'd seen naffies use dogs on homeless people too many times to be comfortable around them. The damn things *wanted* to bite you, he could see it in their eyes. He tugged his disguise straight and made sure the wig was in place. He was actually having fun with the trans persona but could have done without the fake boobs. They were gel, not just padding, which gave a more natural movement when he walked, but whenever he turned quickly it felt like they were going to fly off.

The door cracked open, coming up short on a security chain, and a slightly frail female voice shrilled from the other side of a sliding security barrier. "Oh, stop it you two! First visitors in months and you act like they're here to rob me! Sit, Symphony! Concerto, down!" The cacophony subsided, and the face of an old black woman peered out through the six-inch gap from behind a metal grating. "Dr. Winston, I presume?" A merry chuckle followed.

"Yes, Dr. Donley, but please call me Ellen." Empa smiled at Donley as the woman scrutinized them. "This is my research assistant, Genie Johnston."

"Of course. Just let me get this silly thing open." Keys rattled, and the security barrier squeaked as she pushed it aside.

The door was still chained, and before she could close it to release the latch, a huge canine snout poked through the gap, a tongue the size of a human hand lolling out, a strand of thick drool threatening to drip from the slavering maw. Gippy forced himself not to cringe.

"Back, Concerto! Behave, or I'll lock you up!"

The snout receded, and the door closed. The chain rattled, and it opened again, fully this time. The woman stood blocking the two massive dogs with one hand, smiling at them. "Forgive these unruly beasts. They're really nice, just big and loud. They're good boys."

"I love dogs, actually." Empa stepped forward and bent down to hold out her hands palm up. The dogs sniffed her and licked her hands, both of them wiggling with glee.

Gippy shuddered in disgust.

"And they seem to like you, too. Please come in." Donley backed up and made a motion with her hand to the two massive beasts. "Down. Be good, now!"

The two canines backed up, and Gippy followed Empa into the house. It smelled of dog and a slightly musty, smoky aroma that suggested Dr. Donley smoked weed on occasion. Gippy knew that lots of older people did for aches and pains. Donley closed the door, shot the chain, and secured the extendable steel barrier. Gippy noted where she tucked the key just in case they had to leave in a hurry—part of Empa's training; always be aware of your surroundings, plan escape routes, obstacles, threats...

Right now, the two biggest threats were a pair of Rottweilers the size of small horses. Donley had just locked them all in a cage with the beasts, which felt like a scene from a horror movie.

"Please, come in and sit down. Can I get you anything? Coffee, tea, lemonade?"

"Coffee would be lovely if you have some ready. Don't go to any trouble." The dogs edged around Donley to sniff Empa thoroughly, butts wagging, tongues lolling.

"Symphony, Concerto, come! Leave them alone for two minutes!" Donley bustled into the kitchen. "Coffee for you, too, Genie?"

"Please, if it's no trouble, Dr. Donley." Gippy forced calm as one of the dogs nosed toward him—*steady spirit*—and put down a hand as he'd seen Empa do. The nose was cold and wet, and he wiped the slobber on his jacket. The other beast stuck its nose right into his crotch. The dogs seemed friendly—too friendly, in fact—but Gippy could only imagine how they'd react if any harm came to Dr. Donley.

"Not at all, and please call me Mary. Have a seat in the living room. I'll just be a moment. Ignore the boys. They'll settle down once they get to know you."

Gippy followed Empa into a room furnished in old comfortable chairs and a half-sized grand piano. One entire wall of bookshelves was filled with books, sheet music, and framed photos, everything neat, clean, and organized. There were other instrument cases here and there, and a cello stood in the corner. He wondered if Donley played them all. They took seats, the cushions soft and thick, and Gippy crossed his legs to keep canine noses at bay. Both dogs sat before Empa, panting happily as she patted their huge heads and scratched their ears. He wondered if they picked up on her nature somehow or just got a warm feeling around her as most people did.

Donley bustled in with a wooden tray in hand, her steps short and a little unsteady, the coffee rippling in the cups. "There's milk and sugar on the tray, if you like." She put the tray down on the little table between them and picked up a mug for herself. The dogs nosed over, but backed off with one word from their mistress. "It's instant, I'm afraid, but..."

"No problem, Mary. Thank you." Empa took her cup and sipped.

Gippy spooned sugar into his and stirred. *More flies with honey... Steady spirit. Conversation first, then information.* "I've never seen so many musical instruments. Do you play them all?"

"Not as much as I used to, I'm afraid." Donley sat and sighed, raising one hand, flexing knobby fingers with a wince. "Old age *sucks,* young lady."

"I'm sorry," Gippy mumbled, suddenly embarrassed.

"Don't be." She flashed a smile. "I had a great career and was lucky enough to teach a lot of wonderful young people to appreciate music." She sipped her coffee. "You mentioned Teri, and I had to look her up to remember. She was only one of my students for two years, and non-degree, but what *talent* she had."

"I hope you understand why we need to find her," Empa said. "Our clinical trial..."

"Yes, well, what I know about medicine wouldn't cover a single page. Seems kind of... a shame to test medicines on people."

"A necessity, I'm afraid." Empa sipped her coffee. "I don't suppose you know where Teri is now?"

"I'm afraid not. I remember, now that I read up on her school records, that she left rather abruptly, before the end of spring session. She was in a relationship with a young man at the time, and after she left, rumors went around that they had a falling out. I wanted to ask him what happened to her, but he'd dropped out of the PhD program and vanished." She sighed. "Two promising careers cut short."

Gippy realized she was talking about Father Farrell and asked, "Do you know the man's name?"

She shook her head. "No, but he was... Some said he was a strange fellow. Autistic, but high-functioning. A brilliant scientist, they said. He evidently didn't handle Teri's sudden departure well."

"And she left nothing to let you know where to forward her grades or evaluations?"

"No. Nothing." Donley shrugged. "Would you like to see her file?"

"You still have access to Brown's records?" Gippy felt a surge of anticipation.

"Oh, better than that!" Donley barked a laugh and put her cup aside to stand. "I keep files on all my students. Two hundred and thirty-one of them! I even followed their careers, the ones I could keep track of." She bustled over to the piano and opened the seat lid, pulling out a shiny Apple Fritter, tablet. She tapped the touch screen and logged in. In the time it took her to totter over to Gippy, she'd pulled up her full file on Terisa Timmons. She handed the tablet to Gippy. "Feel free, but please don't delete anything."

"Oh, I won't. Thank you!" Gippy started scrolling, astounded how much information the document contained. "There's a *lot* here!"

"Well, I *do* like to be thorough." Mary turned back to her chair. "Teri, now that I recall her, was brilliant but scatterbrained. A true creative genius with an amazing knowledge of music history, and as talented as anyone I've ever met. She couldn't, however, keep a coherent account of her work to save her life, which was why she was non-degree. She could *never* have managed a dissertation."

"That's a shame." Empa shot Gippy a pointed look and nodded down to the tablet in his lap.

She want me to steal it? he wondered. Then he realized he didn't have to.

Until his time with Empa, Gippy hadn't had much education, and couldn't even read, but months of practice had opened up a whole new world to him, and computers were doorways to everything. She'd taught him caution, of course, for they were always worried about being tracked. The coolest thing about computers, however, was that you didn't have to steal one to take the information they held.

"Mind if I just scan through this while you two chat? There's a lot here, and we might find something we can use to track her down."

"Not at all!" Donley waved dismissively.

The dogs continued to faun over Empa, who scratched them absently while sipping coffee and carrying on an effortless conversation about nothing in particular.

Gippy slipped a hand into his pocketbook, found the Bluetooth thumb drive, and pressed the tab that put it into receive mode. He then pulled down the tablet's settings and enabled its Bluetooth. *Scan for new devices? Yes!* It found his thumb drive in only a few seconds, and he copied the entire Teri Timmons file onto it. Data safe, he disconnected, deleted the record of the device's connection from the tablet's settings, and continued to scan the document. There were a lot of images of sheet music, and copious notes from Donley on Teri's accomplishments, grades, and astounding musical talent. She evidently played at the graduate lounge every Friday night.

Then he found a copy of the university personnel file that Bobby wouldn't let them see. It wasn't much, but did have a social security number—Gippy wondered if that was real—phone number, address in town, and some other personal data. He doubted they were anything more than fakes, smoke and mirrors, but one thing did catch his eye. Teri had a parking permit. She'd owned a blue 2028 Tesla, and parked on campus. The record included plate number, her Tennessee drivers' license number—if not fake, then long expired—and the vehicle's VIN.

Score! he thought, skimming past for anything else they might be able to use. The rest was just more notes and music stuff, none of which Gippy cared about. It was all on his thumb drive, and they could study it in detail later for clues. Empa had found a code in the sheet music Cora had left with Father Farrell, and there might be more clues here.

"Well, that's disappointing." He closed the file and got up to hand the tablet back to Donley. "Nothing much, I'm afraid. Maybe her old landlord will have a forwarding address." Reporting failure seemed safer than telling her what he'd found.

"I doubt it, if the school didn't get one." She took the tablet and set it aside, pushing on the arms of her chair to stand. The dogs whined and nosed over to her, and she absently patted them both. "Can I offer you another cup before you go? I feel like I should have been more helpful."

"You tried, Mary, and that's all we can expect." Empa stepped over to her and held out a hand. "Thank you so much."

"You're welcome." Mary shook her hand, then seemed for a moment to stiffen, as if surprised by something. Then she shook her head and sighed. "I'm sorry I couldn't give you more."

"Well, we had to try." Empa knelt and ruffled the dogs' ears. "And you two are just the best boys in the *world*, aren't you?"

The massive dogs ate up her adoration like kibble, butts wagging and tongues lolling.

"They're spoiled *rotten* is what they are!" Donley collected the cups and took the tray back to the kitchen, her steps straight and quick.

Empa stood, but slowly, stiffly, and Gippy realized what she'd done. The daughter of the angel of healing... sometimes she had no choice but to spread her gift.

Donley reappeared with a broad smile. "Well, I wish you could stay longer, but I know you must be in a hurry. You have my number if you have any more questions. Let me show you out." She moved quickly to the door, her strides longer than before, her hands sure on the locks.

"Thank you for the coffee." Gippy slipped past her onto the porch, staying close to Empa. If she took the woman's infirmity, she might need the support, especially on the icy sidewalk.

They said their goodbyes and made their way slowly to the car, Empa taking short measured steps.

"You took her pain, didn't you?" he asked when they were far enough away not to be overheard.

"Some of it. Not all."

"You okay?"

"I will be." They got into the Buick, Gippy behind the wheel. "I... felt something in her. An echo of Cora, I think."

"Echo?" Gippy glanced at her, a little worried. "What's that mean?"

"Cora spread love with her music. That was her gift. She could make just about anyone happy just by playing or singing. I felt some of that in Mary."

"Really? That's weird." He knew Empa's powers were real; he'd felt them, seen them work. Other Ageless had different gifts, he supposed, but magical music didn't seem possible.

"You had to experience it to understand." Empa shook her head and sighed, still clearly in pain. "Did you get anything?"

"It's all on my thumb drive. Teri...er, Cora had a campus parking permit. I got the tag and VIN of her car. We might be able to track it if she sold it."

"Good. I'll dig into records, and you drive." She pulled her phone, her fingers moving stiffly.

"Where to?"

"Just away for now. I don't want her to think we got anything, and I don't want anyone to know we visited. Nephilim might have found out we were at Brown, but there's no digital record of our visit here, just one phone call."

"Right." Gippy pulled away and drove through the neighborhood, vaguely in the direction of the highway. "If she sold the car anywhere, there'll be a record of the VIN transfer. Even if it was scrapped or stolen, someone's gonna have it."

"Thank God for electronic records," Empa agreed

"Journal Entry eighteen. May twenty-eighth, twenty fifty-two. We crossed over into Mexico at Laredo. Strange that there's no check at the border anymore. Well, not a *real* check, anyway, just a bunch of former Federales in NAFAS uniforms. One big happy fascist empire. It's a wonder they didn't insist on *frisking* me." A coal-emulsion pickup truck blows past me at over a hundred miles an hour, but nobody cares how fast you drive in rural Mexico. I could go offroad and not hit anything but sagebrush for miles. "Good thing they didn't check me too closely, actually, since I've got enough ordinance in the trunk to start a revolution."

Revolution... smuggling muskets into Paris under an oxcart full of manure. The gaunt faces beyond hope... the executions. Never again will I send innocents into the jaws of Hell's minions. We always lose, for war fosters hate even in victory.

"I shouldn't run into any problems, but I'm being careful. I think I'll stick to back roads once I recover my stash in Mexico City. I should probably sell my car and get something that runs on fossil fuel. Monterrey for that, I think. Not as many charging stations down south, and the roads are bad. Maybe a four wheel drive would be best. I'll want to get below the hurricane belt before I start looking for a place to live. The season's getting worse every year. I hope I don't have to go into South America."

I stay at the speed limit, because cops like to pull over out of state plates, not to mention gringo women traveling alone in Latin America. Things aren't as bad as the Middle East, or even most of my first few millennia, but still, I don't want trouble. I'm prepared for it, but the last thing I need is a run in with NAFAS. Strange how some things never change; a woman traveling alone has to take precautions. I've been a slave more than once, and I don't care for an encore performance.

"I'm wondering how long we'll have to live in hiding, but years, certainly. I need someplace remote, someplace a white woman can raise a child without drawing too much attention. I don't know if there's anywhere like that left on Earth, but I think our chances are better the farther south we go, and rural communities are less likely to give us problems."

I cross the interchange with Highway 2 and see a truck stop ahead. My stomach growls, and I'm tired of junk food. My Tesla's battery is below one quarter, too. A meal and a recharge are in order. I pause my recording, unplug and pocket my phone, and move my pistol from the floorboard to the back of my waistband. My car doesn't handle the dirt crossing between the strips of freeway very well; one more reason to trade it in on something with four-wheel drive. I pull into a charging station at the gasolenara, don the bedraggled cowboy hat I scrounged out of a dumpster in San Antonio, and get out.

I've transformed myself once again, a southwest blond in jeans, denim shirt, sheepskin vest, hat, and worn shit-kicker boots. I'll have to change again farther south, maybe dye my hair dark, but here, this works perfectly. I plug in and slot five tencoins for a thirty minute charge. The solar farm behind the truck stop makes me smile... energy straight from the sun into my car. There's hope for mankind after all.

"Need anything, Chiquita?" A beefy hombre leans against the fender of his rig, more gut than brawn. Not my type, and I don't like the way he's looking at me.

"No gracias. Solo algo de sol y comida."

His eyebrows arch at my flawless Spanish, and he replies in kind. "El Rancho has good carne guisada, if you like spicy."

"Gracias!" I wave, lock my car, and start walking across the dusty parking lot for the restaurant, my cowgirl swagger intact and my mouth already watering at the scent of grilling meat on the air. It might not be beef, but it sure smells good, and I'm not squeamish about where my protein comes from.

I step into El Rancho, and the music from a sound system hits me harder than the fabulous scents from the kitchen. My boot heels clack against the linoleum floor as I cross to the counter, weaving my way through the mostly empty tables, unconsciously moving to the rhythmic Latin music. I can count the customers on one hand, which is good. I draw a couple of stares and force myself to quit swaying my hips to the beat. Sometimes I can't help myself.

"Hola senorita." A big Latino in a stained white shirt and apron steps out of the kitchen. "Menu?"

"No necesito." I doff my hat and wave it to cool my face, reconsidering the heavy spice of the carne guisada. I need something that won't upset my newly delicate digestion. I keep the conversation in Spanish just to make it clear that I'm not the average gringo. "Chicken quesadilla with rice, and ice tea, please."

"Coming right up!" He grins and retreats to the kitchen.

The tea arrives immediately, sweet with a wedge of lemon, delivered by a round Latina with a quick smile. "You passin' through?"

"Si. Heading south for winter. Maybe Guatemala or Belize."

"Skip Belize. The storms..." She makes a gesture that needs no translation. Thirty or forty major storms a year have ravaged the Caribbean side of Central America. "Best stick to the west coast or keep headin' south."

"Gracias." I raise my glass to her and sip, then pull my phone and start looking for a destination. I've never been very good at planning ahead, but in this I have to focus and find someplace I can call home for a while. Not Mazatlán or Acapulco, for they're already drowning with the rise of the sea. *Memories of beaches, white sand, reggae music, dark sweaty skin against mine, the sweet scent of ganja...* I shake it off as the music shifts to a salsa tune I know, and I find myself humming along, the rhythm invading my bones.

My food arrives and a refill for my tea. I thank the waitress and eat, continuing to look through maps on my phone for someplace safe, still humming, moving to the rhythm. *Something about Latin music...*

The door chime rings, and I glance up to spot the unmistakable reflection of two NAFAS officers in the stainless steel of the counter's splash board. Their cruiser's parked outside, wide brimmed hats on their heads, torsos bulky with body armor, and belts laden with weapons. My stomach clenches on my half-eaten lunch, but I suppress my wash of fear. I push my plate away and sip my sweet tea. Puking wouldn't be good right now.

The cops take a table, obviously here to eat. They're not after me, but I've got to be careful. My face might be on their radar. The Nephilim probably have allies in the NAFAS police force, and uploading my picture to their search list wouldn't be unlikely. I put on my hat and wave over the waitress.

"No bueno?" She nods to my half-full plate with a frown.

"Oh, *muy* bueno." I pat my tummy and pull two C-notes from my pocket, twice the price of the meal. "Can you pack it up for me?"

Her smile flashes. "Si." She takes my plate to the kitchen.

I gauge the angles to the door and grit my teeth. I'll have to walk right past the NAFAS troopers. The music changes again, and I hum Hotel California, considering my options. They can't see my face from where they're sitting, but cops are observant, and a gringo woman walking past will draw their attention.

"There she stood in the doorway. I heard the mission bell. I was thinkin' to myself..." *This could be Heaven and this could be Hell... Heaven and Hell...* One hand settles on my stomach, for inside me now resides the union of both. *Oh Emil, how can you stay sane with such an abomination inside you?*

The waitress returns, and I push the two bills across the bar. "No cambio."

"Gracias!" She looks surprised, but only briefly, tucking the bills into her apron.

"Baño?" I ask.

She nods to my right, and with one glance, I thank God. The bathrooms are away from the troopers, down a side hall with a door to the outside at the end. I slide off my stool, thank the waitress and cook, and head to the bathroom. I pee, manage not to throw up, and slip out the service entrance. I'm in my Tesla and down the road before the big hombre who called me *little girl* finishes fueling his rig.

I plug in my phone and punch *Record*. "Back on the road after a close call with some NAFAS troopers. Time to start being more careful." I breathe and my stomach settles. "By the time you listen to this, you'll probably already know, but you must never trust the authorities, whether they're police, military, or something else. We're being hunted by Nephilim, and they're very good at worming their way into positions of power. They won't know you, but they have my face and several of my identities. If they ever catch me..." I swallow hard. *Memories of the inquisition, blood, horrors, torture, screams...* "I'll never let them take me alive. I've seen what they can do. I wonder, when you listen to this, if I'm with you still or gone. I love you more than life itself, but I may have to leave you to keep you safe, for they'll never stop hunting me."

6
ELECTRON TRAIL

Score! Monterrey, Nuevo Leon, Mexico." Gippy tapped his phone and grinned to Empa. They were on I-70 east out of Baltimore. She'd taken over driving once they cleared the suburbs, insisting she was feeling fine and he was better at tracing down car facts. "There's a record of Cora's Tesla being sold to a car dealer, Maestro Motors. June second, 2052." He punched up the car dealership and frowned. "Place looks dodgy as fuck."

"*Maestro* Motors? Really?" She looked at him sidelong.

"Really. Why?"

"Because that sounds *exactly* like the kind of place she would pick. Cora was impulsive if anything. She was never very good at planning, so she didn't. Utter chaos."

"How the hell is she still alive?" Gippy knew Empa pretty well by now, and if there was one thing she was, it was prepared. She planned everything, adjusted her plans when the shit hit the fan, and always had multiple alternatives lined up. Preparedness was her method of survival.

"By being unpredictable, I guess. She always said you can't catch what you don't understand. She'd shack up with a street musician, then drop them like a hot potato for a concert pianist." She shook her head with a smile. "She used men for cover as much as anything. Groupie, gaffer, roadie, whoever she could latch onto, which was pretty much anyone she felt safe with. She'd play whatever role felt right."

He gaped at her. "I thought Ageless didn't like hooking up."

"Not all Ageless are like me. I'm... Well, you know from Jeri, I suppose." She shrugged. "When I touch someone, I get more than a dump of their emotional history. I feel what they feel, which makes intimacy... difficult in ways it's hard to explain. Cora's not like that, though she can generally tell if someone's good-hearted. That might have been what drew her to Emil initially. He's unusual, and a truly good soul, but when she first touched him, she would have felt the Nephilim inside."

"That must have scared the shit out of her." Gippy had touched Nephilim, but only felt a little uneasy. When he'd touched a woman possessed by a succubus, however... He shivered all over at the memory of Chaki, the Latina who ran the office of a chop shop in Albuquerque where he'd bought a new tag for their car. He had little doubt that she was the reason they'd been ambushed by NAFAS goons in Memphis days later. Hell's network was extensive, and one call to a Nephilim with their license plate would have been enough to bring the Hounds of Hell baying to their door. That one call had also sent the naffies and a Nephilim to St. Luther's, nearly costing Father Farrell and Jeri their lives.

"Initially, I suppose, but curiosity must have pushed her to find out how he could survive being occupied by a Nephilim without having his soul destroyed. I might have done the same. I've never encountered that before."

Gippy nodded. "And his autism gave her the slippery mind theory. She gave us what we needed to exorcise them."

"Absolutely right. Cora's the reason we have the weapon that tipped the scales."

"Remind me to thank her when we find her." He took a deep breath and asked the question that had been plaguing him for months. "So, if this was Cora's theory, how come she never followed up on it? She knew about Laurence Caldwell. Why didn't she go to the Lady of Healing and look up his records?"

"I don't know. Maybe she did. That might be why Caldwell's medical record was expunged, or... maybe she didn't make it." Empa's voice had taken on a steely tone that meant she was fighting back emotions that would only cloud her judgment.

The lessons of the Five Rings came to him again: High spirit is weak; low spirit is weak; steady spirit. Vigilance is a constant state. Focus on the now. See all things.

Gippy changed the subject. "So, Mexico." He tapped his phone. "South on 340 at Fredrick, and we'll hook up to 81. The freeway should be clear of snow."

"Should be. And we'll need another change of identities, I'm afraid. I need to look more Latina than Afro-Asian, and you need to drop the trans persona."

"Damn, and I was just starting to *enjoy* wearing a bra." He cupped his fake boobs and jiggled them to break the somber mood. High spirit might be weak, but a little humor would break the low spirit. Sometimes he felt like they were always on an emotional teeter totter—hope and sorrow, joy and loss, fear and aggression, loneliness and reunion. His job was to balance them in the middle.

Empa snorted a laugh. "We can figure out something for you on our way through Texas."

"Avoid Dallas," Gippy said flatly, though he doubted that he needed to remind her.

She nodded. "Absolutely. I think we'll need a new car, too, but let's wait to see what we find in Monterey."

"We should at least change tags if we can find another olive green Buick," he suggested. "Too many cameras in Baltimore, and if our questions about Cora set off a search alarm on Bobby's computer, they might be on our trail already."

"Good call. In fact, I think I want to avoid big cities until we do." She squinted at a sign far ahead and moved into the exit lane. "Texas here we come."

"Yee-haw! Find a good sized town and we can hit a drug store or salon." Gippy lowered his visor and checked his look in the mirror. "Damn shame. I put a *lot* into this look."

"And you can't unpluck your eyebrows," she said.

"Right." He thought about it for a while, considering options, all of Jeri's suggestions, and the things they had packed. She'd sketched all kinds of ideas using a cosplay program, and he had them all on his phone. He flipped through several, and came up with a notion. "How about musicians again? We buy cases to carry our long guns incognito, and if we're following Cora, and she was into music..."

"Good idea, but Cora wasn't *into* music, she *was* music." She shook her head, again clearly walling off emotions. "We'll shift our looks in San Antonio. They still have an art and culture district along the river."

"Fine by me." Gippy slouched and reclined his seat. "Wake me when you're tired, and I'll drive for a while."

~

I never thought I'd tire of music, but listening to reggaeton from San Antonio to Monterrey is driving me slowly insane. I glance at Gippy and suppress a smile. He's so into his new disguise he could start up a band. We found a salon in San Antonio, and his new dreadlock weave-in looks natural and covers his ears. We took our time from Baltimore, and he stopped shaving, trimming his scruff into a face-altering wedge goatee. Thick false eyebrows hide his plucked ones, and a scruffy open-necked shirt with a gaudy gold cross necklace and ragged jeans round out his new persona. Not even a NAFAS supercomputer would guess that this person was a hot black trans woman only days ago.

Jeri has been giving him lessons.

I tap him on the shoulder, interrupting his groove, and he kills the music.

"Sup, sistah?" He grins, proud of his practice. Too proud maybe.

"Ease up a little, *brah*." I point to the ridges of mountains ahead. "Monterrey. Punch up Maestro Motors for me."

"Fine. You gotta work on your saucy Latina thing a bit though." He pulls up an address on his phone and syncs it with the car's system.

"You work on you, I'll work on me, okay?" My own disguise was easier: makeup and cheek cushions to make my jaw look wider, darker eyebrows, a wig to hide my ears and neck, dark contacts, and hip padding in my jeans. A padded push up bra with a V-neck shirt, and a flash of midriff for eye distraction, and I'm done. I wonder how Cora would have blended in. She's Greek by birth, but her hair is light and her eyes greenish. Nothing cosmetics can't alter, of course, but her fair skin's a giveaway. *Why Mexico*, I wonder for the hundredth time since Baltimore.

The nav app tells me where to exit, and we leave the highway. The city has sprawled a lot in the last few decades, as most inland metropolitan areas have, absorbing the populations of coastal areas now underwater. The mountains restrict the spread to the south and west, but not to the north and east. Most of the high rise business district has only expanded upward, towering buildings of pharmaceutical, agricultural, and business megacorporations challenging nature's skyline of conical green mountains. The nostalgic downtown remains as it was a hundred years ago, narrow streets and colorful buildings, but the newly developed outlying areas are dismal, flat, unpainted concrete, high fences, trash littering the streets, starving dogs, and stripped cars. Some of the cars have families living in them.

Steady spirit... You can't save them all... yet.

We find Maestro Motors situated between the old and newer districts, a walled courtyard with an iron gate that would dissuade an urban assault vehicle. Two armed guards stand at the gate, currently open for business. Inside, the space is jammed with high-end cars and trucks, most probably stolen, chopped, and now for sale. There's a row of garage doors at the far end where vehicles are modified. With one glance at the place's website, Gippy had said, "Chop Shop."

I turn into the entry. There's a security camera on the wall, but the roof of the car and dark sunglasses hide my face. A guard steps up to the driver's side window and smiles down at me.

"Hola." His right hand stays on the grip of his AK, his thick index finger tapping the trigger guard. His eyes fix on my cleavage and stay there. Distraction accomplished. "Need something, senorita?"

"Depends," I reply in Spanish. "We're looking for a friend who sold her car here a while ago, and we may want to upgrade this." I pat the wheel but have no intention of parting with the Buick unless we have to.

He nods, eyes still on my tits, which was the whole point of my outfit. The guy wouldn't recognize me if someone flashed a picture of me from the neck up. He points to a gap in the row of vehicles. "Park there. Office is the first door on the right."

"Gracias." I pull the Buick forward, shift my Glock to the holster at the base of my spine, and we get out. Thankfully, it's still cool enough to wear jackets. Winter storms fighting Caribbean storms leave little unravaged, but we're currently between the two. The sounds of power tools reverberate through the closed garage doors; business must be good despite fuel shortages. I'm grateful that there's been a huge resurgence in refurbishing old vehicles. It gives us more options and better camouflage. The global crash in manufacturing has been good for something, anyway. A sheet-metal sculpted sign hangs over the office: 'Maestro Motors. Est. 2004. Decades of making your POS beautiful.'

The guards are still looking at us as we get out of the Buick. "Stay with the car, amigo."

"Irie, sistah." Gippy grins and shrugs his shoulders in my old duster, leaning back against the hood of the car to light up a spliff.

"And go *easy* on that," I add in a low warning. The only downside of his disguise is the need for ganja. No Rastafarian would be without, but I don't want Gippy to backslide into chemical dependency.

"No problem." He grins again, taking a shallow drag. "Never was my junk anyway."

That's true, at least. Gippy had been deeper into hardcore narcotics. Weed has no more effect on him than a beer would. I put some Latina swagger into my stride and step into the office, air conditioned and dark enough to force me to remove my sunglasses. The wall to my left is festooned with framed photos of tricked out cars of every make and model imaginable, from low rider Impalas to monster trucks. A long counter with a gate to one side separates the clientele from the racks of file cabinets and shelving. Two flat screen monitors stand on the counter, and two video cameras cover the room from opposite corners. I wish for a hat to block my features, but there's nothing for it now.

I swagger up to the counter and smile at the enormously fat man seated behind. "Hola. Cómo estás?"

"No puedo quejarme." He shifts on his stool and looks me over, his eyes settling predictably on the V of my shirt. "Wha'chu need, senorita?"

"Looking for a friend who sold a Tesla to you a while back." I pulled my phone. "A 2028 M-class. Sold to you in May of fifty-two. I've got the VIN."

His eyebrows climb his thick forehead, wrinkling the skin like a rug under a chair leg. "You NAFAS?"

"No. She's my cousin." Sometimes the truth works better than a lie, and when that doesn't work, money does. I dip two fingers into a pocket and withdraw a thousand NAD bill, holding it up for him to see. "Cash. No questions."

His eyes widen. "Chica, for *that* I sell you my fuckin' mother!"

"Is she for sale?" I say with a smile that doesn't reach my eyes.

He grins back and taps a keyboard. "*Everything's* for sale, chica."

Truer words were never spoken, and it's exactly what I hoped to hear. I show him my phone for the VIN, and he types it in with short, pudgy fingers that dance over the keyboard like the legs corpulent spiders.

"Got it. Teri Timmons. Quite a few years ago. My papa did the deal. Gave her a good trade on a nice four-by-four." He taps again. "She kicked in twenty grand in cash and drove away in a silver 2050 Range Rover. Nice ride."

"Excellent!" I start to hand over the T-note, then hesitate. "You have the VIN?"

"I have the VIN *we* put on it, sure." He cocks an eyebrow and grins. "But that'll be extra."

I pull the tee-note back. "So, you're saying this information is worth *more* than your mother?"

He snorts a laugh. "Chica, if you *met* my mother you'd think so, too."

"All right." I pull a C-note to accompany the larger one and hold the two of them between my fingers for him to see. "Print it out first, please."

"Sure, chica." His pudgy fingers dance, and a printer hums beneath the counter. He pulls the sheet and hands it over.

"Thanks." I slide the bills across the counter in exchange for the paper and turn to go.

"Sure I can't fix you up with a new ride, too?" he asks.

I glance back. "Not at *your* prices, amigo." I squint as I step out of the office into the daylight and put on my sunglasses. Gippy's still leaning on the hood of the Buick, chatting with two grease-covered hombres, everyone sporting smiles.

He shifts to his feet as he spots me. "We good, sistah?"

"We good, brah." I wave the paper and nod. "You're drivin'."

"Irie!" Gippy exchanges fist bumps with the two mechanics and they eye me as I get in the passenger side.

He fires up the Buick and we back out of the courtyard past the grinning guard who will only remember my chest. I'm on my phone before we're around the block.

"So?" he asks.

"Cora traded her Tesla for a chopped Range Rover. I have a copy of the registration. If she sold it anywhere in NAFAS, there'll be a record. Just head for the highway. It's a safe bet that she's headed south."

"Sweet!"

I pull up the illicit app we use for tracking vehicle transactions and begin tapping in the Range Rover's ID. "We're still following a twenty-year-old trail, Gip. Don't get too hopeful."

"Oh, I know, but we have more than we hoped already, right?"

"Maybe." The results come up and I cringe. "Head south. Mexico City. We're going to need a new ride."

"Mex-city here we come!"

7

DOWN COMES THE RAIN

The succubus Duvara stared through Chaki's eyes at the message on her phone and sighed in frustration. *Father, burn me in Hell for ever having this stupid idea!*

After the realization that the boy she'd failed to seduce last year had been with an Ageless, she'd put out feelers to every thrall she'd recruited over the last half century, and circulated their pictures to every chop shop and car thief in southwest North America. In the last five months, she'd received hundreds of leads, but nothing worthwhile. With about a million cars stolen per year, she was looking for a needle in a haystack the size of Mt. Shasta. In the past few months, three more Nephilim had been banished, one only weeks ago. The Hounds of Hell were hunting for the culprits, but this Ageless had evaded every dragnet, every hack, and every assassination attempt they'd mounted. She and the mulatto boy she'd met were still in the winds.

Chaki sighed and pulled up the images attached to the message. The hot Latina with big hair and sunglasses didn't trip any alarms in her memory, but a single shot of a thin black man leaning on the hood of a dirty green Buick tweaked a smoldering recollection. She zoomed in; dreadlocks, jewelry, and sun glasses hid most of his face, but that mouth—and all the things she wanted to do with it—solidified in her memory. *Maybe...* Her fingertips tingled as she sent the security camera photo to the desktop computer. She could still taste the boy on her skin where she'd touched him.

She pulled the photo up on the larger monitor and expanded it. That mouth, his chin, and the strong cheekbones... Chaki licked her lips. *Oh, yes... I see you little boy.*

She messaged the sender back, "Tell me you have the tag on that Buick!"

The response came in less than a minute. "Who's your daddy?" The attached security camera picture showed the back of the dirty green Buick, the plate clear enough to read.

The succubus grinned, and replied, "Reward coming at you. Oh, and you'll meet my daddy later..."

Smiling, she pulled up her contact list and forwarded all three pictures to her Nephilim supervisor with the tag line, "Maestro Motors, Monterrey, MX, yesterday. This is the man who accompanied the Ageless in Albuquerque last year."

Ten seconds later the confirmation came back, "Received. Well done. We'll be in touch."

Duvara smiled and dropped her phone on the desk, leaning back and kicking up her high-heel clad feet in triumph. *An Ageless and her accomplice... Jewels in my crown.* Then she realized what her Nephilim supervisor had said.

"In touch?" Her smile faded. The two were in Mexico. They had nothing to do with her. Why would the Hounds of Hell need to be in touch with *her* for the upcoming hunt?

"Journal entry thirty-seven, June eighteen, twenty fifty-two: We're south of the hurricane belt finally, or most of it. It's still raining like a cow pissing on a flat rock but the winds have come down some." I peer through the windshield of the Range Rover, thanking God once again that I purchased a vehicle that could go virtually anywhere. So far, the roads haven't been that bad; a few mudslides and washouts, but nothing I couldn't muscle through or detour around.

"Rainy season in the tropics has been getting longer and longer every year, but at least it's warm. Oh, we're in Panama now. The border was a wave and a smile. They barely glanced at my NAFAS ID and waved me through. It's weird, this new empire. Some areas have gained in the union of every nation from Panama to Canada, and some have lost. Cities are crawling with cops and cameras, and things are oppressive, but in some of the rural areas the promise of basic needs being fulfilled has come through. People who have nothing are already oppressed, so if you give them power, water, sewer, and access to satellite broadband, they're uplifted. I can't imagine living in a hut in this jungle. I lived 4900 years without air conditioning, but down here, I think it's a necessity, and that means electricity. So, I'm still thinking a small rural community would be best for us, but I don't know if I should settle here or keep going south into Colombia, just to get the hell out of NAFAS. It's a trade-off between safety and anonymity; a gringo woman will stick out like a sore thumb even more in South America."

A northbound tractor trailer hauling Venezuelan fuel blasts past me, the spray blinding me momentarily. I'm taking it slow, limiting myself to eight hours driving per day, and never allowing myself to go below half a tank of gas. The heavy weather provides welcome cover, limiting the resolution of security cameras to a dozen meters or so. My bedraggled cowboy hat blocks high-mounted cameras, and cash transactions leave no electronic trail. This isn't, as they say, my first rodeo.

"More important than anything, I need someplace where I can raise you in peace and quiet." On a secluded stretch of highway, I spot a gas station/tienda advertising fresh caraminolas, and my stomach growls. On impulse, I pause the recorder and pull in. The tiny village is struggling, that's plain to see, and I prefer spending money in places where it will help instead of simply lining the pockets of the rich. Also, there will be fewer cameras here, and poor people don't trust police for good reasons. *Recollections of my hippie years of almost a century ago, police rousting harmless musicians camping out at concerts, arresting people on narcotics charges for smoking pot, the abuses that followed, screams echoing through the jail as men are beaten and woman are raped.*

I no longer look poor; not driving the Rover, and I've traded my sheepskin vest for a slicker poncho that keeps me dry, covers my holster, and hides my shape. I step out into the pouring rain, lock the Rover, and splash across the muddy lot to the door. Stepping inside to the chime of a bell on the door, I shake off my hat and poncho and wipe my boots on the mat. Tinny Latin music blares over blown-out speakers, but the rhythm invades me.

I salsa my way up to the counter. "Hola." The old woman behind looks me over as if I'm crazy. I breathe in the smell of deep-fried wonderfulness and smile. "I saw your sign for caraminolas and couldn't resist."

Her eyebrows arch at my fluent Spanish and she nods, glancing at the case under a heat lamp. "How many?"

"Six, maybe? And gas?" I look around the store. Not exactly upscale by any stretch of imagination, and as I suspected, there are no video cameras. The shelves aren't completely bare either. I'm the only customer, but I hear sounds of a TV from a curtained opening to the back. A child's grimy face peers out, large dark eyes staring at me. The money I spend here will put food in his mouth. "I might do some shopping, too."

"No problem. I'll do some fresh." She taps the register to free up one of the pumps, then gets up and steps into a tiny kitchen open to the rest of the store. "Take a few minutes to get the oil hot. Go ahead and pump your gas. Number two."

"Perfecto! I need to stretch my legs anyway." I step back out into the rain and move the Rover over to the pumps. They're covered, at least, so I can fill the jerry can on the spare tire mount without getting rainwater in it. I start the pump and unlock the five-gallon can from the mount. Ten gallons in the tank, and another five in the jerry, and I'm done. The pump reads two-hundred seventy NADs. *Damn, prices are getting out of hand.* Money's not a problem, really. I've retrieved another of my stashes in Mexico City, and I have another in Panama City, if it's not underwater yet. I make a mental note to check it—maybe I can retrieve it with scuba gear—and lift the forty-pound jerry can back into the bracket, clicking the lock closed and locking the Rover before I splash back inside.

"*Man,* it's raining!" I shake off again and pick up a shopping basket.

The old lady behind the counter snorts a laugh. "Best get used to it, chica. We won't see sunshine for six months."

"*Six* months?" I shake my head. The entire world's in turmoil over rising sea levels and crop failures. Millions are dying of starvation and outright war as billions flee the lowlands. Along the eastern seaboard, New Hope Seawall is being built at a frantic pace, but the sea is winning. The Antarctic ice shelves have collapsed completely, and the Arctic and Greenland are virtually ice free. Miami, Tampa, and Houston are already drowning. New Orleans is gone, and I weep at the loss of that music-rich culture.

I pick some fresh vegetables from bins, scrawny tomatoes, peppers, and the small, sweet bananas that I remember fondly. Some other items—hard tortillas, salt, soft queso blanco, and a hard sausage for protein. I've been trying to eat well, but travelling always seems to induce junk food binging. At the counter, the old lady is putting six steaming caraminolas in a paper bag, the aroma tantalizing.

She rings up my other items and says, "Three twenty-one total."

I peel off notes from the crumpled wad in my hip pocket, knowing better than to flash a wallet or a bankroll in such a destitute environment.

She starts to make change, then looks out the window of the store, her eyes widening. "Mierda!"

I turn and bite off my own expletive. Two men stand at the back of the Rover siphoning gas from my jerry can. I'm out the door before I think better of confronting anyone over five gallons of gas.

"Oye! Pendejo!" One turns toward me, but the other just glances and continues siphoning.

The man facing me grins. "Best go back inside, little rich girl." From under his poncho he pulls a two-foot machete.

My hand moves toward the holster under my poncho. "Just walk away from the—"

Beefy arms clamp around me, pinning my arms to my torso, and a basso voice growls in my ear. "You hand over your keys and maybe we won't take turns fucking you over the hood of your fancy truck, bitch."

I can't reach my pistol, and he's too strong for me to break his hold, but his mouth is close to my ear. I let my knees fold and feel for his feet, then stomp one heel of my shit kicker boot into his instep and slam my head back into his face. His grip slackens, and a fist hits me hard enough to knock me down. My hat flies off, but I have my pistol out and aim up at his gut from the muddy ground.

Before I can say anything, a shotgun blast tears through the air. If my ears weren't already ringing from the blow to the head, they would be now. All three men whirl to face the old woman with the riot gun aimed levelly at them.

"I warned you, Diego! Now go, before you make me mad!"

I scramble to my feet and retrieve my hat, but keep my pistol ready. The man who grabbed me is bleeding from a broken nose, but his hands are out and empty. The man with the machete has lowered his weapon, while the other is capping his gas jug. Shooting into gas fumes could be catastrophic, so I back away out of the line of the shotgun.

"She's a rich gringo, Marta! That fancy truck would keep us fat for a *year*!"

He has a point. The truck is too shiny, and a high-end vehicle in a poor area draws thieves like shit draws flies. I was foolish, but he and his boys picked the wrong target. I level my pistol at his crotch and grit my teeth against the urge to pull the trigger. Robbery is one thing, but the threat of rape...

"Put the gun down!"

I stare at the old woman and the shotgun now aimed at me. I realize I'm still being foolish. These people know each other; I'm a stranger. Her warning shot saved my assailant's life, not mine. I holster my pistol and raise my hands. "Just let me drive away, Marta. I didn't bring this to your doorstep, *they* did."

She purses her wrinkled lips, and the shotgun moves, the muzzle now aimed between me and Diego. "Go, Diego!"

The man glares at me, then nods, and all three men walk away, one carrying a half-full gas jug. Marta lowers her shotgun, her eyes hard on me. "You drive that fancy thing into a place like this, what do you expect?"

"I expect to spend my money where it'll do some *good*!" I tell her flatly.

Her wrinkled lips purse again. "Go, and maybe think about what you're doing next time."

As she turns away, the little boy I saw through the curtain runs out of the store holding a bulging plastic bag. His bare feet splash through the puddles as he dashes up to me and holds up my groceries, his eyes wide. I take the bag from his trembling hands and smile.

"Gracias."

"De nada." He smiles and runs back into the store, as if armed robbery is something he sees every day. Marta holds the door open for him, the shotgun still in her other hand.

I turn away, replace the cap on my jerry can, climb into the Rover, and drive away, cursing myself for being stupid. The scent of the fresh caraminolas tortures me, so I rifle the bag with a shaking hand and pull one out, eating carefully to keep from burning my mouth as my nerves slowly ease. By the time my tumultuous stomach is full, my ears have stopped ringing, and my brain has begun working again. I come to a realization: the Rover is too shiny.

"I need camouflage."

I pick a secluded stretch of highway, take an exit onto a dirt road, and drive far enough to be out of sight. Pulling to one side, I get out and look around for what I need. With a good sized rock and a downed limb, I carefully bash the hell out of my shiny Rover, then scrape one side with handfuls of gravel. When I'm done my hands are raw, but my car looks like a piece of shit that nobody in their right mind would steal.

I consider my work, then smash one of the parking lights with my rock. "Perfect!"

I'm back on the road in minutes, and drive into the small city of David two hours later. I decide to get a motel for the night and pick one near the downtown area that caters to busses and has an attached gas station and restaurant. They also have security. A hard-eyed older man wearing camos and holding a shotgun in the crook of his arm watches me as I approach. He's not NAFAS, or even a local cop, but clearly takes his job seriously. Just what I need.

"Hola." I smile, and he nods. "You have people watching all night?" I gesture to the parking lot.

"Si. *Nobody* messes with anyone's shit here." He doesn't smile, serious as a heart attack.

"Excelente! Gracias!" He gives me a nod as I enter the building.

The interior is a shop, restaurant, and gas station all in one. I approach the counter, and the Latina behind the register eyes me. "You okay?"

I tense. "Fine. Why?"

"You have blood." She touches her own cheek.

"Ah." I touch the spot where the man's fist struck, and feel a scabbed wound. He must have worn a ring. I cringe, cursing myself for not checking myself in the mirror. *Get your head on straight, Terpsichore.* "Just a scratch. I stepped out of my truck and slipped in the mud. Hit the car door. I'd like a second floor room for the night, please."

She nods and pulls a paper register from under the counter. I write down the name I'm using, the Rover's current license plate—I have four more and registrations to match with different names—and pay in cash. She hands me a key card, and I turn away. At the door, a stand of old fashioned newspapers catches my eye. Two of them are local real-estate listings. I grab one of each and tuck them under my poncho.

I move the Rover close to my room and lug my pack and guitar case up the steps to the second floor. The room's clean, but smells like cigarettes. I haven't smoked in years, but the scent triggers a pang. I put my bag down, doff my hat and poncho, toss the real-estate fliers onto the bed, and check my pistol. It's wet, of course, as is the cloth holster. I unload it and lay it on the night table with the cylinder open and the rounds sitting in the ashtray. I'll oil it later. I turn up the air conditioning to dry my things, double lock the door, and sit to pull off my boots.

I suddenly feel like crying and don't know why. I've been in thousands of dangerous situations, most of them far worse than this one. I've been beaten unconscious, shot, bones broken, skull fractured, impaled, burned, irradiated, and deafened by artillery explosions. Why has this simple scuffle unnerved me? I find my hands clenched over my stomach, and realize... *My child...*

"You've got to be more careful, Terpsichore."

I open my backpack and root through to find my backup weapon, another .38 revolver, this one stainless. I check the chamber, set the safety, and take it with me to the bathroom. One glance in the mirror and I understand why the woman behind the desk asked me if I was okay. The man certainly wore a ring of some kind. My cheek is gashed, my eye shot with blood.

"Should have shot the bastard in the balls," I mutter as I wash my face in cool water, but I know that would only have made things worse. Police complicate everything. I'm lucky there were no cameras in the store. I'll put a bandage on the gash later, more for appearances than healing. The Latina at the counter might be freaked out if I show up for breakfast without a mark on my face.

I glance in the shower and cringe. Dirty, and there's an inch-long cockroach sitting on the soap dish staring at me defiantly. "Just don't use all the hot water, okay?"

He doesn't reply. I've had worse roommates. Scorpions freak me out.

I sit at the tiny plastic table in the front room, wondering if I've gone soft with the few years I spent at Brown. An image of Emil rises in my mind, and my hands go to my stomach again. *I'm sorry...* Emotions rage, hormones probably, and I wonder if I'm experiencing more than a normal woman does during the first trimester of pregnancy. This child will be special, certainly. The first offspring of an Ageless to my knowledge. I wonder what their soul will feel like, the progeny of Heaven and Hell.

I've got to keep you safe, my darling...

To that end, I snatch up the two real estate papers, and leaf through them as I eat thick slices of tomato with salt, sausage, and crumbly queso blanco. Most of the listings are in David, people abandoning houses at low elevations. I ignore the scandalously low prices, and look for something higher in the hills. I pull up a map app on my phone and pull up locations of the listings.

Boquete... I've heard of the town, a farming village in the last century that turned into a haven for American expats. Panama encouraged retirees from the United States, offering residency and discounts for any US citizen with a pension. Highway 41 dead ends there, which sounds good. No thru traffic, no NAFAS patrols, and no airport. Only bus stations. There are several listings in the papers. The prices are high, but once again, money isn't a problem. I'll have to be careful not to draw attention, however. I spot an old hacienda with gardens and outbuildings at the end of a long dirt driveway, all surrounded by deep jungle, a former cacao plantation. Twenty-one acres with no access other than the one driveway. It sounds good, maybe too good. I decide to have a look at it tomorrow.

I finish my meal, full and sleepy, but decide to make one final recording in my journal before I fight my insectoid roommate for the shower.

"I had a little incident with some men at a gas station that has opened my eyes to my lack of vigilance. I'm being more careful now. I also think I may have found someplace we can settle. It's isolated but civilized. It looks good. Maybe this could be home."

8
MADE

The best thing about the digital age is that no information is ever deleted. While Gippy drives, I backtrack the vehicle Cora bought from Maestro Motors. The last transaction was five years ago, then again seven years ago, then, lastly, ten years ago when a woman named Wagner sold it. The new owner registered it in David, Panama, which is why we need a new vehicle. The roads are a mess south of Mexico City, so a four-wheel drive is in order.

"Hard to believe a city can get this big," Gippy says as we take the exit.

"Thirty-four million, but there's a lot of sprawl." Mexico City was huge before the migration inland from coastal areas. Now it's a monster.

"Daym! Twice the size of *Atlanta*?"

"At least. It stopped growing about a decade ago, or people started dying as fast as they came in." I shrug and sigh. "They don't do censuses anymore."

"Starvation?" he asks.

"And violence, food and water shortages, dysentery, cholera, and logistical problems. Gangs started looting, and the army intervened. They started shipping people away and executing looters and demonstrators in public." I sigh and try to focus. "Not as bad as Bangladesh, but about ten million died."

"A wonder we didn't end up in world war three."

"It was closer than you might think. Revolutions cropped up during the worst of it, and governments put them down, sometimes with tactical nuclear weapons."

"Like St. Louis?"

"They didn't nuke St. Louis, only bombed the living hell out of it." I've told Gippy about my role in that catastrophe and why I'll never try to raise another army. *So many dead and maimed... because of me.* "Guns and IED's are no match for killer drones and laser-guided munitions."

"One Nephilim at a time, sistah." He punches me lightly on the shoulder, and makes a turn onto a wide thoroughfare, bright lights and neon, one car dealership after another.

Traffic here is moderately heavy, the dealerships sporting shiny new models. "This is too high end, Gip. Keep driving until things look dodgier."

"Gotcha." Gippy drives.

I watch, and my nerves gradually tighten. Too many cameras, too many stoplights, and way too many NAFAS patrol cars. "I don't like this, Gip. Get off the main drag."

"Can't argue with that." He makes a right turn, the street narrower but still bright. Traffic is lighter, but there are still cameras at every intersection.

I crane my neck to look behind us and catch a flash of gold and black. "A NAFAS cruiser made the corner behind us. Turn as soon as you can."

"Fuck!" Gippy swerves around a slow car and cuts them off to make another right, earning a horn and a finger out the window.

I cringe; the last thing we need right now is a traffic accident. "Okay, nice and easy for a minute and we'll see if—" Yellow and blue lights flash beyond the corner behind us. "We're made! Make a left and put your foot down!"

"Shit, shit, shit!"

The Buick's engine races and tires howl as Gippy wrenches us around a corner across traffic, missing an oncoming car by inches. The driver locks up his brakes, and the car behind them slams into their rear end. Gip's only been driving for six months, and his skills aren't as good as they could be. It's hard to practice combat driving.

Lights flash beyond the intersection, and a cruiser howls around the corner, ignoring the accident. "They're still on us. Head west if you can, into the barrios." There are fewer cameras and narrower streets in the old neighborhoods.

Gippy makes a right, sideswiping another car, and curses fluently. "This beast handles like a fuckin' cow on meth!"

"Just drive!" The cruiser makes the corner behind us, and another joins behind them. "Watch for flashing lights! They'll try to cut us—"

"Shit!" Gippy hammers the brakes, and I slam into the dash. He burns the tires in reverse, and I glance forward.

A killer drone is coming right at us, laser sights winking across our hood.

"Evade!" I scream as the machine's armament opens up.

Gippy jinks the wheel hard, and only four of the twenty round burst hit us. Thankfully, it's a small drone, and the weapon's only a nine-millimeter; two rounds hole the hood, one spiderweb's the windshield, and the last gouges the roof. Neither of us are hit. We swerve sideways, and I'm staring out the passenger window right at the drone. The targeting laser winks through the glass three inches from my eyes as Gippy floors the gas pedal. The window disintegrates into a thousand tiny diamonds, and the bullet blasts batting from the headrest of my seat. The backseat window vanishes as bullets zip through the car, and the drone banks to follow.

My Glock is in my hand, and I empty a mag through the back window at the dodging drone, praying for a lucky hit. The things are agile and deadly, but not very tough. God or luck is with me, and one of my shots clips a rotor. The drone veers out of control and hits the side of the alley we're racing through.

I dump the mag and slap in a fresh one. "We're in trouble!

"No *shit*!" Gippy blasts through an intersection, clipping a car in passing. The resulting pile up might slow down our pursuers, but it won't stop another drone... or worse.

"They've tagged this car somehow, Gip. We need to dump it, but we have to get clear first." There's a lot of gear in the trunk that I'd rather not leave behind, equipment that could make the difference between life and death.

"Okay. How?" He sounds calmer than I hoped.

How... Focus. Think! Someplace they can't follow... There's only one option. "The barrios."

"That's like *miles*, E!"

"I know." I glance ahead and spot another alley. The blue and yellow flashes are farther behind us now. "We have a little breathing room. Take the next right, and switch places. I'll drive. You shoot from the back." He's a better marksman than he is a wheel man.

"Okay." He sounds skeptical, but slows to pull around the corner.

We stop, and Gippy scrabbles over the seat to the back. I'm in the driver's seat, and we're moving before he can even pull down the back seat to access our armory in the trunk. I turn off all our lights and bear west at the first opportunity, a two-lane street with lights, but not much traffic. I hear Gippy loading up, then the crunch of him kicking out the shattered back window. I have shards of tempered glass in my hair from the passenger side window. A glance in the rearview confirms he's ready, his headset on, the VR laser sights on his rifle active.

A light turns red ahead of us, and I swerve around the stopped cars to cross before the traffic closes in from the other direction. More horns and screeching tires, and there are cameras on the stoplights. I cock my head and try to filter city noises through my ringing ears. If you think you can fire a pistol in a confined space, then hear worth a damn, I suggest you try it. I barely catch the wail of sirens.

"Too many cameras!" I yell over my shoulder. "They're closing in."

"We need someplace to hide. Someplace they can't see us."

Someplace without goddamn cameras... Technology is our biggest enemy. Imagery from traffic cameras is networked with NAFAS police. They have our vehicle, probably our plate, and they'll get constant updates. We need to change cars, but that requires time we don't have.

I make a turn into a dark alley just to throw off pursuit, then turn again onto a two-lane street to bear west. I glimpse movement above through the shattered windshield, something small and nimble, and swerve instinctively. A puff of flame and smoke illuminates the drone, and I know we're fucked.

"Incoming!" I jink hard and sideswipe an oncoming car an instant before the missile hits.

Shrapnel rips through the right side of the Buick and something slams into my shoulder. If my ears were ringing before, I'm stone deaf now. My foot is flat on the accelerator, and I manage not to hit another oncoming car. Traffic is piled up like a demolition derby, but mostly out of our way. Gippy's rifle barks a three-round burst, then another. He's still with me, at least.

"Got the fucker!" His triumphant curse barely reaches me through the tinnitus.

Okay, maybe I'm not *stone* deaf. "Look for more!" I can barely see through the shattered windshield, so I punch it hard, knocking a corner free from the rubber gasket holding it in place. When I reach up to rip it free, my right shoulder stabs me. I'm hit but too busy driving to see how badly. "We've got about a minute before they drop a missile on us!"

"What was that, a freaking *text* message?"

"I mean a *big* missile!"

"Then we gotta find... Shit! Helicopter!"

Shit indeed. "Take it down!"

As Gippy opens up, I veer into another alley, hopefully narrow enough to dissuade the helicopter. Our tires squeal on the pavement, and I mentally thank the manufacturer of solid rubber combat tires. Without them I'd be driving on rims. I sideswipe a wall, sending trash bins flying.

Gippy stops firing, and I hear him reload. "I hit him, but no joy. He's gone high."

I glance up; the buildings here are only four or five floors. "He'll fire at us. Stay sharp!"

"Any sharper my ass would cut right through the upholstery!"

I snort a laugh and concentrate on evasive driving, challenging in a narrow alley. If they fire at us, I have no room to dodge a missile, and if a car comes the other way, we're screwed.

"What the *hell*?" Gippy's shocked tone sends a chill up my spine. "He's right above us!"

"What?" That doesn't make sense. Missiles have to be fired forward.

"Straight up!" I glance into the rear view; Gippy scrabbling out the shattered back window to lay atop the trunk and aim up. A three round burst, then another. "Stop swerving for two seconds!"

I steady the wheel, and he snaps off another burst, then stops.

"Something... The back of the chopper's opening up!"

The chill up my spine turns to solid ice. "Open fire! He's deploying something!"

Gippy lets off a rip of full auto, then swears. "A whole cloud of shit just flew out the back of the thing! He's veering off!"

"Hang on!" I slam on the brakes, wincing as Gippy swears. We come to a stop sideways in the alley, front and back bumpers wedged against the walls. "Out! Grab everything you can!"

"What the hell are we—"

"Drone swarm!" I lurch out of the Buick. "We need cover right *now*!"

"Fuck, fuck, fuck!" Gippy knows as well as I do what a drone swarm can do; a thousand three-inch square networked fliers, each armed with a single shaped charge that hits with the force of a 410 shotgun. They're used as riot suppression, antipersonnel warfare, or just plain economically murdering large numbers of people. He kicks open the back passenger door, and our two bags and three guitar cases hit the pavement, followed by his boots.

I fling a bag over my left shoulder and grab one case. A metal door fifteen feet away draws me like a magnet, the howl of hundreds of tiny electric rotors above us urging me on. I blow the lock out with my Glock and kick it open.

Behind me, Gippy slings his rifle, hefts a bag over his other shoulder, and kneels to flip open another guitar case.

"Come on!"

"Two seconds!" He lifts out our street sweeper, a semi-auto twelve gauge, and runs after me, slapping in a thirty round drum magazine and jacking in a shell. It will be a good weapon against the swarm if he makes it to the door.

The howl of micro-drones intensifies, and I glance up from inside the door. The swarm descends on us like a mass of angry hornets. Gippy aims blindly into the air as he runs and unloads with the street sweeper. Double aught buckshot rips through the cloud of drones, but there are too many. Behind him, drones land on our car and detonate, blasting holes into the passenger compartment. The rest are coming for us, probably programmed to kill anything that moves.

Gippy skids through the door, and I slam it closed. Drones rattle against the double steel barrier and detonate. The inner wall of the heavy barrier bulges with every explosion, but so far nothing gets through. The noise is deafening, and I can feel the impacts of each detonation through my sore right shoulder. I doubt the barrier will last long, and I blew out the lock. The bots don't mass much, but I can't hold the door closed forever.

I scream over the din, "Jam the door!"

"Right!" Gippy drops a combat knife and kicks the blade hard under the door.

I ease up the pressure on the door, and it holds. "Go!"

"Where?"

"Anywhere!" I rip off my wig and start down the hallway. "Dump your disguise. If they got our pictures, the drones will keep after us."

"*Fucking* technology!" He tears off his dreadlocks—cursing because they're woven into his real hair—and follows me, looking back over his shoulder at the door. "They're comin' through, E!"

I glance back and can see cracks opening with each successive explosion. Every detonation kills a drone, but the door's coming apart. I kick doors, but find only storage, closets, and a bathroom. Hiding here will only get us cornered and killed. The door at the end of the hall is more substantial but not as heavy as the one to the alley. I turn the knob and thank God when it swings open. On the other side, six kitchen workers stare at us in horror.

"Escapar!" I scream, firing a round into the ceiling to get my point across.

If that isn't enough to convince them, Gippy fires six quick rounds down the hallway. "They're through!"

I slam the door and whirl to find the kitchen empty. Drones hit the door and blast holes through, one grazing my neck. "Go, go!"

We dash through the kitchen and into the restaurant. People are fleeing from the sound of gunfire, and the two heavily armed lunatics who have invaded their quiet evening. We join the exodus, sprinting out onto a two-lane street lined with eateries and shops.

"Keep your face down!" I heed my own advice, flipping up the wide collar of my jacket.

Gippy stuffs the shotgun under his duster, but he's still hauling his rifle over one shoulder. "We need a ride, E!"

He's never been more right, so to that end, I step between two parked cars into traffic and point my Glock at the windshield of an oncoming car. The driver slams on the brakes, horror written on his face.

I put a careful round through the windshield left of the driver. "Out!"

He scrambles out of the car, hands raised, babbling pleas not to be killed.

"We only want your car!" I tell him in Spanish. "NAFAS is coming. You should run." As I throw my bag and guitar case into the back seat of the small sedan, the driver turns and runs. I mumble a short prayer that he'll survive.

Gippy's in the back seat in a flash, reloading the street sweeper and scanning the restaurant and street. "Drive, E! There are cameras every-fucking-where! We're made like a ho in church!"

"Time to disappear." I gun the electric motor and we scoot through traffic like a cockroach on hot pavement. The sedan accelerates nicely and handles far better than our massive Buick. I have little doubt, however, that our carjacking was photographed, and our new ride will be on their radar in moments.

As I turn onto a side street, the front of the restaurant disintegrates into a fireball behind us. The explosion shatters windows in several surrounding buildings. NAFAS must have called in an air strike.

"Fuckers are playing for *keeps*!"

"Damn straight, buddy." I slow down and turn again at the first opportunity. "We need to shift cars again. Look for something you can jack. We've been photographed. One traffic cam sees this car, and high-altitude drones will kill it... and us."

"Right!" Gippy leans forward, bringing with him the stink of cordite and sweat. "There!" He points to a late model SUV.

I pull off, and we pile out, grabbing everything and trying to look normal, heads down. This street is less lit, most of the shops closed. I take up a guard stance while Gippy does his magic with a slim jim. He's through the door in seven seconds and working on the ignition. The engine sputters and roars to life.

"Well done!" I jump into the back seat and trade my Glock for my rifle, settling the stock against my left shoulder. My right hurts like hell, and the recoil of the HK might shatter it completely. I run my fingers over my jacket there and feel a shard of shrapnel protruding through the Kevlar. Touching it sends jolts of agony all the way down to my fingers; it's lodged in bone. If not for the armor, it would have pierced my chest. Three inches higher and it would have gone right through my skull. God must be watching over me.

Gippy pulls out and turns off the street into another alley. "West, still?"

"Yes. Get us into the barrios and look for another vehicle. They may have spotted us making the switch."

"Right." He turns west at the next street.

I watch for flashing lights, and spot a cruiser going the other direction at the next intersection. "We may have slipped through the net." The ringing in my ears starts to subside, the laceration on my neck burning like fire. I touch it and my fingers come away bloody and smeared with black from powder burns. "Are you hit?"

"If I am, I'm too freaked out to feel it." Gippy's voice shakes, obsolete nerve impulses fueled by terror. "Those *fucking* drones..."

"Slaughter bots." Memories of St. Louis rise in me like a vile tide: *crowds of fleeing innocents cut down like wheat before a scythe as swarms of the tiny drones latch on and blow holes through human flesh.* "We were lucky."

"Let's stay lucky. There's our ride." He pulls up behind a rusted pickup truck and kills the headlights. "Let's go!"

We're out and into the old truck in moments, our bags in the bed with our long guns stowed in guitar cases. Gippy takes the wheel and props the massive street sweeper between us. We head west toward anonymity at a sedate pace, trying to keep our faces down.

Two minutes later, behind us, the city skyline lights up in a rippling orange conflagration. Three city blocks cease to exist in a fireball of detonating cluster bombs. NAFAS is pulling out the stops, murdering hundreds... because of me. I'm glad Gippy's driving; I begin to shake so badly that I probably would have wrecked us.

9
FRIENDS IN LOW PLACES

Drive or hide?" Gippy gripped the wheel so hard his knuckles ached. When Empa didn't answer, he glanced across the cab at her. She had a graze on her neck, but he couldn't see her right side, the side of the missile hit. "E? You okay?"

"Not really." She sounded stunned, and he wondered if she had a head wound.

"Shit! How bad is it?"

"Physically, nothing serious, but..." Her voice caught in a hoarse sob and she shook her head. "Everywhere I go, innocent people are slaughtered."

Here we go again... When innocent people were caught in the crossfire, Empa took it personally. The lights of a passing car illuminated her tear-streaked face. "You didn't kill them, E."

"I know, but... We shouldn't have come here. I should have known better."

"We had no way to know we'd been tagged. It's not this fuckin' city, it's us. Someone *somewhere* must have IDed us, then put the Buick on their radar. Since we weren't attacked in Monterrey, it probably happened there. Maybe the chop shop or when we got gas."

"It doesn't matter." She shook her head. "We're blown. This mission is over."

"Over?" That shocked him. He wasn't ready to give up yet. Father

Farrell needed to know if Cora had survived, and even more importantly, if he had a child. Empa needed to know what that child was, the first ever union of Ageless and Nephilim. "They know we're here, but they can't know where we're goin'. Hell, *we* barely know where we're goin'. We just need to hunker down, be invisible, and get the fuck out of town. All we need is new faces and an untraceable ride that'll make it to Panama."

"But... We're *made*, Gip! Every car dealer, chop shop, and gas station in Mex City has cameras, and our faces are on their network. We can't stop for *donuts* without earning an airstrike."

She wasn't wrong, but she wasn't entirely right either. "So we get *help*."

"Help? So *more* people can die because of me?"

Gippy gritted his teeth. He'd seen her like this before—she'd been through too much over thousands of years—but knew she'd recover eventually. Her spirit was low, and therefore weak, just like she'd taught him, but you couldn't just tell someone to not be depressed. Pulling her spirit up to make her strong again was her job. All he could do was support her until she recovered. That meant a plan.

"We find someone who the naffies won't have eyes on, someone below their radar." They passed a corner where a lone man leaned against a building, arms folded, eyes watching traffic. He wasn't dressed like a trick, so he had to be a dealer, and the plan came to him in a flash. "I got an idea."

After a long pause, she asked, "What?"

"Easy; who down here hates NAFAS almost as much as we do?" The streets were narrowing, and Gippy scanned the intersections. The few cameras he spotted were missing or broken, street lights often out. *My kind of neighborhood.*

"I don't feel like playing guessing games, Gip."

Come on, E! Get your head in the game! "Fine. So, when NAFAS took over, they legalized recreational drug use, right?"

"Yes."

"That made big pharmaceutical companies a shit-ton of money, and strung out half of North America. But the old school drug lords, their entire *world* collapsed, right? I mean, why buy some nasty shit that'll fuck up your liver when you can buy pharm-grade junk in single-use packets at any dispensary or corner dealer?"

"Drug lords? *That's* who you want to ask for help?" She sounded skeptical.

"Who better? They're still grinding an axe over what they lost. We need help and have cash. In fact, if we need *more* cash, they could help us with a trip to a bank." Gippy grinned at her. "*Trust* me, E. These dudes are pissed and need cash flow. It's a match made in Heaven."

"Made in Heaven..." She pursed her lips and nodded once. "Okay, we give it a try. A vehicle and a bank run. And we shift to new disguises."

"Perfect!" *She's coming around, pulling herself up by her boot straps...* Now all they needed was a tiny shred of luck.

Deep in the barrios now, Gippy spotted another dealer standing on a street corner and pulled over. As the truck slowed, he fished a cee-note from his pocket and folded it between two fingers. He tapped his fingers on the window frame as they came to a stop, drawing the dealer like a moth to a flame.

"Whacu need, ese?"

"Help." Gippy handed over the banknote without hesitation. "A place to crash, a ride, and someone to run an errand." He nodded to the bill as it vanished into the man's pocket. "We can pay."

The dealer glanced into the back of the truck at their bags, a humorless smile twitching his thin lips. "What makes you think we won't just *take* what you got."

"That would be expensive for you, ese." Gippy grinned and produced a grenade from inside his coat, one finger through the pin ring. "*Real* expensive."

The dealer's eyes widened, and he took a step back. But there was more than fear in the man's eyes, there was realization. "Who's after you?"

Gippy nodded back toward the glow of the burning city miles behind them. "Who you *think*?"

The dealer's eyes narrowed, and he fished a phone from a pocket. "Lemme talk to my jefe, ay?"

"Talk fast, ese. Too many eyes up there." Gippy glanced up, and the dealer nodded in understanding, stepping back to carry on a hushed conversation. Gippy glanced at Empa and noted her Glock held low, out of sight but ready. *At least she's on her game now*. He put the grenade away.

After less than a minute the dealer came back and pointed down the street. "Take that first left and go six blocks south, then turn right. Look for the big doors with the bull horns over them on the right hand side of the street. Tell them Carlos wants to see you."

"Carlos. Got it. Thanks."

The dealer nodded and stepped back. "Just be chill. Carlos's one nervous hombre."

"So are we, ese." Gippy pulled away from the curb, turned left, and drove in silence.

"You think this'll work?" Empa asked.

"Should. We have money, they have resources. Business is business, right?"

"Unless they decide to take everything we have and leave us dead in a gutter."

He glanced at her and figured she needed a reality check. "This from the badass bitch who walked into a cult stronghold in Manhattan with nothing but guns and money to bargain with?"

"Well... that's true." She looked pensive, then nodded. "Okay, we play it the same way. If they fuck with us, we fuck back."

"Got it." He counted the blocks and turned right. "You want to do the talking?"

She shook her head. "You seem to be doing fine, and Latinos are still pretty sexist when it comes to business. *Especially* drug lords."

Gippy spotted their destination, a pair of tall wooden gates reinforced with decorative iron work, with a pair of truly massive bull horns mounted above them. He slowed and looked at Empa. "You've known drug lords?"

"A few. They tend to be shrewd and ruthless. Basically modern warlords." She shrugged and winced. "They're not fools, and don't pull punches, Gip. Don't piss them off, and don't show fear."

"Gocha. Time to be bad, I guess." Gippy pulled to a stop, got out, and walked around the front of the truck to a smaller door set into the larger gate. He knocked three times and waited.

A heavy bolt clacked, and the small door opened. Gippy found himself staring at the muzzle of a Kalashnikov leveled at his stomach. The man holding it eyed him from head to toe. "Qué?"

"Carlos wants to speak with us," Gippy responded in English. He nodded to the truck and spotted Empa behind the wheel, ready. "Business."

The man frowned. "Stay here." The door closed.

Gippy waited, one hand holding the grenade in his pocket. He glanced at the truck again. Empa shifted, and he spotted the stock of the street sweeper. She was ready for trouble. He assessed their position, looking for avenues of escape, cover, the rough pavement and cracked sidewalks. He nodded to Empa and shifted his Glock to his right hand coat pocket. If the fertilizer hit the air conditioner, he would dump the grenade and dive into the bed of the truck.

A heavy clank startled him, and the big doors began to swing inward slowly to the hum of electric motors. Gippy backed a couple of steps, hands still in his pockets. Inside, a brick-paved courtyard opened up, shrouded overhead by thick camo netting. Half a dozen rough-looking hombres with rifles stood along the periphery. Across the courtyard, a young man strode forth, seemingly unarmed, wearing a black button down shirt with silver lapel tips and a bolo tie. He was attractive, broad shouldered, and wore jeans with shiny cowboy boots sporting silver toes. His thumbs were tucked in his pockets, his gait relaxed, his mouth set in a subtle smile.

"Bring it in," an hombre beside the door said with an easy wave of his hand.

They didn't look tense, but Gippy knew these people were ready for trouble. He nodded to Empa, and she turned the pickup into the opening while Gippy strode forth ahead of it. He kept his hands in the pockets of his duster, one finger hooked in the pin ring of the grenade.

"You Carlos?"

"Si." The young man grinned and looked him over, still strolling forward. "And you?"

"Gregory." He released his grip on his Glock to hook a thumb back at Empa. "My amiga, Emily."

Empa stopped the truck far enough inside the gates for them to close, which they did. The two hombres stationed there moved to rotate a huge metal bar into place. They were locked in, and from the look of the reinforcing on those doors, their truck wouldn't be able to smash through.

We're ass-deep in it now, Gippy thought.

Carlos walked right up to Gippy and stuck out his right hand. "So, my friend on the street tells me you need help." Very white teeth flashed between the man's lips when he spoke.

"We do." Gippy shook the hand firmly. "A place to crash, an easy errand, and a vehicle. We're gone in twenty-four hours, and you're paid well for your trouble."

"Trouble... Si, my friend said you had some trouble." Carlos's smile remained unabated. He released Gippy's hand and cocked an eyebrow. "Like, *NAFAS* trouble."

"No lie there, amigo." The truck door slammed, and he glanced back to see Empa standing beside it with the street sweeper slung by a strap, her left hand on the grip. He turned back to Carlos. "You probably heard the explosions. The naffies want us bad. We just want to get the fuck out of town in one piece."

"Why?" Carlos shrugged easily. "What did you do to piss them off?"

Gippy snorted a laugh. "That's a *long* list, amigo. We been on their shit list for a long time."

"And you're still alive?" Carlos nodded, still smiling. "Well, we're no friends of the naffie fascists, but we don't like their eyes on us too close either. We try to look legit, and for the most part, we are. Meat shipping instead of narcotics; the money's better, and cows don't shoot back."

Gippy arched his eyebrows. "From the hardware your people carry, I'd guess that cows *do* shoot back."

"We're just careful." Carlos shrugged. "So, a bed, a ride, and an errand. What errand?"

"Just a trip to the bank."

His eyebrows arched. "A *bank*?"

"You *do* want to get paid, right?" Before Carlos could answer, Gippy turned to Empa. "Toss me a down payment, Emmy."

Empa pulled a bar of bullion from her pocket and tossed it without taking her hand off the grip of the shotgun, her face set in stone.

Gippy caught it and handed it to Carlos. "And there's more if you help us. A *lot* more."

Carlos eyed the bar, and his grin finally failed. "Santa Madre de Dios!" He held the bullion up to the light, examined it, then turned to whistle a single shrill note.

As he turned, Gippy spotted the butt of a pistol in the belt of the man's pants, a big revolver, pearl and chrome. Carlos liked shiny things.

A thirty-something Latina strode from the building behind the drug lord, hard-eyed and businesslike, wearing jeans and a vest over a blue silk shirt with rolled up sleeves, and a bolo tie that matched Carlos's. She also wore an automatic pistol at her hip in a speed holster. She wasn't as shiny as Carlos, but attractive with an elegant, no-nonsense Latina air.

"Antonella, check this out." Carlos held the bar of platinum out to her, and she took it, squinting at it. "Tell me if that's real."

"Un momento." She pulled her phone, took a picture of the bar, and tapped. She looked up at Gippy, her eyes dark and scrutinizing. "Si, it's real. Five thousand two hundred thirty-four NAD's worth." She spoke with a thicker accent than Carlos.

"And you get ten more if you help us," Gippy added.

The woman's eyes narrowed. "Fifteen."

Gippy suppressed a reaction. Until now, Carlos had seemed to be in charge, but she hadn't consulted him before challenging his offer, and the flamboyant younger man hadn't even flinched. Antonella obviously carried some clout. "Twelve." He didn't care about the money—Empa's money, actually—but agreeing too easily would look weak.

"Thirteen." She tucked the bar in a pocket. "Not including this one."

Gippy smiled and nodded once. "Done. Half now, the other half when we're good to go."

"Excellent!" Calos grinned and stuck out his hand to Gippy once again. "Forgive my older sister. She's the brains, actually. I just look good and scare people."

Gippy shook his hand again and grinned back. "And you *do* look good!"

"It's a gift." Carlos's grip tightened. "But can I ask you one question, Gregory?"

"Sure." He matched the drug lord's grip, wondering if the man had been offended by the compliment.

"Can you please show me what's in your other hand?" Carlos's grin remained unchanged.

"Absolutely." Gippy pulled his hand slowly from his left pocket, the grenade's ring over one finger. He matched the drug lord's smile. "Just being careful, amigo."

Carlos barked a laugh and nodded. "Good! We'll get along great, then!" Carlos released Gippy's hand and waved his people forward, rattling off orders in Spanish. The hombres approached the truck and pulled their bags and guitar cases from the back.

"Bienvenidos, Gregory." Antonella reached out a hand, unsmiling but suddenly warmer, less guarded.

"Gracias." Gippy shook it firmly and felt Empa move up beside him. She had the money belt she wore around her waist out, pulling platinum bars from the interior pockets.

Antonella turned to her. "And you, Emily. Bienvenidos."

"Thank you." She held out a stack of six more bullion bars. "Half now."

"Thank *you*." Antonella took the bars, but then looked distressed. "You're hurt!" She raised her other hand to brush Empa's neck.

"No es nada," Empa assured her, pulling away from the touch. "Just a graze."

"But it will leave a scar if not tended properly." Antonella waved them toward the house. "We have first aid, and you'll both want to clean up and eat something."

"We have things in our bags, thanks," Gippy assured her. Empa would be healed by morning, of course, but they'd have to put a bandage on anyway, just to keep up appearances. They didn't want to freak out their hosts.

"Get some rest and join us for breakfast in the morning. I insist," Carlos chimed in, grin intact. "Then we can discuss the details of this errand and what type of vehicle you need."

"Thank you. We'd be happy to." Empa didn't sound happy at all, but she seemed to be holding it together for now.

"Good." Antonella looked from Gippy to Empa, one jet-black eyebrow arching. "One room, or two."

Gippy opened his mouth, but Empa beat him to it. "One, please."

"Of course." She gestured again and started for the arched entry. "This way."

They followed her into a hacienda lavishly appointed with crimson Spanish tile and wrought iron, up a curved staircase to the second floor, and down a hall to an expansive bedroom with an attached bath. The suite was decorated in bright orange and blue with pictures of bulls and matadors. Their bags and guitar cases were already there. The window overlooked the street, and was ornately barred with wrought iron.

"Just let anyone know if there's anything you need." Antonella smiled fully for the first time and backed out of the room.

Gippy thanked her, closed the door, threw the bolt, and turned to Empa. "Well?"

"Antonella's honest enough, and curious, but cautious. She resents her brother a little, but loves him. She's got some baggage; their father was an abusive asshole." She propped the shotgun in the corner without unloading it or even clearing the breech, a sure signal that she wanted to be ready for trouble. "Good job, by the way." She shrugged out of her coat, and Gippy saw blood on her arm.

"You *were* hit!" He reached for her, but she flinched away.

"Just a piece of shrapnel. I pulled it out. I'm fine." She dumped her Glock on the bed and started for the bathroom. "I need a shower."

"Okay." Gippy pulled his phone. "I'm going to call in a withdrawal."

"Do that." The door closed, and he heard the water coming on.

Gippy made the call, arranging for a hundred thousand NADs in Swiss bullion to be picked up the following day from a local bank. He received a confirmation code and saved it. He could transfer it to Carlos's messenger for the pickup. He doffed his coat and checked himself over for blood. He had some tender spots where shrapnel had hit his armored coat, but nothing had penetrated. He sat on the bed and breathed deep, calming his still singing nerves, convincing himself that they were safe and trying to forget the deadly whine of slaughter bots.

No high spirit, no low spirit... Steady spirit.

~

"Journal entry forty, June twenty-one, twenty fifty-two: It's not Manhattan, but I think Boquete might just do." I pilot the Rover up the narrow and partially overgrown drive, following the realtor's Jeep. The driveway is torturous, the graveled surface eroded by torrential rains, and my truck moves like a horse over broken ground beneath me, eliciting memories of Catalonia during the revolution, yet another lost cause against Nephilim-fueled fascism.

I spent a day simply looking over the town, eating in the restaurants, shopping, and took a room in a B&B for the night. In the morning, I visited the realtor's office and asked to see the hacienda. He tried to show me a place in town, but I told him I liked my seclusion. With one look at my battered Rover, he nodded and told me to follow him.

"The town's quaint and seems peaceful enough. It's cooler up here, too, but still humid. Not much music scene, but some bars and cafés. A lot of places are closed. The tourist industry's taken a hit here, just like everywhere. They still have a library, so all is not lost. It's still raining, and there are signs of severe erosion, but they're adjusting, shifting to crops that stabilize the soil. People are nothing if not resilient. The markets have food, but not much in the way of manufactured goods. There's still a lot of agriculture up here; even some coffee, thank God. I'm looking at a place today."

The jungle recedes from the rough track, and the drive opens into a formerly gardened area, bougainvillea, hibiscus, and succulents running wild. The hacienda isn't as pretty as the pictures, but the realtor was forthcoming that it would need some work. A single-floor, L-shape, with tile roof and faded burnt orange paint marred by black mold climbing from the ground up.

"The house is a little run-down at first glance, but it's not falling down.

We'll see." I follow the Jeep around a curved drive to a parking area and pause my recording.

Señor Guterres steps out of his Jeep and opens an umbrella. I'm out before he can offer me the cover, immune to the rain in my hat and poncho, my boots crunching on the wet gravel. I look the place over critically and think it might do. Isolated, limited access, concrete construction, and plenty of room. It needs work, but I've got money.

"So, you see," Guterres says with his realtor's grin. "It used to be a bed and breakfast, but the tourists no longer come. The owners, Americans, moved north after the North American Union, as did many ex-pats. It's beautiful but needs a coat of paint."

"And a gardener, a new roof, and a good scrubbing." He had been surprised when we met that I spoke Spanish fluently, his manner changing immediately from slightly slimy salesman to professionally eager businessman. "Water and power?"

"Yes, a well. The pump works, and the water's sweet. Power is sometimes out, but there's a backup generator. The solar works, but these days." He waves at the overcast sky. "Not as good."

And a generator will require fuel, which is becoming more expensive, especially in remote locations. With the increasingly inclement weather, a windmill will supply more dependable power. "Batteries?"

"Yes, but old lithium ones."

I nod, knowing a good electrician can replace them with carbon nanotube models that are now the norm in cars. Having them shipped will be difficult, but again, money will solve that problem. I look around the area, pleased that the jungle has not yet fully invaded. There's at least fifty meters of open and relatively flat ground. Motion sensors would make it impossible to sneak up on the house, and the unobstructed view from all sides of the house means a clear killing field. I hate that I have to think this way, but keeping my child safe is now priority one.

"Let's have a look inside."

"Of course!" Guterres tries to cover me with the umbrella, but it's pointless. Under the broad porch, he shakes it out and punches a code into the key lock box.

The tiles of the porch are slick under my boots, and the scent of mold is thick in the damp air. The lock clicks, and the heavy wooden door swings in easily on rust-free iron hinges. I shake off my poncho and follow him inside. The interior is dark wood, tile floors textured like flagstone, and an even more pungent odor of mold. The furniture still remaining is trash, ruined by years of humidity and neglect, but the dark overhead beams are tropical hardwood, still glossy. I can work with this, but it'll take labor, time, and money.

I stroll forward, my boot heels clicking on the hard floor. "You have local contractors I can hire for the clean-up, I assume."

"Of course! And you'll want a caretaker, and maybe a housemaid. The trick with a place like this is to keep up the maintenance." He waves at the dismal surroundings as if showing me the interior of St. Paul's Cathedral. "A week to clean it out, another to refurnish and decorate. Some minor repairs, I'm sure, and you're good to move in!"

That's bullshit, and I see in his eyes that he knows I know it. I give him a shallow smile. "I'd like to see everything before I make an offer, but I do think this will fit my needs."

His eyes light up. "Of course!" He starts to turn, then turns back. "I'm sorry, Ms. Wagner, but our bank must confirm your financial situation before we can—"

"I'll be paying cash, Mr. Guterres."

"*Cash?*" He looks uncomfortable. "We'll still have to confirm any money order or electronic—"

"Not electronic cash, *cash* cash," I say with the same shallow smile. "With the current state of financial institutions in NAFAS, I've liquidated my investments."

"Liquidated?" He blinks at me as if he doesn't understand.

"Yes, into precious metals, which have performed well with global shortages ever worsening. Krugerrands, to be specific." I pull one from my jeans pocket and show him. "This is currently worth about four thousand North American Dollars. Your clients' bank should accept them as legal currency, yes?"

"Well, yes, but..." He clears his throat. "This is highly irregular."

"Well, so am I." I flip the coin to him, and he catches it with the dexterity of a hawk snatching a dove from the air. "Please have the authenticity of that verified."

"Um... Yes, I will."

"And consider it a bonus for keeping this transaction *confidential*. I'm just seeking a place where I can have peace and quiet, Mr. Guterres. I'm a composer, and I've decided to take a sabbatical. Boquete is exactly what I need. If you spread word that a rich gringo woman is throwing around gold, I'll take my money somewhere else. Do you understand me?"

He nods so fast that his cheeks jiggle. "*Absolutely* confidential, Ms. Wagner."

"Thank you. Now show me my house. When we're done we can negotiate the price."

"This way, Ms. Wagner." He pockets the coin and leads me through the house room by room.

By the time we finish, it's late and I have names of local contractors and suppliers who can get me materials for a complete renovation. Guterres even knows a local carpenter who makes furniture from hardwoods and natural fabrics. He offers to buy me dinner while we negotiate price, and I accept.

On the drive back to town, I resume my recording. "I think the house will do nicely, once it's renovated. It's a good location, defensible, solid, and there will be plenty of space for you to play. The jungle's beautiful, and we can do some plantings and gardening. Maybe a greenhouse." I have visions of walking hand in hand through lush gardens with my child, showing them the beauty of the natural world in safety. I know it's just a dream, but it's one that I think I can make come true. I rest one hand on my stomach and sigh. "I can't wait for you to see it."

Guterres picks a quiet local eatery that serves simple, flavorful dishes while quiet Latin music fills the air. Negotiation proceeds without a hitch, and I talk him into a significant discount for the cash transaction. The former American owners will undoubtedly jump at the chance to keep the transaction off the books. By the time we finish our meal, the deal is settled, both of us content. The guitar has me swaying in my seat, my fingers picking out the chords on the table top as we wait for dessert.

"Do you play?" Guterres asks, nodding to my fingers as we're served sopapillas and coffee.

"Yes. I enjoy playing for people. It... relaxes me." It will also build a relationship with the locals, and spread love. I'll be here long enough, I hope, to make Boquete a flourishing, loving place; exactly the kind of community I need to raise a child.

"You should consider playing around town as a sideline." He shrugs with a wise smile. "You may not need the income, but it will solidify your place here without rumors cropping up. There are many local venues who would be delighted to have you play."

"I probably will." The prospect excites me, an opportunity to change this isolated little town, to infuse love and hope. I can no more resist than I can choose not to breathe.

"I look forward to listening." He sips his coffee and regards me with a curious expression that I can't quite read. I get a feeling for people, and he's not exactly a saint, but he's not plotting my untimely demise, either. "You're very unusual, Ms. Wagner, and clearly an independent woman, but would you take a recommendation from me that, I think, would be wise for you to consider?"

"Sure, and please, call me Tersi." I shrug noncommittally, wondering if he's intending on offering to secure my liquid assets for me... just to keep them safe.

"A woman alone can be seen as vulnerable, whether she truly *is* or not." His eyes narrow, and I see that he knows that I'm aware of what he's telling me. "I know a couple, good people, new parents, who are in need of work. He is resourceful, a former farmer, but competent in many areas. She is my second cousin, and one of the best cooks I've ever known. If you offer them a place and moderate pay, they would be loyal employees and offer you some... protection from rumors and too much curiosity."

I consider the offer seriously, having someone living with me, a family, no less. I'll need help with the hacienda anyway, especially when my pregnancy advances and in the early years of my child's life. *My child...* I touch my stomach subconsciously and make a snap decision.

"I'd love to meet them."

10
SOLACE OF SOULS

I stare at the woman in the mirror and see someone I know from centuries ago. Emiko Kurosawa, consort and onna-musha to Samurai Ronin Miyamoto Musashi. I close my eyes and remember his touch, a warrior's hands, a lover's, and embrace the pain. *So many lost...*

"You okay, E?"

"Yes." I don't think I'm lying, at least not much. "I will be. This just brings back... memories." The disguise is effective, at least. The long, straight black hair hides my ears and the unnecessary bandage on my neck, and makeup intensifies my cheekbones and changes the shape of my eyes, making me look Asian. I also wear cheek pads to round my face and contacts to darken my irises. I am my former self, and I feel the persona like a custom-tailored hair shirt, a familiar torment.

Gippy, on the other hand, has gone cowboy, or at least urban cowboy. For some reason he and Carlos have sparked a friendship. He wears jeans, a big belt buckle, a black shirt with silver buttons, and a bolo tie. A crusty old lizard-skin cowboy hat will hide his face from cameras, and his duster matches the outfit well. He's still getting used to the boots.

He's eying me with concern. Gippy understands me better than anyone else living, even more than Jeri. He knows when I'm in pain, raw and bleeding on the inside from the deaths that weigh so very heavily on my soul. I take comfort from his concern, confidence, and trust in me.

I steady my spirit and nod to him. "We should get gone before the sun comes up." *Gone... So many...*

"No argument from me." He shoulders his bag and guitar case, turning for the door.

I heft my bag and guitar case, and follow. The street sweeper's already packed in our ride.

Our second night at Carlos's hacienda was short but restful, and we're up at midnight to prepare for our departure. The state-controlled news feeds are claiming a terrorist attack in Mexico City, of course. The dark web is spinning conspiracy theories as fast and coherently as a spider on LSD. So far, none of the theories are accurate, and my face isn't on the nets. The Nephilim are keeping this search to themselves. They're still arrogant and powerful, but they know we can banish them now. For the first time in five millennia, they're afraid. That makes them even more dangerous, but lifts my spirits. I have put the fear of God into Hell.

Downstairs, Carlos and Antonella are waiting for us. They've been gracious hosts. Of course, for more than seventy thousand in bullion, they should be. Best of all, they're both sincere about keeping our visit a secret. I felt the fear of NAFAS in Antonella when she touched me. She's a careful woman, as are most of us who have been on the receiving end of abuse. Carlos is the family's face, all charisma and flash. She's the brain. They'll never sell us out.

We hand our baggage over to their men at arms, and I force a grateful smile. "Thank you both."

"Be well." Antonella shakes my hand and gives me one of her rare smiles. "You're good at disguises. I barely recognize you."

"I hope so." *Disguises...* I think of Jeri and my heart aches for the comfort of her embrace. "I had a good teacher."

"Emily, you've graced our humble hacienda with your beauty." Carlos takes my hand and kisses it.

As we touch for the first time, I get him in a rush, more complex and guarded than his outward Latin machismo shows. He puts on a front because that's how he stays in control of his tiny little empire, but he's living under the shadow of a domineering and violent father. Resentment, anger, fear, and a deep love for his sister wash through me. He also would have welcomed me to his bed had Gippy and I not put on the pretense of a relationship. I leave it all there, untouched. Everyone's more complex than they seem, and it's not my place to change them.

"Thank you, and please be careful. NAFAS is still hunting us, and they won't give up easily."

"Pendejos..." He grins. "They've got nothing in this neighborhood. Come on." He gestures, and we follow them out and across the courtyard to the garage.

The camo netting, they've assured us, is high tech, blocking full spectrum surveillance from above. Drug cartels have been evading aerial surveillance for a century, and they've got it down pat. His people have disposed of our stolen truck, and the vehicle they have for us is untraceable. It looks like a piece of junk, the body a conglomeration of rust-splotched Toyota Land Cruiser, Range Rover, and Jeep panels. The upholstery is worn, the dash and controls antiquated. Underneath the rough exterior, the frame and suspension are custom, with high ground clearance and beefy tires that will handle any terrain. The engine is a marvel; a high-compression military design that will burn virtually any hydrocarbon—LNG, propane, gasoline, diesel, kerosene, cooking oil, or coal-emulsion, from three separate tanks—with only minor adjustments. The plates are legit, the VIN for an eighty-year-old Land Cruiser that makes up most of the outer body. The registration is so new the ink's barely dry, and matches Gippy's current ID. These people know larceny like I know my own teeth.

I wonder, as we say our final goodbyes, if we aren't getting the better end of the deal here, even for seventy NADs. I assure Carlos that I can handle the antiquated gearbox, two separate shifters for two and four-wheel drive, and get behind the wheel. Gippy pulls up a circuitous route out of the city on his phone, and we drive out of the courtyard, invisible.

"Good call back there," I tell him. "You saved our lives."

"I learned from the best." Gippy stares at his phone, and I can feel his worry for me. "Looks like about sixty hours, best case. The roads farther south are a mess. Why the hell did they build the only damned highways right along the ocean?"

I know the question's rhetorical, but I answer anyway just to keep the conversation going. "Because nobody ever *dreamed* that the sea could rise to swallow them up."

Gippy snorts a laugh. "Surprise, bitches."

"It shouldn't have been, but yeah, it happened fast." The world has changed so drastically that I barely recognize it anymore. So have I. "I really should have seen it coming, I suppose. Many did. The evidence was all there. Some even tried to legislate meaningful change that would curb the climate crisis. Money and politics thwarted them."

"Think the Nephilim were behind that?" he asks.

"Perhaps. Not in the beginning, but wrecking the environment in general has always been part of their agenda." Centuries of London smog, hundreds of thousands dead and millions ill... "Breeding despair is certainly easier with the entire planet in crisis."

"But there's hope, too," he counters, eying me. "Even livin' on the street, folks got hope." He's speaking from experience, and I take it to heart.

"Yes, they do, and it never ceases to amaze me." Maybe Hell's job is even more difficult than mine, for human beings always seem to sequester a sliver of hope. More than I do sometimes.

I follow the directions mechanically, getting used to the truck's stiff suspension and old-fashioned controls; no flat screen nav system, no LEDs, no satellite radio or Bluetooth, only analog speed, oil, and temp gauges. It reminds me of driving an old WC-54 ambulance through Europe during the war. Those roads were probably worse than anything we'll be facing. Memories of burned-out Panzers and columns of shell-shocked refugees haunt my mind as we turn onto the highway to Puebla.

"So, now that we're out of *that* catastrofuck, how do you think we were tagged?"

"They traced the Buick somehow." I shrug, still struggling to force my mind onto our task, to focus on survival and follow Cora's twenty-year-old trail. "Maybe facial recognition in Baltimore, but that would have been before we traded plates. The chop shop or a fuel stop in Monterrey seem most likely. Too many cameras and too many computers looking for us. NAFAS could have hacked into their network."

"But our disguises were good. I liked the Rasta look better than this, not to mention the music. This cowboy shit's less fun." His upbeat comment is meant to improve my mood, but doesn't.

"They weren't good enough, evidently." That worries me, but I don't see another alternative to changing our identities and moving on. "We should stay to rural routes."

"If you say so, but you might stick out a bit. An Asian woman in rural Mexico?"

"Not so much. China's been subsidizing small town markets in Central America for decades. Even NAFAS hasn't put an end to that."

"Money, money, money..." Gippy taps his phone and it announces a new route, south on 115. "That added a lot of miles to our route."

"Time we've got. I'd rather get to Panama alive." *Panama...*

I remember the days of American pseudo-colonialism there, the tens of thousands who perished from Malaria during the building of the canal. I worked as a nurse then, curing hundreds, but even I had no way to know it was spread by mosquitos. The constant blasting to cut through mountains reminded me of cannon fire. Now, of course, ships pass through the entire canal without going through a single lock, though constant dredging barely keeps up with filling from erosion. Ships aren't what they used to be, either; supertankers and twenty thousand unit container ships can't handle the weather. With the drop in global shipping, the canal is barely paying for the upkeep. *How times change...* I imagine the sea floor littered with broken ships from centuries of sea travel, the dead hulls of bulk ore carriers lying beside those of Spanish galleons, both of which I sailed aboard.

Chaki strutted out of the Mexico City International Airport and flung her carryon bag into the back of the unmarked NAFAS SUV. She was pissed and didn't care who knew it. An Asian man in an expensive suit ushered her into the back seat. When she stepped past, the scalding aura of a Nephilim radiated against her skin like static electricity: crackling hatred, serpentine cunning, and cold malevolence. She knew this one; son of the fallen angel of shadows, and currently Senior Chief Investigator Haitao Zhao, of NAFAS Secret Service.

She scooched across the plush back seat, the leather cool through the rips in her jeans. There was a sound barrier between the back and the front, so they could speak openly. When the door closed, she turned to Zhao. "Why in the name of Hell am I here, Son of Batraal?"

"Because you are *needed*." He looked her over, his gaze judgmental, upper lip twitching. She wore a ripped V-neck tee shirt that exposed her hot pink bra, cut off above the belt of her low-rider pants to show off her ink. He wore a silk Armani that probably cost more than the SUV they were riding in. "We wield the might of the NAFAS *Government*, Duvara, but there are places even *we* can't go. These criminals know our agents and either refuse to speak to them or send them back to us in plastic bags. *Numerous* plastic bags."

"Sucks to be rich and powerful, I guess," she said, mirroring his sneer.

"This is a pivotal moment, *succubus.*" He pulled a slim notebook computer from the seat back in front of him. "You will help us, or I will see you stripped of your crown and cast down."

"You..." She'd started to say he couldn't do that to her, but he probably could. He was a Nephilim, only two steps from the Lord of Hell himself. She was a demon, a made thing, a tapestry of a million depraved souls woven into a single consciousness for a single purpose, to seduce humans into the service of Hell, then torment them for eternity. When the War of Souls was won, and the Earth wiped clean by the Horsemen, she would receive her reward... or her punishment. "Fine. What do you need?"

He tapped the tablet. "We have images of the two you identified in Monterrey. No names, and the license plate of their vehicle was stolen, but traffic cameras found them." He showed her the tablet, as split screen of two blurry pictures, one of the mulatto boy she'd failed to seduce, still wearing that ridiculous dreadlock wig, and the smoking hot Latina he'd been with.

"Yes, I heard. And you blew up three city blocks." *Typical Nephilim move, all balls no brains.*

"In a desperate attempt to destroy them, yes." He tapped the image of the woman, and four more materialized below it, all the same woman with different disguises. She recognized one from a decade-old news coverage of the St. Louis uprising. "We believe this is the Daughter of Raphael, the last of the Ageless. We also believe these two are the ones responsible for the recent banishments of three of my cousins."

Just as she'd suspected. "So, *you* lost them, and you want *my* help to find them."

"Not exactly." He switched the screen to a street cam image of two people carjacking a small sedan. "They took this car from the primary engagement site before we could bring in high-altitude assets." A sweep of the screen brought up a blurry image of the same car beside a dark SUV, the two figures carrying bags from one to the other. "They switched vehicles here, and again here only minutes later." Another picture, even worse resolution, of the SUV behind a rusty old Dodge pickup. "Before our asset could launch a strike, we lost them in the Barrios."

Frankly, she was surprised they hadn't carpet bombed the entire Barrios. "And you think *I* can find them?"

"No, we think they're out of the city. We hope, with your skills in tracking stolen vehicles, you can find out what happened to the pickup, then backtrack to wherever they dumped it. We have no imagery of that truck leaving the Barrios. It's there somewhere."

"It's in *pieces* by now," she grumbled. "Like looking for a specific gnat on a camel's ass."

"We also think they may have had help." He pulled up another street cam photo, this one of a dark Latino in a leather jacket, cowboy boots, and jeans. "This man made a sizeable withdrawal from a local bank the day after the strike. We have no information on the account, but he's a known drug dealer. This doesn't match the cartel's usual behavior, but an Ageless on the run might have needed funds, and paid them to help recover them without exposing herself."

"Drugs? That's not my gig." She looked at the blurry image, then the Nephilim. "You have this pendejo's *name*?"

"Enrico Morales. No address. Long criminal record. He vanished into the Barrios and hasn't been seen since."

"And you don't know who he deals for?"

"Not exactly. There are at least four minor cartels in Mexico City, and our people can't work in the Barrios."

"And you think *I* can?" She muttered a curse in a language unspoken by mortals. "This is fucking ridiculous! Why in Hell's name didn't you drop a nuke on the whole fucking city when you had them here?"

"Because clearance for that kind of strike is complicated, and our asset who had contacts in NORAD is currently burning in Hell." He handed her the tablet. "All the information we have is on that. Don't lose it." He also handed her a stylish leather wallet. "ID, cash, credit cards. If you need anything else, you call me directly."

She took the wallet, pulled everything from it, and stuffed it into her jeans, then handed the wallet and the computer back. "Drop me two blocks from the Barrios and fuck off. I do this *my* way, not yours."

The Nephilim sneered at her, pressed an intercom button, and instructed the driver.

Chaki rode in smoldering silence until they pulled to a stop in a dodgy business district. The door clicked open, then the hatchback. "Thanks for the ass fuck, pendejo." She got out, grabbed her bag from the back, and started walking into the Barrios. She would find Enrico Morales if she had to blow every drug dealer in the city.

"Journal entry one hundred fifteen, January twenty-eight, twenty fifty-three: Motherhood is changing me, I think. Only two weeks and I feel very different. Maybe it's just not being pregnant anymore, post-partum hormonal changes, but seeing you, feeling your soul for the first time when you breathed your first breath, has made me a new person. I feel... protective in a way I've never felt before in all of my centuries. You have become the most important thing in my life, more precious even than my own self-preservation. This both terrifies and exhilarates me like nothing ever has."

I take a moment to shift in the rocking chair, propping my son up a little higher as he suckles, staring down into his blue, blue eyes, feeling his love. "You are *such* a wonder, my son, and that's not just a mother's jaded opinion. Maria and Franko also think so. The most startling thing when you were born was that you didn't cry. Your eyes were open and everything was fine, so I guess you never felt the need. You're as healthy as any baby I've ever seen, and have a piercing gaze that makes me wonder if you're feeling my soul, as I feel yours. Even when you're hungry you just make little sounds or call out in your most *amazing* voice. You are truly my little wonder."

I pause the recording and hum a little tune to my son as he suckles happily. Music is nothing new to him, of course. Before he was born I played in almost every local café and club in town. Now that he's truly here with me, body and soul, I can feel his love for music. His eyes light up when I play for him, and he coos. I think I'll take him with me when I start playing in public again. My music is already having a positive effect on Boquete, and I'm drawn to the love I feel from my audiences. *Hope springs eternal through song...*

"Song..." The word comes to me from nowhere, and I peer down into my son's blue, blue eyes. "You are my song. My greatest composition."

He stops suckling and belches, obviously in agreement. I chuckle and wipe away the spit, shifting him up and patting his back, singing a little tune. "My song, my love, mi Canción..." I haven't chosen a name yet, wanting to truly meet him first, but I sing the word to him, and his eyes light up. "Canción... Canción..."

"So, you've chosen, eh?" Maria puts a glass of ginger tea on the table beside my rocking chair, bouncing her ten-month-old Fernando on her hip. "It fits."

"I think so, too." I jostle him on my lap and sing, "You are my Canción, my sweet music..."

"Ba!" Canción agrees, and Maria and I laugh.

As Canción grows, and I return to my music and working on the constant renovations to "Casa Música," I begin to realize just how unique he is. I document everything in my audio journal, but I try not to freak him out too much. That will come later.

Most curiously, the only time I ever see him cry is when Maria's son, Fernando throws one of his tantrums, and that's brief. Canción doesn't even cry when he's injured. His bumps and bruises heal quickly, as mine do, and Maria and Fernando have noticed. That takes some explaining, but by the time it becomes an issue, they know me and love me, as I love them. We are family. I leave out my angelic origin, but they know I'm special. Eventually, I'll have to tell them the whole truth, but I haven't decided when that will be. Maybe when I tell Canción.

On the rare occasions when Canción does act out, however, he is worryingly violent, usually knocking something off a table or smashing a toy across the floor. Afterward, everything's fine, he apologizes, and he's suddenly happy again. The "Terrible Twos" Maria assures me, but I worry it could be more than a passing phase. He's definitely got a destructive streak, and I wonder if that could be the influence of Azkeel, the Nephilim Emil harbors within himself. Canción is never vindictive or hurtful about this penchant, however, and will spend hours building a sandcastle just to destroy it with Fernando, both boys squealing with glee. Maria assures me this is normal for boys, but I still wonder. I suppose they're just blowing off steam.

He continues to be fascinated with music, too, which is delightful to me. He sings beautifully, and I feel power in his voice. It's not the same as mine, but there is something within him, some energy that is released with his voice. I'm not sensitive enough to know what this power is, or what it might mean, but it's there. He and Fernando are becoming fast friends, brothers at heart, and I'm teaching them both to play guitar. Canción loves to sing more than play, and his voice is enchanting. When I take him out to my performances, he sings at my side, and the audience positively glows.

Canción is inquisitive, as all children are, and asks me questions I don't know if I should answer yet, about his father, people and their feelings, and music. One day, I'll tell him everything, give him my journal, but in the meantime, I find him fascinating beyond measure. I'm constantly torn between protecting him from the world, and showing him the wonders of all humanity. I feel his love for me, for Fernando, for our home, but I also feel his smoldering temper. When other people are angry, or crying, or just being mean, he becomes temperamental, quiet and smoldering, then destructive. He likes Legos because he can build things then smash them with no real harm. He always feels better afterwards, so I never try to curb his behavior.

He is certainly special in other ways, as well. I wonder if he will stop aging, as I did, or grow old. I wonder what his gifts are, when they will fully manifest, whether they will be good or destructive. This child of Heaven and Hell is still, in some ways, a mystery to me.

11

THE LOOMING STORM

Driving becomes more and more torturous south of Oxaca. The numbing cold of North American winter has transformed into the blinding tropical rains of Central American summer in the span of two thousand miles. Hurricane season is upon us, and road maintenance is only for economically viable regions, which Central America is no longer. We drive in short shifts and stop only for fuel and an occasional meal. We sleep in the truck with pistols in our laps, picking small out-of-the-way places, always vigilant for cameras. On the upside, high-altitude aerial surveillance is impossible in this weather.

The highway devolves even further south of the sprawling shanty city of Japala, a once-quaint town on the shores of El Marquéz. Poverty is rampant, the near-constant deluge of the nine-month monsoon season having drowned virtually every crop save the most hardy. Roadside markets sell stunted yautia and taro, cacao pods, breadfruit, and live chickens and goats. Hunger lives in the faces of these people, and armed guards stand at the markets, signs promising the loss of a hand for stealing food in graphic illustration. The promise of mutilation for theft reminds me of my earliest centuries.

"No more maize..." I mutter as we edge out of the city on cracked and eroded pavement.

"Maize? What's that?" Gippy's driving, wrestling us over and around detours that would challenge a Humvee. He's taken a shine to the Mule—

his apt pet name for our chimeric vehicle—and for someone who's had almost no experience with off-road driving, he's learning at lightning speed.

"Corn." I wave absently at the drowned landscape. "An empire once stretched from central Mexico to Panama. The Mayans dominated the region for over two thousand years, and corn was their culture, almost a religion."

"Huh. Never heard of 'em." He diverts around a pothole that would swallow a semi and hammers the horn at a stuck SUV. He knows better than to stop and offer assistance. Stranded vehicles have been the highwayman's oldest trap since before there were highways. Before they invented the wheel, in fact.

"They were a noble and... complicated people, their culture advanced in many ways, but they lacked metallurgy. Drought decimated the empire about a thousand years ago, but some of the culture and people survived. When the Spanish arrived with muskets, steel swords and armor, and diseases they'd never encountered, the rest fell into obscurity or were enslaved."

"Were you here then?" Gippy asks without looking at me. Sometimes my age still makes him uncomfortable.

"Oh, no. I was in Greece, then the Roman Empire, then Africa after Rome burned." Tears sting my eyes with the memory of the flames, the slaughter, and I wrench myself back to the present. "I met an Ageless from here in 1654, near Acapulco. Cadmael. He was a warrior, son of an angel never named in any of the eastern texts, Zoque, angel of wind and lightning. He tried to organize and fight the Spanish, but failed and went into hiding." I remember his touch, electrifying to say the least, and the solace I found with him for a short few years, recovering from Musashi's loss.

"Huh? How did that work? I thought, you know, the Bible covered all the bases."

I snort a laugh. "Not even close. Ageless and Nephilim were born to almost every culture in the world, and there were people here fifty thousand years ago."

"But... I thought they, like, worshiped the sun, the moon... rocks and shit, not God."

"God is the same everywhere, Gip. It's humans that are different." I've wept enough tears to float a battleship over the wars that have been fought between cults vying for their own version of God. "Religions took what they could use for power, and fought wars over whose prophet was right, whose messiah was genuine, whose version of God was real." I sigh sadly. "While the Ageless struggled for unity and community, the Nephilim bred mistrust and division."

"Even back then... Wow."

"Always," I whisper. "Then technology changed everything from warfare to communications to social structures. Species were exterminated just because men had been taught that killing them was masculine recreation. Wars spanned the globe, and fossil fuels began to change the climate before we knew what we were doing." I haven't ever taught Gippy much history, but not because I don't think it would be useful to him. I don't have the heart.

We drive in relative silence for a time, torrential rain hissing against the truck's windows. The Mule's heavy enough that the hurricane-force wind gusts only jostle us. We pass tipped over tractor trailers, long since looted for their contents, some converted into shelters. Humans are still hanging on, scratching out an existence, tooth and nail.

Before we're really out of town, signs direct us west off the old highway—taken by the sea south of here—toward Santa Maria Mixtequilla, another village turned city as the sea advanced to consume the port of Salina Cruz, then inland to swallow Tehuantepec. This once arid land is green, but erosion has taken a horrible toll. We creep down the crumbling road to the river we must cross, passing work crews of gaunt, wiry men in threadbare pants and the Central American equivalent of Ho Chi Minh sandals. They're working with picks and shovels to gouge into the rock hillside, shifting the road barely as fast as erosion takes it away. The Romans, and even the Myans, could have taught them a thing or two about road construction. The Mule's tires crunch over rubble compressed by thousands of trucks. This is one of only three roads south, and it's still an artery for some commerce. Railroads, unfortunately, hugged the coasts, and are long gone.

Miraculously, the dam here is not only intact, but producing enough power to supply Japala, or at least those who can afford to pay for electricity. The construction here is higher tech, workers in hard hats doing maintenance on high-tension towers, transformers, and the structure itself, even as winds and slashing rain threaten to tear them off their precarious perches. On the dam itself, there's a gate guarded by two concrete pillboxes, the snouts of heavy machineguns nosing out of the narrow gaps. They remind me of the war, the horrible toll the Allies paid charging hardened German emplacements, the terrifying rip of Maschinengewehr 42 machine guns firing at 1200 rounds per minute. We pay a toll of one hundred NAD's to cross. Between power and tolls, whoever controls the dam is making a fortune. Maybe hydroelectric power is the new industry of Central America, for if there's one thing they have in abundance, it's water.

We turn south again, and the road here has seen more maintenance than those to the north. We meet traffic coming the other way, trucks piled with foodstuffs and a few small fuel trucks, probably empty or carrying palm oil. Even in the middle of the hurricane belt, there's still some agriculture, it seems. We rejoin highway 190, heading east, then south on 200, which clings to the new coastline like barnacles at the high-tide line. With a break between rain bands, the Pacific Ocean opens up to our right and I catch Gippy gawking at the monstrous waves.

"That's right. You've never seen the *big* ocean, have you?"

He shoots me a sour look. "I didn't even know oceans were a thing a year ago, E."

I point to a turnout that sports a roadside stand advertising chicken and goat, the parking lot half-full of trucks. My mouth waters. "Pull over and we'll grab a bite. I'll drive. You can sightsee."

"Sure." As he pulls in, wind buffets the truck. "Fuckin' weather's turnin' to shit again."

I peer out the rain-streaked windshield to the east at the darkening sky. "Another storm coming, I think."

Gippy pulls his phone, then makes a face. "The fuck? No *signal*?"

"It's the weather." I pull my own and see the same. "Satellites work great until there's enough electromagnetic disturbance in the atmosphere to screw up the signal. We should get something back when the weather clears. *If* it clears."

"Wha-chu mean *if*?" He shoots me a worried look.

"Weather down here's nothing but one continuous storm for most of the year, Gip. The hurricane belt used to be farther north, but it's widened in the last fifty years. If we're lucky, we'll get a signal when we reach Panama. They're still south of the worst of the storm belt."

"How we supposed to *navigate* without GPS?"

I stare at him for a moment, then realize he's serious. *Oh sweet child of the electronic age...* "Before electronics, people used paper maps. We'll find one somewhere along the way, I'm sure."

"Paper?" His brow furrows as if he thinks I'm joking.

"Buddy, I remember when paper was *new* technology! Look on the upside, no drones, no sat photos, and no long-range comms all mean NAFAS has their high-tech hands tied behind their backs. Come on. I'm hungry." I flip up my collar, make sure my Glock's out of sight, and step out into the storm.

~

Carlos collapsed back against the wrought iron headboard, sweat drenching his chest, breath coming in desperate gasps. "You one crazy puta, you know that?"

"Crazy?" Chaki smiled at her new thrall, grinding herself against him, and deemed him ready. She reached back behind her ass to grab him by the balls. "Say that again." She smiled and squeezed, exerting her Hell-given gift.

"Fuck!" The drug lord gritted his teeth, but the power of the succubus Duvara literally had him in her grasp. "Santa Madre de Dios! You're fucking *killing* me!" As Duvara exerted her power, he shuddered and climaxed yet again, his wrists clashing against the handcuffs securing him to the wrought iron. Men were always such idiots to submit to bondage.

"Not *yet*, I'm not." It had taken her three days to work her way to the top of his organization, and now she had him right where she needed him. The time for pretenses was over. "Now, unless you want to eat your own testicles, you'll tell me where the two who came to you three days ago went."

"What the fuck are you talkin' about?" He gasped for breath, still reeling. "Who?"

"Her name is Empa." She squeezed just enough to torture him. "Dark hair, beautiful. She was with a slim young black man. Where are they?"

"Don't know who—" He screamed as she squeezed him harder, forcing another climax. Repeated orgasms were one of her most delicious torments. Men couldn't handle it, and begged her to stop after only a few. This was Carlos's fifth in only fifteen minutes. Much more and his heart would explode. Blood trickled down his wrists from the cuffs, and his chin as well; he'd bitten through his lip.

"Where... did... they... go?"

"Yes! They were here!" His head lolled, and she slapped him hard to keep him from passing out. "I gave them a truck! They just drove away!"

"What truck?" She gripped his bloody chin. "Where did they go?"

He gnashed his teeth and caught her finger, biting down hard.

"Pendejo!" She squeezed her other hand, and he screamed again, releasing her finger. She sucked the blood from her knuckle, immune to the pain. "Now tell me where they *went*, or I'll rip your fucking nuts off!"

"South! Panama, I think! I don't know. The truck's an old TLC! Brown. Puebla plates! Registered to Glen Gonzalez! That's all I know!"

"And that's all I need." She released him and slid off, leaving him lying there. She wiped herself, donned her jeans and a tee shirt, and grabbed her shoes. "See you in Hell, cabrón."

"Wait! Unlock me at least! Jesus, don't just leave me like this!"

She cringed at his use of the name, the Ageless son of the god she couldn't speak of, the one who had changed humanity with his martyrdom. Glaring back at him, she grinned. "Don't worry. You won't have to suffer very long." She pulled her phone on her way to the door and punched the Nephilim's contact.

"Yes?" He answered.

"I have what you need. Pick me up."

"We're a block away."

She ended the call and glanced back again at Carlos, intending one more twist of the knife, but the young man slumped, breathing but unconscious. Chaki trundled down the steps of the cheap hotel on the edge of the Barrios and exited without looking back. She'd intended to find out where he lived, but the man had been careful. Not careful enough, however, and lured easily, as most men were when sex was involved. The demon in a human shell strode out onto the street just in time to step aboard the unmarked black SUV.

The son of Batraal sat there staring at her. "Well?"

"Old Toyota Land Cruiser, registered to Glen Gonzalez. They're on their way south, maybe Panama. You should be able to track it." She shifted on the seat and pulled her phone again, still smoldering from her delicious torment of the cock-sure Carlos. If there was one thing Duvara knew, it was how to track down a vehicle. In moments she had the registration pulled up, and the truck's plate. "Here." She showed him her phone.

"Excellent!" He pulled his own phone and began tapping.

Chaki put her phone away and leaned back. "Do me a favor and dispose of that pendejo, then you can drop me at the airport."

"He's already dead," the Nephilim said, as he continued scrolling and tapping. "But we're not going to the airport."

She narrowed her eyes at him. "Why the fuck not? I did your damn job for you! I'm done!"

"You're *not* done." He didn't even look up from his phone. "You're going with the strike team. I'm handing this operation over to the military, and they're going to hunt those two down. If they're continuing south, the search will be hampered by the weather. They may need your... expertise."

Chaki gritted her teeth, cursing the day she met the angel-touched mulatto boy. She clenched the fist that had tormented Carlos until her nails pierced her palm. If she ever found the companion of the Ageless, she would have him begging to be sent to Hell.

"Panama...," the Nephilim growled. "Could she be searching for her cousin?"

"What?" Chaki's dark eyes focused on him like targeting lasers. "What are you talking about?"

"Empa, of course." He kept scrolling. "We ended one of her Ageless cousins in Panama only eight years ago. She may be trying to find Terpsichore. If she is, we'll have her trapped."

"Good! Then you don't need me!" Chaki snapped.

His eyes slid up to her like snakes in tall grass. "You're going along, Duvara. Quit bitching."

Behind them, thunder boomed as a drone-fired missile struck the hotel where Carlos still lay unconscious, chained to the wrought iron headboard. The blast took out the whole block, obliterating every shred of evidence that she'd ever been there.

"Canción!" I burst into the hacienda like a storm front, dumping my guitar case and satchel, shaking water from my poncho. "Canción, where are you, love?"

"In the back, mama!" his cry comes, his sweet voice as pure as a note from a Stradivarius.

I hustle through the house without regard for my muddy footprints on the rugs. It won't matter anyway. I find Canción and Fernando on the patio, building an elaborate city of Legos. "Canción, I..."

How to explain? He's twelve, and I've not yet given him my journal. I've been procrastinating, prolonging his childhood as long as I can. He knows we're special, and that bad people are looking for me, but not everything.

Now, before he's ready, before *I'm* ready, everything I love most is in danger.

"Mama?" He looks at me, and I can see he feels my distress. He's really coming into his power now, whatever that is, and he picks up on people's feelings to an astonishing degree. "What's wrong?"

"We have to pack up and go, love." I drop to my knees before the two boys as shock and alarm register on their faces. "I'm sorry, but I was careless. Someone recorded my music and posted it on the ultranet. They took video with a phone. It's gone viral."

"That's bad, isn't it?" Canción's a smart boy, but sheltered from the troubles of the world, a loving mother wishing her son a peaceful childhood.

I'm an idiot.

Even in the isolation of Boquete, I've kept abreast of current events. The expansion of the fascist police state of NAFAS, the tyranny, the mass executions, the bombings and demonstrations quashed by air power and facial recognition cameras have all been building to a crescendo. The uprising in St. Louis that resulted in tens of thousands dead troubled me deeply, for the iconic leader of the rebellion I recognized. *Oh, my dearest cousin, what were you thinking?* NAFAS began dropping smart cluster munitions, fuel air bombs, and slaughter bot swarms not to pacify the dissidents, or even exterminate them, but to take out one Ageless. When the dust settled on the rubble of St. Louis, I knew that my cousin was dead.

I'm not going to let that happen here. If the Nephilim would do that to a city to take out Empa, what would they do in a Central American backwater? Our only saving grace is the inclement weather. No satellite coverage, no air support, no drone strikes... We can escape, but we have to move now. As isolated as we are, with the weather now interfering with satellite to ground signals, what little news we receive is often delayed, recordings of newscasts or dark net podcasts copied from phone to phone. I fear that NAFAS may already be on their way.

I have to make Canción understand. "Yes, very bad. They'll be coming for me, so we have to run away."

"Where?" He's getting angry already, I see it in his eyes. "Where will we *go?*"

"Colombia." I reach out to grasp his hands, but he jerks away. "Please, love. It's not safe here anymore. I have everything we need, but we have to go before they hem us in here. There's only one road out of town."

"I don't *want* to go!" Canción lurches to his feet, balling his fists. "I don't want to leave Fernando and our house! I like it here!"

"I like it here, too, but Casa Musica isn't safe anymore. They'll come here with bombs and guns and kill *everyone* if we stay. All of Boquete will be destroyed if we don't flee. Fernando and his family can come with us. They're already getting ready." Fernando's father, Franko, is in town buying up supplies and gassing up our escape vehicle. He, at least, needed no convincing.

"No!" Canción stamps a foot, fists hammering the air at his sides.

I've seen him like this before, right before he throws a tantrum. Fernando's seen it too, and scootches back.

"Canción?" I stand and put my foot down. "We have to *go*!"

"NO!" He whirls and kicks the Lego city with a shrill scream, obliterating it in one sweeping stroke. Blocks fly into the rain-drenched yard, but with the sudden violence, Canción's fists unclench, his shoulders easing their tension in a heartbeat. As usual, his destructive tantrum is brief and harmless. I feel the release of his anger and breathe easier. My panic recedes; he'll calm down now.

He turns to me. "I'm sorry, Mama, but..." He looks around at our home. "I don't want to leave Casa Musica. I *love* it here."

"I love it here, too, my dearest, but we have no choice." I kneel again and hold out my arms. "We'll find a new place and be happy there. I promise."

He hugs me, and I feel his love beating against me with every heartbeat. "I understand."

I wonder, not for the first time, if this is my son's gift, or if he's simply bipolar. The drastic and sudden changes in mood are startling, but he never hurts anyone. Now, at least, he's seeing reality.

"Good." I hold him at arm's length and reach out to Fernando. "Now you boys pack up like I taught you. Just what you need, one favorite toy, and make sure your phones are off. Pack everything water tight."

"Yes, Mama." Canción nods, and Fernando also, both of them remarkably calm.

"Good. Go now, and be quick! I don't know how much time we have." I turn to my own preparations, calling for Maria. She understands immediately and starts packing. I grab passports, money, identifications, weapons, clothes, and a little food for the road. Franko will bring the truck with everything else we need.

I check the weather and cringe. It's storm season, and the mountain passes will be difficult. The highway south of David is impassable, but Highway 10 branches off at Alto Boquete. The road is not good, but we can make it. When I sold my Rover, Franko found an old surplus military JLTV, and outfitted it like an RV. The beast can handle almost anything. Canción named it *A Cappella,* of all things, and painted the sides with music.

By the time we're finished packing, a mound of packs and duffels is piled in the front room, along with several long-gun cases and crates filled with nonperishables and ammo. Twelve years has given me plenty of time to prepare for this day, but still I look around at my beloved Casa Musica longingly. This has been the longest I've spent in a single place in centuries, and my heart breaks to leave it, but I know I'll get over it. We have no choice but to flee.

Maria and Franko know I'm wanted by NAFAS, but not about the Nephilim, or that I'm the daughter of an angel. Not even Canción knows that yet. They do know that I'll do everything in my power to keep them safe. They're my family.

The roar of *A Capella* pulls me to the front porch in time to see Franko racing up the drive. He skids to a stop only meters from the front door and leaps out, his face painted with horror. I know what he's going to say before he opens his mouth.

"Senora Wagner! They are *here*!"

I don't need to ask who he means. The Nephilim have found me.

12
CLOSING IN

I jerk awake as Gippy nudges me. "What?" I reach for my Glock, but he holds up a hand.

"Chill, E. We're just comin' into Panama, I think." He yawns and squints through the windshield. "Rain might be letting up a bit, but it's still comin' down like piss at a kegger."

I blink myself fully awake and work the kinks out of my ass. The memories of the roads of Guatemala, El Salvador, Nicaragua—where the sea has virtually cut the isthmus through—and Costa Rica are a blur of slashing rain, mud, and poverty that reminds me of Cambodia.

"Fuel?" I ask. We've shifted the Mule from coal emulsion to palm oil simply because there is virtually no petroleum this far south. The thing gets horrible milage, and we've nearly run out twice due to faulty gauges in the oil tank. A lesser vehicle, however, would never have made it over the terrain we've traversed.

"We should make David okay, I think. I'm dying for a good night's sleep." Gippy looks haggard, his eyes puffy and red.

"Me, too." We've slept in the vehicle rather than risk a hotel. We skirted San José for fear of cameras, buying oil at a roadside depot for exorbitant prices. "We'll get a room in David. It's pretty cut off. There are no highways open south of the canal."

All the effort to link up the Pan-American Highway seems wasted, but they never closed the Darién Gap anyway, for good reason. I sometimes feel as if Mother Nature is reclaiming the Earth in a fit of petulant rage. Perhaps she is, and I can't blame her.

"Thank God," Gippy murmurs. "I ain't been this funky since you scraped me off the sidewalk in Cincinnati."

I glance at him, remembering the strung-out, half-dead street punk who held me up at gunpoint, a pivotal point in both of our lives. He's come so far, grown so much, I can barely suppress tears. I'm so proud of him it's physically painful. He's given me the one thing no-one has in centuries: hope.

I reach across to lay a hand on his shoulder, taking his aches and pains, and giving him all that I am in gratitude. "Thank you, Gifford."

"What?" He glances at me, but the road requires his attention. I can see that he feels my gift, and is puzzled. "What was that for?"

How do I explain? "For being you. I don't thank you often enough."

"Well, okay. You're welcome, I guess." He clears his throat, clearly uncomfortable with my gratitude, and changes the subject. "So, somebody sold Cora's old Land Rover in David like a *decade* ago, and we're... What exactly *are* we lookin' for?"

"Any sign of her." I've been considering this for some time and have searched the net as we traveled from Monterrey south until we lost satellite coverage. After the sale of the Rover, we've found no other trace of Cora to follow. If she bought a new vehicle, she did it under a different name and with cash. If we find anything, it'll be the remnant effects of her presence. "The only reason I can think for her to come to such a remote area is to find someplace safe to raise Emil's child. That would take some time, a few years at least, until they could travel. If she spent much time here, she would have spread her gift among the populace, giving her love to people through song. I should be able to feel that."

"Okay." He sounds skeptical. "Maybe check out local music shops, night clubs, places she might have played?"

"Not a bad strategy. She was... *is* as addicted to music as I am to healing." I still don't have much hope that she's alive, but if there's anywhere in NAFAS where she could remain undetected, it would be here. "If we're lucky, someone will have known her."

The highway diverts from its original path before we reach David. The raging Pacific has devoured about half of the city. Even this far south, hurricanes rip across the isthmus; unheard of in all the history of mankind. Payback's a bitch.

As we climb over a hill into town, the view is disheartening. They've built a seawall, of course, and the massive buttresses of reinforced concrete seem to be holding up. The sea has risen as much as it can, so the rest of the town might survive. The city's expanded uphill with the demise of lower coastal towns and the influx from Panama City. Most of the new buildings are hovels, some with only one concrete wall and sheets of corrugated tin for a roof. The rain slashes down, and rivulets of filth flow over eroded streets. Hungry faces peer out from the squalor, eying our vehicle with suspicion and desperation.

Deeper into town, the older buildings are in better repair, and there are even markets selling local produce, every single one with armed guards. Agriculture is still possible in the higher country, evidently, and there's a comparatively drier growing season here. I don't see many cameras, and virtually no NAFAS presence, both good.

"This place is almost off the grid, E," Gippy says.

"Yes, and it gives me hope. It'd be a good place to hide. Cora may have settled near here, not in the city, but nearby."

"You think she might still be here?"

"Frankly, no. Emil's child would be twenty by now. Cora would have no reason to stay put. If she did settle here for a time, we may be able to find someone who knew where she went." That's not very likely, for if she fled, she would cover her tracks.

"So, this ain't even close to over, right?" He sounds despondent, and I can't blame him.

"Just getting started, I'm afraid." I spot a bio-fuel and bus depot burning electric lights, three wind generators on the roof rotating so fast I can't see the rotors, power for the taking. They have a restaurant and more serious private security; three badass hombres with shotguns. A large sign proclaims 'Solamente Efectivo,' which is good for us. Cash only means less chance of tracing transactions. "Pull in there. Looks like they might rent rooms, too."

"Food, fuel, a bed, and a freakin' *shower*! Fuckin' a!" He pulls in and maneuvers up to a pump labeled 'fuel oil.'

The pumps are covered, but I don a hat anyway to hide my face before I get out. One of the security hombres eyes us, his shotgun resting on a lanyard, his hand on the grip but relaxed. "I'll pay, you pump."

"Ay-firmative, amiga."

I give the security man a nod, step into the market/restaurant, and stroll to the cashier, inhaling the scent of deep fried food and brewed coffee while tinny Latin music plays over blown out speakers. My mouth waters. Nobody even glances at me. I'm invisible.

"Si?" The middle aged woman behind the counter looks bored and tired.

"Fuel and a room for tonight, please," I say in Spanish with a Mandarin accent, which comes so naturally it startles me. "Pump number four, and the room on the second floor."

"Six hundred for the room, cash first, please." She holds out a hand.

I tease a T-note from the roll in my pocket and hand it over. "If the pump runs over, just let me know."

"No problem." She punches up the sale and slides a key card across the counter with the room number written on it in sharpie. Ironically, the card is attached to an old-fashioned brass deadbolt key by a cable tie. Electronic locks have gone by the wayside down here, harder to maintain than mechanical.

I stroll around the shop while Gippy pumps fuel, looking for traces of my cousin. A stand of maps and local advertisements catches my eye. There seem to be a lot of them, and I wonder why. Then I check my phone. Still no signal. We're still in the pre-satellite era down here until the end of storm season.

Gippy finishes pumping fuel, parks the truck, and comes in. "Room?"

"Yes." I hand him the key. "Let's eat. This place is a way station. Nobody notices or cares about anyone else."

He scans the room and nods. "Yep. Good call."

I get my change from the counter, and we step into the restaurant section. There are a few people at tables, eating absently, clearly passing through. The counter is cafeteria style, stainless steel bins of food, mostly deep fried, behind glass. It's manned by a dour, middle-aged man in a stained apron. He's mixed race, Asian/Hispanic, and eyes me with mild interest. I order carne guisada over rice with black beans, and he dishes up a plate with fried plantains and stewed greens of dubious origin. I don't even ask what the meat is. Gippy picks something deep fried that might be chicken, goat, cat, dog, or bush meat. The tiny label on the glass just says "Carne Frita," but Gippy's never been squeamish about his source of protein. We both order coffee, which the server pours into thick porcelain mugs. Disposable containers are rarer here with the nightmare of shipping anything in. Easier just to wash dishes, and there's certainly no water shortage, though I doubt it's very sanitary. Dysentery and cholera are probably running rampant. I thank him and pay, and we pick a table in the corner facing the parking lot.

We eat in silence, the food surprisingly good, especially the plantains. The coffee's astonishingly good. The music shifts to an eclectic guitar with a sweet tenor accompaniment, simplistic lyrics, but the guitar is sheer genius. My foot taps of its own accord, and I realize this is hauntingly familiar. Comprehension comes in a rush of adrenalin.

"Cora!" I whisper under my breath, my heart pounding.

"What?" Gippy looks around, then at me. "Where?"

"The music. It's hers." I get up and stroll over to the food counter again, smiling to the server. "Señor! This music is beautiful. Do you know it?"

"Si." He shrugs. "It's old. A local woman."

"Do you know her name?"

"Senorita... Tersi, I think. She lived in Boquete."

Tersi. Terpsichore. It's Cora; I can feel it in my bones. "Thank you." The old man said *lived,* not *lives,* but I have a lead, and my steps are light as I return to our table. "Boquete."

Gippy's eyebrows arch. "What's that?"

"A town near here, up in the mountains. I'll get us a map." I shovel food into my mouth, my heart lifted by our new lead. "I think Cora lived there."

"Wow! That was too easy." Gippy peels meat off a bone that certainly isn't chicken or goat. "Can we get a night in a bed before we hit the road again?"

"Sure." We're in no rush. The trail we're following is at least a decade cold.

But Gippy was right that this was easy, far too easy. If Cora's music was out in the world, even locally, it may have given her away. The Nephilim have adapted technology to search for us, and Cora's music is as distinctive as a fingerprint. If there's facial recognition software, there's undoubtedly music recognition software. I fear that this might be the dead end of our search.

Chaki stepped down from the huge NAFAS military APC and was instantly drenched to the skin by the deluge. The weather had turned to shit. She would have cursed the rain, but it was all part of Hell's plan.

Demoralizing humans was easy, all it took was a global climate crisis, and endless supply of cheap narcotics, and a police state. Besides, wet tee shirts were fucking hot.

The column of NAFAS vehicles had pulled over just south of San José, Costa Rica, in the smaller city of Cartago. They'd spent half a day scouring every gas station in San José looking for camera footage of the Land Cruiser. So far, they'd had zero luck. The Ageless was being careful. This little shithole fuel depot sat at the juncture of two highways, one south and one east. It didn't look like it even had cameras, and didn't sell gas or diesel, only palm oil for cooking and burning in converted diesel engines.

NAFAS soldiers advanced on the little station with weapons at the ready. The Nephilim commander, Captain Hernandez, wasn't very subtle —*All balls and no brains*—but they didn't need subtlety at this point. The son of Batraal had handed the operation over to the son of Ertael, fallen angel of martial prowess, a natural soldier for eons. Brute force was his specialty, and he'd been in high demand for millennia, for there was always a war somewhere. The weather here had interfered with satellite networks, so they'd been reduced to canvasing and VHF radios. They'd left a trail of blood and terror south from Mexico City but had tracked the Land Cruiser using traffic camera imagery matching the license plate.

The plate that I got them. She seethed at being forced to accompany this hunt, but if it succeeded, she would be rewarded for her efforts. If they took out the last Ageless, the War of Souls would be all but won. All that remained would be the task of corrupting every last human on earth, Duvara's specialty.

A shrill scream from the gas station drew her like a magnet. She strode over to find out what was going on. The soldiers stepped aside to let her pass, but that didn't keep their eyes from lingering on her. Duvara absorbed their bridled lust like a sweet elixir. They'd been told she was an undercover operative, which was ironically true. Her cover was human flesh hiding the demon within.

Inside the gas station, the Nephilim had the proprietor, his husband, and their two children on their knees, a pistol pointed at the younger boy, a slim tablet in his other hand, the screen turned to the couple.

"Have you seen see this vehicle?" he asked in Spanish.

"Please! We see many cars!" one of the two men pleaded.

The Nephilim twitched his gun and fired, the round missing the boy by inches. The two boys screamed and collapsed, fetal on the floor, hands clasped over their ears.

"Next one goes in the little one's knee! Now have you seen this *vehicle?*"

"Yes! Yes! Yesterday! Traveling east, I think!" the same man blurted.

"He's lying." Chaki stepped forth, fishing her phone from her back pocket. "Let me try, Captain." Brute force threats like his often elicited false information, but she'd noticed the other man staring at the screen and looking away repeatedly. He was being evasive. They needed a more visceral inducement to extract the truth. "They know something."

The son of Ertael glared at her, then stepped back. "Go ahead." He might be a brute, but he knew she had methods that he didn't.

She stepped up to the couple and leaned down, rain water dripping from her nose onto the less vocal one's face. He was the weaker, and his terror prickled her wet skin like an aphrodisiac. "You need to tell us where you saw that vehicle or these two people." She showed him her phone—the pictures of the Ageless and her companion displayed—and caressed his cheek with her long nails. He shivered in revulsion as she shared all she was with him, all the depraved horrors she'd perpetrated on countless humans. "If you *don't* tell me, I'll take your two little boys to a man I know in LA who makes movies. Movies that use *up* little boys and girls until there's nothing left of them. Then I'll strap you two into chairs and make you watch those movies, listen to their screams as they're slowly destroyed. I'll cut off your eyelids so you can't *not* watch, and I'll turn up the volume until the only thing you'll *hear* is their screams." She glanced at the two cowering children, licking her lips at the possibilities. "They're young and strong. They'll last *months* before the end."

"Please," the man pleaded, closing his eyes. "We saw them, yes. The woman paid us, told us NAFAS might be looking for them, that we should tell them we saw nothing, or that they were headed east."

Success... Duvara could feel the truth in the depths of her depraved soul. "And where were they headed?"

"They drove south on highway two, I *swear.*"

He was telling the truth, too horrified by her threat to think up a convincing lie. She straightened and turned to the son of Ertael. "There you go, and we didn't even have to murder anyone. They're headed into Panama."

The Nephilim sneered at her, then fired his pistol twice, killing both men in cold blood. "Saddle up, people! We'll drive through the night! We have them cornered! Sergeant, *sterilize* this place!" He turned and walked out, his men following.

Chaki glanced down at the two screaming boys, their fathers dead on the floor beside them. "Such a fucking waste." She whirled and stalked past the sergeant standing at the door with an incendiary grenade in his hand. "I could have sold those two little shits for *thousands*!"

The dull *foosh* of the grenade immolating the evidence reached her ears over the hiss of rain as she climbed back aboard the truck.

~

Terror and resolve twist my guts into knots with Franko's news. "Where are they? How many?" I thought we had time enough to flee.

"Six military trucks drove into Boquete about a quarter hour ago." Franko glances back at the drive. "They were asking about you, your music, where you lived. They weren't being gentle or subtle. They'll be here in minutes."

And there is only one road from Casa Musica into town, and one road out of town. We're boxed in, rats in a trap. All my careful planning has put us into that trap, and the jaws are closing. All my horrors have come true, my son, the one being on this God-forsaken planet that I care most about, is now under the guns of the Nephilim. But they're after *me*. My heart shatters, and I make the decision that I know I must.

"Franko, take my pack," I pointed to the shoulder bag. "There's enough money in there to set you all up for life, and Colombian IDs for everyone. Take everything you can carry on foot. Go into the jungle. Leave no trace. Go to Punta Peña on the Caribbean side. There's a man, Captain Marko Blanco. He has a boat. Buy passage to Cartagena."

"But..." Franko swallows hard. "But you..."

"They're after *me*, Franko. Right now they're *only* after me." I see in his eyes that he understands.

Maria gasps in horror, also realizing what I'm doing, her hand covers her mouth, her eyes filling with tears. Her son Fernando clutches her belt, already crying, near panic.

"Mama, no!" Canción latches onto me, his little arms hard around my waist. "Come with us!"

"Canción, my love." I kneel and take him in my arms, trying to figure out how to make him understand. "I need you to be strong. The Hounds of Hell, the ones I told you about, are coming. If I go with you, they'll come after us and kill *everyone*. If I stay, I can end their hunt here. It's the only way."

"But they'll *kill* you!" he screams into my shoulder.

"No they won't, love." I grasp him by the shoulders and stare into his eyes, still not crying but filled with horror. "I need you to believe me. They *won't* take me. I've prepared for this." *Flames... just like everywhere else I've fled from.*

He feels the truth of my words, but I see the anger, the denial, the tantrum coming. It builds in him, pulling at me like a sponge absorbing water, filling him, becoming a force. He whirls away and screams a screeching, pure note, and power lances out. My favorite chair, heavy teak with embroidered cushions, shatters, the hardwood splintering, the pillows flying apart in a shower of batting.

Everyone staggers back, including me. I fall on my ass, staring at my son in shock. "Canción! What in the name of God?"

"I'm sorry, Mama, but..." He looks around at the others. "Everyone was so scared, I just... had to take it away."

"Take it *away*?" I realize that my emotions, other than astonishment, are quiescent, and the fear on everyone else's eyes is gone. "How?"

"I've always done it." He shrugs.

I shake my head sharply and struggle to my feet, recalling all the times he's destroyed something in a tantrum when someone was upset or angry. I'd always thought the tantrums simply distracted people from their woes, but now I know... and the epiphany hits me like a bomb. My son can absorb emotions. He expels the negative energy of anger, fear, and sadness in destructive force. I struggle to grasp the utility of his power, but the realization of Canción's gift is incongruous in the midst of our current crisis. The Hounds of Hell are at our door. We have no time.

"Here!" I unzip a pocket of my bag and withdraw two items. The first is a jump drive with my journal on it. The second is a slim .32 caliber automatic in a belt-clip holster. I've been training Canción with firearms for two years, and he finds them fascinating, as most boys do. I hold both out to him. "You have to go. Everything about why is on this drive. You have to be strong for me or *everything* is lost. You have to survive, my son. You're special, more so than you can imagine. *Why* you're special is on this!" I hold up the drive.

He takes it, tucks it in his hip pocket, then the pistol, still calm, accepting, almost as if he knows what's really happening. "I love you, Mama."

"And I love you more than anything in the world, my son. That's why you have to go." I hug him as if the world is ending, which it very well might be. If I die, who will oppose the Nephilim? The answer, I realize, might be embracing me at this very moment. *God's plan...*

He nods against my shoulder, squeezing me, then finally pushing away. His face is calm, tearless as always. He turns to the others. "We should hurry."

"Yes!" Franko grabs my bag, then another, and a long-gun case. "Fernando, your pack! Maria, the other rifle case! Vamos!"

They grab gear, and I hug them all, following them out the back, then standing and watching them jog into the rain-soaked jungle. They're gone in moments, and my tears finally release like the rain that pours from the heavens.

"Canción, my sweet song..." I whirl away and return to the rest of the packed gear, opening a case to arm myself for the coming conflagration. Hell is coming.

13
JAWS OF THE BEAST

Chaki stirred from sleep as the NAFAS convoy rolled into David. The demon Duvara never slept, but the human shell required rest. She yawned, inhaling the stink of twelve sweaty soldiers. The entire expedition was exhausted, running on stimulants and sheer determination. At least the trucks had air conditioning.

Outside, rickety doors and shutters slammed closed as they roared through the dilapidated streets, the vehicles' huge tires sending geysers of fetid water splashing to both sides. Those unfortunate enough to be up at this hellishly early hour dodged out of the way, staring wide-eyed at the unaccustomed sight. Chaki glared out the rain-streaked window of the APC at the sodden hovels of concrete and rusted tin, reveling in the fear and despair in the humans' eyes. *And well they should be afraid; Hell has just rolled into town.* But there were too many eyes on them, and she knew word of their arrival would spread faster than their search.

"We're being too fucking noisy," she hissed to the Nephilim seated in front of her. "They'll hear you coming and vanish into the slums like they did in Mexico City."

"Then we hunt them down." Captain Hernandez snapped orders over the radio, and the other trucks peeled out of formation to cover the neighborhoods. Anyplace with a camera would be interrogated for any sign of their quarry. "There's nowhere for them to go. The highway is their only way out."

"Idiot," she growled, but there was no arguing with the creature. He outranked her.

The center of town wasn't as run down as the sprawl. The intersection of highways sported a big bus stop with food and rooms. It seemed a likely place for anyone to stop for fuel, food, and rest. The Land Cruiser they sought wasn't in the parking lot, however.

Hernandez and his soldiers piled out, and Chaki followed. People scattered like cockroaches. The security guard manning the door to the place just about shit his pants, his hands up and away from the shotgun hanging from his web gear.

"Problem, officers?"

"We're searching for a couple of international terrorists." Hernandez pulled a tablet from beneath his coat and tapped up the single decent picture they had of the Land Rover. "Two people. Gringo woman and a black man, driving this." He showed the man the picture. "Have you seen this vehicle?"

"A lot of traffic comes through here," the man hedged, but Chaki could see in his eyes that he knew something.

"And it's your job to *watch* that traffic, so I'll ask you again, have you seen this vehicle?" He snapped his fingers and two soldiers hurried over, automatic weapons at the ready. "You don't want me to ask a third time."

The guard swallowed. "Si, the truck was here last night. They left early."

"And where did they go?"

"I don't know, sir. That direction, not south." He pointed east.

Hernandez grinned and turned away from the terrified guard. "They're going to Boquete, searching for Terpsichore. That's the only thing that makes sense! Pull the team in, Sergeant! We have them in a box!"

"Or this is a big fucking trap!" Chaki had read the report of the operation that had taken out the daughter of Israfal, and it hadn't gone as planned.

"Two fugitives trap an armored column?" He snorted a derisive laugh. "You have a high opinion of our adversaries, Duvara."

He started to walk past her, but she stepped in front of him, lowering her voice to a harsh whisper. "So, you *want* to be banished?"

Hernandez blinked at her, clearly not seeing the big picture. "What?"

"Listen to me, you arrogant *fuck*!" she hissed through gritted teeth. "Empa has survived five *thousand* years! She's beaten countless Nephilim, and now they've discovered a way to send your kind to Hell *permanently*! These two have banished three Nephilim in the past six months! You ever think for two seconds that *you* could be next?"

"Impossible! Two people couldn't beat an armored column."

"Did you fucking *read* the report from DHS? Terpsichore, a *single* Ageless, took an entire armored task force down with her. Maybe you should talk to the son of Gadriel. He's only eight years old, but he might give you some *respect* for our enemy."

He glared at her. She could see the fear in his eyes and knew that he hated it even more than he hated her. Nephilim didn't fear death, for they respawned. If Chaki died, Duvara would languish in Hell for a time before finding a new human host to possess. Banishment for a Nephilim was forever, and their Lord wouldn't be happy with their failure.

"What do you *suggest*?" Hernandez growled.

"Let me do some recon." She waved a hand at the soldiers. "You all are about as subtle as a Nazi at a bar mitzvah. You send your shock troops in with their dicks in their hands, and they *and* you will be picked off like bugs on a windshield. I can at least verify that they're there, and maybe see if they've set up a few dozen IED's to reduce your *armored column* to scrap metal."

"Fine. We'll secure a vehicle for you." He waved his sergeant forward and snapped an order. "And you'll take a radio. If you find them, you call us in."

She didn't like his tone. "Just don't call an airstrike down on my head."

He sneered pure derision at her. "I *can't*! We have no sat coverage, Duvara. Are *you* not paying attention?"

"I pay attention to *people*, Nephilim. It's my *job*. You handle the techy shit, and I'll find our Ageless." She whirled away before he could make another snide comment, cursing his arrogant blindness.

The road from to Boquete was steep but in surprisingly good repair. Gippy took it slow, vigilant and uneasy. Once they passed the Highway 10 turnoff at Alto Boquete, there was only one road in and out of this place. One of Empa's oldest lessons was to always have an escape route. This town was surrounded by jungle, and the damn rain just wouldn't let up. He felt like he was driving into a trap he couldn't see. He wondered if Empa saw it, felt it.

He looked at her critically. She'd been rattled by the attack in Mexico City but now seemed intent, focused, back on her game. "Think she's alive?"

"I don't know." She glanced at him, and he could feel her anxiety. "She's not here anymore, but that could mean she just moved on when her child was old enough to travel. Cora was very good at blending in, but her very nature made her at least locally famous. The locals will have known her. She played for them."

Gippy didn't really understand why anyone would remember someone just because they played music, but he'd learned to trust Empa. She knew her cousin. He'd never really been into music, though he'd enjoyed listening to reggae for his brief stint as a Rastafarian. The guitar music they'd listened to in the restaurant had been nice, if a bit complex for his taste. It had sounded like two people playing together, but Empa had said it had been only Cora. She hadn't known who sang accompaniment, but the voice had been really high, like a kid's. He wondered if that had been Cora's child.

He slowed to a crawl as they entered the town of Boquete, not because there was traffic, but because there were more people out and about than seemed reasonable considering the weather. They wore ponchos, hats, raincoats, and boots, hunched against the wind-slashed rain, but they also greeted one another on the sidewalks, shaking hands and hugging, laughing and smiling in the covered eateries. Four old men sat at a table slapping down dominoes and laughing, sipping beers. A woman and man played guitars in another open air restaurant, the audience singing along with them. People waved across the street to one another, called each other by name in cheerful greeting.

The town was also in much better repair than David, the buildings painted bright colors, sidewalks and even the gutters clean, no wrecked-out cars or ramshackle shelters for homeless. Everyone seemed to be dressed in reasonably good clothes, too, with hats and even a few umbrellas. It felt like a different world.

Gippy had never seen anything like this before. "This is fuckin' weird, E. It's like they're all on drugs."

"It's *love,* Gip." Empa smiled at him, tears in her eyes. "It's *Cora*. This is what her music does. She was here long enough to bring her love to the whole community. This is her gift."

"Wow." He drove on slowly, trying to take it in. "So, why didn't she just sell her music all over the world? If everyone was as happy as these people, the Nephilim wouldn't stand a chance."

"It doesn't work that way. You have to be with her, hear her directly, to receive her gift."

"Then why not become a rockstar? Go on tour? Play for thousands?"

"Too much exposure. She was famous in Greece about twenty-five hundred years ago, and it nearly killed her and almost destroyed Greece. Another empire, Persia, invaded. We never *really* knew if it was because of her or not, but she had to flee." She shook her head sadly. "Fame is a death sentence for us."

"Right." The inequity of the war, Nephilim respawning when they were killed while Ageless didn't, had always struck a chord of anger within Gippy. It seemed to him as if God wasn't interested in winning.

"She used to hook up with famous musicians and composers just to be around their entourages, to play small private gatherings, but even that was dangerous." Empa chuckled. "She was a sucker for anyone with a musical gift and inspired hundreds of them. She even wrote some of their music but never took credit for it."

He could hear the heartbreak in her voice and decided to bring them back on task. "You wanna stop and start asking around?"

"Sure." She scanned the main street and pointed to a covered eatery. "There. They have a sign advertising live music."

Gippy parked the Mule in front of De la Abuela Café and pulled his hat down tight. The wind wasn't so bad right now, the storm maybe passing. They might get a few days of lighter rain before the next one hit. He moved his Glock from the seat pocket to his back and opened the door to step out. They hunched, collars up, and stepped under the restaurant's wide metal awning. Beneath it, the rain sounded like a snare drum. The eatery was half full, though it was early for lunch. A young man, maybe fifteen, hurried up to them with a broad grin.

"Welcome to Grandmother's!" he said in accented English, obviously spotting them as visitors. "Two for lunch?"

"Please." Empa returned his smile. "A corner table?"

"Si... Yes, this way." He escorted them to a small table in the back where they could see the whole restaurant. "Is this okay?"

"Perfect. Thank you." They sat.

"Something to drink? Cerveza, tea, coffee?" His teeth flashed in a friendly grin. "We have *real* coffee, grown right here on the slopes of our own little volcano!"

"Two coffees, please," Empa said.

"Two coffees. Sure." The boy nodded and gestured to a blackboard scrawled with Spanish. "Our menu is there. If you need me to translate..."

Empa said something to him in Spanish, and he nodded and grinned again, hurrying off.

"They really have a volcano here, you think?" Gippy scanned the room and met a few gazes taking them in. They all looked local to his eye, but none of their interest seemed suspicious or discriminatory, just curious. It gave him the creeps.

"Yes. Volcanic soil's good for crops." She looked around at the other customers, whose interest in them was slowly waning. A few men eyed her with interest, their female companions scowling, and in one case kicking her companion under the table. "These people are doing well. No starvation, no strife, and it doesn't look like NAFAS has a presence."

Gippy had noticed the lack of naffies. "You think Cora's magic ran them off?"

"It's not magic, Gip," she said with an admonishing look. "It's God's love."

"Oh, I know. I just..." He paused as the young man returned with two coffees. They ordered food, Empa translating for Gippy. He sipped his coffee and nearly choked; it was strong, flavorful, and perfect. "Wow. *Good* coffee!"

"There's hope for the world after all." Empa sipped and sighed in bliss.

Gippy people-watched through the meal, content to let Empa take the lead on questioning the locals about Cora. Her way with people, that angel-daddy shit he couldn't quite define, would give her an edge. Besides, the food was excellent and the atmosphere friendly. He imagined living in a place like this, happy people, good food, music, love... Then remembered the howl of murder drones, the roar of explosions, the music of sirens.

Fucking war, he cursed inwardly, trying to imagine a future where humans determined their own destiny without the interference of the Nephilim. *Someday...* That was the future he dreamt of, the future that was worth fighting for, even dying for.

When their young waiter returned to take their plates, Empa asked, "You have musicians play here often?"

"Yes. Most nights, starting after dinner. Tonight is my sister and her husband. You should come."

"We will." Empa gestured vaguely. "Is the restaurant named after *your* grandmother?"

"Yes. Her recipes. And she loves music very much."

"Is she here? Can I talk to her? I'd like to thank her for the meal. It was very good." Empa had her angel-daddy mojo turned on full.

The boy's face lit up like a neon sign. "Sure! She's in the kitchen. She loves to talk to customers. Come with me."

They got up and followed. The kitchen was busy and sweltering hot, an old round woman working over a wood-fired stove, a younger man doing the heavy lifting. Gippy saw the family resemblance between the man and their waiter, father or uncle, he assumed.

"Grandma? A lady wants to talk to you," the boy announced in English.

"Yes?" The woman turned with a smile, spatula in hand. Her face was lined with a thousand smiles, her eyes dancing with delight. She obviously loved her work.

"I'm Emily." Empa stepped forward and held out a hand. "I just want to thank you for the wonderful meal and maybe ask you about a woman who used to live here."

"Oh, you're welcome." The old woman beamed with pleasure, wiped her hand on a towel, and shook Empa's. "What woman?"

"We heard some music in David, a guitar. It was amazing. I was told her name was Señorita Tersi. I thought you might..." Empa paused, and Gippy could see why. Both the old woman and the man suddenly went serious, their eyes hard.

"Why?" the man asked.

"Because I love music, and I'd like to meet her." Empa shrugged. "Is there a problem?"

The man and old woman exchanged a glance, and the woman shook her head sharply. Their young waiter backed away from them both, his face suddenly worried. Gippy stepped away from the door and slipped a hand behind his back. *Steady spirit, see everything...*

"You should go," The man pulled off his apron and stepped forward, his face hard. "Don't ask about Señorita Tersi. She was very special to everyone here, but... she's gone."

"Gone?" Empa didn't make a move despite the man's aggressive demeanor. "Gone where?"

"Show her, Enrico," the old woman ordered, her formerly pleasant voice hard as concrete.

The man, Enrico, glanced at his mother, then fixed Empa with a suspicious stare. "Come with me." He moved to another door, opened it into a store room, and went through.

Empa nodded to Gippy, and they followed. Gippy kept his hand on his belt, ready to reach back beneath his coat. Inside the store room, he spotted another door. It had a lock, so probably led outside.

Enrico grabbed a slicker and hat at the back door, and stepped out into the rain. They followed his brisk pace down a side street, bent against the wind. Gippy could hear a river ahead, the sound of rushing water growing louder with every step. A half a block later, he spotted a bridge and a small park at the edge of the river. The flow was roaring with the rains, the water brown, but Enrico crossed the street and led them into the park instead of over the bridge.

Then Gippy saw the headstone.

Empa's steps slowed as they approached. Enrico stood aside and gestured to the engraved granite marker. There was no date on it. Empa took a knee and placed a hand on the ground in front of the stone.

"When did she die?" Empa's voice sounded as cold and lifeless as the gravestone.

"Eight years ago," Enrico said, his tone softer now.

Empa brushed the inscription. It read, Terisa Wagner ≈ Her song lives on. "How?"

"Why do you care?" Enrico's tone hardened again. "What was she to you?"

Empa stood and faced him. "She was my cousin, and I loved her."

"Your *cousin*?" He sounded suspicious now. "I don't believe you. You're not old enough to have known her."

"I'm older than I look, and she *was* my cousin." Empa took a step closer to Enrico, and Gippy could feel her power swelling. "Who killed her?"

"Soldiers. *NAFAS* soldiers." He said it like a curse. "They came and *murdered* her, burned her hacienda to the ground! It nearly destroyed this community, her loss. We don't like strangers coming asking questions about her."

"I understand, but I need to know... Did she have a child?"

Enrico shook his head once. "No. There was no child."

Even Gippy could tell the man was lying, the answer had come too quickly, too pat, but he left it to Empa. She surprised him by not pressing the man for the truth.

"Where was her hacienda?"

"Follow the main road east. Right at the fork, then right again at the first dirt road. It's overgrown and rough, but her hacienda was at the end." Enrico cleared his throat, obviously uncomfortable, either with the emotional memory of Cora, or Empa's angel-daddy mojo. "She named it Casa Musica."

"Casa *Musica*..." Empa's voice cracked. She turned away from Enrico and strode back toward the main street, tears or rain streaking her cheeks.

"Thank you, Enrico," Gippy offered before following her.

She was walking fast and took the driver's seat, determination hardening her face. Gippy got in. "He lied about the kid, right?"

"Yes, but he wasn't going to give us anything." She pulled out and took them out of town. "His mother knew Cora. I... saw her in the woman's memories, but not her child. Maybe we can find a clue in the ruins."

"Maybe the kid got away?"

"Maybe." She sniffed and wiped her nose. "I pray it's so."

Chaki slowed as she entered Boquete. She'd nearly melted the engine of the little Subaru on the drive from David, but now she took in the rainy streets, tidy buildings, and seemingly happy people with a knot of disgust roiling in her stomach. What the hell did they have to be happy about?

Then she realized.

Eight years ago, an Ageless had lived here, spreading her putrid message of love and hope to these witless fools. The humans had eaten it up, swallowing it down like a squalling child sucking on a tit. And the lie had lasted.

Well, it won't last forever, and this place is about to get a dose of the truth!

She scanned the side streets as she eased down the main road through town, watching for the Land Cruiser. The vehicle would be easy to spot, a chopped mish-mash of half a dozen different makes and models. Twenty years in the chop shop business had taught the succubus more than she ever wanted to know about cars.

She spotted the vehicle parked in front of a restaurant named after someone's grandmother, and damn if the Ageless and her companion weren't heading straight for it from the next corner. The Ageless wore a poncho and a floppy hat, her face altered somehow to look Asian. The mulatto boy who'd resisted her come on in Albuquerque wore a duster, boots, and a ridiculous snakeskin cowboy hat. She only glimpsed his face, slightly different than she remembered, but the two were unmistakable.

She drove well past and pulled off into a parking spot, scrunching down in her seat to watch them in the rearview mirror. They pulled out and continued east, driving past her at a good clip. They must have found something or gotten some directions from someone. When they were well past, she pulled back out, staying just close enough to keep the truck in sight.

She pressed the mic button on the hand-held VHF radio sitting on the passenger seat. "Hernandez?"

"Here. Do you have them in sight?" came the static-garbled reply.

"Yes, they're headed east on forty-one out of Boquete, like they know where they're going." She could barely see them through the rain. With her lights off, she doubted they could see her at all.

"They must have learned something. Follow them. We'll be there in ten."

She gritted her teeth at the order and pressed the mic. "Wait until I know where they're fucking *going*! You spook them, they'll vanish!"

"I *know* where they're going, and there's no way for them to escape," he replied.

"Idiot!" She keyed the mic again. "Maybe, but if you barge into town like a virgin into a brothel, a local might tip them off! They may not be able to escape, but they could put up one hell of a fight! Just let me find out where they're going. I'll call you."

"Affirmative. Standing by," he replied.

She wondered if he would wait or blunder into town, guns blazing. "If that dipshit gets me killed, I'll possess his next mother and teach him some fucking respect!"

14
THE FLAMES OF HELL

Canción stopped climbing when he heard engines roaring in the distance, mistaking it for thunder at first. It wasn't thunder; it was Hell coming to kill them. His legs burned and his back ached from lugging his pack up the trackless jungle hillside, but he didn't care. He looked back at Casa Musica, barely visible through the trees of the steep slope below them. His soul seethed in a steaming cauldron of rage, anguish, and love, but he wouldn't... couldn't let it out. *Not yet.*

The others staggered to a halt as well. Maria heaved hard breaths from swift pace, tears of anguish tracking down her cheeks. Fernando still remained quiet, his fear glowing like an oven in Canción's mind. Franko, at the lead, looked back at them with a hard frown, urgency pounding out in palpable waves with every beat of his heart.

"We should keep moving." Franko wasn't even breathing hard, his rifle slung muzzle down. He had picked out their path, ordering them to place their feet where he did and avoid mud. He knew the jungle well.

"No." Canción took off his pack and leaned over to shelter the contents from the rain with his camouflage poncho.

He pulled the binoculars from the small pocket of his pack and kept them under the brim of his cap as he focused on the hacienda. They were only about half a mile away, the terrain rough and steep. They weren't following any trails, and the thick loam of decomposing vegetation concealed their footprints, but if one of them slipped, the Hounds of Hell might be able to track them. The roar of engines grew louder, and his anger grew with it. He held the rage inside, nurtured it, resisting the urge to take everyone's sorrow, fear, and anguish and expel it all in destructive song. *Not yet...* He would hold it in... for Mama.

"You shouldn't watch, Canción." Maria's hand trembled on his shoulder.

She was trying to protect his feelings, of course. He might be only twelve, but he wasn't stupid. He knew what was coming, but he didn't need or want her protection, and not seeing this would be worse. Not knowing would torture him for the rest of his life.

"I *have* to." He had to know if Mama had lied to save his life, if she would sacrifice herself or somehow escape the trap. "I need to see..."

Casa Musica looked placid in the ceaseless deluge, Mama's little electric ATV parked beside the garishly painted *A Capella,* water streaming from the gutters into the row of big blue cisterns. The greenhouse was still, the huge array of south-facing solar panels gleaming in the rain, the wind turbine's long rainbow-striped blades whirring around in a blur of color.

The sound of diesel engines built to a crescendo. Canción gripped the binoculars so hard his knuckles ached, and the image quivered before his eyes. *Mama... Please... Run!*

Trucks burst from the jungle-shrouded driveway into the open, black and yellow monsters with huge tires and weapons mounted on their tops like the turrets of toy tanks. Six of them broke left and right from the opening, fire flashing from the muzzles of the mounted guns. The sound arrived in a staccato beat like a drum. Debris from the house being torn apart by the guns flew in clouds, shattered tile, concrete, wood, and glass. Something flashed from the house, as well. A streak of smoke lanced across the open space, and one of the trucks exploded.

"Ay Dios mio," Franko murmured.

"She's fighting back." Canción knew Mama had all kinds of weapons secreted around the hacienda. She even showed him some of them but told him never to touch them without her there. He hadn't, but now he wished she'd showed him how to use them, how to fight, how to kill. He wanted to be by her side for the end, to meet God together, hand in hand.

Another of the gold and black vehicles exploded, this one blasted from beneath as it ran over one of the bombs Mama had placed around the open area. The killing field, as she'd called it, was living up to its name. Mama was the most peaceful, loving person Canción knew, but she had survived a very long time. She never told him how old she was, but he knew she was special, could feel it when he touched her, the glowing warmth of her mother, Israfal, Angel of Music, within her. He felt that same glow within himself, but to a lesser degree, along with something darker, smoldering, destructive... the monster he knew he could never let loose.

The vehicles stopped, and soldiers scattered from them, the mounted weapons still belching fire into Casa Musica. The hacienda was being ripped apart, and Mama was still inside. Another explosion amidst the mass of advancing soldiers, and a wedge of them fell, flesh shredded into a red mist by the blast.

"Claymore," Franko said. "Tersi is a badass."

Maria shushed him, but Canción reveled in the destruction, in the swaths Mama blasted through the murdering soldiers who had come to kill her. *Kill them all,* he thought. *Kill every last one, so we can come home.* He knew he was being foolish. They could never go back to Casa Musica. He could never go home, would never hold Mama in his arms again. There were too many soldiers, and they had too many guns, too much hate. He could almost feel it from here, wanted to take it all away and blast them all to ruins like one of his Lego cities.

Strange black things flew from the backs of the remaining trucks, square aircraft too small to carry a person, hovering briefly, then swooping toward Casa Musica. They wove and dodged, but one fell in a spinning arc to crash before it reached the house. The other three didn't.

The suicide drones exploded, sending pieces of the hacienda's roof flying into the rain-streaked sky.

"Ay Dios mio..." Franko muttered.

"We should go." Maria's hand gripped Canción's shoulder harder.

"Not yet." He shook off her grasp, still staring through the binoculars, his hands shaking. He didn't know how he knew, but Mama wasn't finished yet. All the digging, the barrels buried all around the property, helping her mix coconut oil, kerosene, and soap into the nasty smelling goop she called napalm, the detonators and wires she'd buried leading back to the house, and the big red switch behind a locked panel in the cellar... the key she wore around her neck. "Mama's not done yet."

"Canción, it's over." Maria's hand gripped his arm, pulling him away.

He jerked free. "It's *not* over! Not *yet.*"

Canción watched the soldiers creeping forward, more careful now, listened to the sporadic gunfire as they shot into the crumbling remains of Casa Musica, his home. No one fired back. More soldiers exited the vehicles, their uniforms different, one wearing no uniform at all, but all black clothes. He wore no helmet, but a plain black baseball cap. This was their leader. Canción couldn't make out his face, but he knew the man was smiling, and he also knew this wasn't a man at all. This was one of *them*, a Nephilim.

"Die," he whispered.

Fire erupted from where Mama had burred the barrels of homemade napalm, flames spewing into the sky, coating everything in the entire valley. Soldiers thrashed and ran, burning, dying, and the smiling man in black vanished in the inferno. The vehicles burned, more soldiers fleeing them, burning, dying. Ammunition exploded in the flames, the fuel in the trucks igniting, bombs and suicide drones detonating, spewing more flames. Canción watched the soldiers die and felt not a whim of remorse.

Then Casa Musica exploded.

Maria emitted a startled cry, and Franko gasped. Even Fernando whimpered piteously. Canción just watched through the binoculars as his home, his mother, and his life vanished in a pyre that filled the rain-soaked sky.

Finally, when the last shard of wreckage fell to the ground and the flames began to subside, he lowered the binoculars and turned to his only remaining family. "*Now*, it's over."

"Vamos!" Franko ordered, his voice as cold and solid as stone.

Canción lifted his pack to join them. He could feel their sorrow, their fear, their anguish. He also felt the urge to take it away, to transform it into wrath, to destroy it. This time, for the first time in his life, he resisted the urge. He would let them have their sorrow, and he would let his own remain there in his heart with the memories of Mama. They had a long way to walk, and he would listen to her journal, just to hear her voice again. But the one thing he wouldn't do, *couldn't* do, was cry.

"Holy shit," Gippy mutters from the passenger seat as we emerge from the rutted driveway.

The wide open area is overgrown with vegetation, but the hulks of burned out military vehicles and the destroyed structure of a house and outbuildings aren't hard to see. A battle has taken place here, and from the look of it, nobody won.

"The wrath of God." I point to the less-overgrown track of the graveled drive. "Pull up to the house."

"Not much left, E." Gippy eases us up the drive between the burned out wrecks, rock, vegetation, and the incinerated bones of the fallen crunching under the mule's tires. "Don't know how, but it looks like she took 'em all with her."

"Napalm." I can see the epicenters of the explosions, the perfectly-spaced craters where the bombs must have been hidden. "She was prepared for this."

"Yeah, but the house is fucking *gone*." His voice trembles with woe, and I don't know why I'm not feeling it myself. "She blew herself up, didn't she?"

"Perhaps." I point to the burnt skeletons of two vehicles near what used to be the front door of a lovely little hacienda. One is large, a massive US Army surplus MRAP, the other a little electric ATV, probably for quick trips to town. The jungle hasn't overtaken the house entirely, and bits are still standing. "Park there, and we'll have a look around."

"Sure." He stops the mule, and we get out.

The rain has let up a little but still patters on the brim of my hat, a staccato, rhythmless beat. The steps up to the porch are still intact, and I can see portions of the wall pockmarked with bullet hits from heavy caliber weapons, probably the turrets of the APCs. I look back, and notice that one of the armored vehicles is completely shredded, and another is flipped upside down. Cora must have used mines as well as napalm. The house itself has been torn to pieces, but I've seen more than a few bombed out buildings, and there are peculiarities here. Aside from blast damage and bullet hits, there are two deep craters in the left and right wings of the house. They resemble the craters in the front area too much to be anything but placed munitions, probably more napalm. I don't see how anyone could have survived this, and feel my heart slowly breaking in my chest.

"We got company, E."

I turn slowly, cautioned by the tone of his voice. Gippy has his Glock in hand but held out of view. He's facing the non-existent back of the house, once a covered patio, a burned-out greenhouse, the overgrown yard, and the slope up to the dense jungle. Between humps of vegetation that used to be solar panels walks a man in a camouflage poncho and wide brimmed hat. He carries an automatic rifle slung on a strap, barrel down. I can barely see his face, though he seems young and healthy by his gait. He raises his left hand, but his right remains on the rifle's grip.

"What do you want here?" he asks in Spanish from twenty meters away, still walking slowly forward, his eyes barely peeking out from under the brim of his hat.

"We're looking for the woman who used to live here." The truth seems the best choice here, and I can see from his boots that he's not a soldier.

"She's dead," he states flatly, still advancing but even slower, fifteen meters now. "NAFAS soldiers murdered her."

"So we've been told." I see Gippy's nervous with us speaking Spanish, and say. "Do you speak English? My friend has no Spanish."

"Yes," he responds in perfect English. "So, if you were told she's dead, why are you looking for her?"

"Because she was my cousin, and I loved her." This truth stops him in his tracks, ten meters away, his dark eyes hard on us, hand steady on his weapon.

"*Cousin?*"

"Yes. Second cousin, actually. We had the same grandmother." The truth again, and his eyes narrow.

"You're lying." The rifle moves, but Gippy's aiming at his center mass before he can shoulder it. He freezes, but his hand remains on the grip of the rifle. "You shoot me, and you're dead before I hit the ground."

"Then we die together, amigo." Gippy doesn't twitch, but I scan the hillside and spot the sniper half hidden behind a tree, the scope glinting in the wan light.

"Stand down, Gip." I raise both hands empty, and Gippy lowers his weapon. "And I'm not lying. If you knew Tersi Wagner, I'd like to speak to you. I know she came here to raise her child, and I'd like to know what became of them."

"Child?" Surprise flashes on his face for an instant. "There was no child."

"Now *you're* lying," I say without a hint of accusation. "I read her journal. She said she was pregnant. I know the child's father. I'd like to know what happened to them."

He raises a hand and waves off the sniper, but shakes his head. "You can't have listened to her journal, Señora."

"Why not?"

"Because I have it." He takes another step forward and releases his grip on the rifle, his hands broad, scarred, and now empty.

Confusion... "*You* have her journal? I don't understand how..."

"He said *listened* to, E. She must have made an audio journal."

I glance at Gippy and realize he's right, then turn back to the young man. He's now only steps away, but his friend in the trees still has a line of fire on us.

Time for some real truth... I extend both hands palm up. "Please. I need you to trust that I'm telling you the truth, and I need to know what happened to my cousin's child." I take a careful step toward him. "If you take my hands, you'll understand, but I can't force you."

"Miss Tersi once said in her journal that half of her cousins were Nephilim, and the other half were all dead."

That he knows so much astonishes me. "She put *that* in her journal?"

"Yes. It was for her son, but once he'd listened to it, he gave it to me." He nods to me once. "Just in case any of his relatives came snooping around Casa Musica."

"*Son*? She had a son?" My heart leaps in my chest.

"Yes. Canción. We grew up together here." He gestures to the burned out hacienda and steps forward to take my hands, then hesitates and grins dangerously. "But if you're a demon, my father will put a bullet through your head before you can possess me."

"Amigo, she chews up demons and spits out asphalt," Gippy quips, his humor, as usual, timely and spot on target.

A brief smile flashes across his mouth. "Good!" He takes my hands, and we lock eyes.

I delve gently, and see Fernando's love for Canción glowing like a beacon. I see him watching Casa Musica exploding in flames, and Canción's tearless resolve. I see Canción as a young man, surrounded by people whom he cares for, his role as a mediator, a leader. I hear his lovely voice, and my heart longs to meet him. Then I see some of what the union of Heaven and Hell has produced, his ability to take in fear and hate and expel it in a destructive pulse of sound with his voice. The union of Israfal and Azkeel, angels of music and destruction... I give Fernando enough of myself to destroy his doubt of what I am, then take his malaria and festering dysentery and finally release his hands.

"Now do you believe me?" I feel a little weak from his symptoms, but they're subsiding quickly. Hopefully, they'll be gone before I puke.

"Ay Dios mio... How can I not?" Fernando waves to his father in the trees and extends a hand to Gippy. "Fernando. Good to meet you."

"Gifford." Gippy puts his pistol away and shakes the proffered hand. "So, where is he? Cora's son?"

"Cora? Oh, you mean Miss Tersi." He nods. "We fled to Colombia. Miss Tersi gave us money and passports, and we hopped a boat. Here." He fishes a flash drive from a pocket and hands it to me. "Miss Tersi's journal. I've listened to it about a hundred times. Hard to believe, if I hadn't grown up with Canción."

I take the drive to listen to later. "He's special. Like Tersi was special, yes?" I long to know what plan God might have from the union of an Ageless and a Nephilim, for the union of music and destruction. I wonder perversely if he's into death metal.

"He is, but he would say no. He's... very different than her, and different than *you* for that matter." He nods to his father as the older man walks up, his scoped rifle slung. I have little doubt that he would have killed us both if his son was harmed, and can't blame him. Fernando introduces Franko, and we shake hands. I get the peak moments of his life in a rush. Franko has indeed seen a lot and loves his son more than life itself.

"Different how?" I ask Fernando. "I intend to find him, but... I'd like to know who I'm looking for."

"Well, Canción's... got a temper, but you won't know it until it explodes. And I mean literally *explodes*. He doesn't look mad until he's over the top, and when that happens, you don't want to be anywhere near him." He exchanges a glance with his father, and the older man nods. "He's a good man and has worked hard to help people, but when the shit hits the fan... look out."

"Reminds me of someone," Gippy says with a grin and a nod to me.

I know he's kidding, but I shoot him a glare before I turn back to Fernando. "You said Colombia. Where? We need to find him."

"We took a boat to Cartagena, but it was mostly underwater. We settled in Las Brisas. It used to be a slum, but some of the folks from the city resettled there, and it's surviving. We bought a small hacienda with some of Señora Tersi's money and lived on the rest for a few years. Papa taught us how to build; carpentry, masonry, plumbing... but my mother wanted to come back here, to make sure Señora Tersi's love lived on, and that nobody found out where Canción had gone. We told everyone that he died with her, and most believe it. The others... nobody talks about him for fear that he didn't."

"Because the naffies would go after him," Gippy adds, and Fernando nods.

"Exactly." He nods to me. "You're the first of her cousins to come looking for her."

"And I'll probably be the last," I say without irony. "Thank you, Fernando. We should go. We don't want to draw any more attention to this wonderful place than we already have."

"We understand." Franko and his son shake our hands and smile, and I feel Cora's love through them, her music, and their love for Canción. "Travel safely. There's still some boat traffic from Punta Peña. Fast cargo and ferry service to Cartagena and the canal between storms."

"Good! Thank you!" We turn away and stride for the mule. I glance back but Fernando and Franko are already gone, vanished into the jungle.

"Can you drive, Gip? I want to listen to some of this." I fish Cora's journal from my pocket and head for the passenger door.

"You've been wanting to hear her voice for more than a century, E. Of course, I can drive."

We get in, and as he maneuvers through the maze of burned out vehicles into the overgrown driveway, I link the journal to my phone and start at episode one. Cora's voice comes over my earpiece, and my heart breaks anew.

"Audio journal entry one; May eighth, twenty fifty-two. I don't know why I'm making this, or where to begin...

Canción tucked the audio drive away and stood to stretch. He'd heard Franko returning from hunting. The man emerged from the jungle—the ever-encompassing, beautiful, infuriating, maddening, wet, and wonderful jungle that had saved their lives and tortured them for the last month—with a butchered sloth over one shoulder, his rifle slung, and his face grim. Franko had also saved their lives. He knew the jungle like Canción knew the smell and feel of his mother when she hugged him. The memory spurred anger, as it always did, but his love for her, for her music, and the sound of her voice still echoing in his head, calmed the burning rage.

"Did you sleep?" Franko asked, dropping to one knee beneath their lean-to.

"Some," Canción lied. He'd barely slept at all since they watched Casa

Musica explode with Mama inside. He glanced at Maria and Fernando huddled in the corner where the camouflage covering met the ground, snuggled in each other's embraces, more for comfort than warmth. He envied them.

"Good. We travel today. Weather's letting up."

"It is?" It didn't look like it to Canción, unless perhaps the rain had thinned slightly.

"Enough." Franko placed the butchered carcass on their impromptu table, a slab of deadfall he'd barked and scraped with a machete. "We leave as soon as this is cooked. We should make Punta Peña in three days, maybe two if the weather's fair." He drew a short, curved knife and started cutting meat from the bones.

Canción helped by stoking their fire to life, then placing the thin strips of meat on the folding grill to sizzle and pop. The smell of cooking woke Maria and Fernando when their voices and other sounds hadn't. The constant drumming of rain on the lean-to and the overhead jungle canopy masked sounds like white noise. They ate, packed up, including their tiny supply of dry firewood, and started hiking, Franko in front, then Fernando, then Maria. Canción followed, girding his tumultuous emotions as always, concentrating on the good—they were all alive, uninjured, and not starving—not the flames of Casa Musica that still raged in his mind. He wanted to expunge the anger with everyone else's pain, but he couldn't. Not yet. He needed to feel his smoldering rage for a little longer. At the moment, he felt like that was the only thing keeping him alive.

By the time they reached Punta Peña, Canción had listened to the entirety of his mother's journal. Mom was either stark raving loco, or truly the daughter of an angel. He couldn't believe she was as old as she'd said, but what she could do with her music, and what he could do with people's emotions—take in the negative, the hate, fear, pain, anguish, and sadness, and expel it in a torrent of energy with his voice—corroborated her tale. Normal people couldn't do that, but he wasn't normal. That felt unfair, which stoked his rage even more. He wanted to be a kid, irresponsible and fun-loving. He wasn't any longer, and never would be again.

That a war between Heaven and Hell had raged for so long, and was all but lost, was harder to accept. That he was unique in the world, the only offspring of both Ageless and Nephilim, he wasn't buying for a second. It couldn't be true. He wasn't good enough to be that special, not feeling what he felt.

Sometimes, like now, he wanted to burn the whole world to a cinder and be done with it.

They joined the highway some miles from their destination and caught a ride with a friendly farmer delivering a load of breadfruit. At the edge of town, the driver pulled over, and they climbed out into the teeth of the unabating storms of the Caribbean. Canción pulled his hat low and squinted into the wind so hard it made the rain sting against his skin, forcing him to lean into it or be thrown flat.

Punta Peña wasn't much, even by post-apocalyptic standards, with one single exception. They'd built a seawall, but nothing like the one he'd seen in David when Mama took him there to sell their old truck. This one faced the storms of the Caribbean, and withstood category five hurricanes on a regular basis. It stretched five kilometers wide, a hundred meters thick, and fifty above sea-level, solid concrete with the windward side a mountainous slope of rip-rap to subdue the breakers. It seemed excessive to shelter a town of barely five thousand, but from the maps Mama had packed along, this was one of the few surviving ports on the Caribbean side of Central America.

Cancion and his family were here for only one reason: there were boats.

"We're going out *there*?" Fernando sounded more terrified than skeptical, and Canción had to agree. The seas were monstrous, breaking on what used to be islands farther out to sea and still retaining enough might to throw spray over the top of the seawall.

"Their fishing boats go out whenever there's a break in the weather, and this is the farthest south port on North America, not counting the Canal. Cargo ferries make trips to South America." Franko sounded confident, but he always did. His constant rock-solid support felt like a warm fire on a damp night. "There should be a break soon. Maybe tonight or tomorrow morning."

Something his mama had said in her journal came to Canción like a visitation of her ghost. "We need to pay the captain enough that he won't sell us out to the soldiers. Someone in Boquete may have told them about me. They'll be searching."

"Money and guns will keep the captain silent." Franko unslung his hunting rifle and carried it in the crook of his arm.

Canción thought there might be another way to ensure the captain's silence, but didn't tell anyone. If the fear of guns didn't convince them, maybe the fear of God would.

They drew a few stares walking through town, but not many. Refugees and migrants were commonplace enough. The stink of a fish processing plant with inadequate waste disposal hung in the air, despite the storm force winds. The harbor, three massive floating concrete docks accessible by hinged ramps, sported about two dozen rugged-looking boats, each about thirty meters long, with huge metal outriggers stowed upright, nets hung in the driving rain like moss-covered vines from massive trees. There were also two cargo vessels, designed to carry four shipping containers on deck with accommodations forward for passengers. All of the vessels were heavily built to handle the insane seas of the Caribbean.

Franko led them down one of the ramps toward the cargo ships. One was loaded, the name *Perra Dura* scrawled across the high stern. The other was empty, and the flickering light of a welder flashed through the rain from the superstructure. They were doing repairs. The loaded vessel, perhaps fifty meters in length, jostled at the dock, huge ropes groaning and creaking, the hull dented and scratched, rust streaking the remaining paint like blood in the rain. Two armed men stood at the gangway, eyeing them as they approached.

"Cartagena?" Franko asked from the foot of the gangway.

"Si." He pointed to a heavy metal door in the forward section. "Speak to Captain Moreno. You leave your rifles here."

That's not the name that mama gave us, Canción thought.

Franko frowned but nodded, removing the magazine and the chambered round from his rifle before handing it over. "Please be careful. The scope is delicate."

"No problem." The man slung the long rifle over his shoulder, barrel down, and accepted their other one, a short carbine, from Maria. "They'll be here when you come back. If you sail with us, we'll stow them for you."

Franko's frown deepened, but he nodded. Canción knew Franko had a pistol as well and was glad the man hadn't asked for that, too. He wasn't about to hand over the one Mama had given him. The holster felt comforting at his back, and he'd taken good care of it on their long hike through the jungle, just like she'd taught him. They strode across the textured steel deck to the heavy metal door. It was rounded at the corners and had handles all the way around the edge instead of a simple doorknob. Franko turned one and pulled it open with a screech, motioning them inside.

Canción wrinkled his nose at the stink of fuel oil, sweat, and burnt coffee, but the inside was dry, well lit, and relatively quiet compared to the raging storm outside. He could feel the vibration of a motor beneath his feet and wondered where they got the fuel for something this big. They shook off their ponchos, doffed their hats, and stomped the water from their boots. A hallway went forward, a steep stair branching off to the right, a sign "El Capitan" above it.

"Moreno," Canción said. "That's not the name mama gave us."

"No, it's not. We'll see. Maybe the other boat's captain is named Blanco. If this one will take us, we go." Franko climbed the stairs, and they followed.

At the top, a short corridor ran left and right, with two forward-facing doors labeled, "Bridge - Authorized Personnel Only" and, "El Capitan." One more heavy metal door facing aft was designated "Deck Obs," and two more at the ends of the passage "Port Obs" and "Stbd Obs." Franko knocked on the captain's door.

A heavyset man with salt and pepper hair and a weathered face opened the door. Behind him, Canción glimpsed a room with a bunk, a table, and a bunch of electronics. One flat screen displayed a confusing map with curved lines and concentric circles that reminded him of tree rings.

"You looking to buy passage to Cartagena?" The man asked, his eyes flicking from Franko to Maria, then the boys, lingering on him long enough to make Canción's skin crawl.

"Yes. How much for all of us?"

The captain frowned and scratched his stubbly jaw, and Canción could feel his avarice like an itch in his mind. "For crew's quarters, eight hundred NAD's each. For a private room with two bunks, four thousand. No pesos."

"Meals included?" Franko asked.

"No. One hundred per day per adult. Half that for the boys. It's a four-day trip." He smiled, and his eyes fixed upon Canción. "He's not your son. You pick up a stray?"

Franko's eyes narrowed. "Adopted. Why does that matter?"

"It matters because I'm captain, and this ship follows *my* rules," Moreno stated flatly. "People traffic in young boys and make a lot of money on pretty young *white* boys. Colombia has strict laws. I don't break the law."

Canción felt the lie like a splinter of ice in his mind, and the way the man had said 'pretty' made him want to pull his pistol and shoot him in the crotch. Mama had warned him about human trafficking, modern-day slavery, and how they preyed mostly on children. Chances were, the captain *did* offer passage to human traffickers, and was all but telling Franko that he could give him a lot of money for a twelve-year-old white boy. The notion kindled his long bridled anger.

"I'm not a slave." Canción stepped forward. "These are my *family*. The only family I have left!"

"Calm down, little boy. I wasn't saying—"

"I *know* what you were saying!" The man's denial, another lie, added to the pit of rage. "We will pay you six thousand for everything, and you keep your mouth shut about us, or the wrath of God will smite you!"

"*Smite* me?" The man laughed, but he was the only one. Franko and Maria took a step back, Fernando wincing. "God's not going to protect you *here*, little boy."

"No?" Canción drew in a breath, and with it he absorbed all of the anguish, sorrow, and fear from Franko, Maria, and Fernando. Empowered, he took in all of his own festering rage, sorrow, and sadness as well. Lastly, he breathed in the captain's bigotry, his arrogance, and his avarice. He then turned to the heavy steel door labeled "Deck Obs" and let the poisonous feelings blaze out in a single pure note from his throat.

The force of Canción's voice buckled the heavy metal portal, snapping the bolt of the handle securing it. The door flung open with a clang that reverberated through the ship.

"Ay Dios mio!" The captain staggered back a step. Previously unafraid of this arrogant little boy, now the only emotion that filled him was terror.

"Yes, it *is*." Canción turned back to face the man. Though his raging emotions were gone, he had to make sure his ploy worked. "Six thousand. No questions, and you never saw us. If you tell *anyone* about us, I'll know." The last was a lie, of course, but the stunned captain didn't know that.

"Si, si!" His mouth gaped, eyes wide, and he nodded.

"Here." Franko handed over six worn bills with a smile that held little humor. "What state room?"

"Nu-number four. Two decks down." He took the bills with a trembling hand.

"*Thank* you, Captain Moreno," Canción said with a thin smile.

"Just stay away from me!" The captain's stateroom door slammed closed.

Canción turned to his family. "Everyone feeling better? I'm hungry!"

"Ha!" Franko clapped him on the shoulder. "Yes. No more sloth or capybara for dinner!"

"I want ice cream!" Fernando chimed, and Maria laughed.

"Me too!" Canción loved the music of her laughter, the first he'd heard since watching his home vanish in flames.

15
BLOOD AND DAMNATION

With the music of my cousin's voice in my ear, I barely hear Gippy's question.

"So, Colombia, huh?"

I pause the recording, not wanting to miss a word. "Yes. We have to find Canción."

"So, we drive to Punta Peña, then, like a *boat*?" He peers through the windshield at the solid overcast barely visible through the overhanging trees. "On the *ocean* in this shit?"

I recall his trepidation when we crossed the Hudson River in a ferry and smile. "Don't worry. There'll be a break in the weath—"

The blast slams me into my seatbelt, flinging the left side of the truck into the air. The sound numbs my ears instantly, and I glimpse the world spinning outside the shattered windshield, a kaleidoscope of trees, sky, broken glass, and shredded metal. A flash of memory: *inside a Humvee hit by an IED, the driver torn to pieces, screams, bellows of command from Sergeant Getash even before the dust settles. "Move, move, move! Grab your shit! Cover!"*

The roof of the mule hits a tree, and I'm scrambling for my gear before I know where I am. My door's against the ground, but the back window is blown out, and there's enough space for me to squirm through. I grab my pack and guitar case, pushing them ahead of me. I emerge into jungle instead of desert, and I realize that I'm in Panama instead of Syria. I don't know how, but we've driven into a trap. I can't hear, but I try to scream for Gippy to follow me. Something comes out of my mouth, Turkish, I think, but I'm too shell-shocked to know for sure.

My HK in my hands—I don't remember taking it out of the case, let alone loading it and chambering a round—my pack on my back, I'm moving, staying low. Gunfire pops through my tinnitus, sounding like someone snapping their fingers, and wood fragments fly from a nearby tree. I drop, roll, and crawl to a downed log, blinking away blood and tears.

The truck is only thirty feet away, but the jungle between me and it is empty. I'm alone.

"Gippy?"

Beyond the destroyed Mule, NAFAS soldiers advance, weapons ready. I pop the covers off my scope, center the crosshairs on a face, and squeeze the trigger. His head snaps back, and he drops. The others spray suppressive fire and take cover. I have a good position, and they're advancing from the road ahead, backlit by the diffuse light. I hear the roar of engines—my ears are clearing a little—and know I don't have much time.

"Gippy! Where the fu—" I see him, still in the vehicle, hanging upside down from his seatbelt, and my heart seizes in my chest. I can't tell if he's unconscious or dead. If he's gone, I can do nothing for him and should flee into the jungle. If he's alive, I can't get to him in time, let alone carry him out of here. If I leave him alive, and the soldiers take him...

Visions of torment assail my mind's eye: *the Inquisition, the Holocaust, atrocities beyond imagining...*

Mercy...

Once, when I thought I was too broken to continue, Gippy offered to send me to my father rather than let the Nephilim take me. He offered that escape to me out of love. How can I do less for him? I center the crosshairs on the head of my dearest friend in the world, and move my finger from the guard to the trigger.

Something obstructs my view, and I open my other eye. A soldier using the vehicle for cover has stepped between me and my friend. His eyes scan the jungle, weapon ready. I shoot him in the groin, and he goes down screaming. Others bellow for cover, firing blindly. More suppressive fire erupts from the road, a heavy machinegun tearing through the jungle. I've got to go *now*.

I reach around and open the side zipper pocket of my pack. My fingers find the cool metal sphere of a fragmentation grenade. I pull the pin with my teeth—strictly against the instruction manual—and lob the bomb at my enemies, hunkering behind my log. The blast sends more men screaming to the ground, and if I'm lucky—if Gippy is lucky—kills the young man I love like a son.

Before the debris of the blast settles, I'm moving, crouched low, vanishing into the jungle. I blink away tears and fight to focus on survival, to center my spirit, not give in to anguish. *Steady spirit.* "Please, Mother of my father, let him be dead..."

~

Canción stared out of the window of his bedroom at the dying city of Cartagena. The weather had cleared enough to open the storm shutters, and he could make out the decaying remains of the sky scrapers jutting up from the bay like the fingers of a drowning man clawing for air. Another had fallen in the most recent storm, and he wondered how many lives had been lost with its demise. The former icons of industry and high finance surrounded one prominent bastion of dry land, the island of La Popa, the ancient convent and chapel perched atop the high cliffs now girded by a circumferential sea wall.

"Why can't they see what's happening?" The question was rhetorical, but Angelica answered anyway.

"Because they're blind to the truth, set in their ways, addicted to a world that's dying, and just plain stupid."

He looked back at her sardonic smile and made a face. "Yes to all but the last one. They're not stupid; they've been lied to." He liked Angelica; she told him what he needed to hear, supported him even when she didn't fully agree with him, and was an amazing lover. At the moment, she wore a robe... and nothing else, her lustrous black hair disheveled because he had personally disheveled it. "Believing a convincing lie isn't stupidity, especially when people of faith are told lies by religious leaders. They've been *conditioned* to believe it."

"Okay, granted, but it doesn't take a genius to see that they don't have much of a future." She stepped up beside him to take in the view, running warm, smooth fingertips up his bare back. "Living in buildings half underwater, scrounging metals, eating nothing but fish and expired packaged junk food?"

"They're inured to the truth. Their faith in God has blinded them." Canción sighed in frustration. He had helped build Las Brisas into a viable community, but never once had he used religion to seduce people into following him. Hard work, love, dedication, and his gift to remove fear, anger, and hate, yes, but never the fear of God. He'd only done that once before, and in the eight years since, not once. That would have been a betrayal to his mother's legacy. The War of Souls wasn't over, and his only weapon was the hope he could give people struggling to survive.

"Not their faith in God, their faith in Bishop Vargas." Her lip curled. They were nice lips, and she was right again.

Angelica was a few years older than him, but that didn't matter. Canción might be the unofficial mayor of Las Brisas, but she'd taught him more in the two years they'd been together than anyone else could have, and not just about intimacy. Her father had been a leader, an organizer, a mediator, and she'd learned at his side. When she was twenty-three, he'd been murdered. She'd wanted vengeance, convinced that Bishop Vargas's people were behind it, even though the death had looked like a gang killing. Canción had known it hadn't been one of the gangs; he'd been negotiating with them since he was fifteen. Murdering the man who was helping to broker a beneficial arrangement between the community and the gangs had thrown everything they'd been building into the sea.

Angelica had wanted to declare war. He'd tried to persuade her to choose a different path, peace instead of blood. She hadn't wanted to listen, especially to an eighteen-year-old white guy. Then he took her rage away and held her while she cried out her sorrow.

Since then, they'd carved out a fledgling government for Las Brisas, working with the gangs instead of against them, making deals with the burgeoning city of Turbaco to support everyone on the island. The complex relationship between the three entities wasn't official, but it worked.

Canción was really nothing more than a negotiator and mediator, when he wasn't helping rebuild homes, farms, and infrastructure. The relatively new island of Villanueva, where Las Brisas was located, along with its twin to the northeast, Barranquilla, were isolated from the mainland, but they had assets the other smaller islands didn't: farmland, skilled workers, and commerce with Bogota. Las Brisas sported a sheltered ferry terminal that harbored vessels from Panama and traded manufactured goods for Venezuelan fuel. The town might be little more than a shipping terminal, but they were more than surviving; they were prospering. There were perhaps twenty thousand residents on the entire island, that many more on Barranquilla, and another five thousand in the outer islands with whom they traded for fresh seafood. The local representative of the

Catholic Church, Bishop Vargas, however, was their biggest opponent, insisting that La Popa governed all of it, and the Cardinal in Bogota backed him.

How ironic, he thought, *that a bishop would oppose the grandson of angels...* Of course, no one here knew of his true nature, even Angelica, and he wasn't about to tell them. One lesson he'd learned well from his mother was the need for secrecy.

"What are you thinking?" Angelica nudged his arm. "You've got that look."

"Look? What look?" Canción blanked his face. "I don't have a look."

"Oh, you *really* do!" She barked a laugh. "Like you're looking into the mind of God, or thinking about sex, I can't tell which it is."

"Well, not the *former,* I promise you." He leered at her. "And I'm twenty years old. I think about sex every three seconds, but I don't have time to do anything *about* that right now. The Bishop's puppet is coming to negotiate."

"Father Mateo?" She made another face, this one of disgust. "I'm sure *that* will go well."

"Well, the Bishop never leaves La Popa, and I'll be damned before I walk into *that* lion's den." Frankly, if he did, the likelihood of him ever leaving would be next to zero. The Church wasn't above using force to achieve their goals, and the only thing keeping them from exerting that force were the armed thugs that Canción had made a deal with. The gangs weren't anything like a police or military force, but they had weapons and weren't timid. He'd rather negotiate with them than the Catholic Church. "I've never met Mateo. What's he like?"

"Like a sanctimonious prick with spines like a sea urchin." Her scowl intensified, and she folded her arms in a defensive posture he'd come to recognize. "What's on your agenda?"

"I want to offer homesteads to the Cartagenians, and the Bishop's pushing back."

She snorted a disgusted laugh. "Of *course,* he is. You're taking money out of his pocket."

"I'm offering people a life instead of indentured servitude to a man who has less to do with God than he has to do with using his position for power!" Canción breathed deep and bridled his anger. Angelica knew he had a temper but also that he'd never hurt anyone who didn't try to hurt him first. "Sorry. Anyway, I'm negotiating compensation to the Church. We help strip the buildings for anything useful, and they get the proceeds.

His parishioners can continue to donate to his coffers, and I'll even offer to arrange ferry service to La Popa for masses. I'd like to demolish the skyscrapers before the sea does it on her own, killing thousands of people."

"That's generous, but he'll never take the deal. He's got the Cartagenians isolated now. If they see they can have land and a life of their own without his interference, they'll eventually stop donating to the Church entirely." She gave him a tolerant look of skepticism. "You don't think he's stupid enough not to know that, do you?"

"No, but I can try, can't I?" He shrugged. "I've got to start somewhere, and the scrapers are coming down eventually. If they fall when there are people in them, the Church loses everything. That's how I'll pitch it to him, or Father Mateo, I guess. I'm hoping they'll see it as a foot in the door to the mainland."

She pursed her lips. "Still not enough. Offer to build them a church in Las Brisas. He can station one of his priests here to keep his claws in his parishioners."

"Good idea." He didn't know where the land would come from, but it was another inducement.

"Well, I wish you success, but don't get your hopes up." She stepped in between him and the view and kissed him. "Just don't make me stand in the same room with Mateo. He gives me the creeps."

"I won't." He smiled and checked the time. "I better get down there."

"Comb your hair first." She ran her fingers through his hair, which he hadn't cut in two years. "You look like a wild man."

"I was trying for the JC look." He fingered his thin beard. "I thought a man of the cloth might appreciate it. No?"

"You're way too white, gringo. And maybe put on some decent clothes. The pajama bottom look is pretty hot, but it's not likely to get you anywhere with Mateo." She kissed him and whirled away, dodging his swat to her backside. "When you're done with Mateo, go see the Martinezes. They're arguing again."

"Okay. Thanks." Canción went to the bathroom, ran a comb through his hair, tied it back with a thong of braided leather, put on a pair of clean cargo pants, a loose button-down shirt, and headed downstairs. He didn't bother with shoes; this was his house and he'd dress how he liked. He'd bought it outright with his mother's money, refurbished and modernized it, and named it Casa Musica in remembrance of her. It was nice, but hardly palatial, two floors of reinforced concrete construction, salvaged tile from dozens of flooded estates, a huge cistern and water filtration system, and two wind turbines to power everything. He used it for his work as well as pleasure, with an office, meeting room, and workshop, but he did have a music room, and played regularly. Music was his therapy, his safe place where the concerns of the world went away. Unlike his mother, he didn't like playing for audiences.

"Ah! Canción! Father Mateo's boat has landed, and he's taking a taxi up the hill now." His housekeeper/assistant/cook Isabella patted the hand-held VHF in her apron pocket and gave him a critical head-to-toe inspection. "You should put on shoes."

Canción made a face. "In my own house? I never wear shoes in the house."

"He will, and you don't want to insult him." She crossed herself and lowered her voice. "He's a piece of work, you know."

He knew she was right on both counts. "So I've heard. Thank you, Isabella." He trudged to the foyer, slipped on a pair of sandals that he'd abandoned beside the door, and went out to wait for his guest.

The rain was light, but it wouldn't stop for at least six more months. From under the covered drive, the misty air thick on his skin, he looked to the hills rising behind Las Brisas, checkered with carefully managed farms. The best they could hope for was enough diffuse sunlight between storms to grow some shade-tolerant summer crops. They'd carved terraced rice paddies into the hillsides, which produced a staple starch crop. Most of the houses had small greenhouses with LED lighting to grow greens that supplemented their diet. For protein, they had fish, chickens—which kept the cockroach population under control—and goats. He'd helped build dozens of farms and houses since they arrived here. Franco had taught him construction and agriculture, instilling a work ethic, and helping people made him feel good, as well as spreading hope.

A covered bicycle taxi struggled up the hill, the driver's legs pumping hard. Canción recognized him, Adrian, a hard worker, and raised a hand in greeting. He grinned to Canción, braking to a stop out of the rain, and jumped off the bike to open the door for Father Mateo. The priest stepped out, all in black, his shoes shiny, his coat immaculate and freshly pressed. Even his wide brimmed black hat looked freshly cleaned. He ignored Adrian, brushing non-existent dirt from his clothes, and looked around as if inspecting the hacienda for purchase.

With one look at the man, Canción knew he wouldn't like him, but he also knew he couldn't show his disdain. *More flies with bullshit,* he thought, and this was one instance where he had to fork on a thick layer of the stuff. Flattery placated small-minded men of power more effectively than calling them out for what they were.

"Father Mateo. Welcome to Casa Musica." He nodded respectfully, but held off from the customary reverence. "I hope you had a smooth crossing."

"It was dreadful." His brow wrinkled, eyebrows arching. "You do well for yourself Señor Canción. Very well indeed, for one so young." The priest emphasized the last word just enough to show his disapproval. As if anyone outside the Church living in anything but a hovel or a crumbling skyscraper was committing a sin.

"I refurbished Casa Musica with what little I inherited from my mother, God rest her soul." He often thought of his mother playing her music for the angels and all the good souls she had brought love to during her immeasurably long life. It brought a genuine smile to his lips. "It's comfortable." He gestured to the door. "Won't you come inside?"

"Of course." Mateo walked toward the door, still ignoring the taxi driver's expectant look.

Canción fished a fifty peso coin from his pocket and handed it to the driver. "Stay, Adrian. I'll have Isabella bring something for you while you wait."

"Thank you, Señor." The man grinned and shot a glance at the priest's back, rolling his eyes.

Canción hurried to open the door and usher Mateo inside, but when he passed close by the man, he felt something strange, as if a chill had invaded his bones. Then Mateo was past and the curious feeling vanished. He shook his head and followed, closing the door behind him. Isabella was there, and took the priest's coat and hat without any compunction. Maybe he'd imagined the chill.

"This way, please." Canción waved the priest into the room he used for meetings. It was furnished with a table for large groups, leather upholstered chairs spaced here and there with low coffee tables strategically placed between them, and a fireplace that they rarely used. Isabella had already set one of the coffee tables up with refreshments. Again, passing close to the priest, he felt that strange chill and shivered. Something was wrong, but he had no idea what it could be. He'd never felt anything like it before, as if Father Mateo radiated cold like an open refrigerator door.

"Please have a seat. I've got a proposal that I think would be beneficial for both the Church and Las Brisas." Canción took a chair and poured coffee into two cups, black and strong. As Mateo sat across from him and their eyes met, he felt that chill deepen, as if a cold hand rested on the back of his neck. He ignored it and forged ahead. "I'd like to thank you for coming to listen to it."

"The Church will always *listen*, Señor Cancion, though we may not agree with your agenda." Mateo smiled and added three heaping spoonfuls of sugar to his coffee, stirring the brew slowly. "I'll tell you right now that we will not allow the Towers of God to be torn down."

Canción smiled back, dampening his ire and the building unease with this man's proximity. Naming a bunch of ruined skyscrapers the Towers of God was not only disrespectful, in his mind, but blatant propaganda. "Eventually, they *will* come down, Father. Nature will have her way, as she does with all the works of mankind. If they fall with your parishioners still living inside, Bishop Vargas will find himself without parishioners."

"The Towers of God will never fall," the man said calmly. "God will not allow it."

Arrogant ass... "So said the Egyptians, the Greeks, the Romans, and every other nation of the Earth. Time and the elements will have their way. History has taught us this. The greatest creations of every empire in the world succumb, without proper maintenance, which in this case is impossible. I'm offering the Church an option that would be good for you *and* your parishioners." He lifted his cup and sipped. "Will you listen to my proposal?"

Mateo stared at him for a long uncomfortable moment, his gaze feeling like icy spiders along Canción's nerves. Then he nodded once. "I'll listen."

"Thank you."

Canción made his pitch, thorough and heartfelt, logical and obviously beneficial to the Church both in the short term and the long. The resources salvaged from the dying towers—structural steel, copper wiring, conduits, machinery, and even some electronic control systems—could be sold to manufacturers in Bogota or put to use in reinforcing the island of La Popa. Las Brisas would help the residents settle and learn new trades at no cost to the church. Throughout his presentation, he avoided the priest's eyes. He still felt that bone-deep chill, but not meeting the man's gaze helped suppress the discomfort.

Father Mateo looked skeptical but thoughtful on some of the points, and when Canción finally finished, he sighed and shrugged. "Your proposal is interesting, I'll admit, but I find it hard to believe that you'll welcome so many into your community without any compensation."

"The compensation will be in their contributions over time to the entire community. We all work together, and many hands make light work. Additions to the community are not simply more mouths to feed, they're more hands to grow more food to feed everyone. We've proven this."

A sour look crossed the priest's face. "All I can do is present it to Bishop Vargas. The final decision is his."

"Of course," Canción said, thinking, *And that decision will be 'No.'* But Mateo had listened, and for that he had to be grateful. He stood, finally meeting the man's gaze again, and extended a hand. "Thank you for listening."

Mateo stood and smiled for the first time, reaching out to take Canción's hand. "Listening is the *least* I can—"

When their hands met, the unease that Canción had felt earlier lanced through him like an icy spear of malevolence. Something was very wrong with Father Mateo, something that he'd never encountered before, something of pure, unadulterated evil.

Canción gripped hard out of reflex, strong with years of labor tearing down ruined buildings, constructing new ones, clearing jungle, tilling the soil, helping people survive. He met Mateo's gaze, and the smoldering malice within the man blossomed into an icy nova, glowing in Canción's mind, a putrid, vile thing coiled like a festering serpent waiting to sink its fangs into living flesh, injecting venom to infect the soul. He felt that venom now, penetrating him to the core through the man's touch, and the priest's lips curled back in a rictus of victory.

"No." Canción's refusal, a single whispered word, enveloped that venom and absorbed it, pulling it in like the line of a harpoon that had speared a lurking leviathan. He drew it in as he did people's harmful emotions, taking in the hate, fear, rage, and spite, and containing it within himself. But this wasn't simply a frightened man's fear, this was deeper, a nameless horror, a seemingly bottomless pit of malice.

Mateo's dark eyes widened, this time in sudden terror, his grin failing, mouth gaping in shock. "Wha..." He tried to pull free, to break the connection forged in their locked gazes.

"No!" Canción continued pulling in the evil writhing within the man, refusing to release his grasp.

It wouldn't have mattered now if he did release the man's hand; he had a grip on the malevolence, and he wasn't about to let go. He *couldn't* let go, couldn't allow such a vile thing to exist. Their gazes were locked more firmly than their hands.

More... more... take all of it. A mental scream of sheer terror reverberated within Canción's mind, a thousand tormented evil souls crying out in anguish as they unraveled within him. A memory formed in his mind, something from his mother's journal... *There are demons in the world, my son. They look human, but they are merely the vessels for the minions of Hell. You'll know them when you find them, for they're pure evil, sent from Hell to infect the souls of humans. They seek only to defile, torment, and corrupt.*

This was a demon. Canción knew it like he knew a sour note of music when he heard it.

"Be *gone*, demon," he said, his voice a song that shredded the evil coiling within himself. As with harmful emotions he took in and destroyed, a core of remaining energy remained there, much stronger than the hate, anger, and anguish he took from people. It no longer had a will of its own. It was destroyed. Later, when it was safe, he would expel the energy in destructive force. For now, it pulsed within him like a held breath, safely contained with some minimal effort.

Father Mateo convulsed as the last of the demon was wrenched from his body, his eyes rolling up in his head and his knees folding. He crashed into the coffee table between them, but Canción had a good grip on his hand. He lowered the poor man to the floor and called out for Isabella.

She burst in, eyes wide, hand over her mouth. "My God! What happened to him?"

"He collapsed. I don't know what's wrong. Call Dr. Hermosa." He checked the man's pulse, which was racing, then his eyes. The pupils were pinpoints, but equal. "A heart attack, maybe. I don't know."

Isabella fumbled the radio from her pocket and called out a medical emergency. Las Brisas didn't have a hospital, or even a clinic, just one old semi-retired family practice physician who did the best he could. Canción held Mateo's hand, feeling the human soul within. He was alive, but his mind reeled in panic, lost without the demon that had possessed him for so long. How long, Canción had no way to know, nor what to do for the man. This wasn't the panic of fear, something that he could take away, but the panic of sudden release. For the first time in who knew how long, Mateo had control over his own body.

By the time Dr. Hermosa arrived, Mateo was conscious, moving, shaking his head back and forth, and mumbling hysterical nonsense. The doctor frowned and withdrew a stethoscope from his bag, asking Canción to give an account of what happened while he performed a quick examination, listening to heart and breathing, checking eyes and ears, and feeling around his head, probably for signs of injury.

"We were through talking and stood to shake hands. He didn't show any signs of... *anything* really. Then his eyes went wide, and he went rigid for a second, like a seizure of some kind, and his legs just folded. I caught him before he hit the floor." All of that was basically true, but he wasn't about to tell anyone about the demon he'd torn from the man's soul. A priest, no less. Nobody would believe him.

"Did he eat or drink anything?"

"Yes. We both had one cup of coffee." Canción pointed to the pot and two empty cups. "He had sugar, I didn't."

Hermosa sniffed the sugar bowl, then tasted it, and shrugged. "His heart's beating fine, and his blood pressure's high but not dangerously so. His pupils are equal, which doesn't *completely* rule out a stroke. With the sudden onset, hemorrhagic stroke's more likely, but without any patient history, I can't make that diagnosis. He's a healthy middle-aged man, and shows no signs of pre-onset trauma, so that doesn't seem likely. Turbaco has no proper hospital, only a clinic, so they can't do a CT, and transportation to the nearest imaging facility would take days." He sighed. "We should contact La Popa, tell them what happened."

"I'll call them," Isabella offered, hustling from the room.

Hermosa stood and turned to Canción, worry written plainly on his face. "This won't go over well with Bishop Vargas."

That took Canción aback. "What's he going to do, accuse me of *poisoning* his priest?"

"He might." Hermosa's frown deepened, and he shook his head. "This won't end well, Canción. This won't end well for anyone."

"I'll deal with it," he promised, unsure if he could. If the bishop accused him of murder, and the cardinal in Bogota backed the accusation, they might convince the police to investigate, even press charges. Even though there was absolutely no evidence of poison or any assault, Canción wasn't so naïve that he thought something couldn't be manufactured.

"They said to put him aboard their boat," Isabella said from the doorway. "They'll take him to La Popa."

"And do *what*? They don't have any more medical facilities than we do." Dr. Hermosa looked angry.

"I mentioned the clinic in Turbaco, but they said no," Isabella said. "They said he was one of theirs, and they would care for him."

"They'll probably pray for his recovery." Canción put a hand on the doctor's shoulder and took his anger away, a bare whisp of additional effort to contain compared to the seething mass of energy that had been the demon. "Like they said, he's theirs. We have to respect their wishes."

"Yes, of course you're right," Hermosa agreed. "Help me take him to the taxi."

Mateo walked with help, and they lifted him gently into the taxi. Dr. Hermosa agreed to ride down to the ferry terminal with him. Canción paid the driver again, and they started down the hill at a careful pace.

Isabella leaned close. "What *really* happened?"

"I wish I knew," he said numbly and quite honestly. Canción had never encountered a demon before and had not known he could wrench one right out of the possessed human like a weed from a garden. This whole situation terrified him; that he could destroy a minion of Hell. The implications were too much for him to wrap his head around. "I need to walk this off, Isabella, and the Martinezes need some help. I'll be back this afternoon." He started off, but she grabbed his arm.

"Don't you *dare* go trapsing off without a hat and poncho, young man!" She dashed back into the house and grabbed the garments, scowling at him in a motherly fashion. "You'll catch your death!"

"Thank you, Isabella. I don't know what I'd do without you." Canción had never been sick a day in his life, but he donned the poncho and hat anyway. He walked out into the rain, through the streets of Las Brisas, the community he'd helped to create, and tried to reconcile what had happened.

His mother's words rang in his mind: *You are unique in all the world, my son, and I don't know how the will of God or Hell might move through you. You must be careful, for I feel you may possess powers that no Ageless or Nephilim can match.* Again, it was too much. He didn't want it.

His strides took him without thought exactly where he needed to go, a run-down building that they were slowly demolishing. The former owner, a rich banker, had murdered his family and blown his own head off with a shotgun when the economy crashed, and nobody wanted a house where a man had committed such atrocities. The only answer was complete demolition. Sixty-year-old reinforced concrete, however, was putting up a fight against picks and sledgehammers.

There were no workers here at present—everyone taking the brief break in the weather to help farmers tend their fields—so Canción could do what needed to be done without anyone seeing. He worked his way through the wreckage to the solid concrete retaining wall pockmarked with chips from hammers and chisels. With one more glance around to make sure nobody was nearby, he stood about five steps from the wall and took a deep breath, concentrating on the seething mass of energy within him.

In a single shouted musical note, Canción expelled the destroyed demon in a spear of destructive force, fogging the rain into mist before him. The pulse of energy struck the retaining wall with the impact of a battering ram. The concrete fractured outward from the point of impact, pieces falling away in a minor avalanche, exposing the lattice of rebar within.

Canción smiled, feeling instantly better. Whenever he took the harmful feelings of others and expelled them, he could also expel his own worry, fear, and anger. The evil was gone, and he'd made the workers' job easier. A win-win. He turned and strode off toward the Martinez house, wishing all of his problems could be solved so easily.

Gippy woke to a skull-splitting headache, unable to move his arms and legs. His neck felt like hot knives had been thrust into his spine. *Paralyzed?* he wondered, but he clenched his hands and felt his fingers respond. With no clear memory of the attack, he wondered how he'd been hurt and where he was. He tried to lift his head. The hot knives stabbed deeper, eliciting a groan, and he realized he was sitting in a chair. Blinking his eyes open revealed thick black cable ties on his wrists and forearms. With the light, more hot knives pierced deep into his brain, intensifying the high-pitched whine that rang in his ears.

"What the fuck?" he tried to say, but it came out less than intelligible.

"He's conscious, sir," a deep male voice said, but Gippy couldn't lift his head to see who it was.

"Good." A hand grasped his hair and wrenched his head upright.

Gippy cried out at the searing agony blazing up his neck into his skull —half-groan half-scream.

"Good morning, terrorist." The man gripping Gippy by the hair had hard, weathered Latin features, dark eyes, and wore black military fatigues with gleaming gold bars on his collar. His black baseball cap also had two gold bars on the front. His mouth was set in a grim smile. "Glad you could join us."

You're in deep shit, Gip, he realized. Two more soldiers stood behind the officer, also wearing NAFAS fatigues. They held military rifles and wore combat web gear instead of police flak vests and belts. He sat in the middle of a motel room, a door with a security chain and peep hole to his left, and no other visible furniture. Resolution struck through the piercing pain in his skull. *Not getting out of here alive... Not if you're lucky.*

Gritting his teeth against the pain, he groaned, "Can't say much for the room service."

The NAFAS officer's smile widened, then he released his grip on Gippy's hair and slapped him. It wasn't very hard, but pain lanced through Gippy's neck, up into his brain and down his spine. Stars popped behind his eyes and his ringing ears rang louder.

"You're going to answer some simple questions, terrorist, or you're going to learn new definitions for pain. Do you understand me?"

"Can't hear a word you sayin'," he groaned. "My ears ringin' too fuckin' loud."

The man gripped his hair again, shaking his head hard and eliciting more agony. "I said, you will answer *questions*!"

The abuse sent electric jolts down his spine and along every nerve in his body, all the way to his fingers. His neck was hurt bad, maybe bad enough to send him on his way if he taunted this sadistic jackass a bit more. "Okay... Got it. Questions. The answer's B, or forty-two if it's not multiple choice."

The officer slapped him again, harder this time, and the lights popping behind Gippy's eyes reached new heights.

Even as his head slumped, he grinned to himself. "Okay. Not multiple choice, then?" Gippy knew his brief future would only be defined by how much pain he would have to endure before the end. The way his neck hurt and his ears rang elicited memories of Empa's lessons on trauma medicine. *C-spine injury. One wrong twist and it'll be over.* A few more hard blows to the head should do it. The officer didn't seem too bright. Maybe he could trick him into killing him quickly, rather than slowly. "Are you into BDSM, then? Is this foreplay? You're kind of cute for a butch fascist, but I really don't feel like—"

The captain jerked him up by the hair and punched him in the nose.

Something in Gippy's neck cracked as his head snapped back, and the room went hazy, darkening at the edges like someone had the lights on a dimmer. He tasted blood, and the room darkened further, his head drooping forward, the ringing in his ears so loud he barely heard the other voice, a different voice.

"You kill him, we get nothing." The voice was feminine, and plucked strings of memory and deep revulsion through Gippy's semiconsciousness.

"I'm not going to kill him. We're just getting started." The captain grasped Gippy's hair again and lifted his head. Something wet splashed into his face. "No passing out, now, little terrorist."

Gippy blinked away the water, the darkness receding to the edges of his vision, lurking there, ready to pounce. *Just a little bit more...* "Thanks for the drink."

"Where is your companion going? Why were you here?"

"Companion?" *She's alive,* he thought, hiding his relief. *She escaped!* "Who?"

"The woman with you. Empa. We know who she is. Tell us where you were going?"

"Oh, *her.*" Gippy swallowed blood and blinked. The room was still blurry, and he saw two of everything. *Getting close now...* "She picked me up in... Laredo. I traded some sweet ganja for a ride. She said something about... Panama City, I think? Yeah, wanted to pick up... something. Coke, I think."

"He's lying." The revolting feminine voice said.

"I *know,* Duvara. I've conducted *thousands* of interrogations. They always lie... at first." The captain grasped one of Gippy's fingers and bent it backward in one swift snap.

Gippy screamed, which made his head explode with more pain than the disjointed finger. The room darkened again, his head drooping forward, which only hurt his neck more. He spiraled down a maelstrom of agony, wishing his heart would simply stop beating, that God would take him, release him from torment... a just reward for helping his granddaughter.

"He'll only lie again. We need information, not fifty different red herrings to chase!"

"You suggest we *coddle* him into cooperation?"

"No, but if you continue this, he'll taunt you into killing him. He has a concussion and neck injury. It won't take much to push him into a coma."

"What then? We need what he *knows.*"

"Let me do what I was *made* to do. Give me a day, and he'll be ours, body and *soul*."

Even through the shock and pain, that statement gave Gippy pause. He raised his head slowly, inch by agonizing inch, trying to focus though the haze fogging his senses. Where had he heard that voice before?

"A day..." The NAFAS captain stared down at Gippy in disgust. "We're already at a disadvantage. She's in the jungle, and we have no air support, shitty sat-comms, and insufficient personnel to conduct a ground search. She could be miles away by now!"

Thousands of interrogations... He's a Nephilim, Gippy realized. That put a new spin on things. Nephilim weren't stupid but, according to Empa, they tended toward arrogance. Could he use that to provoke the thing?

"And this young man is our only lead." The owner of the revolting feminine voice finally stepped into Gippy's view, tight ripped jeans, snug V-neck tee shirt, curvy, with dark hair and sultry eyes. But there was cruelty in those eyes, and he knew them. Chaki smiled down at him, cruel lust burning there as plain as day. "If he dies, we have nothing. If you let me flip him, we have *everything*."

"You think you can?" the Nephilim asked, eying her, his previous derision suddenly absent.

"I *know* I can." Her smile widened, her tongue running over her upper lip. "Give me *one* day."

With the thought of her touching him, Gippy felt like he might puke. He'd rather be tortured by the Nephilim.

"Fine." The captain turned to his men. "Everyone out. Find me some communications. We may need reinforcements."

The soldiers filed out, and Gippy caught a glimpse of familiar rain-streaked streets though the open door. They were in David, the same motel he and Empa had stayed at only... Had it only been last night? He still had no memory of the attack or being injured, but he recalled the burned out hacienda, meeting two Latinos, one young with smoldering eyes, the other older, weather beaten, hard. Both had F-names, father and son, and they'd known Cora's son, but he couldn't recall anything after that. Maybe that was for the best, considering what the next 24 hours would bring.

The door closed, and Chaki leaned down, her face only inches from his, her stale breath warm on his clammy skin. "We meet again. Do you remember me?"

Gippy swallowed hard. "I know what you are, succubus."

"And I know what *you* are." She ran long fingernails through his hair, and shuddered all over. "Angel touched... You resisted me before. Not this time."

Her touch felt like something decayed and slimy, a parody of sensuality. He tried to pull away, but his neck was killing him. "Fuck off, demon."

"Oh, I'd rather fuck *you,* little boy." She reached into the pocket of her jeans to withdraw a pearl handled folding knife. She opened it with the practiced flip of her thumb, and her smile widened even further. "It's play time. Where shall we begin?"

Gippy closed his eyes and muttered a silent prayer. This wasn't going to be fun at all.

16
LOST HOPE

I move through the jungle as fast and quietly as I can, thanking God for the inclement weather. If the skies had been clear, I'd have been targeted by drones scanning with infrared and eliminated before I made it a mile. My only hope is to put distance between myself and the Hounds of Hell before they can call in reinforcements. I make my way east, climbing the steep hills, memories of Southeast Asia and the Philippines tweaking my subconscious, old survival habits coming back. *Move, stop, listen, move. Don't follow trails. Don't leave footprints. Never stay put. Steady spirit. Vigilance.* My heart aches for Gippy, but I have no choice but to flee. I pray that he awaits me in Heaven, that his death was swift and painless.

When I stop and listen near the crest of a hill, a sharp whistle freezes me, two notes, almost like a bird, but not quite. I lower myself slowly to the ground, trying to discern the direction of the sound, inching to the cover of a massive tree's buttress roots. Straining to listen over the hiss-patter of rain through the high jungle canopy, I pick out the sounds of something moving through the undergrowth. I raise my rifle, but gunfire will draw more pursuers. If I'm lucky, there's only one nearby. I unsnap the strap of my combat knife and wait. *Steady spirit...*

Another whistle, the same quick two notes, from far to my right. There are two, at least. Luck seems to have evaded me. I sweep my scope slowly over the landscape, and spot the near one, broad hat, camouflage poncho, rifle held low. My finger moves from safe to trigger. If I take him down, the other might expose himself. Then he turns, and I see his face.

I release the breath I'm holding. "Fernando!" I pitch my voice to carry only so far, for sound echoes among the hills.

He freezes, turning toward me. "Miss Empa?"

"Yes." I secure my knife and rifle, and stand, hands out. "How did you find me?"

"Tracks." He whistles a three-note song, and receives the same in reply.

So much for not leaving tracks. My jungle warfare skills are a little rusty, it seems.

He approaches. "You have nice boots, but you're alone. Where's your friend, Gifford?"

"Dead..." *Please, God, let him be dead.* "...or captive. I don't know. They mined the road. He was still in the truck, but I couldn't get to him. I tried but..." I gasp a sob. "I don't know... if..."

"Easy now." He approaches and puts a hand on my arm.

I realize I'm crying and draw a deep breath. *Stop it! Steady spirit...* I think of Musashi, then the sword he gave me, that I gave to Jeri. *Jeri... Shit! She'll hate me.* "Fernando, I need you to find out what happened to Gippy. If they took him alive, they'll interrogate him, and he'll break. I need to get online to warn our friends."

"We can help with that." Fernando nods to his father who is approaching, moving through the jungle like a ghost. He briefly explains what I told him.

Franko nods. "I'll take her to Camp Two. Find out what you can and join us there."

"And communications?" I ask, grateful for the help, but barely keeping my panic under control. *Think! Focus!* If he's alive and captive, I have no doubt that Gippy will crack under the hands of a skilled interrogator... eventually. Even if I can get ultranet reception, I dare not use my phone. If Gippy's survived the attack, the naffies have it, and my contact is in it. So are Jeri's and Emil's. If they hack into it, a ping to those numbers will bring down all nine shades of Hell. "If they have him, my friends will die. I need—"

"I have a friend with an old Ham radio. He's on the nets every day. We can patch a call through." Franko grabs my arm and nods to his son. "We need to move, *now*. They have patrols."

"*Thank* you!" I sling my rifle and nod, forcing my spirit to steady state. I have a plan, allies, a mission.

Franko points up the hill. "Go that way. I'll be right behind you, muddle your tracks."

"Be careful, Fernando," I say to his retreating back.

He nods back. "Always."

With Franko's guidance, we reach a camouflaged camp in less than an hour. My legs are burning like fire from the hills, but I feel sure that even a pack of bloodhounds couldn't follow our trail. Franko knows this jungle like he knows the scars on his own hands. I collapse on a camp stool, and he starts up a propane stove, pouring rainwater into an old-fashioned perk coffee pot. Two heaps of near-black ground coffee go into the basket, and he puts it on to boil.

"I'll call my friend." He pulls a VHF radio from a pocket.

"Careful. They'll be monitoring radio traffic." I pull an oily rag from my pack and start checking my rifle. Old habits, and the routine sooths me, lessons of old wars rising in me. *Your rifle is your best girl. Treat her right and she'll save your life. Treat her wrong, and she'll betray you when you need her most.* Jungle isn't as bad as desert for the fine moving parts, but the combined gunk of moisture, powder residue, and general grime can cause misfires and jamming.

Franko grins. "Not in *these* hills, they won't."

I realize he's right. VHF is line of sight. His friend must be close. I service the HK, listening to him talking to his friend, Miguel, and the man's quick, clipped replies. He heard the explosions and gunfire and is worried about soldiers, as am I. He has no news from Boquete but is willing to let me use his radio. I replace the magazine I used and chamber a round, topping up the old one and rapping it smartly to align the cartridges. The rifle's action works smoothly. I warm my hands by the propane flame, and glory in the scent of boiling coffee.

"Here," Franko returns and pours two tin cups half full, handing me one.

"Thank you." I sip, burn my tongue, and thank God for caffeine.

Franko nods. "My friend, Miguel, will help, but he's a little paranoid."

"Rightfully so." I stand and stretch, most of the aches from the explosion already fading. My ears aren't even ringing anymore.

"Here." He hands me a towel he's dampened from the rain. "Your face is bloody. We don't want to leave a trail."

"Thanks." I wipe my face and the towel comes of mired in blood. I find a gash in my scalp, but it seems to have stopped gushing. "How far to Miguel's?"

"Five miles, across the valley, but there are trails. Two hours if we hump it." He looks around, and finds what he needs, a dry erase marker and a scrap of clear plastic. "I'll leave Fernando a note to meet us there. We can leave whenever you're ready."

"I'm ready." I down my coffee and heft my rifle.

"Okay, then." He scrawls a note, places it where it'll be seen, and shoulders his gear. He dons his hat and frowns. "Sorry I don't have a spare hat."

"No matter." I'm already wet to the skin. "Let's go."

He nods, and I follow. The slog through the jungle is only slightly easier than our previous trek. In just over two hours I spot a dilapidated shack tucked into a hillside, the winding trail snaking up a clear area that's cultivated with passionfruit vines so thick they're impassible. Wires are strung all over the place, among the vines and from tree to tree above us. The high ones, I realize, are antennas. The low ones support the vines, but also might be trip wires. We stay on the path and wind our way up the trail, fully exposed to anyone in the shack. I glimpse a face in one of the windows.

The door opens as we near, and an old man eyes us, a big revolver in his hand. At least he's not pointing it at us. "Who's your friend, Franko?" His English is almost without accent.

"Emily." He gestures to me. "She knew Señora Tersi."

Miguel's face changes from grim to passive, and he steps aside. "Please, come in."

We enter, and the interior of the shack is a surprise; clean, dry, and orderly, larger than I expected, cut deeply into the hillside, but with a homey feel.

"Marta, something for our guests," Miguel says in Spanish.

A round young woman hurries to a tiny kitchen. "Coffee and fritas. Just a moment."

"Please, don't go to any trouble," I tell them in Spanish. "I just need to use your radio."

"It's no trouble." She pours water into a pot and oil into another, turning dials on a surprisingly modern induction range. "Just leave your wet things by the door and make yourselves comfortable."

"Thank you," I place my rifle beside the door and doff my poncho, then unlace my boots and kick them off. My socks are wet, so I take them off as well to avoid tracking damp across the immaculate floor. "You have a lovely home. Very modern and comfortable." Discussing décor seems inane to me, but being personable helps calm my nerves, and my hosts' as well, I hope.

"We have a wind turbine on the hilltop." Miguel gestures me to his ham station, which occupies a nook in the back of the house. "It's not a good time of day to connect very far north, but I can get through to Mexico City, and they can relay. What do you need?"

I'm not an expert with ham radios, but evidently Mexico City's not far from Boquete. "A cellular patch or an ultranet connection, if you can manage it."

"No problem." He grins. "I have a modem converter. Is text okay?"

"*Yes.*" Again, I'm surprised. Miguel probably has better connectivity than NAFAS down here. While VHF is short range, and sat com bands are susceptible to interference from violent weather, some ham bands propagate better when the atmosphere is full of ionization.

He sits and tunes the radio, his fingers moving like a virtuoso over his instrument. He talks briefly with someone, then someone else, the connections scratchy. He adjusts his antenna array, tunes it again, and the signal clears. Then he uses a modem converter to connect to an ultranet uplink in Mexico City, and stands up.

"There you are. Text only." He arranges a keyboard and a tiny grayscale monitor. "Just type in the phone number in that box, and you'll get a text window."

"God bless you, Miguel." I sit and type in Jeri's number, and the text, "Carbuncle Freeway!" and send it. I send the same message to Emil Farrell. The message is our scramble code. It means we've been compromised, and they could be targeted by NAFAS or Nephilim assassins. I doubt that Gippy has cracked yet, but if he's alive, it's only a matter of time. If they're already into his phone, I could be too late. Lastly, I dial my bank, tapping in the long alphanumeric of my password in lieu of a voiceprint identification. I transfer the bulk of my ready cash account to another, leaving fifty thousand NADs behind in the unlikely event that Gippy's alive, and even less-likely, that he somehow escapes and needs money.

I mutter another short prayer that he's dead and turn back to our benefactor. I have one more vital need. "Do you have a kit of small tools. I need to destroy the sim card in my phone." I've kept the thing turned off for days, since we had spotty ultranet connections at best. If the weather clears, I might be able to use it, but I don't want to be tracked. If our pursuers have hacked Gippy's phone, my own would become a perfect GPS beacon for a missile strike.

I see through the scope of my rifle again, my friend hanging upside down in the Mule, helpless. *Mercy... Please, God, let him be dead.*

"Oh, sure!" He opens a drawer and I find a full set of electronics tools. "Do you need a new one?"

"A new *sim* card?" I blink away tears to stare blankly at the seemingly incongruous question. "Are you serious?"

"Sure! Here." Miguel grins and fishes a small plastic case from another drawer. He opens it to reveal about fifty sim cards of various makes and carriers. "Nobody much uses ultranet phones down here, and I scavenge parts. Take whatever you need."

"You're a godsend, Miguel." I pop the back off my phone and lever out the sim card with a plastic tool. As I work, amazing aromas of fresh coffee and fried breadfruit waft through the cabin. When I'm done, I turn to find the table set for us.

Marta gestures to a chair with a smile. "Please. Franko said you knew Señora Tersi?"

"Yes. She was my cousin. I hadn't seen her in years." I sit, and she pours coffee. The fries are sizzling hot and spiced with a local blend. I try one. They're amazing. Food and coffee make everything a little brighter. I feel my spirit settling into absurd normality, considering the situation, and I'm grateful. "These are delicious. Thank you."

"We have to wait until Fernando comes," Franko explains. "And you'll need your strength, whatever you decide to do."

Whatever I decide... I don't want to dwell on the possibilities if Gippy survived, but I must. I sip the wonderful coffee and try to think. One more dire realization surfaces through my grief: Gippy knows where Canción is. I turn to Franko. "Is there any way you can contact Canción?"

"Not by phone or radio directly. We might be able to get a message to him." He looks to Miguel. "Las Brisas, Colombia?"

Miguel purses his lips. "Maybe Bogota or Medellin, but Cartagena's totally off grid, and there are no active hams in the area that I know of. I can have a telegram sent, but the only way there is by ferry. It'll be slow."

Franko nods and turns to me. "We can try to warn him, but... Canción's not one to run away and hide."

"He's going to have to *learn*, then," I state flatly. "If the... my enemies find him, there will be Hell to pay." I don't know how much Miguel and Marta know about Cora and Canción.

"But NAFAS has no jurisdiction in Colombia," Franko counters. "That was one of the reasons Miss Tersi chose Cartagena."

"That might slow them down, but..." I don't want to freak out our hosts by talking about Nephilim, but I have to get the point across that national boundaries won't make a difference. "They undoubtedly have allies in Colombia that they can mobilize. I'd like to get word to him if I can, just to warn him. They'll want him *very* badly."

"I don't understand," Marta says. "Why all the interest in Señora Tersi's son?"

Before I can speak, Franko interjects. "NAFAS murdered Señora Tersi because she was... special. She countered their tyranny with her music, spreading love instead of hate. Canción's also special, and they'll hunt him down if they can."

I couldn't have said it better myself, so I simply nod in affirmation.

Marta looks horrified, and Miguel grim. He nods. "Let me see who I can contact. What message do you want to send?"

"Tell him the Hounds of Hell are coming." I fix Franko with a meaningful stare. "He'll understand that, won't he?"

"Yes. Yes, he will. Sign it FFM. He'll know it's from me."

"I'm on it." Miguel takes a seat at his radio and starts tuning his antennas.

"More coffee?" Marta lifts the pot from the stove.

"Please." I force a smile I don't feel. "You have no idea how much you're helping me here. I don't know what I would hav—"

We both start at a knock on the door, and I spill boiling hot coffee on my hand. I'm up with my Glock out, but Franko gestures for calm. Miguel rises from his chair, pulling his revolver, and Marta backs toward the kitchen, reaching for a butcher knife as long as my forearm.

A voice from the other side of the door, "Miguel? It's Fernando!"

Franko moves to the door and cracks it, then widens it for his son to enter. He looks exhausted, breathing hard, soaked and muddy.

I holster my pistol and advance on him, my heart in my throat. "News?"

"Gifford's alive, but they have him." Fernando removes his hat and wipes his brow. "I'm sorry, but I couldn't get close."

"Where?" I'm in his face, shaking, ten thousand atrocities playing through my head. *No, no no! Not my dearest boy...* "Where did they take him?"

"David, I think, but we can't even get there. They've blocked the road at the Highway Ten intersection. Four armored cars and maybe twenty soldiers. They left one car in Boquete with a squad, and four more took off toward David. Gifford was with them, but the people who saw him said he was unconscious."

"Fuck!" I grit my teeth and start to pace, my hands clenched, trembling. "I've got to get to him! How can I—"

Fernando steps in my path, his hands on my arms. "Empa, you *can't*. They'll surround him with soldiers. There's nothing we can do, but you can still escape."

"You need to get to Canción before they do," Franko adds.

My heart is breaking, but they're right. And I don't have much time. "Gifford won't break quickly, but he'll break. I need to get to Colombia. *Fast.*"

"The road's blocked," Fernando points out. "They're letting no traffic through. If we have to go overland, it'll take *weeks*."

"*One* road is blocked," Miguel says, and we all turn to him. "The old country club road is still passable, but not by car, and it's not on many maps. They may not know about it. It's a mess, but... I know a guy with horses."

"Antonio!" Fernando grins and turns to me. "Yes! We can do this!"

"Horses?" I blink at him, baffled. "We can't beat them to Punta Peña on *horseback*."

"You won't have to." Miguel turns the dials of his radio. "I can have a truck waiting for you where the road hooks up with Highway Ten. We can get you to Punta Peña by tonight! There might even be a weather window for the ferry! I can pull down GRIB files from the NAFAS weather service."

The chance to reach Canción before the Nephilim and the torment of leaving Gippy in their hands clash in my head for a moment, but Fernando's right. I can't fight through a hundred solders to free him.

I nod. "Okay. We go!"

"I'll go with you," Fernando offers. "Papa, contact Antonio. Tell him we'll pay."

Pay... While Franko pulls a hand-held VHF, I fish a bar of bullion from a pocket and turn to Marta. "Here. Take this." I press it into her hands, and her eyes widen. "For everything you've done for me. Please." I close her hands on the bar of platinum and touch the peak moments of her life. Her love for Miguel, her joy with the baby she's carrying, her hope. I remove every vestige of infirmity from her, though she's remarkably healthy, and try to smile. "Thank you."

"Go with God, Señora."

The irony helps me smile. "I always do."

"Come on!" Fernando holds out my poncho and boots. "Vamos!"

We're out the door in two minutes, jogging down the zig-zag path through the passionfruit vines, rain trickling down my neck, and prayers for Gippy ringing through my mind.

~

Chaki's interrogation techniques weren't what Gippy expected. Instead of parting his flesh with the pearl-handled knife, she meticulously cut his clothes away, promising a thousand delicious torments with every slice. Her touch disgusted him even more than her threats. He'd never known that sex could be torture, but Chaki had educated him.

"Does your Ageless whore do *this* for you?" She slithered against him, skin on skin, and laughed.

He gritted his teeth against the revolting sensations her touch elicited. At first, he thought he would be able to ignore her attempts—she disgusted him on a visceral level—but again he'd been wrong. She forced him again and again with just a touch of her hand, until he thought he would pass out.

"Tell me where she is, and I'll let you rest... for a few minutes."

"Fuck off!" he growled through gritted teeth.

"Okay, then..." Her hand tightened on him, and he thrashed against the cable ties, howling, crying, begging her to stop, but she wouldn't. She laughed as he tried to pull away, to evade her touch, to resist.

Gippy tried to concentrate on something else, on Empa, on Jeri, on *real* love, not this perversion of sex into torture. He cursed and prayed and begged, but she would not relent.

"Do you hate me yet, little boy?" she teased, giving him a breath of rest.

"I hated you before, demon!" he growled. "I'll send you to Hell for this!"

"Oh, but I've *been* there." She chuckled and leaned over him, her face close to his. "Would you like a taste of what you'll experience there?"

"Fuck off! You kill me, and I get a one way ticket to Heaven, bitch!"

"Not when *I'm* through with you, you won't." She kissed him hard, and he bit her reflexively, blood between his teeth. She squeezed his testicles, and he screamed.

"*Now* you're learning!" She laughed, blood dripping down her chin from her torn lip. "Now you're *really* starting to hate me."

Gippy spat her blood out, disgusted and ashamed, but she was right. He hated her with every fiber of his being.

"You want to hurt me, don't you?" she teased, straddling his lap, grinding him into her.

"*Yes*, I want to hurt you! I want to rip you limb from limb!"

"Good!" She pressed her breasts to his face. "Do it, then."

And he did. Her blood tasted rancid, like rotting meat, but he couldn't stop. Flesh tore under his teeth, and she laughed, howling as if she was climaxing. He screamed and bucked her off, and she laughed at him, lying on the floor bloody and bitten.

"You liked that, didn't you?" She smeared the blood over her skin and stood. "The taste of my blood?"

"You're *disgusting*!" He spat again, refusing to look at her, wishing he could die, wanting to rip her apart, and knowing that was what she wanted. She wasn't just torturing him, she was trying to corrupt his soul. He closed his eyes, muttering, "I am God's warrior. You will burn in Hell, and I will laugh at God's side."

"Not quite ready yet, then," the succubus cooed, and Gippy knew that her torments had only just begun.

17
BREAKING FAITH

Three hours on horseback kindles a lot of memories. It was the fastest mode of transportation for most of my life. Fernando is shocked when I rub my spirited mare's neck, whisper in her ear, exhale into a nostril, and vault aboard without even mentioning the lack of a saddle.

"I'm sorry we have only bridles," Antonio apologizes. "The constant damp has ruined all of my saddles. Everything made of leather rots, and I can't get more.

"No matter. You're helping us more than you know." I caress my mount's neck, patting her affectionately. I miss horses; they're so strong and willing, and will give their lives for you. "I can ride without one well enough."

Fernando has more trouble than I do, but he makes do. We ride along an overgrown dirt road, wet limbs slapping us, pushing our charges as hard as their noble hearts will sustain. The concentration and motion distract me from thoughts of what Gippy must be going through.

Unfortunately, when we reach the highway and clamber into the back of an open pickup truck for the three hour ride to Punta Peña, I have nothing to do and far too much time to think. By the time we reach our destination, I'm a wreck, ready to highjack the vehicle and drive into a swarm of NAFAS soldiers in a hopeless attempt to save my friend. I know

I can't, but I feel like a traitor for not dying with him, as I know he would have for me.

The storm-worn town greets us like a testament to human survival. It grips the embattled shore like a limpet to a rock, the massive seawall worn but holding against the storms, the people resigned and wary. We get out of the truck near the docks, our rifles barely drawing a lingering glance. The vessels remind me of North Sea workboats, but they've seen better days, the steel hulls dented between the frames. When Fernando starts to follow me down the ramp to the jostling dock, I turn to confront him.

"I thank you for your help, but I don't need an escort anymore, my friend." I hold out a hand, but he just stares at it for a moment, then shakes his head.

"I'm coming with you. I know Canción *and* Las Brisas."

I grit my teeth, unwilling to put him in any more danger. "I'll be fine, Fernando. I've survived longer than you can imagine all by myself."

"Maybe, but I'm going anyway." He shrugs. "I haven't seen Canción in four years. He's my brother. I *want* to go."

I turn away without another word. I can't stop him short of violence, and his familiarity with Las Brisas and Canción will admittedly help. I've been to Cartagena once before, but I imagine it's changed since 1724. There is only one cargo ferry at the dock, the other rests at the loading terminal, half-sized tractor trailer tankers being lifted by a derrick crane onto the massive concrete quay, a bare trickle of fuel by past standards, but commerce. The vessel at the dock is loaded with four shipping containers, a thin trail of smoke streaming away from her stack. There's been a slight break in the weather, but the seas are still huge. I wonder if the ship will risk a crossing before the next hurricane hits.

Two men meet us at the gangway, one raising a hand. "No long guns permitted."

I open my mouth, but Fernando beats me to the punch. "We're booking passage to Cartagena. You'll stow our rifles?"

"Sure." He gestures to a deck locker, and we board.

I'm reluctant to give up the weapon, but I have my pistol, and if something happens my Glock is probably better aboard a ship than my beloved HK. Still... "We've been traveling rough. I'll need to clean this before it's stowed."

"Once you arrange passage, you'll be allowed to, but we'll keep the ammo." He gestures insistently.

I unload my rifle and stow it in the locker. There are four other weapons inside, and I wonder if they belong to passengers or the ship. The thought of high-seas piracy is almost laughable in this era of global storms, but one never knows. I recall the days of my own acts of piracy, the futile effort to unite the islands in the face of European imperialism. Not the first time I banded together with a bunch of murderous fools, and not the last either.

"See Captain Estrada on the bridge." He waves us forward.

When we're out of earshot, Fernando tells me, "This is the same ship we crossed on eight years ago, but a new captain. I don't know him."

"Please let me do the talking this time." I step inside and doff my poncho, hanging it with the crew's raingear. I untuck my wet shirt to cover my pistol.

"Sure." My unwelcome companion follows my example, and we climb the companionway to the bridge deck.

I knock on the captain's door first but receive no answer. At the bridge door, I knock again. When I'm about to reach for the handle myself, it opens.

A young man looks us over. "Yes?" His English is heavily accented.

"We're to see Captain Estrada to book passage to Cartagena."

He looks surprised at my perfect Spanish, but nods. "This way."

He leads us along a short passage, past an open door to a radio room, and onto the bridge. It's typical of many vessels I've seen, all painted metal, worn and chipped near the handrails, smelling of stale sweat, lubricating oil, and burnt coffee. The ship's captain, however, isn't what I expected.

Captain Estrada turns to us when her junior officer announces, "Passengers to see you, Captain."

She's middle aged, her pock-marked face set in a permanent scowl, clearly hard as nails. "Fine. Two thousand NADs each for a stateroom, or one for crew berths. We leave in thirty-six hours. If you're not aboard, we leave anyway."

"Emily Grant, Captain." I smile and extend a hand.

She shakes it out of habit, and I get the peak moments of her life in a rush. A hard woman indeed, but there are details I can use, if necessary.

"Welcome aboard, Ms. Grant. The price of passage hasn't changed, however."

I release her hand and give her a tight smile. "How bad is the weather right now?" My question catches her off guard.

Her iron gaze hardens. "Sixty knots, ten meter seas twenty-five seconds apart, and a nasty chop, but dropping, if that means anything to you. Why?"

"So, for this vessel that would be... *uncomfortable,* but not life threatening, yes?" I've been in worse aboard a Spanish galleon. That had been life threatening.

Her eyes narrow. "I suppose, but we have no reason to risk it. We leave in thirty-six hours."

"And if I *gave* you a reason?"

Her eyes widen slightly at my emphasis. "We could leave tomorrow morning, eighteen hours, but it would have to be one *hell* of a good reason."

"How about two reasons." I slip two bars of Swiss Bank bullion from my hip pocket and hold them out to her.

Her narrow eyes widen further, then narrow again. I can see her doing the math in her head. I'm holding over ten-thousand untraceable NADs in my hand. Her eyes flick up to mine, penetrating, calculating.

"How about *three* reasons."

I hesitate. For once, money is a concern. I doubt I can access my accounts from Las Brisas, and I'm down to less than half of my usual stash. Still, I have another card to play, and I learned to haggle before actual currency even existed. "Okay, *these* two reasons and a NAFAS Military column probably arriving in Punta Peña within twelve hours." I've thought long and hard about how long Gippy might hold out, and what information he will give them. He'll send them on wild goose chases at first, but eventually they'll get the truth from him. My worst case estimate is less than a day from the time they took him, for that's when fatigue and pain truly begin to affect the mind. I know this from experience, unfortunately.

This really opens Captain Estrada's eyes. "I don't harbor fugitives."

"I'm not asking you to. I'm just warning you." I smile, every eye on the bridge now watching us. "Come now, Captain; half of your crew are probably Colombian nationals without proper papers, just like you." I've seen her time in prison and know she would die before she went back. "NAFAS is coming whether I'm here or not, and they'll arrest everyone aboard."

"Why would they?"

"Because they're going to want passage to Colombia, just like I do. I'm giving you the opportunity to evade arrest and make a tidy profit." I still hold the two bars of bullion in my hand.

I watch the muscles bunch and relax rhythmically on her acne-scarred cheeks. "Mister Flores, how soon can we depart?" Her eyes don't leave mine.

"Um, maybe an hour?" one of the men answers, probably the mate. He doesn't sound happy about the prospect.

"Do it. Rig her for heavy weather and make sure our other passengers are aboard. Tell them there's a change in the forecast." As the deck officers hurry to comply, Captain Estrada reaches out and takes the two bars from my hand. "State room four. Now get the *hell* off my bridge."

I give her my most insincere smile. "*Thank* you, Captain."

Her face flushes scarlet. "You're lucky I don't have you shot."

"It wouldn't be the first time I've been shot, Captain." I turn to exit the bridge, and Fernando follows.

When we're down the companionway and in our state room, he releases the breath he was holding. "You play for keeps, don't you?"

"I play to fucking *win*, Fernando." *A lesson I learned from Gippy.* My heart shatters a bit more. "You *still* sure you want to come along? Hanging around with me is dangerous."

"Oh, I'll tag along." He sits on a bunk and sighs. "I was getting bored in Boquete anyway."

I put my pack down and think of the pending days aboard ship with nothing to do but think of Gippy. "I'm going to clean my rifle." I search through my bag for what I need and am out the door before Fernando can say a word.

"I would *love* to be a fly on the wall in La Popa." Angelica stood at Canción's window staring at the burgeoning sky above the distant isle of the convent. Beside her stood their spotting scope on a tripod. With the recent break between storms, small craft had been coming and going from the towers to the island at a feverish pace. They'd done little but watch and speculate what was going on for the last twenty-four hours. "You still not going to tell me what *really* happened?"

"I told you. I shook his hand, and he had a seizure of some kind." Canción paced. He hadn't slept well. Rumors were spreading: he'd poisoned Father Mateo; the priest had attacked him, and Canción fought back; the man had been so angry he had a stroke... So far, none had come closer to the truth than what he'd just told Angelica. If Mateo had told the bishop the real truth, and Vargas believed him, what would Vargas do? Why a demon-possessed priest would even be in La Popa left Canción deeply troubled. The bishop was a jackass, but to harbor demons under his roof felt like a harbinger of doom. "Dr. Hermosa was right; no good will come of this."

"Well, I don't *like* the man, but—"

A knock rattled his door, and Canción knew it was Isabella by the cadence. "Come in." She did, and he saw the bad news on her face. "What?"

"News from La Popa, and a letter for you."

"A *letter*?" That was odd. The postal service wasn't dependable in the best of times.

"By courier." She held it out.

"What news?" Angelica asked as Canción took the sealed envelope.

Before he could open the envelope, Isabella stopped him cold.

"Father Mateo died." Isabella crossed herself. "They say a heart attack, but Dr. Hermosa says that's all but impossible."

"Dead? How in the name of Heaven and Hell?" Canción suspected foul play of some kind. If Mateo had told the truth, having him killed might hush it up, but would also cause suspicion. The death made him wonder about the Bishop. For all he knew the entire Church had been taken over by demons. He stared at the envelope in his hand, which bore a courier's stamp and his name and address. *Who the hell sends letters these days?* He tore off the end of the envelope and slipped out a single sheet of paper. It was a telegram, typed on a single sheet of yellow paper with no sender information. It read, "The Hounds of Hell are coming. FFM."

"Franko, Fernando, Maria..." He stared at the note from his only remaining family and believed it, but he didn't know what it meant. He remembered his mother saying the same thing when NAFAS was on the way to murder her. "The Hounds of Hell..."

"What?" Angelica turned to him, her eyes wide.

Canción hadn't realized he'd spoken aloud. His mind spun. Could this be a coincidence? But Franko couldn't know about his confrontation with La Popa. Did the note mean NAFAS knew about him, or worse, the Nephilim?

He crumpled the note. "An obscure note from my family. I don't know what it means. We have enough to worry about."

"What do they say?" Both Angelica and Isabella knew his family well, and Angelica wasn't the type to be blown off so easily. "It must be important if they went to the trouble of sending a courier."

"It may be, but we've got to figure out what to do *here* first." He waved a hand at the view. "If they try to charge me with murder..."

"No one's talking about murder yet, Canción," Isabella assured him.

"And if they try something so foolish, Las Brisas will *not* let them take you," Angelica added.

Canción frowned and gritted his teeth. "The Church has power, and I've been a thorn in Vargas's side for two years. The cardinal in Bogota will—"

"Bogota's a long way away," Angelica interrupted. "And Colombia has no navy, or even a coastguard anymore. If they send police, they'll have to take a *ferry* across from the mainland. They won't risk helicopters in this weather for something like this."

Angelica was right, but Canción feared worse than a boatload of police. After watching what NAFAS did to his home in Boquete, he wondered if the Colombian military *would* send helicopters. Not the friendly kind, but gunships. "The Hounds of Hell..." Could his family have somehow known what was coming? That didn't seem possible.

"Canción? What are you talking about?" Angelica looked concerned, as if she thought he might be losing touch with reality.

Maybe I am, he thought, but then shook his head emphatically. "Nothing. I'm not going to stand behind the people of Las Brisas if they send police to arrest me."

"You think they'll stand aside and *let* you be arrested for this?" Isabella snorted a laugh and waved a hand. "You're a good man, and I love you like a son, Canción, but sometimes you're an idiot."

He glared at her. "What do you mean?"

"I mean this community is not going to let the Church take you from us!" she snapped back. "You may have helped build this place, but you don't have a say in what the people do or don't do. Especially your gang friends. They take their roles seriously."

He gritted his teeth harder, a deep dread growing. "I watched my mother murdered by the NAFAS military. I'm *not* going to watch that happen here!"

"Let's all just calm down and take a breath, shall we?" Angelica stepped up to put a hand on his arm. "We have eyes in La Popa. We'll know what they plan to do before they do it."

Canción nodded and asked Isabella, "Do you have any details about how Mateo died?"

"Only that he arrived, seemed confused, and was ushered to a private audience with the Bishop. He walked under his own power, but looked distraught. They spoke for less than an hour, and Vargas called for help. Mateo had collapsed, and they couldn't revive him."

"So he was fine until he spoke to the Bishop. If they charge anyone with murder, it should be *him*!" Angelica was grasping at straws now.

"You know that's not going to happen, Angelica." Canción squeezed her hand. "Keep listening to your friends, Isabella. We can't take action until we know what they're planning."

"I will."

She turned and left the room, but Canción remained troubled. He stared out across the rain-lashed waters of the bay at La Popa, wishing he could see into the mind of Bishop Vargas.

Gippy writhed in a sea of sleep-deprived torment. Chaki wouldn't let him sleep, teasing him with only brief moments of rest, then torturing him anew. But her torment elicited more than one type of pain. Her constant taunts made him question his faith, his devotion to Empa, the war itself, and he felt himself slipping closer and closer toward madness.

"You owe that Ageless whore nothing. Tell me where she went, and you sleep," she promised.

Lies... He knew the voice in his head was right. He wondered where it came from, but he believed it. Chaki would continue to torment him even if he told her the truth, because she *enjoyed* it. "F...uck you."

"You *are*." She ground herself into him relentlessly, forcing his body to respond, for the power of the succubus elicited unrelenting carnal desire that no human could deny.

"Please... *stop*." He wept openly, pleading, begging, cursing. The answer she wanted was there in his mind, it hung like a ripe fruit that he could pluck and eat, washing away his torment, but *She* wouldn't let him. *The demon lies, Gifford,* the voice said. Sometimes it was Empa's, sometimes his mother's, his sisters', or Jeri's, but it was always Her. *Peace, Gifford. You cannot bargain with Hell. Don't give in to hate. You'll be with me soon, and the torment will end.* He wondered if the voices in his head were God, or if he was delusional.

"Don't drift off, now!" Chaki lifted his chin and smiled at him, her lips still bloody but already healing from his assault. "Tell me, or you'll never sleep again, never rest, never escape me. I'll follow you to Hell and do this for ten *thousand* years!" She squeezed him hard with her other hand.

He cried out, trying to bite her fingers, but she just laughed.

"You want to hurt me again, don't you? You want to *kill* me. You want to choke the life out of me, *don't* you?"

"Yes!" He couldn't deny it; he hated her with his entire being, wished he could tear her apart. The voices in his head didn't mean anything anymore. He saw visions of ripping her throat out with his teeth. The rage swelled in him like a tide, filling him, banishing the voices. "I want to fucking *kill* you!"

"Then do it, if you think you can, little boy."

Something jerked his right wrist, then his arm, and the limb fell free from the armrest of the chair where his fingernails had dug furrows in the plastic. He blinked away tears and looked down. His arm was free. The little pearl handled knife moved in her hand to his other wrist.

Snick! The cable tie parted at his wrist.

Snick! The other was severed, both arms now free.

It was a trick. Deep in his soul, he knew it was. She still had the knife. If he tried to throttle her, she'd stab him.

Death... Release... Gippy saw his only escape, the door to Heaven looming, and the rage in him built to a crescendo. He didn't give into hate, he *became* hate.

"Die!" With a strength he didn't know he still possessed, Gippy lurched up and grabbed her by the throat with both hands.

She fell back, and he landed on top of her, his ankles still secured to the legs of the chair. Her legs wrapped around him, holding him, refusing to let him pull out of her, but he didn't care. Gippy squeezed for all he was worth.

"Die! Die! Die!" He glared into her bulging eyes, and the chasm of hate within him opened up...

And something filled that void.

Gippy felt like he was falling into himself, as if the world expanded, or he shrank, or something pulled him down. He knew instantly that he had been tricked, but not as he'd thought. He screamed, but his mouth, his voice, were no longer his to command. Neither were his hands, his legs, or the rest of him. He saw it all, felt it all, but couldn't act. He was trapped within his own body, a prisoner.

His hands fell away from Chaki's throat, and she smiled.

"Hello, Ardat." She grinned with bloody teeth. "Welcome to your new host."

Host... oh, God, please... No, no, no... Gippy felt it then, the filth filling him, sheer lustful malevolence, bottomless and insatiable. The trick had been a trap, a means to open him up for possession, and he'd fallen right into it.

"Hello Duvara," the demon within Gippy said with his voice. "Took you long enough."

"He was... *resilient.*" Her heels smacked his backside. "Now, tell me everything he knows."

Something wrenched within Gippy's mind, and the demon said, "Cartagena. The Ageless, Terpsichore, had a son. The get of a Nephilim, if you believe it. Empa seeks him."

Chaki's eyes widened. "Fucking Hell! *What?*"

"The boy's name is Canción. We must call all our allies together to apprehend this child of Heaven and Hell." The demon, Ardat, rose on Gippy's arms, but Chaki wouldn't release him.

"You haven't possessed a human in *centuries*, Ardat." She grinned and raked her nails down Gippy's chest. He felt the pain, but the demon didn't. It felt Gippy's agony, however, and reveled in it. "Are you *sure* you don't want to indulge yourself a little before we martial our forces?"

Gippy felt his mouth stretch into a grin. "Well, it *has* been a long time..."

No, no, no! Gippy screamed within himself, unable to look away, unable to not feel, unable to even weep any longer. He'd fallen into Hell's snare and would know only torment evermore.

18
A SONG IN THE RUINS

We leave the ferry only slightly worse for wear. The crossing from Panama to Colombia was tumultuous, and Fernando was seasick. Alas, that's one malady I can't cure. I paid my dues in that regard aboard a Greek trireme in the Aegean, three centuries before God sent her son to be crucified by the minions of Hell. Our transit was luxurious by comparison; three meals a day, a dry bunk, and only a few cockroaches. My own ordeal was one of inactivity, my thoughts ever returning to Gippy, my poor lost son. All things considered, I wish I'd been back aboard a slave galley. Only Cora's journal kept me sane.

After a perfunctory check of our papers by the harbormaster at the ferry landing—there are no customs or immigration officials in Las Brisas—I stare at the drowned towers of Cartagena and remember Manhattan, and our desperate foray into that dying metropolis. *Gippy... my savior...*

"Taxi!" Fernando is still a little weak from his ordeal, but also stoic. As are most young men, he's resilient, cocksure, and convinced of his own immortality. I've seen too many young men and women die to be impressed.

A ramshackle bicycle taxi squeaks up to us.

"*Fernando?* Is that you?" The driver's forty something, prematurely gray at his temples, his clothes tatters from the ceaseless wet. He staggers off the bike, gaping at my companion, holding out two hands.

"Adrian! Good to see you!" He shakes the man's hands warmly, beaming with pleasure at the renewed acquaintance. "Can you take us to Casa Musica?"

Casa Musica... Cora's son has named his new home after the one that burned with his mother inside. This, at least, speaks well for him.

"Of course!" The driver looks past Fernando and sees me, his eyes widening again. "Introduce me to your friend, and I won't even charge you!"

Latin men... Their libido just never shuts up.

Fernando gestures me forward. "Ellie Grant, this is Adrian. Don't play cards with him."

"Adrian. Good to meet you." I shake his hand and feel his carefully bridled yearning, and also the pain in his knees and hips from decades peddling his taxi. There's no hate in him, only determination to provide for his loved ones and some genuine awe with me. I don't know if he's picking up on my nature, or just smitten. I also feel a haze dampening his pain, and from the condition of his teeth, suspect cocoa leaves. Because it's an undeniable part of my nature, I take the worst of the torn cartilage and inflamed tendons from his knees and hips. "And we'll pay. I insist."

"If you insist." He doesn't react to the sudden easing of pain in his legs, probably due to the cocoa.

I try not to limp as we board the taxi, but the pain is as familiar as an old friend. It reminds me what I am, and helping good people helps me. I also feel as if I deserve it; penance for leaving Gippy in the hands of Hell's minions.

He pedals off at an impressive pace, and I take in my surroundings as we ride up the winding streets. It's easy to see that Las Brisas is a healthy community. There's pride here in the care people take in their homes and gardens, though the latter here is probably for necessity, rather than simple beautification. As we round switchbacks, climbing steadily, the pain in my joints slowly eases.

Fernando points out all the improvements since his last visit. "Canción's been busy!"

He's told me stories for four days at my request, both to distract me from my mood and give me a good picture of who Cora's son is. Canción's a good boy but temperamental, and his ability to absorb emotions and vent them in destructive energy is a little alarming. He seems to take negative emotions like I take injuries, but while I heal them, he expels them violently. He's truly had a positive influence here, and the people seem content and prosperous, if not exactly happy. Fernando calls out to old acquaintances as we climb the hill to a hacienda near the top. It commands a view of the bay and looks well kept. Canción is skilled in construction and demolition, it seems, tearing down the old and building the new. I find hope there, for this is something the world desperately needs right now.

The bike's worn brakes squeal to a stop under the covered drive, and I pay our driver.

Adrian gapes at the hundred NAD note I press into his hands. "This is too much. *Much* too much!"

"Nonsense. Buy your family something nice with it, and maybe some new brakes for your bike." I fold his fingers over the bill with a smile I don't feel.

"Thank you, kind lady." He looks at me strangely, as if wondering what I am, this comely yet bedraggled woman carrying a pack and battle rifle.

I let him wonder and follow Fernando to the door. He pulls a chain, and bells chime within. A middle aged Latina answers, and her eyes widen in shock.

"Fernando!" She lunges forth to grasp him in a crushing embrace. "My God how you've grown!" She holds him at arm's length, her features flushed with glee. "Canción will be delighted to see you!"

"Isabella, you're as lovely as ever!"

"Oh, you stop that!" She slaps his arm and ushers us in, her gaze roving over me. Suspicion, surprise, and caution radiate from her like an aura.

I follow them into a well-appointed foyer, high ceilings, tile floors, and a wrought iron balustrade up a curving stair. I hear a guitar in the distance. I know without thinking that tune is one of Cora's compositions, and my breath catches in my chest.

"Is he home?" Fernando askes. "Did he get our message?"

"Yes, and yes, though your telegram was too cryptic to understand. You might have been a bit more *specific*. How did you know?"

"Know?" Fernando pauses from putting his rifle in the rack beside the door, looking puzzled. "Know what?"

I see the worry in the woman's eyes now and know something's wrong. "What's happened?"

Isabella looks at me with one arched eyebrow. "And who is this?"

"Oh, I'm sorry! Ellie Grant, this is Isabella." Fernando doffs his poncho and bends to unlace his boots. "She helped raise us, Canción and me." He kicks a sodden boot over to a shoe rack beside the door, and I notice that Isabella's wearing house slippers.

I extend a hand to the woman. "Nice to meet you, Isabella. Canción's mother was my cousin."

"Miss Grant." She shakes my hand, and I feel her suspicion full force. She's very protective of Canción, the son she wanted and could never have. She's not afraid of me, but wary, thinks I'm too skinny, and hides a small pistol under her apron. I like her instantly.

"Can you tell me what's happened here?" I clear and rack my rifle and hang up my poncho. "We hoped to warn you, but thought we would arrive before the danger."

"We've had some... *difficulties* with Bishop Vargas, the prelate of La Popa. I'll let Canción tell it." She gestures to the shoes beside the door. "If you could please remove your boots. The damp, you understand."

"Of course." I bend to unlace my boots, habits of previous centuries reasserting themselves.

The guitar music ends, and a throaty, melodious male voice calls out from the stairs. "Isabella? Is that..."

I look up and see him, tall, wavy long hair the color of summer wheat with a thin beard. He has his mother's beauty and Emil's startling blue eyes. A wary-eyed Latina descends the stairs at his side, close enough to him that I know without thinking that they're intimate. I try not to stare at Canción as I hurriedly finish with my boots.

"Fernando!" Canción trundles down, his face splitting into an elated grin.

"Canción!" Fernando meets him with a hard embrace, laughing and pounding his back. "You look well, but what's this?" He tugs at Canción's scraggly beard. "No razors in Colombia?"

"Just too lazy to shave." He spots me, and his gaze lingers for a moment, curiosity written across his brow. He introduces the Latina with him, Angelica, and starts to ask about the obscure warning Franko sent.

"First, there's someone you should meet." Fernando extends a hand to me, and I approach, my bare feet cool on the tile floor. "Ellie Grant, this is Canción. She...um..."

"Your mother was my cousin, Canción." I resist extending a hand in greeting, knowing he'll understand what I am, and unsure if he'll want to reveal too much of himself to me. I've thought a long time about this meeting. The last thing I want to do is estrange him. I've come too far, lost too much to get here, to meet him, to discern God's plan in all of this. "Your father's a dear friend of mine."

"My..." His mouth gapes open with the news as he clearly tries to wrap his head around all the implications of what I've just told him. "I don't..."

"She's your cousin, Canción!" Angelica jostles his arm. "Don't just *stare* at her! I'm Angelica. Welcome to Casa Musica." She steps forward to extend a hand to me, and I take it.

"Angelica." The irony of her name catches up to me, and my smile is mostly genuine. I feel her love for Cora's son, though she has no idea what he truly is. She's a confident, friendly woman, and I feel no animosity in her at all, just caution and mild curiosity. I wonder if that's Canción's influence, if he's stripped away all of her negative feelings. "Thank you."

"You... *can't* be my cousin," Canción states flatly. "Mama said..."

"She *is*, you insufferable dork!" Fernando claps his arm hard and grips it. "And she's *literally* come through Hell and high water to find you, so greet her properly before I knock some hospitality into your thick head!"

"I'm sorry, I..." He looks abashed, but still confused. "Mother said all of her cousins were gone."

"I thought the same. Then I stumbled across your father and saw Cora's...um, Terisa's picture on his mantle." I smile and extend my hands to him, rethinking my strategy. He doubts my nature, and I have to show him. "I've got so much to tell you, but I need you to trust me first. Please."

Canción frowns, clearly reluctant, but finally nods and takes my hands.

He is like no human, Ageless, or Nephilim I've ever touched. I perceive the peak points of his life like mountaintops through clouds: Cora, her music, her love, watching his home destroyed with her inside, his love for Fernando, his reticence to love Angelica. When I reach deeper, however, I find myself facing a wall of resistance. For the first time in five millennia, I can't delve into a mortal's soul. He, however, plunges into me like a diver into calm water, a spear of determination and suspicion. I have no way to resist the intrusion—other than knocking him on his ass—and don't want to. I need him to know who and what I am.

Then, from nowhere, my anguish for Gippy's loss is wrenched from me. I gasp for a breath, feeling the removal of my sorrow like a violation. Before he can do more, I twist free of his grasp.

"Don't *do* that, please." I tell him. "Not to me."

"What did you—" Angelica's eyes are wide and accusing, flashing like dark daggers between us.

"I'm sorry, but you..." Canción glances at Fernando, then Anjelica, who is still staring at him accusatively.

"It's all right." It really isn't, but I need to smooth this over. I feel the void where my sorrow once was like a missing tooth. I need to speak to him privately, but I don't want to alienate the others. "We're a bit ragged from our journey, and..."

"Of course! Where are my manners?" Canción steps back and waves a hand. "My home is yours. We have plenty of room. Not as many modern conveniences as you may be used to, I'm afraid, but hot showers and fresh clothes. Then we'll have a meal together and catch up. I'm afraid you've come at a difficult time."

"*Difficult?*" Angelica scowls at him and opens her mouth, but he interjects.

"We'll explain once they're settled, Angelica. Please, Isabella, show them to the guest rooms." He endures a glare from his companion and waves us upstairs. "We've obviously got a lot to tell each other, but it'll be easier over lunch."

"Thank you." I doubt it'll be any easier at all.

We retrieve our packs and follow Isabella upstairs, harsh whispers between our host and hostess following us. I ignore them, still rattled by what Canción did. I feel as if I've been violated, but I know he meant no harm. Just as I took the taxi driver's injury without asking, he took my anguish. The latter seems more personal, however. I have to come to grips with his astonishing abilities, and how this could be part of Gods plan... if there is one.

The rooms are comfortable and well appointed, and I compliment Isabella. "You must work constantly to keep everything so beautiful in this climate."

"It does keep me busy, but I love my work." She shows me the attached bath. "Please conserve hot water. We have only cisterns and wind generators for electricity. This time of year we have more of both than we can use, but we provide for others with the surplus. There are towels, and you can leave your soiled things on the floor here. I'll bring you some fresh clothes and clean the rest."

She has a nice way of telling me I stink, and I smile my gratitude. "Thank you."

She leaves, and I divest myself of my pack and jacket, bundling my pistol in the bottom of my pack to keep it out of sight. There will be no such thing as privacy in this house. Canción isn't what I expected, and the intrusion of him removing my sorrow for Gippy's loss took me by surprise. Someone less attuned to the power wielded by Ageless might not have felt it, but I'm an empath. I also carry more emotional baggage than any living person. That's a part of who I am, and I don't want it torn away from me by someone I barely know. I don't know who I would be without it.

I recall something Gippy said to me in the midst of an emotional crisis. *It's supposed to hurt...* Without the pain of loss, I fear I'll be nothing but a shell.

The shower eases my nerves and washes away a week-long funk. I take the time to brush out my hair, don a robe, and find fresh clothes laid out on the bed; a blousy white shirt and draw string pants that are too long, probably Anjelica's. I dress—down to my last pair of clean underwear once again—and clip my holstered pistol in the back of my pants. I roll up the cuffs, slip into a pair of thin-soled house slippers that are too big, and step out into the hallway.

"Feel better?" Fernando leans on the wall, looking and smelling freshly scrubbed.

"Yes." I finger the lacy neck of my shirt. "Not exactly my style, but it feels nice to be clean."

"Come on. It'll feel even nicer to have a decent meal." He ushers me downstairs, obviously eager, having been barely able to keep down toast and porridge during our voyage.

The scents of cooking greet us as we enter a small but cozy dining room, the north wall an arc of windows overlooking the bay and half-drowned towers, ghostly in the slashing rain.

Canción stands from the table, Angelica at his side. I was hoping to speak to him alone, but that will have to come later. "Welcome." He gestures to two more seats. "Coffee?"

"Please, and thank you for the clothes." We sit, and he fills our cups from a silver service, the brew so black that it looks like tar. I sip, and it's glorious, stirring memories of years I spent with an Ottoman warlord after the fall of Constantinople. "Lord, that's wonderful. You have no idea what passes for coffee in NAFAS these days. You could make *millions* exporting this."

"Colombia barely harvests enough for local consumption, I'm afraid." Canción sips his, still eying me curiously. "You'll forgive me, Ellie, but...

I'm still having trouble accepting that you're my cousin. Mother was so sure she was the last of her... extended family."

"I hadn't seen her in a long time, and with things the way they are, keeping in touch was dangerous." I feel waves of suspicion from Angelica. She's probably thinking I'm too young to have known Canción's mother. I can't do anything about that right now. "I'm sorry for your loss, Canción. I loved your mother a great deal. She was very special to me."

"Thank you, but you're not here to simply touch base with family, right?" He nods to Fernando. "Your warning was a little cryptic, but something tells me you weren't referring to *our* current troubles."

"No. We don't know what's happening here." Fernando nods to me. "NAFAS soldiers tried to kill Ellie, and captured her companion, Gifford. They probably know about you by now, Canción, and will come looking for you."

"What?" Angelica looks startled. "Why would NAFAS be interested in Canción? And Colombia's out of their jurisdiction. They can't just *invade*!"

"They're interested in Canción because of his mother, I'm afraid." It's difficult to hedge around the elephant in the room, with three of us knowing so much more than Angelica. "She was special, as are all of our family. We've been hunted for... a very long time. Canción's of interest to them, and they'll—"

Isabella enters the room through a swinging door, a huge platter in her hands. She serves us without a word, and Canción thanks her. I wonder if she's been listening at the door. The fare is simple, the delicious aromas tantalizing; breadfruit, goat cheese, chick pea tortillas, and a savory chorizo dish. We all begin eating—Fernando like a starved wolf.

I pick up where I left off. "So, suffice to say, those who were after me won't be dissuaded by jurisdictional restrictions, and they won't *ever* stop. I don't know what's been happening here, however."

"I still don't understand why they'd be after Canción." Angelica's sharp, dark eyes flick from me to Canción and back. "And what do you mean that your family was *special*?"

"That's not my tale to tell. At least not to you." I nod to Canción. "It's his."

Angelica glares at him. "So *tell* me." She clearly has a temper and doesn't appreciate being left in the dark.

This is going to be difficult for Canción; he's been keeping a very big secret from her. I've been through it hundreds of times, but I'm not going to help him unless he asks or things go badly. It's not my place, and he needs to learn. Or maybe I'm just being a bitch for what he did to me.

Canción sighs and shakes his head. "My mother had the ability to spread love with her music, and not just by making people happy. It was... a gift given to her by... her father. I never really knew how special she was, or that I was also... gifted, until I just..." He sighs, pushes his nearly untouched meal away, and looks to me. "I'm not very good at this."

No, he certainly isn't.

"Gifted. What gift are you talking about?" Angelica's glare intensifies, and I can feel the conversation slipping into accusations and denials.

I intercede, finally. I can't allow our hostess to run screaming from the house. "You need to tell her, Canción, but I understand your reticence." Telling mortals of us, and all the implications of the War of Souls, rarely goes well.

"My mother told me to keep it a secret, that people would be after me if they found out."

"I know. I listened to her journal." I nod to Fernando.

Fernando swallows a half-chewed bite and washes it down with coffee. "When I found out Ellie was your cousin, I thought she should know everything. I hope you don't mind."

"Would all of you stop talking about this like I'm not here!" Angelica's temper flares like a beacon, and Canción winces. "Tell me the *truth*!"

"I... don't know how, honestly," he says, and I remember just how young he is.

"I do," I offer, "if you'll let me."

Canción nods. "Please, but before she does, Angelica, you have to understand, I was told to never tell *anyone*. Only Fernando and his parents know this. It's... kind of hard to swallow."

"Let *me* decide that, please!" Her eyes snap to mine. "So?"

I lay it out as simply as I can. "Canción's mother was the Ageless daughter of Israfal, Angel of Music."

Angelica's mouth drops open.

I continue before she can call bullshit. "Her birth name was Terpsichore. She was named one of the legendary muses of Greece, sometime around the beginning of the Bronze Age. I'm the daughter of Raphael, Angel of Healing and Empathy. I was born over five thousand years ago in the Middle East. There were two hundred of us begotten by the Seraphim all around the world, but with the death of Cora, I'm probably the last."

Angelica just stares at me, clearly disbelieving my story.

"She's telling the truth," Fernando interjects.

Angelica turns her gaze to Canción. "And *your* gift? What is it?"

"Um..."

"You need to understand something first," I interrupt. "Canción is the first of his kind, as far as I know. Ageless, like me, are generally unable to procreate, but his father was... different. He harbored the soul of a Nephilim, one of the agents of Hell, within himself, but it was unable to devour his soul due to his autism. Somehow, the union of an Ageless and a Nephilim produced progeny." I nod to Canción. "He can absorb negative emotions—hate, fear, anger, sorrow—and later expel them."

"Fucking *hell* you can!" Angelica's chair screeches on the tile and she lurches to her feet. "You didn't! You can't!"

Oh shit... I realize now that I was right in my earlier surmise; he's been stripping away her negative emotions without her knowledge or consent. This could go very, very badly.

"Angelica, please. I can't bear to see people in pain. I... do it without thinking. When your father was killed, I—"

"Bullshit! I don't believe you!" Her dark eyes flash to me. "None of it!"

I sigh in frustration; denial is pretty normal at this stage. "Angelica, please, just wait a moment." I've seen this before, and there's no way around it. I have to show her the truth to keep her from simply running away. "Fernando, can I ask you a favor?"

"Anything," he says without pause.

I hand him the small, sharp knife from a plate. "Could you cut your thumb for me, please."

"Sure." He slashes the little blade across his thumb without hesitation, blood welling from the cut. He doesn't even wince, Latino machismo intact.

I turn to our wide-eyed hostess. "Look at the wound, Angelica. I need you to believe it's real."

She does, trembling, pulse pounding at her throat, and nods.

I hold out my hand to Fernando, and he places his in mine. "Now watch closely." I take the small injury, and it appears on my own thumb, blood welling from the cut.

Angelica gasps and staggers back another step.

Fernando wipes the blood away, showing his healed thumb, and I show her mine.

"I'll heal this cut in a few minutes. I can do the same with disease and psychological trauma." I press the wound hard with a napkin, and the bleeding stops. I show her the parted flesh and feel her confusion, doubt, denial, and fear. "You're not hallucinating, Angelica. This is real."

Her reaction isn't what I expect.

Angelica's dark eyes flash to Canción. "You *fucker*!" Her open hand connects with his cheek squarely, hard enough to leave a red imprint. "You took my pain away! You didn't even *ask* me!"

"You wouldn't have believed me, and I was told to keep it a secret." Canción rubs his cheek. "But I probably deserved that."

"You did," I tell him. I can't really feel sorry for his plight; he has to learn to control his impulses. "I can't say I've never used my gift without consent, but healing infirmity or disease is different than psychological trauma. That, I've discovered the hard way, is generally not a good idea without consent." I hold a hand out to Angelica. "Will you sit and listen?"

"I... don't want *either* of you touching me. My feelings are my own." She sits, edging away from Canción.

"I understand completely." I withdraw my hand. "What neither of you know yet is that the Nephilim control most of NAFAS, and are actively hunting me now more than ever because Gifford and I discovered a way to exorcise and banish them permanently. This is the first time in five thousand years we've had a weapon against them, and they're afraid, which makes them even more dangerous. Now they probably know about Canción, whose very existence is unprecedented, so they'll never stop until they find him." *Probably... unless Gippy died before he gave me up.* But I know they would be careful breaking him, and there are many ways to inflict torture without lasting physical harm.

"Not the *only* weapon," Canción says.

It's my turn to stare at him in surprise. "What do you mean?"

"I..." He hesitates, casting another glance to Anjelica, and I feel his reticence. "The Bishop of La Popa sent his senior priest, Father Mateo, to negotiate with me over plans for the towers in the bay. They're still occupied, and the Bishop has... He calls the buildings the Towers of *God*. I want to dismantle them before they fall and kill people, but they're his... power base."

"Sounds typical," I offer. There's more to this story; I can see it in his eyes. "Please continue."

He does so haltingly. "Anyway, I'd never met Father Mateo, but he seemed strange to me. Cold, like opening a freezer whenever he was close."

"A *freezer*?" A ball of anxiety blossoms within me. "Tell me what happened."

"I tried to ignore the feeling. I thought I was just imagining it. The negotiations went nowhere, but he listened, so I thanked him, and we shook hands. When we did..." Canción glances at Angelica, then stares down at the table. "He felt wrong, inhuman, like a snake of ice coiled inside him. I felt it... him trying to infect me, so... I took it away."

"Mother of God," Angelica mumbles.

I have a different response, for this sounds like a possession. "Tell me, did he survive this?" If this was a possession, and he expunged the demon, the implications are huge, and perhaps a glimpse of God's overarching plan.

"He collapsed, but yes. He was confused, mumbling, barely coherent, but walked out with help." He glances at Angelica again. "I... destroyed the thing, and expelled it later where it couldn't hurt anyone. It was the most powerful and putrid thing I've ever contained, like a million insane, hate-filled minds all screaming at once. I didn't know what it was, but..." He looks back to me. "Could it have been one of the Nephilim?"

"No. The Nephilim destroy the soul of their host at birth. This was a demon of some kind, one of Purson's minions, from your description, but there are millions of them. That you destroyed it *completely* is... unbelievable." I wonder if he could do the same with a Nephilim; they have a much firmer grasp on their host's body than the other minions of Hell.

"Tell her the rest." Angelica's still upset, but holding it together. She's stronger than most. I've seen Saints run screaming when they learn of the War of Souls.

"Oh, yes, well... Father Mateo died later. We sent him back to La Popa at the bishop's insistence, and they said he had a heart attack." He shrugs. "There have been accusations against me. Murder, poisoning, even some rumors that I..." He shakes his head.

"Bishop Vargas accused him of being in league with Hell, that he cursed Father Mateo." Angelica sounds disgusted, her opinion of the bishop clear.

"We don't know if the Bishop's the source of the rumors, but they're spreading like wildfire among the residents of the towers, his followers." Canción rubs his eyes, clearly frustrated. "I've tried to talk to them, take their suspicions, but they won't listen."

"Accuse your opponents of the very crimes you're guilty of." I nod and sigh. "The oldest strategy of Hell." I realize that I've become sidetracked by these developments, and although they're enlightening, they're also irrelevant to our current situation. It's time to lay down the cold, hard truth. "None of this really matters. We need to decide where to go."

"Where to *go*?" Canción looks puzzled. "Why would we go anywhere?"

I see the confrontation before it even begins; he won't want to leave everything he's built here. He's young, confident, secure in his own little empire. I have to break it to him gently, but firmly.

"Canción, an army of NAFAS soldiers will be here in a matter of days, perhaps less. They're hunting me and they probably know about you. You can't fight them. We're lucky it's storm season, or we'd probably already be dead. *All* of us would be. These people don't pull their punches, and they command the North American Strategic Defense Network."

"You're saying they'd drop a *missile* on Cartagena?" I hear his disbelief.

"To eliminate me? Yes. In a heartbeat. They'll probably want to *capture* you, however. Trust me when I tell you that you don't want that to happen." Visions of what has undoubtedly happened to Gippy rise up, and my sorrow begins to fill the void that Canción left behind. "We have to go."

"But... everything I've built here. I can't just *abandon* these people."

Oh, sweet summer child... I have to explain, and flipping the argument on its head seems the easiest way. "If you stay, all these people will be slaughtered, Canción. I've seen it before. *Millions* of people have died trying to fight this war for me, and I don't want you to bear that burden." *Ireland, St. Louis, Cambodia, Constantinople, Europe more than once...* I see their faces in my mind, hear their screams. "If you don't want to watch your people die, you need to leave."

"I'm not leaving." He says it with all the surety of youth.

I feel like getting up and walking out, but I can't. I've paid too much, lost too much, to find this blend of Heaven and Hell, this piece of God's plan. There is one more thing that I can say to him, however.

"Then you're a fool, and you'll watch everything you've built here go up in flames."

"I can't abandon them," he counters, and I know the argument is lost.

"Fine. But I hope you're prepared to watch all your friends slaughtered, all you've built razed, all you love utterly destroyed." I stand and drop my napkin onto my plate. "Thank you for the meal. I hope it's not our last."

As I walk away, I hear them whispering, Angelica and Fernando adamant, pleading, and Canción's stoic refusal. I pray that they'll convince him, that he won't have to go through what I have. I doubt that God will grant my wish, however. She doesn't work that way.

~

Gippy viewed the world through a haze of rage and smoldering lust, feeling the thoughts of the incubus Ardat in his mind like an infection in his soul, slowly grinding him to a pulp. He'd never imagined such vile depravity, the longing to despoil every human soul, to seduce them into Hell, damn them all to an eternity of suffering. He'd tried to pray at first, but thoughts of God wouldn't congeal through the fog of hate. The memories of what Ardat had done to Chaki, what *he* had done to her that opened the door for the demon, sickened him on a visceral level. And then, after, he'd told her everything, or Ardat had. With the incubus constantly in his mind, he was having difficulty parsing out his own thoughts from the demon's, the burning need to corrupt all of humanity, to seed corruption in their souls.

Only thoughts of Empa, her lessons, her grace, kept the darkness at bay. *Steady spirit...*

They'd found no trace of her in or around Boquete. Interrogations yielded little, even under the demonstrated threat of violence. They left the town cowering in terror and headed for Punta Peña.

"You better be right about this, Ardat." The Nephilim wasn't the sharpest sword in the armory, but war required blunt instruments, too.

"Right?" The demon who occupied Gippy sneered at the dolt. "Even if Empa's gone to ground, we need to find this... *thing*, this get of Ageless and Nephilim. But she *will* try to find him. I *know* she will." And Ardat knew because Gippy knew. The demon knew *everything* Gippy knew: Jeri, Emil Farrell, the slippery mind theory, Fernando and his father, and Terpsichore's son.

Canción...

That was the true revelation here, the real puzzle, and perhaps a weapon for Hell to wield. The Nephilim who had been sent to take out Terpsichore hadn't known about a child, but Gippy had told them of Cora's journal, her relationship with Emil Farrell, and the astonishing result. What powers the offspring of Heaven and Hell combined might wield hung like a burning golden ring. And what was more, if they could capture Empa, they could make more. Gippy felt his mouth stretch into a sadistic grin as the demon's thoughts ranged into all the depravities he would rain upon the Ageless if they managed to take her alive. If Terpsichore could raise her half-Nephilim child to be loving and caring, the minions of Hell could raise them to be equally vile. They would breed an army of warriors, corrupt them from birth, and lay waste to humanity.

Run, Empa... just run...

The NAFAS convoy hit Punta Peña like the storm front that followed the brief calm between hurricanes. Locals fled, hid, and huddled in fear, as they should. The Hounds of Hell had the scent and would stop at nothing to find their quarry. The vehicles howled to a stop at the harbor quay, and soldiers piled out into the storm, weapons at the ready.

"Secure this shithole, Sergeant!" the Nephilim captain barked over the radio. "Find out if the terrorist was here!"

"I need an ultranet connection." Gippy stepped out of the vehicle into the slashing rain and buffeting wind, the hurricane-force rain stinging his face. Of course, Ardat felt no pain, but Gippy did. The lingering ache a broken finger, neck trauma, concussion, and his time with Chaki still plagued him.

"Why?" The Nephilim's eyes narrowed, almost accusative.

"To root out the Ageless' network," Chaki said derisively. "You're not the only hound on the hunt."

"And to empty her bank account," Gippy added. They'd tried to find some way to access the net in David but hadn't even found an old fashioned land line that worked. Satellite connections were spotty at best, and every time Gippy tried to call Empa's bank, the call failed before he could log in. One of the downsides of the climate apocalypse was that violent weather interfered with technology, their greatest weapon. "We need to remove her resources. This is a shipping terminal. They must have communications of some kind."

The captain nodded once and snapped his fingers. "Fine. Corporal, assign two men to go with them."

Gippy and Chaki staggered around the storm-lashed little harbor toward the small shipping terminal, hunched against hurricane winds. The terminal yard was empty, the last shipment of fuel from Colombia already trucked out, but a light burned in the single building's windows. The door was locked, but a soldier's boot solved that.

"Who the fu—" The fat man behind the cluttered desk froze in mid-protestation, his pendulous jowls quivering, eyes bulging at the rifles leveled at him. On his desk sat an old-fashioned flat-screen and keyboard.

"We need communications," Gippy barked in Spanish, a language he didn't know. Ardat spoke dozens of languages, some long dead, however, so Gippy could as well. "A land line, an ultranet connection, a radio link. Anything. Now!"

"I have only a shortwave connection, but it's spotty." He nodded to the tangle of electronics cluttering a shelf behind his desk. "And a Packet modem."

"Packet modem?" Gippy had no idea what that was, and neither did Ardat, having been in Hell for the last century or so, but Chaki did.

"A radio computer connection. Slow, but it'll do." She stalked around the desk. "Move your fat ass."

"Sure! Whatever you need!" He lurched up and staggered away, his hands up, fingers like sausages shaking.

Gippy watched Chaki expertly navigate the technology, finding a radio band that could support modem traffic, relaying through stations in half a dozen cities before connecting finally to the network of low-orbit ultranet satellites. She could communicate, though at a snail's pace. He gave her addresses, phone numbers, and account logins as fast as she could type them in. NAFAS authorities would be deployed to Jeri's and Father Farrell's addresses. Pinging their phones, however, resulted in a no-show. They were completely out of service, which didn't bode well. When they accessed Empa's bank account, the balance showed only fifty-thousand NADs.

"She's cleaned it out and warned them," Gippy said. "Leave the money there. If we take it, she'll know her minion cracked under interrogation. Her lover and the priest are long gone."

Hope flickered in Gippy's tortured mind. *Jeri... Thank you, E...*

"Fuck!" Chaki slammed her fist down on the desk. "We're fucked!"

"Not yet." Gippy pulled a hand-held VHF radio and pressed the mic button. "Captain Hernandez, we're online. You can contact your people in Cartagena."

"Excellent! They left here three days ago. We're securing transport."

"Transport?" Chaki looked up at him. "Does he mean a *boat*?"

"No other way to get there, is there?" There were no roads from Panama to Cartagena, and nothing could fly through the storm.

"We don't *need* to go! Hernandez can contact Bogota and send a fucking *army*!" Chaki reached for her hand-held, but before she could key the mic, the Nephilim burst through the door. She stood and confronted him. "You're *insane* if you think we can take a boat to Cartagena in this shit! Contact Bogota and let the Colombians take care of it."

"No. This is *my* hunt! Get out of my way!"

"Idiot!" Chaki backed away. The Nephilim was calling the shots here, but if they all drowned trying to make it to Cartagena through a category three hurricane, the hunt would end and the Ageless would escape.

Gippy tugged Chaki aside, speaking in a whisper only she could hear. "When he's through, text your contact in LA. This is bullshit."

She nodded. If their human hosts perished, at least someone would follow up where they left off.

19
CARTAGENA BLUES

Canción stared at the smoldering ruins of his neighbor's home, hurricane winds hammering against his back, the relentless rains quenching the flames of the bomb that had been meant for him. "How can people *do* this?"

"Don't be a fucking idiot!" Angelica was still angry with him, though he still couldn't fully understand why.

Empa had been the first one to ever actually feel what he was doing when he delved into her mind. Even his mother hadn't known he was infiltrating her soul until after, when her fear and anguish were suddenly gone. Now Angelica knew what he'd done, and didn't trust him to even touch her, wouldn't let him take her pain, her anguish, her hurt.

Maybe she shouldn't trust me. He could feel her raging emotions and longed to remove them, to gather up all the fear, anger, and sorrow spreading like wildfire through Las Brisas and expel it in a torrent of destruction that would blow La Popa right off the map. But he couldn't. Angelica had told him flat out that taking people's pain without their consent was wrong, a violation of trust. He clenched his fists in impotent rage and ignored her comment.

"I hate to say I told you so, but..."

Canción glared at Empa. Her constant haranguing wasn't helping; it was only stoking his anger. "How the hell was I supposed to know the

Bishop's cultists would strap *bombs* to themselves and try to *assassinate* me?"

"Because I *told* you." She fixed him with that smoldering, calm stare that unnerved him.

He'd felt what she was and couldn't deny her angelic origin. Empa reminded him of his mother in that, if nothing else. She was much more of a warrior than his mother had been, insisting they go armed wherever they went, fortifying the house, carrying that rifle of hers anytime they stepped out the door. He had felt how much she loved people; she was just more brutal about it than his mother had been. Or at least more brutal than she had ever been with him.

"This is your fault as much as Bishop Vargas's," Empa added, twisting the knife of guilt.

"This was *not* my fault!" The unfair accusation tipped him over the edge. Two steps, and his hands closed on the collar of her poncho, her rifle pressed between them as he lifted her up onto her toes, his nose an inch from hers. "I didn't *kill* these people!"

"Canción!" Angelica snapped, but he wasn't listening.

"Brother..." Fernando's hand settled on his shoulder, but he ignored it.

Canción just glared into Empa's deep hazel eyes. He wanted to rip away her arrogance, her self-righteousness, her sanctimonious accusations...

"Let go of me, Canción," she said calmly, and he felt the aura of her heritage, his own heritage, impelling him. He also felt something sharp prodding him in the groin. "Or I'll cut your dick off." She prodded harder, and knew she wasn't bluffing.

He released her and stepped back, still angry, still glaring. "This was *not* my fault!"

"You're young, brash, and overconfident." She slipped the combat knife back beneath her poncho and rested her hand on the grip of her battle rifle, calm as still water, which was even more infuriating. "I told you they would come after you, that you'd have to watch friends die, see everything you've built here burn, and you refused to believe me. Now you're paying the price. I'm sorry you had to learn this lesson the hard way, but sometimes you have to experience failure to learn wisdom."

"Don't *preach* to me," he growled through clenched teeth. "These people were my *friends*! I helped build this house with my own hands! I watched their children play."

"I know." Still, she remained calm, poised, as if ready for him to fly off the handle again, but there was pity in her eyes. "I've been through this a thousand times, Canción. If we leave, Vargas's cultists won't have a reason to murder your friends and reduce Las Brisas to a pile of bombed out buildings. Stay, and they'll continue. The equation's simple."

"It's not an *equation*! These are *people*!" He didn't understand how someone like her, his mother's cousin, could be so cold.

"It *is*, and being emotional about it won't help you make a decision. You have to see this logically." She shook her head sadly. "High spirit is weak. Low spirit is weak. Steady spirit is strong. Don't show your spirit to your enemies."

"I don't need lessons on my *emotions*!" he growled.

"Yes, you do, more than anyone I've ever met, because of the power you wield." She turned away, shielding her eyes from the stinging rain, scanning the sodden neighborhood. "We should go home before another cultist decides to murder you. This could have been a ploy to pull you out into the open."

Canción hadn't thought of that, couldn't think of anything clearly through his rage. Maybe she was right; anger never helped, it only blinded you. He couldn't absorb his own anger, however, couldn't expel it in destruction. Only when he took someone else's negative emotions first could he expel his own, and nobody would let him. He could do it without their consent, but that would only make things worse. He longed to lash out, to blame someone for all of this, but he knew deep down that Empa was right. If he'd left Las Brisas, this wouldn't have happened.

"Fine." He turned away and led them back up the hill toward Casa Musica, hating himself and everyone else for this. He'd never asked to be the first child of Heaven and Hell, had never wanted this gift, or curse, or whatever it was.

They trudged back up the hill, bent against the wind and slashing rain. Few others were outdoors in this weather, but there were faces aplenty peering down at them from behind cracked storm shutters. The explosion had rattled windows for a block around the destroyed house. Six people he had known were dead. He remembered their elation when they moved into the newly rebuilt home, the children's glee with the clean, dry, safe space of their own. All that was destroyed now, his fault, and no place was safe.

Canción turned onto Casa Musica's stone-paved drive, his thoughts a muddle, ignoring his surroundings and the accusatory faces of the people he loved, guilt drowning him like the unrelenting rains. He mistook the gunshots for the crack of close-by thunder, but something tugged hard at his arm, spinning him to his right. Then, to his left, Angelica started to fall. At a glance, he saw the spray of blood through the rain, her blood. He opened his mouth, trying to move, to catch her, to react, but stood frozen. She hit the paving stones bonelessly.

A rifle roared, six rounds so fast it sounded like a roofer's nail gun, but deafening. He felt the shock of the muzzle blasts, saw the flash of his own shadow, strobe-like against the bloody paving stones. Empa knelt close beside him, her battle rifle aimed back down the street. Fernando fumbled for a pistol from under his poncho. Fifty feet away, a woman lay on the ground, a pistol in her hand, her back a mire of blood and torn meat.

Empa stood up, rifle still poised, sweeping the street. "Anyone hit?"

Hit? Everything suddenly registered, gunfire, blood, pain...

"Angelica!" His knees hit the pavers beside her, and he reached for her, but his left arm wasn't working. He touched the two holes in her back with his right hand, bloody, and she wasn't moving. The cracks between the paving stones beneath her ran with bloody water.

"Shit!" Empa handed her rifle to Fernando. "Check the shooter and cover us! There could be more." She knelt and placed a hand on the back of Angelica's neck. "She's alive, but critical. We need to get her to the house, now!"

"Canción's hit," Fernando said.

Empa turned to him. "Your arm. Here!" She reached for him, and he remembered her taking the cut from Fernando's thumb.

He jerked away. "No! Help Angelica!"

"I *will*, Canción, but I can't lift her, and Fernando's covering us. Let me take your injury, then you can carry her to the house. I'll make sure she doesn't die on the way, but if I heal her here, I'll be incapacitated, and you can't carry us both!"

He couldn't believe how calm and pragmatic she sounded, like explaining the rules of a game to a confused child. But it made sense. He nodded. "Okay."

She put a hand on his arm, and the pain vanished in an instant. He hadn't known how much it hurt until it was gone. She winced, cradling her now injured arm, and nodded to Angelica.

"Roll her over gently and lift her. Try to keep her spine straight." Empa looked over her shoulder. "Fernando?"

"Road's clear. Shooter's dead. Four to the chest, one to the head. Nice shooting!"

"Okay, we're going. *Now*! Roll and lift!" Empa rested a hand on Angelica's slack face as Canción rolled her over.

Two much larger exit wounds in her stomach and lower right chest had leaked a horrible amount of blood onto the paving. She didn't respond as he lifted her in his arms, her face deathly pale. They quick marched to the door, Empa bent over, staggering. She must have taken some of Anjelica's injuries as well.

Isabella was there, her face ashen, a pistol in her hand. "My God! Oh, my God!"

"Just lay her on the floor there," Empa instructed.

They shouldered past Isabella, and Canción lowered Angelica gently onto the floor. She coughed blood, her head lolling.

"Fernando, secure the doors, all of them." Empa knelt again, blood dripping from the fingers of her left hand. "Now, Canción, *listen* to me! I can't take all of her injuries, but I can stabilize her. I'll take the rest later. If I pass out, prop me up in an armchair. If you don't, I'll drown in my own blood. Do you understand me?"

"Yes. Yes, no problem. Just help her, *please*." Canción hated the panic in his voice. This was his fault, all his fault.

"Cancion? What happened? What's she talking about?" Isabella stood close by, still holding her pistol.

He didn't have time to explain. "Someone started shooting at us, and Angelica was hit. Ellie's going to help her. It's..." But Empa was already laying her hands on Angelica's face.

There was no glow or anything visible. Empa just groaned and slumped to the floor, barely catching herself. The once shredded flesh that he'd seen through the bloody fabric of Anjelica's shirt now shone pink and unblemished.

"Mother of God!" Isabella crossed herself and stepped back.

"Granddaughter, actually," Fernando quipped as he dashed from one room to the next, Empa's rifle still in hand.

Angelica's eyes fluttered and she coughed again, more blood. Canción wiped her mouth with his sleeve and sat her up. "Angelica?" He patted her face, and she blinked, swallowing hard.

"What... happened?" She looked around, clearly dazed. "My chest hurts."

"You were shot. Ellie healed you, but not completely." He lifted her again and took her to the hallway divan. "Just rest here for a moment."

She nodded, staring blankly down at Empa, who lay with her head supported on one arm, blood trickling from her mouth. "Is she all right?"

"She said she would be. I've got to move her. Just rest." He hurried back to Empa and lifted her. She coughed a spray of blood onto his shirt, and there was more on the floor beneath her. "Isabella, throw a towel over the den chair. We have to keep her upright."

"Yes... yes." Her paralysis seemed to break, and she hurried away, stuffing the pistol into a pocket.

By the time Canción reached the den, Isabella had four large kitchen towels spread out on the deeply cushioned chair. He laid Empa into it gently, and found her eyes open and staring at him.

"Now... do you... understand?" She coughed again, her breathing ragged. "They'll never... stop coming... after you."

"I understand." And he did. He was being stupid, and Empa's calm in the midst of such violence quenched his rage like the storm had quenched his friends' burning house. *My fault. All my fault.* "We have to leave Las Brisas. As soon as there's a break in the weather, we'll take a ferry to the mainland."

"Good." She closed her eyes and patted his hand, leaving bloody fingerprints. "Thank you."

~

Gippy strode beside Chaki into the Convent of Santa Crus, de la Popa, soaked, aching, and weary from the tortuous crossing. At least he felt the chill, pain, and fatigue, but he doubted the demon Ardat felt anything. The commandeered ferry they'd taken from Punta Peña had suffered badly, but the NAFAS soldiers crammed into the hold had suffered worse. Neither Gippy nor Ardat cared in the slightest, just about the only thing they had in common. He had prayed without hope that the vessel would be overwhelmed by the storm and they'd all drown. At least that would have saved Empa's life and maybe his soul.

Slowly, inexorably, Gippy felt that he was losing the battle with the incubus that occupied him. The constant assault of lurid, violent, hateful thoughts was wearing him down. He could feel himself giving in to the evil. His spirit was slowly sliding down a slippery slope, and he couldn't stop it.

A priest bowed in greeting as they stepped into the foyer, his long black coat spotless and freshly pressed. "Bishop Vargas received your message, Captain Hernandez. He's requested a private audience to discuss a cooperative effort to bring these devil-worshiping terrorists to justice."

"Good! Take us to him." The Nephilim barely broke stride.

Gippy and Chaki shared a glance and followed, at the mercy of the Nephilim. The plea for intervention that she'd sent up the chain of command had been met with a resounding, "Shut the hell up and do as you're told." Neither of them was happy, but maybe the Nephilim that posed as Bishop Vargas would be more cautious. Fifty centuries of invulnerability had taught the Nephilim hubris. Now that they were being banished permanently, maybe they'd learn some prudence. Ardat, having known dozens of Nephilim over the centuries, doubted it.

Their guide paused before a pair of lofty doors guarded by two men in monks' robes. Gippy could see the bulges of weapons beneath the coarse brown cloth. "No weapons are allowed in His Excellency's presence, I'm afraid."

"Of course." Hernandez handed over his pistol and nodded to Gippy and Chaki.

She carried only the folding pearl-handled knife, and handed it over. Gippy had kept the Glock Empa had given him, since he was familiar with it, and Ardat knew nothing of modern firearms. He pulled the weapon, ejected the magazine and the round in the chamber, and handed them and his combat knife over to one of the guards. The priest nodded politely and opened the doors.

The audience chamber was lavish in the extreme, red velvet and gold adorning the walls, the furniture, and even the floor. The man sitting in a deeply upholstered chair with gaudy gold accents was clad in a black house cassock with a crimson sash. The necessary gold cross lying upon his chest made Gippy's skin crawl, and he realized this was the first time Ardat had felt any discomfort at all.

Demons don't like crosses... Good to know. He wondered why the Nephilim wasn't bothered by it. Demons were different than devil-spawn, evidently.

The bishop himself was ancient for a human, flesh sagging on skeletal features, eyes deep and dark rimmed, lips like shriveled lemon peels parting to reveal teeth the color of weak tea with too much milk. A hand like a knobby claw twitched as they approached, and a young nun came forward with a silver tray bearing a crystal carafe and four glasses.

"Thank you for the audience, Your Excellency." Hernandez bowed, then motioned to Gippy and Chaki. "These are my assistants, undercover agents in our service. Both have personal experience with the terrorists we seek. I hope we can work together to solve this debacle quickly."

"Have some wine, Captain, please," Bishop Vargas offered. The nun proffered the tray to him and filled his glass with a curtsey, her dark eyes downcast.

Through the incubus, Gippy could feel the woman's fear, though she hid it well. The demon fantasized about her, wondering if she was having sex with the Bishop, and how often, and if she enjoyed it. The demon's memories of previous possessions, the corruption within the church that he'd helped foster, the young choir boys castrated to keep their voices high and pure, and the priests who regularly abused them. Gippy, disgusted, felt a nascent erection as Ardat planned to indulge himself later with the nun, corrupt her utterly as he had so many before.

"Thank you, Your Excellency." Hernandez took a glass, and the nun expertly filled it.

As Gippy and Chaki followed suit, he caught the nun's eye briefly, and the incubus felt her fear intensify. "Thank you." Ardat sipped the wine. "Quite *delicious*." Gippy felt her shiver of terror through the demon's supernatural perceptions, could see in his mind what Ardat wanted to do to her, and it made him sick.

Steady spirit, Gip. That's not you. You wouldn't do that... He prayed that Ardat wouldn't have the opportunity, both for the nun's sake, and his own.

"Leave us, sister," the bishop rasped. "Father Vasquez, please wait outside. We wish to speak to our guests in private."

"Yes, Your Excellency." The priest motioned the nun out and backed out of the room. The doors boomed closed, and they were alone.

"Nice little empire you've carved out here, Son of Samsaveel." The Nephilim captain raised his glass to the bishop with a mocking smile. "Well done."

Samsaveel... As before, everything the incubus knew, Gippy knew. The image of a terrible mass of blackness looming to blot out the sun flashed into his mind, Samsaveel, the Angel of Darkness and Deception. Ardat had met the Nephilim in previous incarnations, and his father, the Grigori, in Hell. Taking the position of a Catholic bishop, hiding like a wolf in a herd of sheep, the Nephilim obviously took on the traits of his sire.

"Deception and despair are my specialties, Son of Ertael." The Bishop sipped his wine with a quavering hand, eying Gippy and Chaki with rheumy eyes. "Who are these two?"

The captain nodded to them each in turn. "The succubus Duvara, and the Ageless's former companion, newly possessed by the incubus, Ardat. He's proven a most useful ally."

"Who *I* recruited," Chaki interjected.

"Yes, well..." the Nephilim bishop grinned at her, "succubi *do* have their uses."

Another arrogant fuck, Ardat thought, though he held his tongue.

The Nephilim captain ignored the interruption. "What's been done here to neutralize the Ageless?"

The bishop's grin faded. "Many things, none of them successful, but you failed to warn me about the other one's capabilities. Before the Ageless even arrived, one of my minions was either banished or utterly destroyed."

"Canción." Ardat took a step, suddenly intent, and Gippy could feel a core of fear smoldering within the incubus's corrupt soul. "What happened?"

"I sent one of my dybbuk-possessed priests to corrupt him under the guise of negotiations, and he came back to me empty. I don't know how, but the boy has some... power."

Gippy felt the incubus rifling through his memories. "This is new. Formerly, he seems to have been able to absorb emotions—fear, anguish, anger—and expel them in destructive energy. If he can do the same to a demon, we're in trouble."

"*You're* in trouble," the son of Ertael scoffed. "Demons are a dime a dozen. He wouldn't have the same luck with one of *us*."

"Arrogant ass," Chaki hissed. "You said the same thing about being exorcised, until four of you were banished to Hell permanently!"

The NAFAS captain opened his mouth, but the bishop raised one gnarled hand. "She has a point, cousin. We should tread carefully here. The problem is, Las Brisas is now well defended. Canción has allies, former gang members he's recruited as muscle. They're armed and are now turning away any boats we send. We can't call in air support from Bogota with this weather, even if I *did* have sway with the military, which I unfortunately do not. We have agents within the government, but none highly placed in the military. Assaulting the island directly on our own would be costly."

"We have soldiers to spend," the captain insisted. "Can't you contact the Cardinal for support? He could convince the president to..." He fell silent at the old man's shaking head.

"The cardinal is a truly devout man, I'm afraid, and he's been suspicious of me for a very long time. Supportive because he has to be, but there have been some... incidents in my past that he's learned about." The old man's tone brimmed with resentment. "That's one reason I was sent here, to the ass-end of this country."

"Fortunate that the Church is as good at hiding its own transgressions as it is at corrupting choir boys," Ardat said. Memories of previous possessions—priests, inquisitors, monks over the centuries—and all the depravities the demon had committed, rose up in Gippy's mind like a tide of filth.

"Indeed, but I can't wage war on Las Brisas. We've sent assassins, but to no avail." The bishop finished his wine and put the glass down on a tiny table beside his chair. "We need a surgical strike to take them both out."

"You're both missing an opportunity here, I think," Ardat interjected once again. "Canción's unique in the world, the first union of Ageless and Nephilim, and he has a unique power. We can *use* that."

"He's incorruptible," the bishop insisted. "I've been trying for years."

"Perhaps, but from what I've learned, he has a temper, too," the incubus pointed out. "If we can provoke him to act rashly, then exploit the opportunity to neutralize him and *capture* the Ageless, we could create more like him and corrupt them from birth."

The two Nephilim stared at him without a word, as if astonished that a demon could plan something so elegant. In fact, Ardat couldn't, but the incubus knew Gippy's deepest terrors, and exploited them.

"That would be dangerous," the son of Ertael said. "The Ageless is capable and experienced in combat. She killed four of my soldiers and evaded us in Boquete. She won't be taken easily."

"But the human I've possessed *knows* her," Ardat insisted. "She'll be with Canción; he's the whole reason she's here. If we can provoke him into doing something rash, she'll remain with him. We could take them both, or kill him and capture her."

"Provoke him *how*?" the Nephilim captain asked.

"He has a temper. We do something that will ignite it." He looked to Chaki and grinned. "I'm sure we can think of *something*."

"Yes..." The sheer malevolence in the bishop's voice sent a shiver through Gippy's soul. "Yes, I do believe I have an idea. My followers in the

Towers of God have had an adversarial relationship with the islanders to the south. I've labeled them infidels and pagans. I suggest we use them."

"What else are humans for?" The son of Ertael nodded to Ardat. "Give my soldiers a day to recover from our trip, and we'll round up some peasants for you."

20
ROCK AND A HARD PLACE

"A boat has arrived at La Popa," Isabella announces as she enters the sitting room with a tray of coffee and sopapillas. "Our spy says they're NAFAS. Two large armored vehicles and a number of soldiers, but there are two others with the captain in charge who aren't soldiers, a man and a woman. They say they're spies."

"A boat in this weather?" Canción looks doubtful. "That's insane."

"Or desperate." I shift in my chair to accept a cup and one of the pastries.

Canción's housekeeper impresses me; the epitome of someone who isn't what they first appear to be. Isabella is a motherly hostess, and I'm taking full advantage, still recovering from the injuries I took from Angelica. She also has connections all over Las Brisas, Turbaco, the outer islands, and even within La Popa. She's Canción's spymaster, though she would deny it. She also accepted what I am without panicking, which might also have been Canción taking her fear away.

The more time I spend with him, the more he worries me. I don't know whether he's compelled to destroy negative emotions, or simply addicted to his own power. It took me centuries of dealing with panicked humans to learn impulse control, and even now, sometimes, I can't help myself, as with the taxi driver, Adrian. I am my father's daughter, and Canción is the grandson of music and destruction. I remember his sweet voice from the recording we heard in the restaurant in Boquete, and I wonder now if Cora's ceaseless love stabilized his penchant for violence, if without her he's devolving.

Then I recall what Isabella said about two people with the NAFAS captain. "Do you have descriptions of the other two?"

"Yes." Isabella continues serving the others as she speaks. "A Latina who likes to wear tight ripped jeans and tee shirts, and a slim black man, young and attractive but frightening."

My cup hits the floor, shattering with my soul. "Oh, dear God... Gippy..."

Isabella's there in an instant with a dish towel, her eyes wide with concern. "Who's Gippy?"

I swallow my horror. *Steady spirit.* "My... companion who was caught and interrogated in Boquete."

"Your friend Gifford?" Fernando looks puzzled. "Why would he be helping them?"

"He wouldn't." I force myself up from the chair to help clean up my mess, but Isabella's already collected the shards of my cup before I can kneel. "I'm sorry. It's just..." Her description of the Latina with Gippy spurs a memory of his interaction with Chaki, the succubus at the chop shop in Albuquerque. All the pieces fall together—how they found us through our vehicles, the unrelenting pursuit, and now, Gippy... and why he's helping the Nephilim. "He's been possessed. The woman's a succubus. Somehow, she's..." Exactly how a succubus would have tormented my friend to the point where a demon could invade his soul comes to me in a wave of revulsion and sorrow. "Oh, my poor son..." My knees quake, and I lean on my chair to remain standing.

"You need to sit." Angelica's at my side, gently forcing me back into my chair. She's not much stronger than me at this point, since we're both weak from blood loss.

"Then they know everything about us." Fernando begins to pace the room, his hands flexing rhythmically at his sides. "They'll come for us all."

"Yes, they will." I turn to Canción imploringly. "We need to flee *now*."

"We have to wait for a break in the weather," he insists. "The boats aren't running."

"La Popa's are," Isabella says, and we all look to her with questions in our eyes. "They're conducting raids on the islands with NAFAS soldiers, kidnapping people. It's random."

"Hostages?" Fernando looks worried and angry.

"Maybe, but..." Canción looks at me, curiosity and horror vying for supremacy on his face. "What are they planning?"

I shake my head, unwilling to speculate, unable to force my thoughts away from Gippy, my poor lost son. The chasm of sorrow that Canción emptied is now full to overflowing.

~

Canción glared through binoculars at the crowded, pitching boat, his dread building. "Fifteen prisoners, four soldiers, one officer, and a priest on deck." He swept the lenses forward. "Two people in the wheelhouse. I can't see them very well."

"May I?" Empa held out a hand, and he gave her the binoculars.

He felt her soul-crushing sorrow like a chill aura, wishing he could take it from her. He'd even asked, but she'd refused. She was in that deadly calm state that he'd seen before, ice water in her veins. He watched her focus on the boat motoring against the wind and chop a hundred meters from Las Brisas's ferry dock. They'd sheltered in the harbormaster's office a block up the hill, but a crowd of locals lined the quay wall despite the unrelenting storm.

"It's them," Empa said, her voice as steady as her grip on the binoculars. "Gippy and the succubus." She handed the lenses back and reached for her battle rifle.

He stared at her as she removed the scope covers and leveled the weapon, aiming through the window. "What are you doing?"

"I'm going to free him." The rifle jostled minutely. "Hold fucking *still*!"

"Wait, please," he said.

"No." Her finger moved from the guard to the trigger.

Canción put a hand on the barrel and pushed down. "You're not going hit a man from two hundred yards, on a pitching boat, through hurricane force winds, and two panes of storm glass."

Her eyes bored into his, cold and hard as a glacier. "Take your hand off my weapon."

"If you start shooting, they'll—"

Isabella's radio crackled, and a voice came through.

"People of Las Brisas, this is Father Vasquez of La Popa. You are harboring two international terrorists. The man you know as Canción Wagner is an emissary of the Devil. He placed a curse on Father Mateo that resulted in his death. The NAFAS authorities here are pursuing a woman calling herself Eloise Grant, one of her many false names. She, too, is an agent of Satan, a foul witch who lies with demons. Bring these two forward, and we will release these poor infidels. If you continue to harbor these minions of Satan, the Church will have no choice but to execute one prisoner per hour until you hand them over to us. If you bring them forward, you will be rewarded in Heaven. Refuse, and you will all burn in Hell."

"*Now* will you let me shoot?" Empa's eyes had never left his through the priest's speech.

"Do you really think you can hit—"

"We have a problem." Fernando nodded through the window.

A scuffle had broken out among the spectators on the quay, and a number of people had broken away to advance on the harbormaster's office. Several of them were armed. He recognized a few of the ganger security force among them, but they didn't seem to be urging restraint. In fact, they looked like they were out for blood.

"Now we're in deep shit." Empa slung her rifle and pulled a pistol. Fernando already had one in his hand.

Canción wore one at his hip, but didn't draw it. "Let me talk to them. We're not going to start shooting our friends." He hurried to the door.

"And if *they* start shooting?" Empa asked, one dark eyebrow arched.

"They won't. Trust me." He heard Empa mutter a curse before he stepped outside and the wind tore the rest of her words away.

Canción faced the small mob, hands raised. "Friends, neighbors, don't do this."

"Devil worshiper!" a woman in the fore screeched, pointing a shaking finger at him.

He recognized her. "You know better than that, Loretta. I helped build your house, broke up the pavement for your garden. And you, Horatio, I built your chicken coops. Benito, I installed your cisterns and helped you with the pluming."

They kept coming, but there was doubt on some of their faces now.

"Father Vasquez said you were a devil worshiper!" Loretta continued.

"And you *believe* him?" Canción spread his hands in helpless supplication. "He threatens to kill your neighbors if you don't hand me over to their NAFAS dogs, and you think he's telling you the *truth*?"

"They blew up the Conseco's house trying to kill you!" another man said. "If we don't hand you over, they'll kill us all!"

"Bernardo, I understand that you're afraid. So am I, but the Church is supposed to be *good,* not evil. Is it *good* to take hostages and threaten to murder them if you don't hand me over to NAFAS soldiers to be tortured and killed? Is *that* the right thing to do? Is that what Jesus Christ would do?" He hated invoking religion, but at this stage he'd use any weapon he could get his hands on.

"But if we don't, they'll murder our neighbors!"

"And *that* is an evil act, murdering innocents. If I could wave my hand and stop them, I would, but I can't. I'll also not give myself up hoping to stop them, because it probably won't." He pointed to La Popa, barely visible through the storm. "*There* is the evil, my friends. If they capture and kill me, do you think they'll treat you all any better? Vargas sends his own followers to murder me with explosives strapped to themselves. Do you think he'll allow word of his atrocities to reach Bogota and the Cardinal?"

That brought them up short, and Canción could feel their mood shifting. He stepped forward slowly, peacefully, and met the gaze of their ringleader, Loretta, with his own. "You don't make bargains with evil, my friends. If you do, you *become* evil."

"Are you saying we should fight them?" Bernardo asked. He was a former gang member, but now had a wife and two infant children. His knuckles were white on the grip of his shotgun.

"If they attack, we fight, and I'll fight by your side. We'll inform Turbaco of what's happening here, and Barranquilla as well. We'll help our friends on the islands resist their kidnappings and murder. We'll send word to the cardinal in Bogota, and he'll intercede." Canción didn't know where the plan had come from, but it calmed the mob. Some of them nodded, but others were still afraid. He had only one more ploy to diffuse this situation. "You are my friend, Loretta. I helped build your house. Put the gun away and take my hands in friendship." He stepped closer, hands out, palms up.

She looked down at the gun in her hand, and nodded once. "I'm sorry, Canción. I... know some of the people they're holding hostage. I buy fish from them." She holstered the pistol and took his hands.

"So do I, Loretta." Canción took her fear, and with it, his own and all of the others' nearby. It smoldered in him, waiting to be expelled.

A distant gunshot, and they all turned, several of the locals crying out. Canción watched one of the prisoners topple into the storm-tossed water, the NAFAS commander still holding the pistol that had killed the man.

Then a rifle boomed from close behind them, and they all whirled, some reaching for weapons.

Empa stood in the lee of the harbormaster's office, her battle rifle braced, aimed at the boat from La Popa. Everyone on the boat's deck ducked, but Canción didn't see anyone fall, and couldn't tell from his position if she'd put a round into the wheelhouse.

Empa lowered the weapon and turned to face him, her features blank. "Nice speech. Did you mean it?"

"Every word," he assured her. If she'd really just put a bullet into her former companion... Damn that woman was cold.

"Then we need to get busy." Empa opened the door to the office. "Isabella, send word to Turbaco. Tell them what happened here and have them relay the news to Barranquilla. Then ask around if anyone has a radio that'll reach Bogota. Everyone who owns a gun should be armed at all times, and if they own two, arm someone else. This is going to get *really* ugly."

Canción wondered how it could get any uglier, and realized he was being naïve again. He turned to the stunned group. "You heard her. We fight. Tell everyone."

Their fear gone, they all nodded and hurried off.

Canción started for home. The boiling pit of energy within him needed to be expelled, and he didn't want to show anyone what his curse could do.

Gippy hit the side of the wheelhouse and fell to the floor, his mind reeling with the concussion of the bullet that had grazed his skull. For a moment, as the pain of the injury arrived, he felt like he had control over his body, that the incubus's hold on him had slipped. For that moment, he was looking at the world through his own eyes, not the demon's. He reached for the pistol at his belt...

Just two seconds... He pulled the pistol free, his finger on the trigger.

Gippy's control melted like a snowflake on a hot skillet. Ardat reestablished dominance before the muzzle of the weapon reached his chin, and holstered it. Gippy would have screamed in frustration if he'd been in control of his own mouth. One more second and he could have finished what the sniper had started.

"Well, if *that* isn't a flat-out 'fuck you!'" Chaki looked down at him dubiously, crouching out of view, below the window the bullet had blasted through. "You dead?"

"No." The demon pressed a hand to the side of his head, and it came away bloody. His skull throbbed in time with his heart. "An inch to my right and I would be. That bitch can shoot!"

Empa, Gippy realized through the splitting headache. *Mercy...* He wished her bullet had hit its mark.

Ardat started to stand, then stopped, latching onto Gippy's thoughts, rifling through his memories like pages in a book. "Duvara, call Hernandez in here. I need to talk to him."

"Afraid to show yourself?" the succubus said with a sneer.

"No, I want Empa to think she killed me. It'll give us an advantage, but I need that dolt of a Nephilim to play it right."

Gippy felt the plan forming in the demon's mind as it sifted through his memories for details. He tried to resist the intrusion but had no way to keep Ardat at bay. Chaki stepped out of the wheelhouse and called for the NAFAS captain, who stepped in with her a moment later.

The Nephilim grinned down at Gippy. "Damn near got you, eh?"

"Damn near, but I want her to believe she succeeded." Ardat pressed hard at the bleeding headwound, a gouge just above his left ear, and Gippy felt exposed bone. "The locals won't give up Canción and Empa, but she'll fall into a depression if she thinks she's killed her friend. She's weak that way. She loves too much and carries a lot of baggage. If she's convinced she killed him, she'll be distracted and less careful."

"What makes you think they won't hand her over?" the Nephilim asked derisively.

"Because she *sways* people. It's what she *does*." Ardat grabbed a rag from a shelf beside the wheel and pressed it to the wound to stop the bleeding. "And Canción absorbs negative emotions, *remember*? He'll take their fear, and she'll heal their trauma. Between the two of them, they've probably convinced everyone in Las Brisas that they're fucking *messiahs*."

The NAFAS captain's lips pursed as if he was actually thinking it over. "Okay, so how do we exploit the Ageless' state of mind?"

Again, Gippy felt the incubus rifling through his memories for details.

"Empa will be staying with Canción, and she likes her comfort. Get floorplans of his house, and we'll know where he sleeps and where she'll be. We send a small team in quietly at night and take them both. We use Tasers and drugs to immobilize them." Ardat checked the rag, but the bleeding had barely slowed. "I'm going to need something to cauterize this, Duvara."

"I'll check the tool box." She turned to rummage through a locker.

The Nephilim shook his head. "We already have a floorplan of the house, and it's fortified. Locking storm shutters, reinforced doors, storm glass windows. We'll have to blow a door to get in, and that'll wake everyone up."

"No, we won't." Ardat gritted Gippy's teeth to keep from calling the Nephilim an idiot, intensifying the pain lancing through his skull with every beat of his heart. "We take our time and get a door or window open some other way. Pick a lock, remove the hinges, cut the glass and reach through to unlock it." Gippy felt the demon sorting through his memories again. "This human was a thief. He's skilled at breaking and entering."

"*You're* going?" The Nephilim scowled at him.

"Of *course*, I'm going. If Empa sees me, she'll be shocked enough to give me an edge. I'll Taser the shit out of her and whack her up with enough Ketamine to drop a mule!" Ardat grinned, and Gippy reeled with the lurid, sadistic fantasies raging through the demon's mind.

The captain finally nodded. "Fine. What do you need from me?"

"Four soldiers who'll follow orders and won't trip over their own dicks, and a way to get into Las Brisas without being seen."

"Here." Chaki knelt beside him with a small butane torch made for soldering and shrinking electrical insulation. She pulled the trigger and a half-inch blue flame blossomed from the end. "Pull that rag away."

"And execute another prisoner. Tell them it's in retribution for my assassination." Ardat removed the rag from the wound, and Chaki applied the torch. "An eye for an eye..."

Agony and the nauseating stench of burning meat and hair filled Gippy's entire being, and he couldn't even scream.

21
ASSASSINS IN THE NIGHT

The storm lashes against the shutters of my room, relentless, violent, but not malevolent. Not like me. *Gippy...* Sleep is impossible. All I see when I close my eyes is my friend through spider-webbed storm glass, spinning, toppling, as my shot takes him down, kills him, frees him... *No choice... I had no choice.*

I check the time, 2:23 am.

Fuck this! I lurch out of the comfort of my bed, warm sheets, soft pillows, luxuries I don't deserve, pulling on a shirt and jeans with jerky, angry, sorrowful motions.

I know I had no choice. I couldn't let him live for decades with a demon corrupting his soul. I'm more familiar with Gippy's soul than any other living person. He's a good man, a warrior for God, a loving and caring person. It would have taken time for the demon to corrupt him fully. Now, free, he's with God. I wonder if he's watching me right now, if he blames me. I can't imagine he would, but I wouldn't fault him if he did.

It's supposed to hurt... Well, he was right. It hurts. The temptation to ask Canción to take away all these emotions that are torturing me gleams like a lighthouse in the darkness. Maybe I will. I wonder who I'll be if I do.

I clip my holstered Glock to my belt, grab my Everlite, and leave my room, my bare feet pat-patting the smooth tile. The hacienda is cool, damp, and dark, but I don't want light or warmth. I'll check the doors, touch base with Fernando on watch, and maybe take over for him. I descend the back stairs and smell coffee, hope kindling in my soul. *With coffee, everything's brighter...* I remember saying those words to Gippy after I told him of the War of Souls. The memory makes me smile and brings tears to my eyes at the same time. I step into the kitchen, a single red LED illuminating the coffee maker, and pour myself a cup, inhaling the life-giving aroma.

I sip and leave the kitchen through the dining room, still in darkness, my eyes barely making out shapes. I'll have to be careful. It would be embarrassing if Fernando shot me. Out of the dining room into the hall, I feel uneasy, as if the hacienda is wrong, too quiet, too cold. I haven't survived five thousand years by not trusting my instincts. I slip into battle readiness with one breath, listening, tasting the air, feeling the floor beneath my feet. My bare feet on damp tile send shivers up my spine, the roar of the storm outside beating on my mind like battering rams on a castle gate. I put my coffee down on a credenza and ease across the foyer one careful step at a time.

One foot slips slightly on the damp tile, and I freeze. *Damp?* I pause, breathing deep through my nose and mouth, attuning my ears, feeling the house through my bones. I can barely hear my own breathing over the storm outside, but the air is too humid, and there's another scent, something familiar but too faint to pin down, like burning electronics and rare steak mingled together. Sultry night air brushes my cheek, a draft, but from where?

Something's horribly wrong.

I draw my Glock and begin prowling. I can't hear a thing with the storm raging against the shutters, but my other senses are screaming: *wrong, wrong, wrong...*

Entry hall, clear, sitting room, clear, meeting room, and the draft and scent of blood and scorched electronics are stronger. I step around the meeting table and find Fernando on the floor.

No, no, no! I kneel, avoiding the still expanding pool of crimson beneath him. I can't see details, but checking for a pulse at his neck tells me he's gone. A chasm of sorrow opens up in me where I didn't think there was room for any more, but I suppress it. *Steady spirit...* Emotions now will get me killed.

My fingers come away bloody from his neck. His throat is wide open. I risk my Everlite, shielding the glare with my hand to preserve my dark vision. His pistol is in his hand, and two thin wires trail across the tile floor from his torso. A Taser. The draft comes from the corner window, the storm shutter is closed, but the window is up. They're inside.

I consider firing a few rounds to wake everyone up, but reconsider. They don't know I'm awake, and alerting everyone will only turn this into a pitched battle with my allies all groggy from sleep. *Planning... strategy... See close when far, far when close. Awareness is a constant state.* Musashi's lessons give me strength and calm. Sorrow melts away, focus blinding me to my emotions.

I scan the rest of the room. Water on the floor reflects my light, droplets and booted footprints. A trail leads out the other door. I keep my light shaded with my left hand, and follow as quickly as I can, avoiding the wet tiles. The footprints cross the entry hall where I'd found one with my foot and ascend the stairs. I missed seeing them in the dark. I follow them upstairs, straining for the sound of a footfall or the clatter of combat gear. At the top, the wet footprints turn left, the master's wing of the house. They're after Canción. If they have night-vision goggles, they'll spot me before I see them, and my flashlight will only make me a target.

I turn off my Everlight and hurry, soft-stepping, bare feet on cool tile silent beneath the constant white noise of the storm. At the corner to the cross hallway I pause, leaning around just far enough to see. Canción's door is open; two darkly clad figures stand in the portal facing the room, bulky with body armor and wearing helmets. They also wear balaclava masks and night-vision rigs over their eyes, which will block their peripheral vision but allow them to see in the dark. Each carries a military carbine and a sidearm. I still don't know how many there are, but the time for stealth is over. I have the advantage of surprise, and I intend to use it.

Swift strikes are decisive. Show your enemy no mercy. Mercy is weakness. Focus only on victory. Steady spirit.

I'm barely fifteen feet away, but I take two long strides to reduce that to ten. Body armor and helmets mean I have to be accurate. I ready my Everlite, knowing the muzzle flash will blind me and them if they look straight into it with light-intensifying goggles. As my finger moves to depress the trigger release, a sharp crack reaches me over the roar of the storm. A Taser.

Two rounds from my Glock catch the farther of the pair in the neck and ear. The pistol is deafening in the enclosed space, the muzzle flash like a strobe in the dark. My thumb clicks on my Everlite as the other turns, and I put two bullets in his face. I bolt forward, pitching my Everlite into the room ahead of me, eliciting a hail of gunfire. I bound off the doorjamb into the room in the opposite direction of my flashlight decoy. I can't see well, but muzzle flashes draw my aim, and I drop another soldier to the right. A fourth figure stands beside the bed, Taser one hand, a syringe in the other. A shape thrashes under the sheets, Canción. A fifth soldier to the other side of the room sweeps his weapon toward me.

I dive and roll while firing, but hit nothing. Neither does he, bullets from the carbine chewing up the wall above and behind me. The figure standing beside the bed turns toward me... and I see a dead man.

Gippy! My aim wavers and I freeze, my mind numb for an instant. *How...* I saw him fall, shot through the head.

He drops the syringe and pulls a pistol, his grip steady, just like I taught him...

A hand reaches up from the thrashing covers to grasp the hand holding the Taser. Gippy goes instantly limp, toppling like a ragdoll, his Glock falling to the floor. Canción lurches up, and a sound like nothing I've ever heard issues from his throat, a single note, pure and perfect, the power of it shivering the air. The last soldier is reloading, and the blast of Canción's gift hits him like a speeding car. He's flung so hard that his gear goes flying, and hits the wall with an impact that shatters plaster. He crumples like a broken toy soldier.

I'm up, checking the soldier I dropped. One round makes sure he's dead, then I turn to aim down at Gippy. He's lying on the floor, trembling, fetal, stunned perhaps. I have my shot, and I won't miss this time. My finger moves to the trigger, depressing the safety lever.

"S...stop!" Canción's still out of it from the Taser, but it must have hit him off center. His right arm is still convulsing, but his left is clawing at the sheets. Thankfully, Angelica has chosen to sleep in another room. "D...don't shoot him."

"He's *possessed,* Canción. I have to—"

"No! He's... *not* p...possessed any...more." He struggles up, barely able to sit. His right side is in spasm, and two darts are still wedged in his shoulder and hip. "I t...took it away." He waves vaguely at the crumpled solder lying beneath the shattered wall. "It's gone."

"Gippy?" I lower my pistol and kneel to touch him. The horror of being possessed, his own actions under the torture of the succubus, the fear, the pain, are incapacitating, but he's free of the demon. His memories of what the incubus planned for me are sickening, the dread in him mind-numbing. I drop my pistol and take his hands in mine. "I've got you, Gip. You're free!"

"E?" His eyes snap open, unfocused for an instant, then horrified. "Oh, God! E! I..." He shudders, wailing a piteous cry. "Oh, *God*! I... can't..."

"I've got you, Gip." I pull him into a tight embrace. "You're safe."

"K...*kill* me! Do it!" Sheer terror shudders through him; both with his ordeal and the knowledge that I know what he's been through, what he did, what the incubus planned for me, and what that would have done to him. He's shaking so hard I wonder if he has brain damage from the gunshot wound that left a bone-deep furrow above his ear.

I take his physical injuries away. A blinding headache, fractured finger, neck trauma, and a dull ache in my groin assail me; a ruptured testicle. Lucky I don't have any, but I feel like an ovary just exploded. I hold his face between my hands and look into his, but his eyes are tightly closed. "Gippy, look at me. Let me help you."

His eyes open, and I delve into his soul, a pit of horrors no one should ever experience, shattering guilt, self-disgust, suicidal thoughts. He truly wants to die. I take all the trauma I can encompass, all the evil that he believes is his, put there by the incubus that infested him. I pull it all away as gently as I can, and his tremors ease. The disgusting mess writhes inside me like a metastasizing cancer, but I constrict it in a tightening sphere of my angelic gift, squeezing the life out of it.

"I've got you, Gip. You're safe now. It's gone."

Angelica bursts into the room with a pistol in hand, Isabella right behind her with a rifle. They're wide-eyed with terror, but seem steady. My Everlite still illuminates the room in a glaring radiance and stark shadows. I nod to the fallen soldiers without easing my grip on Gippy. "Check them, Angelica. Isabella, secure the window in the meeting room." I don't tell them about Fernando. Not yet. "Canción's been Tasered, but—"

"I'm fine," he insists, struggling to rise and failing. He curses fluently and manages to jerk the Taser darts out, leaving blood on the sheets. "Just a little shaky."

Angelica starts to check the fallen soldiers, and Isabella hurries out. Gippy's still sobbing into my shoulder. I can't take his memories away, just the psychological trauma. I hope he'll be able to deal with it, but it'll take time. Then I realize... *Memories!* He knows everything our foes are planning, and probably their forces and deployment. We've just gained an advantage, and they don't know it, but we'll have to act quickly to exploit it.

I pat his back. "Gip, are you with me? I need you, buddy."

He nods, his fingers still clamped onto me, holding on for dear life. "You... fucking... *missed*!"

"Huh?" He sounds angry, accusative. "Missed what?"

He pushes me away, and I let him. His face is streaked with tears, and his fingers brush the side of his head, a hairless strip where I took his injury away. "This. One... fucking inch, and... I wish you hadn't missed."

"Right now, I'm glad I did." I pull him in and press my forehead to his. "A hundred meters, hurricane winds, a pitching boat, and safety glass, and you're getting all *judgy*?"

"Excuses? *Really*?" He sniffs in a sob and coughs out a laugh, the most glorious sound in the world.

"I can take his horror away," Canción offers, shifting to English.

I fix him with a cold stare, then reconsider. In this case, it might help. "Gip, it's your choice. It might be easier for you."

"I... don't know." He shakes his head, still dazed. "Maybe, but let me get my head on straight."

"They're all dead," Angelica says, pointing to the one that smashed the wall. "That one looks like he's been crushed flat."

"They'll know we... um... *they* failed in about an hour. There's a boat waiting." Gippy speaks in flawless Spanish, surprising me.

"Gip, you're speaking *Spanish*."

"Am I?" He shakes his head, clearly as shocked as I am. "I... remember *everything*, E. That thing was in my mind. It... told them everything, and everything it knew is still there. I really wish it wasn't." He sounds steadier, but still shaken. "We were supposed to capture you and kill or capture Canción. They wanted to... make more like him with you."

I feel a little sick at that prospect, but it's what I might have predicted if I'd been thinking a little clearer. I realize now how much Gippy's loss affected me. Pulling the trigger to end his life and save his soul wasn't the hardest thing I've ever done, but it was close. Now, with him here, safe, whole, I feel as if I've been delivered from a dark storm into a bright dawn. I can see everything now. *Strategy, tactics, advantages, high ground, vantages, weapons...*

I stare down at one of the dead soldiers, the body armor, helmet, balaclava... and the pieces fall together like a jigsaw puzzle. A plan to exploit our brief advantage blossoms in my mind. "How about we let them think they've succeeded?"

"What?" Gippy and Canción both say in unison.

"You take me back in cuffs, and we take those fuckers *down*!" The sheer vengeance in my voice startles me, but the opportunity is real, and I feel energized by Gippy's rescue. "We can get close to whoever's running this horror show and *end* this fucking nightmare."

"E, you need to chill." Gippy heaves a breath and struggles to his feet, still shaky but physically hale. "We can't barge in on two Nephilim, a succubus, and about *thirty* NAFAS troopers."

"*Two* Nephilim?" I try to stand and pain lances through my lower abdomen.

"Vargas and the NAFAS captain, Hernandez." He holds out a hand to me, and it's remarkably steady. "Sorry about the... um..." He grins in sympathy.

Before I can answer or even get to my feet—I hurt in places I didn't even know I had—Isabella returns, her face ashen and streaked with tears.

"Fernando's dead." Her voice quakes with horror, waves of anguish radiating from her. Angelica gasps, and an inarticulate cry escapes Canción's mouth. Isabella's eyes fix upon me. "But you *knew* that, didn't you?"

"Yes, I did." I take Gippy's hand and manage to stand, my head swimming. The ache in my abdomen feels like I've been kicked between the legs, but it's easing off. "I'm sorry. I should have warned you."

"Yes, you should have, but *you* didn't kill him." The muzzle of her rifle shifts toward Gippy. "*He* did."

I step between Gippy and Isabella. "He was possessed by a *demon*, Isabella."

I see her doubt, but Canción intercedes before she can speak.

"She's telling the truth. I took it, like I took the one from Father Mateo. It's gone." He finally makes it to his feet, and the calm from him is startling. His adoptive brother is dead, and he's not crying. I feel no outward emotion from him. He's either bottling it up or feels nothing. This clashes with the volatile temper I've seen previously. "And Empa's right. We have an opportunity to strike back."

"What?" More doubt but also a sudden eagerness radiate from Isabella. She loved Fernando like a son.

"*We?*" The last thing I want is Canción with me in a firefight. He's unpredictable and has a temper, even though he's not showing it now, which is even more worrisome. "I don't think that's a good idea."

"Why not?" Canción's penetrating eyes fix on mine, and I feel uncomfortable under that piercing scrutiny. I've faced down emperors, kings, queens, and demons, and this twenty-year-old man unnerves me. "I just saved your life *and* his." He squares his shoulders, and I realize just how beautiful and captivating he is; his mother's beauty and his father's warmth and caring eyes, but an intensity of his own, too. He extends a hand to Gippy, still quaking from the aftereffects of the Taser. "I'm Canción. You must be Gifford."

"I'm sorry for Fernando." Gippy shakes his hand. "And for shocking the shit out of you."

"It wasn't you." Canción's head cocks curiously. "I can take all of your—"

"Canción, stop it!" Angelica steps forward, her dark eyes hard. "Messing with people's emotions isn't helping! We need to figure out what to *do*."

"And what do you mean strike back?" Isabella adds, tears still flowing down her cheeks.

Everyone looks at me, and I grit my teeth, which only intensifies my pounding headache. "Nothing personal, but Gippy and I are a team. We've worked together in combat. I don't know you all that well, and I don't know your capabilities or if you're going to fold under stress."

"I won't, and we need to end this," Canción assures me.

"We *could* use a couple more, E," Gippy says. "Two alone wouldn't be very convincing."

I feel like smacking him. "I don't want to risk your lives. You're not soldiers."

"*Anyone* who's fighting for their survival is a soldier," Isabella snaps.

Wiser words were never spoken, and I understand. *She* understands. If we don't end this, Las Brisas will burn and everyone they know will be slaughtered. But still, even five against such a force is a no-win scenario. Still, we would certainly have the element of surprise. I need intel desperately, and we have no time to argue about this.

"Fine!" I step back and rake them all with a cold stare. "Gippy, you're going to be our point man. They know you and will still think you're possessed. I'm your captive, and you three will wear the NAFAS soldiers' gear and weapons. Body armor and balaclavas will help, but no talking and keep your eyes down. I'll give you all a quick once over on their weapons. We've got about thirty minutes, and I need details from Gippy before we go. Our focus is to take out the NAFAS captain, the succubus who corrupted Gippy, and Vargas, but we need to take the NAFAS captain and Vargas *alive*."

"Why?" Isabella's already reaching for one of the dead soldiers.

"Because they're Nephilim." Gippy picks up the Taser and syringe he dropped, and holds them up. "And these are their one-way tickets to Hell!"

~

"Mission accomplished!" Gippy motioned the others aboard the big, black panga, and Canción handed Empa over to the two NAFAS soldiers they'd left as guards. The boat would have been all but invisible in the narrow mangrove channel without the light-intensifying goggles, not only sheltered from view but the wind as well.

He'd refused Canción's offer to remove his fear, anger, and loathing. Empa had taken the mental trauma, but the memories of being possessed, and what the demon Duvara had done to him to push him over the edge into madness, percolated inside him like a vile stew. He needed those memories to keep him sharp for what they had to do tonight, but he also had to keep his head on straight. They'd all agreed that if things went sideways, he and the others would secure Empa's escape. Empa had argued, but Gippy had flatly refused. If she died, the whole world would eventually spiral into Armageddon. If escape was impossible, none of them would be taken captive.

"You're one man short, and where's the other prisoner?" one of the soldiers asked, barely audible over the hiss of the storm-lashed trees overhead.

"Both dead. The freak killed our man, and I wasn't going to fuck around." Gippy clambered aboard last. "She's more important, so don't damage her. Now, *go*!"

The local pilot gunned the twin outboards in reverse, and the long, heavy boat lurched back off the muddy shore. They didn't have room to turn around in the narrow channel, but he backed masterfully out of the tunnel of thrashing mangroves, the claw-like roots scraping both sides of the hull. Emerging into the open, the wind slammed into them, and they all hunkered low against the stinging spray. The engines roared, and they wheeled around and slammed forward into the teeth of the wind, the heavy hull hammering down with numbing force every time they topped a wave.

Gippy gritted his teeth and hung on for dear life as they passed the towering, rotting skyscrapers of the drowned city of Cartagena. The pilot routed them to take advantage of the relatively calm water in the lee of the structures, and lights flickered here and there, some fires, some electric. They reminded him of the towers of Manhattan. There were also a few specks of dry land here and there, built up with massive seawalls and bunker-like concrete buildings, but the towers loomed like dying sentinels amidst the roaring seas. He wondered how the towers remained standing, but some obviously hadn't, nothing but twisted iron girders sticking up from the waves.

Gippy decided that he hated boats almost as much as he hated being possessed. Not, however, as much as he hated Duvara. Seeing that creature utterly destroyed would go a long way to making him feel human again. He glanced at Canción and marveled at his own deliverance. *A weapon that can destroy the minions of Hell...* The possibilities were endless and inspired hope he'd not experienced since being saved by Empa. *A chance to really fight back...*

The crossing was wet, tumultuous, and terrifying, but without incident. The pilot had been born to this and knew his business. After half an hour of pounding torture, they pulled into the lee of the isle of La Popa and into high-walled cove, soaked and pummeled, but otherwise unhurt. Everyone but Empa lurched to their feet, and Gippy made sure to keep track of his team as they debarked, since they were dressed identically to the other two soldiers. Canción was taller, but he couldn't tell Angelica or Isabella from the others, much less from each other, at a glance. He checked on Empa, but she remained motionless, limp and soaked, shivering. Of course, she was wide awake and armed to the teeth under the voluminous poncho, but they had to play the game a bit longer before the shit hit the fan.

Workers took dock lines, and they hoisted Empa ashore. "Mission team, with me for debriefing. You two, back to the rectory." The two guards didn't argue, and Canción heaved Empa over his shoulder like a sack of grain. Gippy winced at the rough treatment. He knew she was hurting after taking his injuries, but she'd assured them she could take it without crying out. If there was one thing in the world she knew, it was pain.

They slogged up the pitching ramp to the quay wall where a canopied pickup truck and a full platoon of soldiers awaited them. Captain Hernandez, the son of Ertael, and the succubus-possessed Chaki sat in the cab with a driver behind the wheel, while the soldiers stood in the rain guarding the cove. This was the tricky part.

Gippy motioned his team toward the back of the vehicle and tapped on the passenger window. It lowered a few inches. "Lost one trooper, and Canción was killed. We got Empa. She's wacked up and cuffed."

"Excellent!" The Nephilim jerked a thumb toward the back. "Make sure she stays out."

"No shit!" Gippy bowed his head against the slashing rain and made his way back to the tailgate. The altercation had been far easier than he'd hoped. Evidently, the Nephilim couldn't feel the absence of the incubus.

Canción, Isabella, and Angelica sat on the bench seats, divested of their night-vision lenses, but still wearing their helmets and balaclavas. Empa lay on the floor, limp and motionless, heavy cable ties securing her wrists and ankles. The restraints were rigged so she could pull free, but they looked tight. He clambered over the tailgate, pulled the tarp down, and slapped the metal bed twice with his palm. The truck lurched into motion, and they pulled out of the shelter of the island's peak onto the twisting road up the hillside. The howling wind hammered the taut canvas covering loud enough to make conversation impossible.

He gave the others a thumbs up, and knelt beside Empa, bending close enough to put his mouth near her ear. "You okay, E?"

She nodded minutely.

"Good. We're on our way to the convent. Ten minutes."

She nodded again.

So far, their plan had gone without a hitch. Inside the convent, things would change. They needed to get Chaki and Hernandez alone before they sprang their trap. After they disposed of the succubus, they would make contact with Isabella's spy and find Bishop Vargas. He would be under guard, so their plans would have to be fluid. Isabella's spy was a nun and knew the convent intimately. If anyone could find a way to get them close to Vargas, she could. He wondered if she was the same one who had served them all wine, and cringed. She'd been terrified of him, and he couldn't blame her. He was thankful that the incubus had never been able to get her alone.

Even if they were successful, getting two unconscious Nephilim off the island would be the biggest challenge of the mission.

They rode along without speaking. One of the women, probably

Angelica, fidgeted. Isabella seemed more solid. Gippy would rather have done this with people he knew wouldn't freak out under fire, but allies were short of hand, and Isabella, Angelica, and Canción were all determined and at least knew how to handle guns. He checked his Glock one last time, and Canción took off his gloves in preparation.

When Empa asked how he'd taken away the demon infesting Gippy without making eye contact, as she had to do to delve someone's soul, he'd explained that touching someone possessed by a demon was evidently different than taking harmful emotions. While he had to make eye contact to absorb a person's anger, hate, or sorrow, doing so was like opening a floodgate, allowing him to pull in emotions from everyone nearby, including himself. Gippy found that creepy beyond belief. Just touching someone possessed by a demon, as both he and Canción had discovered only an hour ago, was like grabbing a live wire. The floodgates opened without making eye contact.

Gippy had felt that first hand—a violent wrenching utterly unlike his experiences with Empa gently removing his emotional trauma—and they'd worked it into their plan. Of course, there was also a Nephilim to deal with. *Son of Ertael, fallen angel of martial prowess...* Ardat had witnessed that martial prowess in previous lives; the Nephilim was a badass in every sense, with weapons or without, and personally responsible for the deaths of numerous Ageless. They'd have to take him by surprise.

Gippy unclipped the strap restraining his Taser. He would only get one shot at the NAFAS captain, and he had to make sure Chaki didn't touch him before that. His experience as a captive within his own body had taught him that the demons could feel one another with bodily contact, as well as the souls of the humans they touched. That was how Chaki recognized him as 'angel touched' when they first met in Albuquerque. After so long possessed, he wondered if Chaki would be sane after her demon was gone. Frankly, he doubted it.

The truck rumbled around one last sharp switchback, and the pavement changed from asphalt to brick. The winds buffeted the canvas even harder as they crossed an open courtyard, then abated completely as they entered the covered garage of the convent's motor pool. Gippy released the tiedowns on the tailgate and flipped up the canvas to look around. Four other vehicles were parked here, two armored cars, a black Southafricar sedan plugged into the wall, and another pickup modified with a glassed-in rear compartment for the bishop to tour around La Popa and wave to his cultish parishioners. The metal roof of the garage rumbled with the storm, but everything in this place was built to withstand the weather. The building itself, a chapel and convent originally, had stood for centuries, assaulted by pirates, the Spanish, and dictators, each time rebuilt and reinforced to withstand the next attack. As the sea claimed Cartagena, and sequential hurricanes began to lash the north coast of South America, it had been transformed into an even more stolid fortress, the inner courtyard roofed, and the outer walls and windows reinforced.

"Out!" he ordered. They piled out, and Canción lifted Empa in a fireman's carry, her bound arms and legs hanging limp. "Follow me." Gippy rounded the driver's side of the truck to avoid close contact with Chaki. "If she gives one twitch, let me know."

"Why do you need the soldiers along?" Chaki asked, as she and the Nephilim rounded the front of the truck.

"Because she's more dangerous than you can imagine. If she comes to, she can drop whoever's carrying her. Don't get too close to her." Not exactly true, but it hopefully would make them keep their distance. "We should have arranged a stretcher."

"She's bound hand and foot," the NAFAS captain said. "How could she—"

"With her *gift*," Gippy insisted. "I've seen her do it."

The Nephilim scowled. "Nothing we have on her suggests she's capable of incapacitating someone that way. She's a *healer*, not a telepath."

"You don't *know* her. I do. She's an *empath*," Gippy reiterated. "It might not work on you, but she can turn a human's mind inside out in a second. How the hell do you think she's *survived* so long?"

"Fine. We'll keep her restrained and sedated." The Nephilim led the way toward a steel door with Chaki on his heels.

Gippy motioned the others to follow and brought up the rear, keeping as far from the succubus as possible. The captain pounded on the door and it opened. Inside, two of the bishop's guards snapped to attention, disheveled and poorly equipped compared to the NAFAS soldiers, but armed and alert. They'd been told to expect the returning mission and stepped aside, motioning them through without a word.

The Nephilim spoke to them in Spanish. "Notify Bishop Vargas that the mission was a success. We have one of the terrorists, Empa. The other was killed."

"Yes, sir." The guard pulled a hand-held radio from his belt and spoke into it.

The Nephilim continued down a hall into the convent proper, and they followed. "We've set a room aside. As soon as we get a break in the weather, we'll arrange for transport to Bogota then back north."

"What? Why not take her north ourselves?" Chaki shot Gippy a suspicious look over her shoulder that he knew too well; demons were lesser minions of Hell, subservient to the Nephilim. Both Duvara and Ardat despised their status and their overlords. Then again, demons hated everything and everyone, reveling only in torment. Captain Hernandez had never mentioned working with the Colombians before, so this came as a surprise.

"I thought you said this was *your* hunt," Gippy added. "She's *your* prize."

"It *is* my hunt, and she *is* my trophy, but..." The Nephilim turned to look over the disguised soldiers as they rounded a corner. "...Bishop Vargas insists. He—"

Canción stumbled, emitting a half-grunt, as if in sudden distress.

"What's wrong?" Gippy pulled his Taser. This had to be Canción's play to neutralize both Duvara and the Nephilim at the same time, but it was shitty timing. They were too exposed in this hallway, and barely out of sight of the door guards. *Fucking amateurs...*

"Is she waking up?" Chaki took a step back.

The Nephilim captain whirled and pulled a pistol as smoothly as if it was choreographed. "Tase her! Now!"

"No, I've got her, sir." Canción stood straight and shifted his load, Empa still inert. "I'm fine, sir."

The captain's eyes narrowed minutely, but he holstered his pistol. "Don't *drop* her, private." Hernandez turned away and continued his explanation for the change in plans as they proceeded deeper into the convent. "The bishop has a plan for an alliance between Colombia and NAFAS with *her* as the linchpin. We've captured a terrorist responsible for thousands of deaths and untold damage to our nation with the help of the Church. With the aid of the Colombian government, we'll cement an alliance, and Vargas's position in the church will be strengthened."

"He wants to be cardinal," Gippy surmised, well aware of the machinations of Nephilim. The higher they climbed up the chain of power, the more humans they could influence, the more despair and hate they could foster.

"Politics." Chaki flashed a sarcastic smile over her shoulder that turned Gippy's stomach. "Some things never change. You know the game."

"I do," he said, thinking, *And your game's just about over, you sadistic monster.*

They passed numerous doors, small chambers formerly for the housing of nuns or monks. Gippy didn't know where they were planning to hold Empa, but he hadn't been to this part of the vast building before. The farther they progressed, the more trapped he felt. Finally, the captain paused at a door and knocked. A latch clicked, and the door swung inward onto a landing, and two more armed guards snapped to attention. A stone stair lit by dim LEDs descended into living rock.

"Why down here?" Gippy asked, uncomfortable with the narrow stair. Empa had taught him to avoid places with limited escape routes, and he would bet his ravaged soul that this was the only way in or out of here.

The Nephilim glanced back from the top step, his mouth stretched into a sadistic grin. "Peace and quiet for our *guest.*"

The sheer malevolence in the man's voice sent shivers up Gippy's spine, and he realized the true reason for the seclusion. *So nobody will hear her screams.* He forced a grin through his disgust. "Perfect."

They followed the Nephilim down into the depths, and the guards closed the door behind them. Gippy felt like every step brought him closer to Hell. He didn't want to think about how dark it would be if the lights went out.

22
A SONG IN DARKNESS

Hate hammered against Canción's thin mental armor as he carried Empa down the stone steps. The demoness was bad enough—sadistic lust radiated from her like heat from a furnace—but the Nephilim... *Mama said I'd know them when I met them.* But Terpsichore had never said they emitted hate like radioactivity from a melting-down nuclear reactor. He'd felt it in the garage when the Nephilim had first stepped out of the vehicle, an assault on his soul. Then, inside when he met the captain's gaze for just a moment, the intensity of it had staggered him. *So much hate...*

The visceral desire to take it away, to destroy it, worried on him like an inexorable pressure in his mind. But could he do it? The demon, yes; one touch, and he could rip the thing out of the woman, just as he had with Mateo and Gippy, but the Nephilim was different. *It feels like Empa,* he realized, *or Mama... but corrupted.* Instead of love and caring burdened by eons of conflict and trauma, these Nephilim were burdened by nothing. One eye-to-eye glimpse, and he knew this creature wanted nothing more than to beat every living human to pulp, to make them bleed, to subjugate through physical violence. And there was nothing else there, no core of a human soul possessed by evil. *A human shell occupied by the offspring of a fallen angel.* Canción didn't know if he could take that away. He'd only ever done it for humans, removing their hate and sorrow, or—

as with Father Mateo and Gippy—a corruption. This was a being of nothing but malice.

At the bottom of the stair, they paused at another door. The Nephilim knocked again, and two more guards opened it and ushered them through. Inside, a long table draped in a thick black cloth centered a rectangular chamber. The walls were lined with human skulls and sconces displaying statues of saints. *A catacomb,* he realized. Upon the table lay an array of gold accoutrements of the Catholic faith, bowls, crosses, small coffers, and incongruously a set of steel manacles bolted to the surface. Whether this was something new or a holdover from the inquisition, Canción didn't want to know.

At the other end of the table stood a high-backed chair inlaid with gold. Upon that gilded throne sat an old man in a black and red cassock. A ruby-encrusted gold cross suspended by an equally ornate chain rested upon his chest; a red cap perched upon a head of wispy white hair. He also wore a smile, and even from across the room Canción could feel an aura of darkness. This was Bishop Vargas, the other Nephilim, son of Samsaveel, Fallen Angel of the Eclipsed Sun.

Canción kept his eyes averted but felt Empa tense on his shoulder. Maybe she felt it, too.

"Captain Hernandez, your plan has borne fruit." The bishop's grin turned Canción's stomach. "Put your burden down there and secure her."

"*His* plan?" Gifford played the demon-possessed minion almost too well, his tone brimming with wickedness. "The plan was *mine,* Bishop, and I was the one who risked my ass pulling it off."

Vargas waved one bejeweled hand in dismissal. "Your assistance is noted. Now secure our prisoner."

Canción stepped around the table and shifted Empa off his shoulders, lying her down on the smooth surface, amazed that she could remain limp with so much evil in the room. She'd said she could feel the proximity of Nephilim, and the twin auras of hate emanating from them were slowly driving Canción mad. He didn't know how long he could keep his eyes averted, and if he locked gazes with either of them, he didn't know what would happen.

Or maybe he did know. *Either they're destroyed, or I am.*

Unfortunately, this was where their careful plan began to fall apart. They'd assumed the captain would want her restrained, but there were two Nephilim in the room instead of only one. The captain seemed the greater threat, but Gippy only had a single Taser. Angelica and Isabella could handle the two guards, but there were two more at the top of the stairs, and no other way out. Canción was supposed to take down the succubus, and Empa and Gippy the captain, but not *two* Nephilim.

As he pulled a combat knife to sever Empa's bonds, a desperate idea came to him. He'd used the energy from the incubus that had possessed Gippy on one of the NAFAS soldiers. He could at least give them an edge by doing the same against one of the Nephilim. Empa wanted to immobilize them, but one at a time. Even if they could take down both, getting them out of here would be impossible. Gunfire would bring more soldiers, and they were trapped at the bottom of a hole.

No, he decided, *take one of them out of the picture and follow through with the plan.* If they struck quickly, taking out the four guards, they might get out of here with one of the Nephilim.

The knife snicked through Empa's leg restraint, then the one on her wrists. Gippy had a hand on his Taser, and stood only a few feet from the captain, his primary target. Canción had no choice but to stick with the plan and embellish on his own.

As he took Empa's arm and fumbled with one of the manacles, she grabbed his wrist hard, the signal to spring their trap. *Now or never...*

At her touch, however, a curious calm swept into him, like the refrain of one of his mother's melodies, laughing water flowing over stones, the trickle of the refrain calming his singing nerves. He had his part to play in this performance, and he played it.

Canción staggered back toward Chaki with a convincing gasp of shock, and all hell broke loose.

The Nephilim captain had his pistol out before Canción even went to his knees. Chaki, instead of reaching to help him up, stepped back, her eyes fixed upon Empa. The two guards at the door shouldered their rifles. And at the other end of the table, the Nephilim bishop lurched to his feet.

"Tase her!" the captain ordered.

Empa rolled off the table away from the NAFAS captain, pulling her pistol from under her poncho.

"Don't shoot her!" Gippy stepped into the line of fire between the captain and Empa, pulling his Taser. But instead of firing at Empa, he turned the weapon on the captain and pulled the trigger. The Nephilim's pistol barked even as the two barbs of the Taser lodged into his flesh and fifty thousand volts convulsed every muscle in his body. Gippy swore and folded over, fumbling for his pistol.

"Kill them!" the bishop bellowed, but before the guards could fire,

Isabella and Anjelica unloaded, their rifles deafening in the confined space. The two guards beside the door dropped without firing a shot.

Empa vaulted over the table, her pistol barking three times, the bullets slamming into the bishop's torso hard enough to force him back into the chair. *Damn,* that woman could shoot, and she evidently had the same idea of how to alter their plan as Canción. She landed beside Gippy and the twitching Nephilim captain.

Canción lunged up and reached for Chaki. The succubus met his charge with a short knife, stabbing at his stomach, but the blade couldn't penetrate his body armor. He snatched her wrist, ten thousand lurid scenes of violent copulation flashing into his mind, not unlike what he'd felt when he touched Gippy. He ripped the vile thing free of its host, surrounding it with his gift. As Chaki crumpled to the floor, a thousand tormented souls screamed in his mind. He shredded the essence of the demon, transforming the evil essence into pure energy and silencing the screams.

Canción turned to face the bishop, thinking that the man was probably dead already, but he was horribly mistaken. The man stood, blood marring his vestment where the bullets had struck, and in his hand... a phone.

Canción stared in shock. How could he even be alive? "What the fu—"

With a tap on one aged finger, a deafening alarm blasted through the room, making the gunfire seem quiet by comparison. Canción cringed at the noise, then gaped as the bishop pulled something else from beneath the folds of his cassock. The Nephilim dropped his phone and reached for the ring dangling from the top of the grenade.

"No!" Canción unleashed the energy of the destroyed succubus, smashing the old man backward through his gilded throne. The bishop of La Popa struck the wall of human skulls, shattering several before he fell to the floor. Canción tore off the helmet and restrictive balaclava, drawing a ragged breath. Chaki lay in a fetal ball at his feet, and the bishop was now certainly dead. The fight was won.

They had not, however, escaped yet.

Gunfire rattled from up the stairs, bullets ripping through the door to ricochet off the stone floor into the table. Isabella and Anjelica stood to either side of the portal, smart enough to assume the guards from above would attack. Firing through the door from above without a target seemed stupid, but maybe they'd heard the bishop's command and weren't particularly bright.

"Check him!" Empa shouted over the din of the alarm and gunfire. Gippy lay on his side, and she crouched beside the NAFAS captain, pushing a syringe into his leg.

Canción wondered who she wanted him to check, but she pointed to the crumpled bishop. He wondered why she wanted him to check a dead man, but she obviously had more experience with Nephilim than he did. If the old man had survived, maybe she intended to perform another exorcism on him.

When Canción rounded the end of the table, he realized he'd been wrong yet again.

Bishop Vargas leaned against the wall of shattered skulls, a bloody rictus grin splitting his ancient face in a mien of malice and mirth. "You've failed, idiot child of a dead god."

That the Nephilim had survived was shocking enough; that the creature knew who and what Canción was terrified him; his claim that they'd failed trumped both.

"Failed?" Canción wondered how the man could think that when he lay broken and his cousin was their prisoner. Then he saw the grenade still clutched in the old man's gnarled, bloody fist.

"Yes, *failed*!" The old bishop coughed a bloody laugh, grin intact as his other hand reached for the pin of the grenade. "You will all die here, and I will live again to corrupt and deceive your precious humans into *oblivion*!"

Canción lunged at the trite bastard, but one bloody and bent finger fitted into the ring and pulled. He slammed into the old man, hands strong with years of labor grasping the hand that held the bomb. He squeezed the bloody hand with all his strength, not sure what else to do. Then the Nephilim heaved beneath him, obviously not only alive, but *strong*. Forced to roll, he managed to keep his grip on the creature's hand. Nephilim were evidently much tougher than they looked.

A fist slammed into his ear, hard enough to stun him, then another, ringing his already ringing ears. He squeezed harder, unable to fend off the blows, but knowing if he let go, he would die.

Through the ringing, he heard music... The thrill of a guitar riff, masterful and pure, the memory as clear as the chime of crystal in his mind. *Mother...* Her comforting music infused him, her smile, her love...

Canción blinked away blood and tears. The Nephilim grinned, his wizened face only inches from his, bloody teeth a rictus, eyes filled with malice and victory. Hate beat at him with more force than the man's fist. But in those eyes, Canción saw a portal, a window into that terrible soul forged in the union of a fallen angel and a human. Canción shattered the glass of that window and plunged through, down into the pit of hate. He surrounded the seething malevolence, and ripped the vile thing from its fleshy shell. The bishop's eyes widened, horror registering for a moment, then the body convulsed. The evil essence of the Nephilim filled him to overflowing, but Canción surrounded it with his gift and *squeezed*... The hate that filled him died, leaving only a burning energy waiting to be released, exponentially more power even than consuming a demon had given him.

A last sigh escaped the bishop's bloody lips. Without the force of Hell's minion to keep it alive, the aged and broken shell expired. The bloody fist gripping the grenade went slack, but Canción maintained his hold. If he tried to find the pin and replace it, he might slip.

How ironic would that be? he thought. *To be killed by a dead man.*

But it wasn't a man he'd just killed; it had been the corrupted grandson of God, the offspring of a fallen angel. His own distant cousin. An even deeper irony dawned: the entire War of Souls was nothing but a family squabble between celestial beings with all of humankind caught in the conflagration. Canción wondered for a moment if releasing his grip on the grenade might be the wiser choice; end the war in one violent conflagration and let the Four Horsemen cleanse this poor, tortured planet of humans.

The only thing that stopped him was the music still echoing within his mind, the memory of his mother's love, her lifelong struggle to bring happiness and joy to people. He couldn't betray her. He'd been forged by the union of Heaven and Hell, a weapon that would tip the balance of power one way or the other. He would tip it the way he knew Terpsichore would have wanted, not out of vengeance for her death, but out of love.

I flip the twitching Nephilim onto his face and place a knee between his shoulder blades. My hip hurts like hell—half of Gippy's gunshot wound—but I manage to secure a cable tie around the man's wrists before he can recover from the Taser. *Note to self: send another thank you note to the Taser manufacturer.* They might be surprised that their products are used against the minions of Hell, so maybe I'll leave that part out. I secure his legs at knee and ankle, and return to Gippy.

"You okay?"

"Fuck no! I'm fucking *shot*! That bastard was fast!" He winces as he tries to get up, but brushes off my hands. "Check on Canción. I'll live."

"If he tries to break free, Tase him again. The ketamine should kick in soon."

"Got it. Go." He fumbles in a pouch for another Taser cartridge.

I stagger to my feet and hobble to the far end of the table, wary of the sporadic gunfire that's reducing the door to Swiss cheese. I find Canción lying with the Nephilim half on top of him, both hands clenching the fist that grips a live grenade. He's bleeding from one ear and seems a little dazed. The Nephilim's dead, unfortunately, but I'll take a bird in hand over being blown to bits. I kneel and reinforce his grip, worried that Canción might pass out and kill us all.

"Find the pin," he says, unbelievably calm considering the circumstances.

I flinch as more gunfire rips through the door, some of it striking the table behind us. They're working their way down the stairs. "Better idea. I'll take the grenade. Just let me get my fingers under yours."

"What?" He stares at me like I'd asked for a kidney. "Why?"

"Because I've got a *use* for it!" I work my fingers under his, pressing down on the lever. "I've got it. Let go."

He does, and I take a one-handed grip on the deadly little orb, endless hours of training clicking into place without thought. I recall my first experience with a hand-held bomb, a pottery device with a waxed fuse, often as dangerous to the thrower as the target. Technology hasn't changed that, for if my grip fails it'll likely kill everyone in the room.

I push myself to my feet with my free hand and nod to the door. "Now, give me some suppressive fire when I get in place. Use the table for cover and stay low."

He nods, still remarkably calm. Maybe he expelled all his fear with the essence of the succubus. Handy trick, but worrisome; fear is self-preservation. I work my way past Gippy and our captive Nephilim to where Isabella and Angelica stand beside the door. They've both removed their masks but kept their helmets, carbines at the ready. Angelica looks a little unhinged, but the dead soldier at her feet has two holes through his head; evidently her nervousness isn't affecting her aim. The door is well and truly riddled, barely holding together, but the stairs beyond are darker than the room, so I can't see movement through the bullet holes.

I lean close to Isabella, pitching my voice loud enough for her to hear over the din of the blaring alarm. "When Canción makes them take cover, open the door quickly." I show her the grenade.

She nods, her eyes wide, and shifts her carbine to a left-handed grip.

I motion Angelica back, turn to Canción, who's kneeling with his carbine braced over the tabletop, and nod.

From thirty feet, he fires half a dozen quick single shots through the upper half of the door. Not bad shooting, or at least good enough. Shouts from up the stairs, and their guns go silent. Isabella reaches out and jerks half of the riddled double door open. I step out far enough to see where I'm throwing, because hitting someone in the chest to have the bomb roll back down the steps would *really* suck. Four guards are in the act of retreating from Canción's barrage, and one looks back in time to see me pitch the grenade underhand over his head. The horror in his eyes is sad, but I can't allow myself pity for these poor deluded fools. There have been so many thousands like them over the centuries, the unwitting Hounds of Hell.

I take cover, gratified to see everyone else doing the same. Gippy's even pulled our Nephilim prisoner out of the way.

I open my mouth and cup my ears. The explosion is muffled a little by the four bodies between us and the detonation, but some fragments get past them to mar the already damaged table. Canción's well hunkered, and pops up the instant the rain of metal and bloody bits of soldier subsides, leveling his carbine over the table. I doubt there's anyone left for him to shoot, but risk a quick glance.

"Four down!" I can barely hear my own shout over the alarm and tinnitus. "We need to move before more arrive. Canción, can you lift our prisoner?"

"Better idea." Canción slings his weapon and strides over to where Gippy kneels awkwardly beside the Nephilim. He unceremoniously flips the struggling captain over and grasps the collar of his uniform, hauling him up. The ketamine's kicking in, but the captain's still cursing in several dead languages. Canción stares into the Nephilim's face briefly, and the aura of hatred that has been hammering against me since we stepped out of the truck suddenly vanishes. The body goes utterly limp, and he drops it. "There. It's done."

"Done?" I stare at him open mouthed, struck dumb. "You..."

"I took it. Now we don't have to haul his ass out of here." He reaches down and pulls Gippy to his feet. "I hope you can walk."

"I can fuckin' *run*, pendejo." Gippy snatches up the captain's radio.

I'm still stunned. "You... *took* it? The *Nephilim?*"

"Yes, and the other one, too." Canción helps Gippy toward the door. "Sorry, would you rather I hadn't?"

"No, I..." The implications of what he's done—not simply banished but utterly *destroyed* two Nephilim with little effort—leaves me speechless. *God's plan...*

Gippy, not so much. "Fuckin' *A!*" He grins through the pain and points to one of the fallen guards. "What say somebody grabs me a rifle and we get the ever-lovin' *fuck* out of Dodge?"

"Good plan." Isabella hands him a carbine and rifles the corpse for magazines.

I've searched for a weapon against the Nephilim for five millennia, and finally found a way to banish them. Now this young man can eliminate them with a glance. Five thousand years of fighting flashes before my eyes, fire, blood, the hellscapes of battlefields... It all fades away.

Where is your spirit, Emiko? a voice says in my mind's ear.

Steady spirit, Musashi~san, I reply.

The sound of the alarm penetrates the fog, and urgency clicks my brain back into combat mode. I'll have to postpone my nervous breakdown for later.

"Right!" I take the other spare rifle and pocket ammunition. I'll figure out what to do with this amazing new weapon that could alter fate of the Earth later... if we survive. "Everyone on me. Isabella, on my left one step back. Gippy in the middle. Canción, if Chaki can walk, let her. If she can't, fireman's carry. Angelica, cover our asses. Come on!"

My hip complains up the stairs, but pain is an old friend and helps clear my head. I steady my spirit and focus on getting us out of here alive. Later, this new weapon of God we will put to use.

23
THE WRATH OF GOD

Canción was sick and tired of being the mission's requisite beast of burden. He'd pulled away Chaki's terror, anguish, and fear—a pittance compared to the pulsing energy of the two Nephilim humming within him like a dynamo at full power—but she remained catatonic. This was more energy than he'd ever held within himself before, but he found that he could continue to contain it with minimal effort. The pressing desire to expel it nagged at him, however. He longed to blast the entire convent to rubble, but there were too many bystanders, nuns and monks who had little to do with the evil machinations of their hell-spawned bishop.

La Popa seethed like a kicked anthill, but the convent didn't house a large contingent of soldiers. Empa, he had to admit, was more than competent enough to spearhead their escape, and the few guards they encountered either ran or fell to her deadly aim. The alarm finally silenced right before they cracked the door into the garage, the howl of hurricane winds buffeting the metal structure incongruously quiet by comparison.

They all staggered to a stop and stared at the vehicles in sudden horrified realization.

"I don't suppose anyone has *keys*?" Isabella asked.

"Fuuuck!" Gippy growled through clenched teeth, obviously still in pain.

"Check them all! Look under seats, behind visors, glove boxes, everywhere!" Empa limped toward the nearest vehicle.

"If they're keyless, just try to start them," Gippy added. "If they left a fob inside, they'll fire right up. Canción, look around for a lock box or key safe."

While the others tried doors and searched interiors, Canción eased Chaki down to the floor and flexed his aching back. The garage was dark, but his stolen carbine had a light. He flipped it on and began searching. The garage seemed to double as a maintenance bay, with a workbench and toolboxes. He started rifling through boxes for keys.

"Can you hotwire one of these?" Empa asked.

"No way on the electric, and the pickups are push-button start, computer ignition, snip one wire and you're locked out like a cheating husband. The armored cars, maybe. Let me have a look." Gippy hobbled over to one and wrenched open a door. "Jesus! Not only electronic ignition, but a *hybrid*? Sorry E. No joy."

"Then we need keys!" Empa slammed a door and began looking under wheel wells.

Cancion pulled on the handle of a wall-mounted metal box, but it was locked. "There's a lockbox here."

"Jimmy it!" Empa snapped.

"How?" He had no experience in breaking and entering.

"I thought you liked to *break* things!" Empa limped over and pulled a combat knife from under her poncho.

"If *I* broke it, there wouldn't be anything left," Canción retorted, stepping back.

She fitted the point of the blade into the steel door near the lock and hit the butt of the haft with a wrench. Prying hard deformed the face of the box enough to fit a short crowbar in, she popped the lock. Inside, a row of six key fobs, several electronic key cards, and a number of old fashioned metal keys hung on hooks.

"Score!" She snatched the fobs and started thumbing buttons. Lights blinked on the electric, the glass backed pickup, then one of the armored cars. "Yes! Everyone in the armored one!"

They stowed Chaki in the back and piled in, three crowding into the back seat while Empa drove and Gippy took the passenger side forward. The big diesel roared to life at the touch of a button, and Empa squealed out of the garage into the storm, the huge tires growling on the brick pavement as she wheeled around. After a moment to locate the windshield wipers—and some inventive swearing in several languages Canción didn't know, probably regarding automotive design—she gunned it in forward, and they tore down the hill toward the first switchback.

The headlights flashed on a stark white obelisk at the corner, the cross at its apex glowing in the darkness like a beacon. Canción wondered at the irony of a minion of Hell hiding behind the cross of Christ, and how many times in history the Nephilim had taken on the disguises of priests, nuns, bishops, cardinals, or even popes.

"E, we got a serious problem!" Gippy's announcement shattered Canción's revery, and Empa braked to a stop halfway around the corner.

Headlights ascended the winding road far below, three switchbacks down the steep incline. The lights of the second vehicle illuminated the one in the van, a huge armored personnel carrier with top-mounted lights and dual heavy machineguns.

"Someone must have radioed down." Empa muttered in yet another language Canción didn't know, but her words didn't need interpretation. They were trapped.

"Where the hell did they get *those?*" Angelica asked.

"Naffies brought two aboard the boat we came in," Gippy explained. "Nothing we've got will scratch them, E. Not unless there's an RPG in the back."

"There's nothing in the back but a former succubus," Canción informed them. "And there's only one road down."

"Then we are *royally* fucked," Gippy added.

"Can we defend the convent?" Isabella suggested.

Empa shook her head. "Wouldn't be the first time I've done it, but there's probably thirty soldiers in those things. They'll spread out and come at us from too many angles under cover of the heavy guns."

The seething energy within Canción begged for release, and gave him an insane idea. "Back up the road to the courtyard and shut off the lights." He pushed his door hard against the wind to open it and jumped down, handing in his carbine as the storm-driven rain drenched him once more.

"What the *hell* are you doing?" Empa glared over the seat at him. "Get back in here!"

"No. Now back up and shut down." He pointed at the switchback. "That's the narrowest point, and they'll have to slow. I'll take care of them."

"*How?*" She stared at him in horror.

"You said it before; I like to *break* things." Below, the armored vehicles rounded the last corner before the final switchback. "Now, back up and let me do this." He slammed the door and strode back up the hill far enough to allow both of the oncoming vehicles to make the turn before facing him.

Empa backed the smaller armored car up the hill to the brick-paved courtyard and shut off the lights, plunging the scene into darkness. Canción turned to face down the hill and waited. The lights of the oncoming vehicles illuminated the final switchback and the alabaster cross. He squinted through the storm-driven rain down at them as they roared up the road, black and gold in the headlights, ugly and armored, coming for them. They were big enough that they would have to come around the last switchback in single file.

Perfect, he thought, *unless they gun me down without stopping.*

Canción let his anger, his sorrow, and his thirst for vengeance merge with the seething mass of energy from the two Nephilim. These were the same as the ones who had murdered his mother, destroyed his home, killed Fernando, tried to abduct him... *Let them come,* he thought, raising his arms into the hurricane winds, slashing rain stinging his face. He had taken their hate, their demons, their unceasing desire to corrupt all of creation. It was time to give it back.

"What the hell is he *doing*?" Angelica is torn between horror, fear, and love; I feel her conflict beating on me from the back seat.

"Using his gift." I back the car up as far as I dare, turning sideways so that the rear wheels touch the curb, the rear bumper nudging the guardrail at the edge of a two-hundred-foot cliff. If this doesn't work, and we have to flee, I'll drive us straight off the other side. It's less steep than the sheer cliff, and we might not tumble end over end... maybe. And maybe it will work. "You saw what he did to the Nephilim after taking the demon from Chaki. He transforms evil into energy, a weapon."

"Enough to take out an APC?" Gippy asks.

"The *hell* if I know." I wonder not for the first time if he could do the same to me, rip my soul from my body and expel it in destruction. Could he do that to a normal human being? Perhaps only a loving upbringing has made him a weapon for God instead of an instrument of Hell. If the

Nephilim gained this weapon, what would they do? Would anyone's soul be safe?

God's plan, I realize. *The keys to Armageddon or the salvation of the Earth...*

I watch, helpless, as the two NAFAS APCs come around the corner, their floodlights silhouetting Canción. He stands with his arms up and empty, like a backlit Christ on the cross. The 15-ton vehicle in front screeches to a stop only a few meters from him, but he doesn't move. The heavy gun turret atop the beast swivels, dim red lights blinking, a targeting laser twinkling like a shaft of crimson starlight in the rain.

"They're going to shoot him down!" Angelica reaches for the door.

"Wait! Let him do this!" Isabella pulls her back, her stoicism impressing me once again. She loves Canción like a son, and perhaps she's always known he was special. Now, she's watching him face down certain death for us all, and trusting him.

So must I, for with Gippy and I both injured, there's no way we can flee down the hillside on foot, and the convent itself is a deathtrap.

We sit and watch through the hurricane, impotent, rapt. The second vehicle brakes to a stop right behind the first, the road too narrow for it to pass. I can only imagine what they're saying to each other over the radio. A door opens in the front vehicle, folding down, and a figure with a rifle jumps out.

His boots never touch the pavement.

A hypersonic pulse of energy blasts the rain to fog in a narrow cone before Canción. As I saw when he blasted the soldier who would have killed me in his bedroom, there is no recoil from this pulse of force. Canción stands immobile, a statue in the storm. Unlike that blast, this one packs a vastly greater punch.

The shockwave hits the grille of the nearer APC with the force of a bullet train, smashing the engine compartment into the cab and flinging the entire vehicle backward on its rear wheels. The man who jumped out is blasted to a fog of crimson mist. An image forms in my mind; *a soldier standing beside a foxhole fifty meters from me when a round from a Soviet-made Howitzer detonates at his feet.* There wasn't enough left to put into a body bag.

The destroyed APC slams into the one behind it hard enough to tumble it end over end through the obelisk supporting a white-painted cross. Thirty tons of twisted metal, armor, and the soldiers inside cartwheel into the building at the end of the switchback. I pray there's no one inside.

Gippy, as always, is most poignant in his assessment. "*Fuuucking* hell!"

"Not Hell, buddy." I jam the car in gear and burn the tires on the slick brick courtyard, wheeling us around down the hill hard enough to hurt. "The Wrath of God!" I race down the steep incline to where Canción still stands, his arms raised.

We screech to a stop, and Angelica flings the door open. "Get in here!"

He looks at her as if dazed, then smiles. "Sure!" He climbs aboard and closes the door. "Everyone okay?"

Silence... We're all stunned speechless.

I drive, once again baffled by this young man, this creature of Heaven and Hell sitting in the back seat, capable of taking the lives of thirty soldiers with a power beyond anything I've ever witnessed, then smiling about it.

"What's wrong?" he asks, and I see the puzzlement on his face in the rearview mirror.

"Seriously?" Angelica edges away from him as if he might catch fire. "You just blew the shit out of two freaking *tanks* with your *voice*, then smile like nothing's *wrong* with that?"

"Angelica, I've *always* done it, ever since I was a boy. Just to a lesser degree." He looks puzzled at her. "That's how I help people, how I mediate. I take their fear and anger, and they feel better."

"You *rip* people's emotions from them!" she snaps.

"Yes, because their emotions are *hurting* them." Canción's still calm, still puzzled, which frightens me more than a little. "I'm sorry if you think that's some kind of... intrusion, but it's who I am. I can't stand to see people in pain, so I take it away."

"You're *mind* raping them, you mean! Taking what *you* think is hurting them!" Angelica's really worked up, and I can't blame her, but I can't let this get out of hand.

"Can we please put off this discussion until we escape this clusterfuck?" I wheel us around a corner so fast that everyone in the back seat is scrunched together, and I watch Angelica fight not to touch Canción. "Please! Everyone just focus on getting out of here."

"Just don't touch me," Angelica says, her bridled anger and fear palpable to me. She thinks the man she loved is a monster.

I'm trying to figure out if she's right or wrong.

24
REVELATIONS

Gippy stirred from fitful sleep as the door to his room opened. He blinked and recognized Empa's outline from the hall light. "Hey." He tried to sit up and winced. "How goes the war?"

"Interesting choice of words." She closed the door and turned the light on low, moving to the foot of the bed without any visible limp. He checked the time. Six hours since they escaped La Popa, and she was right as rain. "Angelica's locked herself in her room, Isabella's feeding everyone within an inch of their lives, and I'm trying to figure out what the hell to do with a man who can demolish two M1119 APCs with a *shout*."

"Right?" He shifted to take the weight off his hip. "What about Chaki? Is she... uh..."

"Sane?" She shrugged. "Canción stripped away a lot of what she was feeling. I don't know if that helped or hurt her. She's not exactly catatonic, but not much better. I tried to help her, but she's a shell."

"A shell?" Gippy shook his head. "Like, *empty*?"

"Well, not completely. She's eating and drinking with help, anyway. There's still a human soul there, but... Well, you probably know better than I do what she's been through."

"Yeah, I do." He'd thought long and hard about his time possessed and didn't know how anyone could have remained sane through decades of that type of torment. "You think she'll ever recover?"

"I don't know. I've seen post trauma patients regress into their own minds and put up walls, try to forget, to deny what they've been through, what they're feeling, even their own memories. Sometimes they recover, sometimes they don't. Canción took all of her horror, pain, and guilt away. Now she's got walls with nothing inside to contain." She shrugged. "Chaki isn't like you, Gip. She *let* the demon in. She wanted it, or was seduced into wanting it."

"That's fucked up," he said, unable to truly feel sorry for anyone who would ask for that filth to possess them. "Think she knew what she was getting into, or... what was getting into her?"

"Probably not. She had a really rough childhood, abused, ran away, hooked for a few years, and got strung out on narcotics. Then an incubus found her and seduced her."

"I know that tune," he muttered, thinking of his sister Jame, wondering if the pimp who had taken her away had been a minion of Hell. "But she could be dangerous, right? If she *willingly* invited Duvara in, might she do that again?"

"Maybe, but if she does, we'll know, and right now she's valuable. She knows the Nephilim network, who they are, where they are, how they communicate."

That, at least, he couldn't argue with. He'd learned a lot from Ardat, but the incubus had been languishing in Hell for the last century. Duvara had built a network of thralls in the modern world. Only one question remained.

"What do we do with her?" he asked. "Babysittin' a psycho's like a full time job."

"She's not psychotic, or at least not yet, but you're right. We can't leave her alone. She knows too much about us and might sell us out." Empa shrugged. "For now, we'll keep her close and make sure she's okay. If she recovers and we can... convince her to help us, she could be a valuable source of information."

Gippy thought that putting a bullet in her brain might be the kinder solution, and wondered how much of that was the thirst for vengeance, but he knew that his possession and the torture he'd endured at her hands hadn't been her doing. Still, she was there when it happened.

He changed the subject. "What about Canción?"

"He's agreed to go with us as soon as the weather breaks. Maybe tomorrow, depending on if we can convince the ferry captain to take us back. I don't have much cash left, and Canción's leaving everything he has here to Angelica."

"Back to Punta Peña?" He shook his head. "Not a good idea, E. It's full of naffies now."

"No, I figured that. I think we can slip into the canal and pick up the highway at the bridge. It's still standing, and we can vanish in the city, maybe find an ultranet connection, a bank, pick up a ride, and make it back to Boquete. We need to tell Fernando's parents about him, and maybe show Canción his mother's grave before we head north."

That sounded risky to Gippy, but he trusted Empa to call the shots. Even so, he could make a suggestion. "The ferry captain won't like seeing me or Chaki again. Maybe keep us out of the negotiation."

"Definitely. Oh, and Isabella's all over the radio net. She's something else, knows everyone everywhere. Her spy in La Popa's telling everyone the NAFAS soldiers assassinated Bishop Vargas, and since we were wearing NAFAS uniforms, the story's getting some traction. It might turn into an international incident if they play it right." She got up and stepped around the bed to his side. "So, enough about everyone else. How are you?"

"I've got a bullet in my ass, E. How do you think? Why is it I'm always the one who gets shot?" He grinned at her and saw the fatigue in her eyes. "You need sleep."

"I do, but I figured I'd take your injury before I sack out. That way you can watch over me, be my guardian angel." She smiled and held out a hand.

"Give up on the irony, E." He put his hand in hers and nodded. "And I will. Watch over you, I mean."

"Thanks." She took his injury in a flash, but that was all. He knew she could see everything he'd been through. She'd scoured away the worst of the guilt and emotional trauma, but now that he was on the mend, she left him to deal with the rest. As the physical pain left him, he saw it arrive in her eyes.

"Here." He got out of bed and pulled the covers back for her. "I warmed it up for you."

"Keep an eye on things for me, Gip. Touch base with Isabella." She lay down and sighed deeply. "We're going home, Gip. Or at least to our new home."

"Home is where the people you love are." He grabbed a robe and his Glock, and left the bedroom, turning off the light on his way out.

The smell of food and coffee drew him downstairs like a magnet. He found Canción at the dining table, several covered dishes arrayed around, and two empty place settings.

"Morning." Gippy took a seat, smiling at the man's nod and mumbled reply through a mouthful of food. "Never got around to thanking you last night for... what you did for me."

"It was the least I could do... after you shot me with a Taser." He grinned, clearly making the least of his actions.

"Not the way I usually break the ice." Gippy smiled back, poured coffee, and started filling his plate. "Seriously, though, don't take anything else from me without my permission, okay?" He ate a bite, flavors exploding in his mouth. Damn, Isabella could cook. Maybe they could take her with them.

"I won't." He sighed and washed down a bite with coffee. "I learned my lesson with Angelica. She hates me now."

"No, she doesn't. She's just scared of you." He sipped the strong coffee and decided on a little honesty. "So am I. So's Empa. You gotta admit, stripping away people's emotions is pretty... *invasive*."

"I never thought of it that way growing up. Mom didn't even realize what I was doing. I just did it, and people felt better." He shook his head. "I felt like I was helping them, didn't know I was doing anything wrong."

"Just *ask* next time, all right?" Gippy settled down to his meal, then reconsidered. "Unless there's a demon or Nephilim involved, then rip that motherfucker out by the roots."

"I will." Canción met his gaze with one of complete sincerity. "I think that's why I am what I am."

"Gotta say, what you can do with Nephilim will change the war." Gippy swallowed and gauged the young man. He seemed well adjusted considering what they'd all been through, maybe too well adjusted. Gippy started to ask if he'd removed all of his own hurtful emotions as well as other people's, but reconsidered. What Canción did within his own head was his own business. Instead, he decided on a different tack. "So, did E tell you about your dad?"

Canción shrugged. "Not much, only that he was a priest, and his autism kept the Nephilim from consuming his soul at birth."

"Yeah, you need to know more than that." Gippy continued eating, and began telling the young man about his father. "He's one of the finest human beings I've ever known..."

~

Boquete seemed smaller than Canción remembered, less vibrant, more guarded, but familiar. Home. He hadn't wanted to come back here, but knew he had to tell Franko and Maria about Fernando. Leaving Las Brisas, not to mention Angelica, had been difficult, even knowing he had no choice. He'd apologized to Angelica a dozen different ways, to no avail. In the end, he couldn't blame her. He gave her Casa Musica and the rest of his mother's inheritance, encouraging her to stay and be the mediator the community needed. She agreed, but still hated him for what he'd done. Even though he truly didn't understand why, he didn't argue. It would only cause them both more pain.

The eight days getting here had been a trial in endurance and patience. The ferry's captain, all but imprisoned aboard his own ship by the NAFAS soldiers, almost left without them. Empa's money had changed his mind. Chaki was still a mess, but eating on her own and talking a little. He could feel her fear of him and wanted to take it away, but Empa made it clear that he shouldn't. She had to heal on her own, and they couldn't let her out of their sight.

Gippy parked the rattletrap SUV they'd bought in New Panama City in front of De la Abuela Café, and Canción recalled all the times he'd sung here while his mother played her music. He thought the memory would hurt, but it warmed him instead. He remembered the joy in the people's faces, the love his mother had given them, and him.

They got out and hurried into the cover of the café, travel weary, hungry, and grungy. Empa stayed close to Chaki, a hand on her arm. So far, the woman had been cooperative enough, telling Empa and Gippy whatever they wanted to know about the enemy, which turned out to be less than they hoped. Demon-possessed humans didn't know much about the bigger picture, it seemed. Their job was corruption, while the Nephilim ran the war.

Inside, they doffed their ponchos and hats. Something seemed off to Canción, fewer customers, and a somber atmosphere. Also, there was no music playing. He couldn't remember a time when there was no music at De la Abuela's.

A bright-eyed boy met them with a smile. "Four for lunch?"

"Please." Canción recognized him, Enrico's younger son, Emanuel, but the boy's eyes focused on Empa.

"I recognize you," Emanuel said warily. "You came here right before the soldiers."

"Yes, we did." Empa stepped to Canción's side. "They tried to kill us.

We didn't know they were following. They won't be following us this time. Can we speak to Enrico?"

Emanuel nodded. "Father's in the kitchen. Here. Sit down and I'll tell him you're here."

"Thank you."

They sat at a corner table, Empa and Gippy with their backs to the wall. Chaki seemed oblivious to the exchange. Less than a minute later, Enrico came back with Emanuel, his face dark with anger. Then he recognized Canción.

"Ay Dios mio!" His features paled as Canción stood, his palpable anger melting away to surprise and joy.

"Enrico." He stood and faced the man with a grin. "It's good to see you again. I'm sorry for—"

The man slammed into him, a hard embrace pinning his arms to his sides. "Canción, my boy! The prodigal son!" Enrico grasped his shoulders and beamed at him. "You've come *home*!"

"For a while, Enrico. I need to see Franko and Maria." Canción clapped the man's shoulders and smiled as warmly as he could. "I'm sorry for the trouble my friends brought here. They had no way to know the soldiers would come looking for them."

Enrico's face fell, and he leveled a cold stare at Empa. "Yes, well, they came looking for your mother and asked about you. I never thought in a million years they'd find you." He gestured back to the table. "Please. Sit! Anything you want!" He turned to Emanuel. "Put on some music! One of Señora Tersi's recordings."

"Si Papa!" The boy had been staring at Canción in awe, recognition finally dawning. He hurried off, and a moment later, the music of a sweet guitar filled the room, and with it, the high tenor of a boy's voice.

Canción's voice... A sea of memories threatened to drown him.

"I'll contact Franko, but they live up in the hills. Maybe half an hour?" Enrico wrung his hands, scanning their faces, probably looking for Fernando but reticent to ask.

"Thank you. We'll be staying one night, at least, but please keep it quiet. We don't want to draw too much attention."

"Oh, yes, of course! Good!" Enrico's grin returned, and he hurried off.

A moment later, young Emanuel returned with coffee to take their orders, still in awe of Cancion.

When he'd left, Empa sipped coffee and asked, "The music, is that you?"

"Yes, before my voice changed." He shrugged. "We used to play all the venues in town. Mother was a local hero. Everyone loved her."

"Looks like they loved you, too," Gippy said.

Again, he shrugged, the music and the voice of the boy he had been slowly torturing him. He was dreading talking to Franko and Maria. He'd expunged that guilt, but it seemed to have returned. Maybe that was the true problem with his gift; he didn't cure people's problems by expunging their fear or grief, he only removed a symptom. The underlying memories always replenished the harmful feelings.

Their food arrived, and Enrico's mother, the café's legendary Grandmother, came out and hugged him with tears in her eyes. He felt her sorrow and her joy at seeing him again. Reflexively, he started to take her sorrow away, but then stopped himself. Long conversations with Empa about emotions and psychology—one subject his mother had no expertise in—had taught him that some negative emotions like anger, sorrow, and fear were important to mental health. Simply taking them away wasn't necessarily a good thing, and could even cause long-term harm. He wondered if he'd damaged himself over the years, always expunging his anger and sorrow. So, he resisted the urge and let her cry into his chest, her tears wetting his shirt.

They settled down and ate, the old-school Central American fare spurring an entire cascade of memories in Canción, the years he spent here with his mother, Maria's wonderful cooking, his brother Fernando...

Then Franko and Maria arrived.

One look, their eyes flicking over the faces at the table, and he saw that they knew. As he stood, he saw the horror in their eyes, felt it beating against him like waves on a shore. "I'm sorry," was all he could say.

"Oh, Canción!" Maria bustled forward, already crying, and embraced him.

Franko was only a step behind, his strong arms encircling them both. "Ah, my son... My dear son..."

Canción held them, felt their gut-wrenching grief, but also their love for him. He didn't cry, couldn't, but he held them both, his adoptive parents, and shared their heartache. In time, their sobs subsided, and they sat, wanting to hear what happened.

Thankfully, Empa told the tale, how Fernando had become her protector, her warrior, stoic in his determination, willing to do whatever it took to help them. How he was killed protecting them. They were surprised to see Gippy, and Franko remembered him, how he'd been injured and taken by the NAFAS soldiers.

"Didn't think anyone could survive their interrogations," Franko said.

Gippy shook his head and glanced sidelong at Chaki. "Neither did I, but Canción saved me."

They both looked shocked but withheld their questions.

"Have you seen your mother's grave?" Maria asked, clearly changing the subject on purpose. "It's not far, in the park by the bridge."

"No, not yet." He glanced at the others.

"Let's go." Empa stood and gestured for Gippy and Chaki to stay. "Relax. We'll be back in a few minutes."

"Sure." Gippy glanced at Chaki and shrugged. "No problem."

So the four of them donned ponchos and hats and braved the storm, yet another hurricane, but not as powerful as Canción had grown accustomed to in Cartagena. The ridge of mountains east of Boquete took some of the energy of the storms away. They bent against the wind-driven rain and slogged along to the riverside park. There, a granite gravestone stood half his height. There were flowers there, planted in the lee of the stone, struggling to survive. Maria knelt and prayed, and Franko wrapped one strong arm around Canción's shoulders.

"It was here when we returned," Franko explained. "The community wanted to do something."

Canción stared at the stone, the inscription with its hidden meaning. "Her song lives on..." For some reason, he felt like destroying it. He didn't feel like he wanted to live on. If he died, he'd be with her again. Maybe that would be better. It would certainly be easier.

A hand settled on his arm, Empa. "It's all right to grieve, Canción."

"I know. I just... never learned how." He met her eyes, and felt her sifting through his emotions. "I always just purged it, didn't want it. It seemed... easier." Maybe that was part of his problem; he'd always taken the easy path.

"Gippy taught me something about grief that I think you need to know," she said, still holding his gaze.

"*Gippy* taught you?" That seemed unlikely.

"Yes. He... saved me, in fact, from my own grief, but not by taking it away." She smiled then, and he felt her dark humor. "He offered me mercy when I didn't want to live anymore. He told me one thing I'd forgotten over the centuries. Grief is *supposed* to hurt. The pain is how we heal."

That seemed backward, wrong, contradictory, but he couldn't imagine her lying to him. "How?"

"Think about how physical pain protects us. If we didn't feel pain, we wouldn't avoid injury. That's how living things evolved. How they survive. Why they fight to continue." She gestured to the stone. "Remembering the ones we love who are lost hurts, but it makes us stronger, more resilient. The grief we feel is like the scouring of a wound. It aids healing."

Canción tore his eyes away from hers and stared at the stone again. Destroying it would be wrong. It wouldn't help him heal, and would only hurt the people of Boquete who had erected it in memory of his mother. This was their monument to the love she'd brought to their community.

Maybe he could learn to heal like they had.

Canción knelt in the muddy grass and placed a hand on the grave beside the struggling flowers. He felt nothing and closed his eyes, struggling, reaching out for something that wasn't there within himself. He reached down into the soil beneath his fingers with his mind, feeling for the echo of his mother's music, for something, anything...

Nothing.

A sudden realization dawned, and he lurched to his feet. "She's not here."

All three of them looked at him like he'd slapped them.

"*What?*" Franko looked shocked.

Empa's eyes widened. "You mean..."

"I mean she's not here. There's a body, but no echoes, no... feeling of her. I don't know why, but I would feel... *something*. There's nothing." He looked around, knowing suddenly that they were being observed, and spotted Enrico and his mother watching from the corner. From fifty feet through the slashing rain, he could see in their eyes that they knew.

Canción advanced on them with long, determined strides, and Enrico stepped in front of his mother, concern etching his features. "Canción, you have to understand..."

He stopped a step away, and felt Empa at his shoulder, ready. "*Tell* me what I have to understand."

Enrico swallowed hard and nodded. "Señora Tersi survived. She had an escape tunnel under Casa Musica rigged with explosives. She hid for a week in a hole before she came out and found us."

"What?" Empa stepped around him, her tone hard. "You *lied* to me!"

"Yes, we did." Enrico's mother stepped to his side, her aged round features set in stone. "For her, for Señora Tersi, we *all* lied. She had to leave, to go into hiding, and if word got out that she survived, the NAFAS would come again. We buried one of the NAFAS soldiers, a woman burned to cinders, and Señora Tersi bled into the grave just in case they exhumed the body and did testing. We gave her all we had to get her to safety." Her eyes slipped from Empa's to Canción's. "To protect your mother, we even lied to you. She said to, that if you found out, it would put you in danger."

"Where is she?" Canción asked, but not as forcefully as Empa.

"We honestly don't know," Enrico cut in. "She said it would be safer if we didn't, for her *and* us. She took two horses and went north, overland through the jungle."

Empa whirled away and stalked toward the café, obviously upset. Canción turned back to Franko and Maria. "I've got to get this squared away, but we'll be spending the night here. I don't want to cause a problem, but—"

"You'll stay with us, of course," Maria stated. "We insist."

"Thank you." Canción glanced back to Enrico and his mother, felt their worry, their fear. "And thank you for telling me the truth."

"Of course." Enrico glanced to his mother, and she nodded. "Whatever you need, we will give."

"Thank you." With another nod he hurried back to the café to find Empa leaning with her fists on the table.

Gippy looked shocked, but Chaki still looked blank, like none of this mattered to her in the slightest. Empa spoke in low tones, but as he neared, she turned to face him.

"We think we can find her!"

That surprised him. "How, after eight years and a cold trail?"

"We found *you*, didn't we?" Gippy pointed out.

Canción had to admit he was right. "Okay, so..."

"She was researching something before she came here," Empa continued. "She didn't continue her research, but she probably will eventually. We know where she'll start looking and can leave a message for her. It might take some time, but—"

"Then it'll take time." Canción shrugged and sat back down. "We're staying with Franko and Maria tonight, so sit back down, and we can talk it over." He glanced at Gippy and cocked an eyebrow. "And we should probably discuss how to break this news to my father."

Gippy's eyes widened. "Holy shit! He's right, E! Emil's gonna *freak*!"

"Yes, he will, but he needs to know." Empa sat back down and waved to their young waiter. "Tres cervesas, por favor."

"*Cuatro*, cervesas," Chaki chimed in, catching them all off guard. Her dark eyes flicked from face to face. "And let me help."

Empa and Gippy eyed her suspiciously, but Canción couldn't feel any malice in her, and nodded. This was the first interest she'd taken in anything. Helping them might help her, give her a purpose. "Sure. With what you know, and what Empa and Gippy know, we might have a chance to find her."

Empa pursed her lips in thought. "Okay, but we're going to have to hack into a secure medical facility's database to leave our message. I don't have those skills, and neither does Gippy. We might be able to find someone who—"

"I have a black-hat hacker on speed dial," Chaki interrupted.

"Well fuuuck me," Gippy grumbled.

Chaki looked at him, and her eyes narrowed. "No *thanks*."

Gippy shot her a sour look. "It's a figure of *speech*."

Canción could feel the animosity between them, the baggage of what happened when they were both possessed, and he longed to tear it away, to free them of the fear, anger, and mistrust. He couldn't. Not without alienating Empa, and he needed her. She knew where his father was.

"Enough, you two. What's done is in the past. Focus. We need to think this through and be careful about it." Empa paused as Emanuel delivered four icy cold bottles without labels. She thanked him and sampled one, her eyebrows arching. "This is *really* horrible."

"Any port in a storm," Gippy sipped and grimaced.

Chaki grabbed a bottle and drank deeply, her throat working swallow after swallow. When she put the bottle down, it was half empty. She was definitely coming around.

Canción sipped his beer but didn't think it was that bad. "So, where do we start looking."

"We go to San José and get some cash first," Empa said. "Then Charlotte, North Carolina. We have friends there. From there, we contact your father and put out some feelers." She nodded to Chaki. "And we secure the services of a hacker who'll keep their mouth shut about this."

"There's one more thing you should know." Chaki took another deep drink and sighed. "Hell's going to know Duvara and Ardat are gone, not just banished but *gone*. When they investigate, they'll find out two Nephilim are also gone. When they do, the shit's going to *really* hit the fan. Banished or exorcised is one thing, *destroyed* is... Not even the Grigori knew that was possible."

That Duvara had actually met the fallen angels hit Canción like an epiphany. What other secrets of Hell might Chaki have learned over her decades of possession? "This is going to stir up Hell like a kicked anthill."

"True that! They'll be running scared, E," Gippy agreed. "They're gonna be even *more* dangerous!"

"Yes, they will be." She frowned and glanced at Canción. "And they're going to know we have a new weapon."

EPILOGUE

I move through the starlit night like a wraith, clad in flat black from head to foot, soft shoes barely scuffing the carpet of pine needles covering the hard-packed earth. Seven years living rough in the jungles of Central America has reacquainted me with my feral self. Memories of pre-colonial Africa served me well there. Here, not so much. At least there are no lions, or hyenas, or jaguars in the high ponderosa forests of Arizona, and the wolves and mountain lions of yesteryear are long gone. I would weep for the loss of those beautiful creatures, but I'm beyond weeping. The only predator in these forests is me.

It took me a year to reintegrate myself into civilization, find one of my old stashes, regroup, rearm, and reassess. Now, skulking through this unfamiliar wilderness, I feel the dry air like an alien thing on my skin, the scents unfamiliar, the thin air hard to breathe. I'm out of my element, but I have no choice; my exile is ended, and my quest must resume.

Canción... I wall off those emotions for now. I can't afford them. I have a purpose, a goal, and I must focus.

Twenty years I've been out of touch. How strange that I took that sabbatical to bear and raise a child, only to be discovered by my enemies and forced into solitude. My greatest nemesis of all now is loneliness. *Canción, my boy...* Not a day goes by that I don't think of him, wonder if I could find him, become a family once again. *Twelve glorious years...* But I know it's impossible. He's either a grown man now or gone; either come to the full of his strange power and mastered it, found his place in the grander scheme of Heaven and Hell, or not. I have no way to find him and would only endanger him if I did.

I also often think of Emil Farrell, what my abandonment must have done to him. I searched the nets for him, but his isn't an uncommon name. Searching for a needle in a haystack would be pointless. He would be near fifty now, and I can't imagine he'd be happy to see me.

Besides, I have a job to do.

Computers have evolved in the last twenty years, both to my benefit and detriment. I, too, must adapt. Money isn't a problem, and anonymous online shopping is one of the few freedoms that remains in this totalitarian empire. Banking is dangerous, but the wealthy have the privilege of identity security, while the poor are scrutinized. Using the ultranet to find where Laurence Caldwell received his treatment, the exorcism that either gave him a brain aneurism or exorcised the Nephilim within him, wasn't simple, but helped sharpen my IT skills. Hacking into medical records, however, has proven impossible, at least for me. I dare not enlist help for fear of exposing myself, so it's time for some good-old-fashioned breaking and entering.

This, at least, is familiar ground.

I've broken into a lot of places over the centuries, sometimes to rescue works of art or original music that were stolen, other times to recover what was once mine. I even once broke into a private home to steal jewelry stolen from a duchess, sheerly out of self-interest. Said duchess was most generous in her thanks for the return of the necklace, and her reward set me up for decades. This is the first time I've broken into a Catholic mental institution, but I've never tried to hunt down an exorcised Nephilim before either. Luckily, mental hospitals aren't big on high-tech security. What is there here to steal, after all? There's only one camera on the gate and motion sensor lights and cameras on the doors. These pose only a minor inconvenience.

My soft shoes crunch gravel as I skirt the building to find the window I intend to use. Nothing on the net ever goes away entirely, and schematics of the building's construction when it was a private ski resort weren't hard to find. Granted, they've remodeled, but most of the windows and doors are still where they were originally.

The window is thermal-pane, but I'm not going to be cutting glass. It also probably hasn't been opened in a decade. I'm lucky it's not painted shut. I look over the latches with a red pen light and smile behind my black ski mask. I fish a small battery powered Dremel from my bag, already fitted with a diamond bit. It's nearly silent, and I go slow. The bit pierces the aluminum frame like a rapier through silk, and I slip a thin steel probe through the hole to push the rotating latch. I do the same to the upper latch, which resists a little, but it pops open with a little coaxing, and the window slides up in relative silence. I clean up the metal shavings, put my tools away, and climb through.

I'm in an office, diplomas and certificates decorating one wall, a bookshelf the other. I'm pleased to see more medical texts than ecclesiastical ones. I crouch and listen for any alarms I might have tripped, or a telltale clatter of boots on linoleum that would undoubtedly follow the triggering of a silent alarm. When I'm greeted by only silence, and armed guards fail to burst through the door, I close the window and check the frame for any sign that I might have triggered something. Nothing suspicious catches my eye, so I tiptoe around the desk to the door. In the hall, I turn right and creep along, straining to hear anything at all. Distant music comes from the entry hall, an interesting mix of techno and grunge, not a typically secular mix. There's an information desk there, so I assume the music is from the night watchman trying to stay awake. If anyone walks rounds this late at night, it will be in the patient wing, and I'm not going there.

At a room labeled "Records," I check the door, which is predictably locked. It's not electronic, thank God, and my picks click it open in about three minutes. Inside, I find three workstations, all antiquated and turned off. The central server is still up, however. I power up a workstation and wait a painful five minutes for it to boot. There's a login, but the administrator of Our Lady of Healing isn't very imaginative. His home computer has the same login. I may not be a cutting edge hacker, but time and patience serve me well. I'm in their records repository in seconds.

My first query, however, comes up blank.

What the hell?

I try different iterations of Laurence Caldwell's name and get nothing. I know he was a patient here from public records and news archives, but there's no record of him at all. Someone has scrubbed it. I feel the footprints of Nephilim in this, for why scrub the medical record of a man who died during an exorcism if he wasn't somehow important? And a low-level politician isn't that important, even if the circumstances of his original injury were suspicious. And yet, I found enough about him on the net to confirm that the procedure resulted in a flat-line EEG and subsequent death. The obituary and accident report weren't deleted, but there's nothing here. This makes me wonder why whoever scrubbed the records wasn't more thorough, but obliterating public records is harder than patient data files. And the public records didn't include details about the procedure. Exorcisms don't generally work on Nephilim—I've tried more than a few—but this one evidently did. If it didn't, why delete the evidence? The details of the procedure, specifically medications, must be what they were trying to get rid of. Unfortunately, it's also exactly what I need.

"Crap and damnation," I whisper in ancient Luwian, my birth tongue, long dead. I recall years spent in museums, making my living translating archeological scripts that were younger than me, earning a pittance and the enmity of *scholars,* jealous men who resented an educated woman showing them up.

"Focus, Terpsichore! Your search isn't over yet!"

I know the date of his procedure, and pull up records of all the attending priest physicians here at the time. One stands out. Father Martin Pederson, DPH, vanished from the records only days after Laurence Caldwell's death. This can't be a coincidence. I suspect for a moment that he might have been murdered by Nephilim trying to cover his success, but that would have drawn attention. Perhaps he quit or moved on to another facility due to his failure, or maybe he was let go in an attempt to cover up malpractice. I have a trail to follow, for if anyone knows the details of Laurence Caldwell's exorcism, it will be his attending priest-physician.

I log off, shut down the workstation, and lock the door on my way out. The music from the foyer has changed to techno hip-hop, and I have to suppress the urge to move to the intoxicating beat. I'm not a techno fan, but music is music, and it all sings to my soul.

I'm through the office and out the window in five minutes, covering up the holes I drilled with a dab of filler that will harden by morning. I can't secure the latches from outside, but whoever discovers them open probably won't think twice about it. After all, nothing's missing, and I've left no trace.

I strike out through the forest under starlight, planning my next move.

Martin Pederson will be over sixty now, but might still be alive, and nobody ever truly vanishes in this new world of technology and digital identities.

Nobody but me, Terpsichore, Ageless daughter of Israfal, Angel of Music.

ACKNOWLEDGMENTS

As always, I'd like to thank my wife, Dr. Anne L. McMillen-Jackson for her input, patience, and keen eye for all the things wrong with my first drafts. (And there was a lot) Another huge thanks to the Falstaff crew for editing, cover design, and all the unseen work they do. A massive amount of research went into this trilogy, from western religions and history, to all the science of climate change. Many thanks to all of those who put their knowledge online for others to use and enjoy with no compensation whatsoever. You all make my job so much easier and fun!

ABOUT THE AUTHOR

Sailor, SFF fan, career biologist, gamer, and author, Chris has a diverse bibliography of science thrillers, nautical fantasy, epic fantasy, science fiction, horror, post-apocalyptic fantasy, and RPG tie-in stories. His game tie-in work includes Pathfinder, Iron Kingdoms, Shadowrun, Arkham Horror, and Traveller RPGs. He has over 30 novels in print and has won numerous awards, including the 2020 Scribe Award for best tie-in short story. His most recent works from Falstaff Books include the War of Souls post-apocalyptic fantasy trilogy, and the high fantasy Seeds of Darkness trilogy.

ALSO BY CHRIS A. JACKSON

(with Anne L. McMillen-Jackson)*

From Jaxbooks

A Soul for Tsing

Deathmask

Blood Sea Tales

The Pirate's Scourge

The Pirate's Truth

The Pirate's Bane

Ash Walker

Blood Walker

Death Walker

Weapon of Flesh Series

Weapon of Flesh (also on Audible)

Weapon of Blood (also on Audible)

Weapon of Vengeance (also on Audible)

Weapon of Fear *

Weapon of Pain *

Weapon of Mercy *

The Cornerstones Trilogy

Zellohar *

Nekdukarr *

Jundag *

The Cheese Runners Trilogy (novellas – also on Audible)

Cheese Runners

Cheese Rustlers

Cheese Lords

From Shadow Alley Press

Pacifica

Stratos

Vesuvia

From Falstaff Books

The Dragons of Boston Trilogy

Dragon Dreams

Dragon's Nemesis

Dragon's Legacy

The War of Souls Trilogy

The Last

The First

The Eternal (Spring 2025)

-

From Paizo Publishing (also on Audible)

Pirate's Honor

Pirate's Promise

Pirate's Prophecy

From Privateer Press

Blood & Iron (ebook novella)

Watery Graves

From Fantasy Flight Games

The Deep Gate (hardcover novella)

From Catalyst Game Labs

Crocodile Tears (ebook novella)

FRIENDS OF FALSTAFF

Thank You to All our Falstaff Books Patrons, who get extra digital content each month! To be featured here and see what other great rewards we offer, go to www.patreon.com/falstaffbooks.

PATRONS

Dino Hicks
John Hooks
John Kilgallon
Larissa Lichty
Travis & Casey Schilling
Staci-Leigh Santore
Sheryl R. Hayes
Scott Norris
Samuel Montgomery-Blinn
Junkle

www.ingramcontent.com/pod-product-compliance
Lightning Source LLC
Chambersburg PA
CBHW050152120726
47903CB00002B/591

* 9 7 8 1 6 4 5 5 4 3 0 8 4 *